"This cowboy romance with Native American characters delves into issues of abuse surrounding Native women and tugs at the heartstrings. The authentic rodeo setting drew me in so deeply I could see the arena and hear the bulls and the horses. The many references to Native culture were deftly woven into the narrative and warmed my heart."
—Debby Lee, author of *Beneath a Peaceful Moon* and *An Evergreen Christmas*

"If you enjoy poignant stories of strength and resilience, this book has it. Peone transports the reader into this world of ranches and rodeos while keeping true to her message of hope and love. There are moments of heartache and angst, all with an undercurrent of faith in the face of hardship."
—Sara R. Turnquist, author of the Convenient Risk series

"Happiness is knowing a great story comes in a book series. Carmen Peone continues the story of Sydney and her family's Seven Tine Guest Ranch. When Rita comes to the ranch for help, morals, love for humankind, and strong faith bring this family together to fight for what is right."
—Linda Wommack, 3-time winner of the Will Rogers Medallion Award

"This romance series is unfolding with sound conflict, delicious entanglements that draw the reader into the story, and deep, meaningful overlays of contemporary issues that reveal the pain young Native women suffer at the hands of their abusers. This series is highly recommended for young women facing life choices, as well as readers of the romance genre and social reformers who desire to see another aspect of Rez life written by an authentic voice."
—Anne Schroeder, award-wi--- 'hor

D0746633

"An edge-of-the seat, heart-pounding ride, *Broken Bondage* is another strong story of breaking the cycle of domestic abuse. Carmen Peone has created a feisty character who, in spite of feeling she is damaged goods, perseveres to find trust in God, rekindle her faith, and heal from victimhood to find victory. I couldn't put it down!"

—Heidi Thomas, award-winning author

"Peone weaves a harrowing rescue journey, vivid details of Reservation life, rodeo and ranch activities, budding romance, and Rita's personal spiritual journey to furnish a top-notch contemporary western novel."

—Teddy Jones, author of *Marva Cope*

"Native American women are two to three times more likely than women of any other race to experience violence, stalking, or abuse. Yet, the atrocities on Indigenous women still stand at a crisis level. Drawing on her own heritage and life on the Reservation, Carmen Peone has chosen to shine a light on the truth in *Broken Bondage*. This novel is so real—so genuine—that Peone makes it hard to ignore the problem. Her characters are well-written and authentic, giving the reader a safe place from which to experience the victimization that needs to stop. This page-turner will stay with me for a long time."

—K. S. Jones, award-winning author of the
True Hearts of Texas series

"I'm just coming up for air after reading *Broken Bondage*. In this gripping story, Carmen Peone is shining a fearless and much-needed light into dark places. There are too many Ritas in the world, abused and devalued by the men in their lives. But, as Rita found, there is hope in the Lord, there is help available, and there are honorable men. I'm grateful that Carmen is using her God-given talent to give a voice and hope to women who are living in bondage, and to those who can reach out a hand to help."

—Milla Holt, author of *Into the Flood*

"An immensely enjoyable story of wounded, vulnerable hero Rita Runninghorse. The magic of Carmen Peone's writing is in her realistic and wonderfully flawed characters coming together with crackling chemistry. Along with secrets and snappy dialogue, the story carries the heartbeats of faith, courage, and community as Rita grows to trust again."

—B. K. Froman, award-winning author of
Hardly Any Shooting Stars Left

"An abused woman on the run learns to lean in to her faith for deliverance and in to a saddle bronc–riding cowboy for protection in Carmen Peone's contemporary Christian romance novel *Broken Bondage*."

—Betsy Randolph, author of The Cat Carlyle Mysteries
and Noah Pool Adventure Series

"Peone shines the light of hope on a very dark subject. My heart raced alongside Rita and Robert in their cross-country journey to elude Rita's demons."

—Kathy Geary Anderson, author of the
Wind River Chronicles series

"Once again Carmen Peone has spun a wonderful and engrossing tale of the reality of abusive relationships and the salvation that can come when one has faith and support."

—Roni McFadden, award-winning author of
The Longest Trail

"At times gut-wrenching, suspenseful, and tragically terrific, *Broken Bondage* is a true hero's story of hope."

—Kim Russell, author of *Photo Finish*

"*Broken Bondage* is another tour de force by Carmen Peone in the Seven Tine Ranch series. It's both a love story and a tale of domestic violence that sears the reader from page one. Rita Runninghorse, a Native American woman from the Umatilla Reservation must escape her abuser if she's to have any hope of a decent life. 'Bronco Bobby' comes to her rescue, but they must first track down the man stalking her and bring him to justice. *Broken Bondage* is as unforgettable as it is haunting. Truly a memorable read!"

—Carol Craig, author of *A Walk in the Dark*

"What kind of fear makes a woman run from the man who promises to kill her if she leaves? How much courage does it take for her to follow the trail to find a haven of safety where she can learn to trust anyone, especially those closest to her? In this brilliant game of predator and prey, Carmen Peone shines a light on the vicious cruelty that lives in a dark closet of the human soul. She makes you feel the terror born of generational abuse, a terror none of us deserves."

—Michelle C. Ferrer, award-winning writer

"A sweet story of the true meaning of love and the triumph of a survivor."

—Jennifer Purcell, author of *The Red Ear*

BROKEN BONDAGE

CARMEN PEONE

BIRMINGHAM, ALABAMA

Broken Bondage

Iron Stream Fiction
An imprint of Iron Stream Media
100 Missionary Ridge
Birmingham, AL 35242
IronStreamMedia.com

Library of Congress Control Number: 2022950027

Cover design by For the Muse Designs

ISBN: 978-1-64526-362-3 (paperback)
ISBN: 978-1-64526-363-0 (eBook)

1 2 3 4 5—27 26 25 24 23

To all the women who desire to be free from the bondage of abuse.
May they draw courage from this passage:

Let us burst their bonds apart and cast away their cords from us.
—Psalm 2:3

CHAPTER 1

Early October
Umatilla Indian Reservation, Eastern Oregon

"You dirty bugger, git over here!" Henry, the red-and-white calf Rita Runninghorse had secretly named, darted sideways as she winced at the pain in her sides, gathered her lariat, and tried for another loop.

Her head pounded from when her fiancé, Bowie Dark Cloud, had slammed her against the door of his pickup earlier that morning and crushed her against a stall door two days ago.

Concentration eluded her, and her timing dragged like the sludge of cold cowboy coffee at day's end. Dusk's chilly breath hovering over the rolling hills of the Columbia Plateau country on her father's ranch failed to help matters.

"Come on, Opal, let's get 'im this time." She swung her lasso overhead and spurred her smokey grulla mare into a gallop, close on the calf's tail. With her horse staying on him, she landed the loop over its head and reined her mare to the right. The jerk of the rope when her horse skidded to a halt caught her breath.

The calf balked on the other end of the rope as Rita jumped off, and her backside landed on the wet ground. Could this day get any worse? She pushed to her feet, wobbled toward the wide-eyed little one, and flopped him to the ground with a deep groan. Good grief. Her father could've built a smaller holding pen.

"Sorry, little man," she said, thankful for the fall calf's small size. "You shouldn't have run from me."

Rita pulled a short piggin' string from her back pocket and tied the critter's legs together. Seconds later, he finally quit fighting her. The cut on his leg was nastier than she'd suspected. She went to one of her saddlebags and retrieved a syringe and a bottle of penicillin. His round eyes watched her while she cleaned the crusty wound, a low bellow escaping his mouth.

Inhaling his earthy scent, she gave him a shot of antibiotic, massaged the injection site, and untied his legs. "All better now."

He shot to his feet, bawling for his mama, and loped away. Come spring, she'd make sure some 4-H kid would get a nice steer to show at the Umatilla County Fair.

Her sides throbbed and her vision blurred as she staggered back to her mare and found a pain reliever in a saddlebag. She struggled to pop the lid off the container. "Stupid . . . childproof . . ." Once the top broke loose, she took two pills and chased them down with a swig of water.

Rita slipped her tan, buckaroo-styled cowboy hat from her sweaty head, rested the side of her face against her mare's steaming rump, and inhaled the glorious horse scent. Scratching Opal's damp hide, she whispered, "You're a good girl."

"You almost done?" Bowie's impatient voice boomed behind her.

She stiffened like the steel blade he often sharpened while pegging her with his ash-colored eyes. *Not today, Lord.* "Almost. I need to put the supplies away."

"Hurry up. There ain't much light left." Towering over her at six-foot-four and wearing a black Stetson, Bowie watched the ranch hands work near the barn with appraising eyes. With a sudden movement, he pinned his arms against her in a coarse embrace, the hair on his black goatee scratching the side of her neck. She scrunched her nose at the stench of cigarette smoke on his breath. "I'll escort you back."

Bowie traded horses for a living. Although she wasn't a veterinarian, he often asked her to check them out before hauling them to various auctions. She regretted the day she'd quit working at the vet clinic—all because he'd shown up uninvited there and threatened and humiliated her in front of her coworkers. She couldn't handle the embarrassment.

Rita forced a smile, detesting his jealousy. Love and respect were key to marital success. Or so her youth pastor had drilled into her teen group. Too bad all she knew of marital bliss included her father shoving her mother against a wall, his red face in her pale one. His tone had been low and sharp and scary as he claimed how worthless she was— especially to little girls watching from the shadows.

How had she allowed herself to get saddled with the same kind of strong-fisted man? How could she walk down the aisle with someone so violent? Someone who didn't trust her? She swallowed the lump in her throat. She needed to get away from him. Cancel the wedding. And survive doing so when research showed most women died trying to flee.

"Where's your ring?"

He squeezed her hand a little too tightly, and she winced. "At the cabin. I don't want to ruin the diamond."

"You need to wear it. There's too much riffraff around here."

Quivering, she gathered the used supplies and stuffed them into her saddlebag. Her hand brushed against the stiff leather carrying case of her Leatherman multi-purpose tool. Why hadn't she attached it to her belt for self-protection?

"I don't like the way your dad's hired hands gawk at you. There's only one thing they want, and you know what it is." Bowie patted her bottom. "That sweet little body of yours."

"They're harmless." The words burst out before she could stop them, and she flinched.

He grabbed her arm and raised his chin as though he were going to strike her, then seemed to think better of it, and dropped it with a cold sneer. "You trying to tell me what to think now?"

Why did she give him an excuse to rough her up? She ran her hand partway down her gritty, waist-length side braid and held on to it as though it were a security blanket. "Of course not, I—"

"Then you better get going." He shoved her forward.

Rita caught her balance and jerked her thumb at the calves. "I have to doctor them too."

"Too bad." He strode toward the barn with her arm in his viselike grip.

She stumbled for a few steps and grabbed her mare's reins for balance. The snap of pressure from the reins to the bit jerked the horse's mouth. Opal pulled back, shaking her head, and finally succumbed to the weight of the headstall's leather bands behind her ears.

"I'll talk to your dad," he said.

She faltered and lost her grasp on the reins as he pushed her along.

"Quit messin' around." He yanked her to her feet.

"I'm not . . . I mean . . . I'm sorry. My boot caught on a rock." She gathered the reins, her hands trembling, and with a soft tone, coaxed her mare to follow. She had to get away from her fiancé. And soon.

How'd he go from Saturday night dancing under the moon, Monday morning flowers, and midweek picnics—all the things she'd dreamed about before her teenage rape—to accusing her of cheating and leaving bruises where no one could see them?

Was she simply Bowie's stepping-stone to her father and his successful cattle ranch? The wedding was scheduled for the following weekend. What then? More beatings? Less freedom?

No thank you. Right then and there, she vowed to get away from him. No matter what it took. No matter what it cost. She had to believe her life was worth more than a good beating.

CHAPTER 2

Colville Reservation, Eastern Washington

Robert Elliot took a clipboard from Sydney Moomaw Hardy, his half sister and CEO of the Seven Tine Guest Ranch. "Here are the lists," she said. "We'll be back in a month. Sure you can handle all this on your own with Glenda gone?"

Their sister, Glenda Williams, was home recovering from an appendectomy. After four two-year terms on the tribal council, she'd come to work with her sister and half brother at the ranch as the administrative assistant.

"I'm absolutely sure." He hated her distrust of him. When had he ever let her down? Needing to jump on a few broncs before the dinner rush, he checked his watch.

"I need to *see* you make this place a priority."

"Like I said, it is. But so is the rodeo. I've got three weeks until the finals. I need to keep riding." He'd had his sights pinned on winning the Indian National Finals Rodeo, INFR, in Las Vegas for years. For him, it was the pathway to obtaining his pro-rodeo status.

"Saddle bronc riding is sitting on a rank horse and hanging on for eight seconds. Anyone with half a brain can do that." She gave him a playful grin.

His hand flew to his chest. "Oh, that hurts."

"Good. Maybe it will knock some sense into you." Sydney patted his shoulder. "I know you can handle this, or we wouldn't be leaving you in charge." She turned to the maroon GMC Sierra with the Seven Tine Guest Ranch logo, a seven-tined elk shed over a T, emblazoned on the side-door panels. Her husband and daughter were waiting inside, rocking out to Garth Brooks's song "The Thunder Rolls" leaking from a cracked-open window.

"Just remember rule number one: honesty and integrity." The Seven Tine's foundation.

"I know, I know. And lead by example." Robert tapped the side of his head, trying not to make fun of her. "I got your little manifesto memorized. Trust me." His attention shifted to the movement among amber-colored trees on a knoll behind the barn.

Sydney hugged her brother. "Thanks for this. We desperately need family time. Even though it's work related."

"Anything for you guys. Helping me get back the practice broncs was pretty generous." After their parents had passed away over a year ago, they had to sell most everything and go bare-bones to save the ranch. They were now beginning to build it back up—thanks to the new barn being an event venue and the gift shop in the lodge, not to mention Trey Hardy's successful photography business.

She waved as she strode to the truck and hopped in. A light haze of dust rose as the pickup rambled down the long lane.

"What are the other . . .? What did you call it? Man—something?" Mandie, the small-but-fierce ranch cook, said as she parked herself beside him, slipping her hands into her light-jacket pockets.

"Manifesto. Anyway, gotta give her credit as it seems to keep us all on the same page." He headed for the double-winged, sixteen-thousand-square-foot log lodge with a half rock-and-wood column portico. Manicured flower beds with daisies and fall-colored mums, dahlias, and zinnias greeted everyone, and smoke swirled from the stone chimney.

"So, what are the other parts to the ranch's philosophy?" Mandie flung a hand towel across her shoulder and strode alongside him, her short legs keeping pace.

"You want me to recite them? Why not just go into the office and read the gigantic photo . . . thingy . . . Trey created?" He hopped up the half-log stairs and strode past a horsehead bench.

"Yeah, I do. And I agree Trey's one heck of a photographer. Syd's lucky to get a gift that fine on their first anniversary."

Robert spun around and grimaced at her sarcasm. "You aren't going to give up, are you?" He let out a ragged breath when she shook her head. "'Respect and enjoy each other and the land we live on.' Which might be a stretch for you, Short Stack." He ignored her scowl and continued, "'Make goals and prepare for ruts in the road. Stand on your word.'"

"Yep. 'Stand on your word.'" She set a hand on her hip. "'And make sure every horse and cow and invested owner pulls their own weight while everyone else is gone.' So go pull your weight, Bronco Bobby. Practice can wait." She snapped the hand towel at his leg and slipped inside, her cackle trailing behind.

"You drive me crazy." Robert followed her through the warm, boot-lined foyer and into the great room to the aroma of freshly baked chocolate chip cookies.

"Sorry. But I promised Syd I'd look after you. Just wanted to make sure you knew the rules."

"Suggestions."

"Rules and you know it."

He tapped the clipboard. "If you don't mind, I have work to do before this weekend's rodeo." He studied the list. "When does the next crop of guests check in?"

"Crop? Really, Bobby? Good grief." She rolled her eyes. "I hope you got someone to cover you for your rode-ay-oh this weekend, pretty boy."

"You know I do."

"Who?"

Robert stretched out his arms, one hand white knuckling the clipboard. "Chad and Rich have a buddy—"

"Good old Chad and Rich. You'd be a mess without them."

"We've got one another's backs."

"You mean because they don't have a life?"

"They're the best buddies a guy could have."

"Whatever." At a toddler's screech, Mandie fast walked toward the kitchen and disappeared through batwing doors.

Robert strode into the ranch office located on the north side of the bay window–lined common room, yanked off his pullover, and dropped it on the worn leather couch Sydney refused to toss out. Placing the clipboard on the desk, he was pumped to ride a handful of broncs before the next batch of guests arrived.

Not that he needed the practice. But the extra rides would keep him on top of his game. Besides, Short Stack didn't have the right to boss him around. She was the cook, not his coach.

A landline phone on the cedar desk Grandpa Moomaw had handcrafted rang. He groaned and answered the call with the usual, "Seven Tine Guest Ranch, how can I help you?" He shifted his weight and registered a family of five for the following month.

He started for the door but stopped by the thirty-by-forty-inch canvas hanging on the wall above the ugly sofa. The photo was an aerial view of the property with the Seven Tine statements of wisdom stamped on it.

The canvas, though beautiful, reminded him of how large the ranch was and how overwhelming it felt. Like now.

"This is gonna be a long month," he grumbled and walked out.

CHAPTER 3

Umatilla Reservation

Rita cringed at the heavy stench of manure and urine. The mixture was piled high in the corner of Bowie Dark Cloud's grimy, six-stall horse barn on his run-down, five-acre ranch. Most of the overhead lights had been out for weeks, and dusk's glow was little help. "Which horse do you want me to look at?" Three equine-filled stalls lined each side of the wooden barn, and none of them offered turnout lanes. This wasn't a bad thing, considering the sale horses weren't around long enough to need exercise.

"She's over here. A real beauty. Like you." He rubbed her back as they walked.

She stiffened at his touch as they made their way down the lane and stopped at the second stall on the right. After setting her layman's medical tote on the ground, she blew warm air into her cold hands. A horse with a light-colored head poked its nose at Rita's shoulder. "Hi there." She rubbed her soft face.

"You do have a way with them." Bowie stood close enough that his rank breath brushed her neck.

She inched away, trying not to be obvious. "You're right, she's a beauty." She slid the door open and when she went to turn, Bowie slammed her against the door's sharp edge. The side of her face bounced off it, and her teeth caught her upper lip. In an instant, a metallic tinge filled her mouth as he pinned her in place.

He grabbed a handful of her hair and jerked her head backward. "I know your dad's hired hands want a turn with you. I heard the way you told them 'Have a good evening' in your sweet, sappy tone. I bet you wouldn't mind fooling around with 'em, huh?"

Oh, God, not again. The pains in Rita's sides went from stiff aches to sharp stabs, and her head burned from his grip on her hair. She clung to the icy latch, bracing herself. He held her face in a crushing grip with his number one rule—never leave a visible mark. Concentrating on not showing fear, she said with an even tone, "I'm not interested in them. Please believe me."

"Not interested in them?" He slammed her with a few choice names. "I saw the way you smiled at Carson." Bowie's deep voice sliced the space between them as he lifted her hand. "Like I said before, you should have worn your ring."

Rita tried to steady her voice. "I'm afraid it will get ruined. But I'll wear it from now on. I promise. I didn't mean anything by it. You know how my dad expects us to be considerate to the ranch hands."

Bowie dropped her hand and pressed his rough lips to her neck. "You're a little more than considerate. You preach about waiting until marriage. Claim it's your family's belief. But I see how you flirt with them. You're nothing but a tease."

"I'm not trying to tease anyone. I . . . I . . . only want to be with you." She would do whatever it took to keep him calm.

"Then prove it." His eyes danced. "Let's go to the house." It was a single-wide trailer. He leaned down, pulled her head back farther by her hair, and kissed the length of her neck. His other hand roamed.

Pushing against him, Rita squirmed. "But that will take away from our wedding night. I want it to be special, don't you?" She forced herself to stay put, and when he lightened his grip, she tucked her head under his scratchy goatee so she wouldn't have to look at him or smell his breath.

He lifted her chin with his finger and dropped his mouth to hers. She stuffed down a gag when he deepened the kiss. She took advantage of the space between her and the edge of the door to spin out of his embrace. "Let's look at this horse. Trust me, babe, there will be plenty of time for romance once we're married." No way could she go through with the wedding. Her dad pushing her to marry, in his words, "such a fine catch" didn't help.

Good Lord, what on earth did her father see in him? Besides being the son that he'd never had who was into horses. Why did her father have to be so blind?

Bowie backed off, scowling as he jerked a halter over the mare's head. "You make me hurt you, Rita. You know that, right?"

Any response stuck in her tight throat. *Please keep him away from me.*

A stocky palomino stood tall in its stall when Bowie led her into the aisle. The mare's pale mane and tail highlighted her dark, soft eyes.

"She's a beauty all right," Rita said, struggling to keep enthusiasm in her voice.

For a quick moment, admiration for the animal soothed her sore sides and split lip. She winced as she picked up her medical tote and took hold of the lead rope to take the horse outside into the dimming natural light.

This one she'd call Lemon Drop and would keep it to herself. Bowie would only accuse her of getting attached, and she wasn't up for added tongue lashings. The mare had kind eyes. "How old is she?"

"According to her papers, six." Bowie gave her a stethoscope and lit a cigarette. "Hurry up. I'm hauling horses to Hermiston in the morning, and I got other stuff to do tonight, now that you're not staying."

Other stuff meant gambling at the Wildhorse Resort and Casino in Pendleton with his buddy, Gary Fullmoon. But Hermiston meant he'd be gone all day. She chewed on her tongue to keep from smiling.

She listened to the horse's heart rate, strong at thirty-three beats per minute, and her gut sounded clear. Her temp came in at ninety-nine degrees. So far, Lemon Drop appeared to be in fine shape. Keeping her elbows close to her sides to ease the sting, Rita disinfected the thermometer and placed it back in her tote. Bowie shifted from one foot to the other, causing her insides to clench tighter, and took a drag of his smoke.

The palomino's legs were cool to the touch. She had Bowie walk the mare away from her, walk in a small circle, and come back. The mare's steps seemed normal, with no hitches or a bobbing head. Rita ran a hand over the mare's back for signs of soreness.

When satisfied, she pointed the red dot of an engine temperature gauge at each hoof, checking for heat from potential founder or abscesses. Overfeeding or embedded gravel in a hoof could cause permanent damage. At least overfeeding wasn't something she'd have to worry about with Bowie's skimpy equine feeding program.

Rita examined two more horses, hoping to finish before the last thread of light. She was thankful he sold quality stock and not abandoned horses whose scrawny hides would end up at a canner.

"She seems to be in perfect health. You should get a good price for her." Holding her breath against the burn in her sides, Rita combed her fingers through the flaxen mane. "What did the owners use her for?"

"Not sure." Bowie blew out smoke and flicked the cigarette butt to the dirt. "Don't care either. As long as I can get a hefty fee." He stomped on the smoldering stub.

She nodded.

"Don't get any ideas. You can't keep her."

"I know. I'm only imagining how she'd move across our rolling hills. Like I said, she seems sound."

"I'll put her away, then take you home." He gave her a sassy smile. "Unless you've changed your mind and want to stay the night."

She wasn't about to stay the night. She forced a grin and sweetened her voice, despite wanting to retch. "Now, Bowie. You know I love only you. And as I've said before . . ." She went to reach up and caress his black goatee; after all, that's what had attracted her to him in the first place. But a sharp pang in her side made her flinch and drop her arm.

Instead, she took hold of his hands, having learned a little affection defused him. "We need to wait so our wedding night will be full of surprises. You don't want to ruin that for us, do you?"

For a moment, his expression seemed to darken. Then he smiled. "I have to admit, I love surprises." He pulled her close and gave her a sloppy kiss before putting the horse up for the night. Once all was locked up, he strutted to his brown Ford F-150.

She eased into the passenger's side. When Bowie scowled at her, she inched over to the middle of the bench seat. Her leg pressed against his as it straddled the four-wheel-drive console. Sidling up to him made her want to puke. But she did it anyway, longing for a peaceful ride home.

Thirty minutes later, they pulled onto her father's two-hundred-and-fifty-acre cattle ranch. By then, her stomach had twisted into a huge knot. The pickup rattled past her folks' place, complete with ranch-style house and eight-stall horse barn, wound down the lane another couple of miles, and stopped in front of a modest log cabin. Her father had built it a few years ago and said it was "to keep his girls in arm's reach."

The glow of an entryway light illuminated planters holding colorful mums, asters, clematis, marigolds, and bee balm adorning every inch of dirt around the cabin. Her younger sister, Hazel, had the green thumb. A wooden porch welcomed guests with the ding of wind chimes made of old silverware, clay pots, and brass tubes of various lengths and tones—also her sister's doing.

The door creaked open, and Hazel stepped out in a long-sleeved tee and sweats. Her hair appeared to be pulled back in her usual ponytail, and she wore a white-and-maroon floral baseball cap. Squinting against the headlights, she frowned.

Rita gave Bowie a quick kiss for good measure, took hold of her tote, and got out. A sharp groan escaped her lips as her feet hit the dirt.

"Remember, honey, you say anything about tonight, and I'll have to take it out on her." He tipped his chin to Hazel.

Her pulse racing, she nodded, shut the truck door, and walked to the cabin as though nothing had happened. She'd do anything to protect her sister. *Lord, help us both.*

CHAPTER 4

Colville Reservation

A giggly, brown-haired girl of about six spoke to Robert as he led her around the arena in the twilight, "I love riding her."

Robert tipped his eagle-feather-adorned Stetson like a gentleman. His mind flipped to the ranch value that stated, "Enjoy each other and the land we live on" before he answered, "Good."

He should be riding broncs, not leading a six-year-old in mindless circles in the arena. But thanks to Mandie, who was terrified of horses, he wasn't. She had invited her cousin over, knowing he had plans to jump on some bucking horses before dark.

So what if the gal was from the west side of Washington in the quaint, fishing town of Aberdeen? So what if the manifesto said to "Stand on your word"? Darned if Mandie hadn't held him to it. Why had he promised to help out when his plate was so full? Why did she have to bring the attractive woman and her cute little girl to ride tonight?

He feared the cousin and her daughter would be hanging around for the few weeks they were visiting, vying for his attention when he needed to concentrate on his rides.

The girl's high-pitched squeals of delight rang in his ears. Once more and he swore he'd drop the lead rope and walk away. The girl waved at her proud-faced mom. Mandie sat on the railing, clapping and cheering, smirking at Robert as they passed by. Heck, she should be the one leading her cousin's daughter.

Integrity. Respect. Good grief. Why did the manifesto have to haunt him? When Mandie let out an obvious snicker, he stopped, told the girl he'd be right back, and gave the reins to Mandie. "Later."

"What? Where you going?"

Robert strode past Chad, one of the ranch hands, who was also snickering and holding out Robert's chaps. "Got the broncs ready?" He yanked the chaps out of Chad's hand, wanting to rip those scruffy sideburns off his face.

"Sure do, boss. Fire Dancer's ready for ya in the chute." Chad chuckled. "Unless you'd rather go back to the girl and her pretty little mama."

Robert rounded on him. "Shut your face or I'll knock your lights out." Still wearing a grin, Chad held up his hands. Robert headed for the chutes, buckling the front of his chaps as he strode, the dangling leather slapping his legs.

"Want me to get Mandie and her family to cheer ya on?"

"Best friend or not, you're looking to get yourself decked."

"Loosen up, Bobby Bronco. Or is it Bronco Bobby?"

"You heard that?"

"Sure did. And so did half the guests." He let out a war whoop and jogged ahead.

Minutes later, Robert hunched as he sat deep in his saddle, pulling his Stetson low, his spur-covered boots above the sorrel's shoulders and his toes pointed outward. He inhaled the horse scent and exhaled his fury as one hand grasped the smooth buck rein, the rope nestled between his pinky and three fingers for a binding grip, and the other held on to the panel of the chute. He nodded and hollered, "Outside!"

Rich pulled the gate rope, and the chute flew open. Fire Dancer burst out, breaking into several jumps. Robert flew off and hit the ground, just shy of the eight-second mark. A groan and bits of dirt sputtered out of his mouth.

Chad waved a flag from the back of one of the ranch's bulky blue roans. "You missed him out, man."

Robert stood and wiped dirt off his chaps. "Did not!" Certain his spur rowels were above the point of the horse's shoulders when his front hooves hit the ground, he fetched his black Stetson out of the dirt and dusted it off against his chaps. He straightened his eagle feather before pushing it back on his head.

"Yeah, buddy, you did." Chad waved the flag at him as Rich concurred. "Your spurs were below the bronc's shoulder."

"You need to rest, bro. The rodeo's this weekend," Rich said. "Give your body a break."

"No way." Robert spat in the dirt. "I got a lot riding on this win."

"Let's go again, then." Chad spurred Big Blue until it came alongside Fire Dancer and unbuckled the flank rope, but the bronc kept running. He flung the rope at Robert who caught the bronc and led him through a gate leading to a holding pen.

Robert retrieved his bronc saddle, strapped it on another horse, and sat deep. He'd cover this one or die of humiliation. Good grief. Eight seconds wasn't asking too much of him. "Let's go." He nodded and gritted his teeth.

Rich pulled the gate open and rushed to the side. The bronc exploded out of the chute and bucked hard. Yes. His feet had stayed in place. But the bronc's power nearly threw him between his ears on the next jump, tossing him about like a rag doll.

Every time the horse kicked up his hind legs, Robert flicked his right arm back and sent his legs toward the animal's shoulders, elongating his torso as he spurred the bronc's neck. As the horse came down, he swept his feet backward and focused on lifting and centering his rein arm, trying to keep his balance.

Half a dozen jumps later, Robert was slammed to the ground.

"Seven point seventy-four." Rich held up a stopwatch.

"What? No freaking way." Robert jumped to his feet and found his Stetson, adrenaline rushing through his veins. "Lemme see." He marched over to his partner and checked the timer. Sure enough, he was a hair under eight seconds. "Let's go again."

"You wanna break?" Chad hollered from across the arena. Above him, a dusk-to-dawn yard light buzzed to life.

Robert circled his pointed index finger in the air. Turning toward the gate to get his bronc saddle, he met Mandie's harsh gaze.

"How ya doing, Bronco Bobby?"

"Quit calling me that, Short Stack."

"Why'd you ditch my cousin and her poor little girl?"

He tried to open the gate, but she blocked him.

"She came all the way from the coast."

"I know she did. But I got a lot going on here, so cut me a break."

Mandie dropped her gaze to the ground. Oh, how he hated when she made that pitiful face. "Sheesh. Fine. Tell them to come back tomorrow and I'll take them for a private trail ride after breakfast."

She squealed. "You're the best, Bobby!"

He pushed her out of the way. "Remember that when I need a favor from you."

CHAPTER 5

Umatilla Reservation

R ita peeked out the window to make sure Bowie was gone. "Thanks for having my back, Sis. I'm glad you stepped outside to show him you were here so he wouldn't come inside. I'm tired and just want to go to bed." She hid her face by dipping the brim of her buckaroo hat.

"You bet." Hazel rubbed her sleepy, brown eyes. "What happened to your lip?"

Rita fingered the swollen cut. "I tripped over a pitchfork and fell into a stall. It's no big deal."

"Okay, well, I'm headed to bed. Dad's got me up early to help round up cows so you can do your healing magic." Hazel yawned. "Your fiancé gives me the creeps. He's got some crazy control issues. Don't you see the tight leash he keeps you on?" When Rita didn't answer, she yawned again and walked away.

Yeah, she saw it.

She detested her looming marriage to the dirtbag. But she had to protect her nineteen-year-old sister from him— had to protect her from all the bad men. Maybe if she left, he'd leave Hazel alone.

When she was sure Bowie's truck was gone, she dragged herself to her room, shut the door, sank to the bed, and flinched from the sharp pain. She inhaled a breath, snapping her hand over her mouth to keep from crying out. After a long moment, she released the breath.

As a young girl, she had vowed to never let a man hurt her. Now she was about to become her mother and repeat the cycle of abuse.

Rita had believed Bowie's lies. It was the same deception her father used on her mother. She should have known better. Both men lived in circles: promised love, offerings, jealousy, rants, rage, violence, sorrow. Then it'd start over again.

She kicked off her boots and rolled onto her side, then curled into a ball and stayed that way, wanting to scream at her Creator for not protecting her. But she knew He hadn't chosen this life for her. It was all her doing.

If she hadn't been so naive.

Her youth pastor used to offer encouragement. She could call him and see if he had any sound advice. Reaching for her phone stung her ribs, but she did it anyway and made the call. She groaned when someone else's name and voice left a greeting. She hung up and swiped the screen. Had he moved? She tapped his name in a search engine and gasped when his obituary popped up. He had died six months ago, leaving behind a young wife and baby.

Oh, God, no. She tossed and turned most of the night, pain racking her midsection with the slightest movement. Nightmares haunted her until she woke, drenched and feeling suffocated.

Oh, Lord, she needed to get away from Bowie. Nothing good had ever come from being married to a woman beater. If only she had extra time to plan an escape and convince Hazel to come with her. But would her sister agree to leave the ranch? Or would she remain behind, feeling responsible for their mother's safety? As usual.

Her mind reeling, she rose, shuffled into the bathroom, and ran hot water. Rita eased down onto the toilet seat and leaned over to pull off her socks. "Ow." She sucked in a deep breath and held it for an instant.

The mirror reflected an image she didn't recognize. Her right eye and cheek were swollen and stained with a plumb-like color. Lifting her shirt revealed smudges as though someone took a handful of huckleberries and washed one side of her torso with them. The other side was beginning to turn green.

He'd gotten his shorts in a bind over her thanking a ranch hand for saddling her mare because she'd been late. Bowie had dropped her off after they'd gotten back from lunch. After the hand had ridden off on his horse, Bowie slammed her against the edge of her mare's partially open stall door.

"You give him a piece of you for that?" he asked.

She was convinced that a woman's ribs were his spot of choice. And no one ever saw him hurt her because, most of the time, they were conversing alone in either her father's barn or his.

But now and true to her research about domestic violence, his thrashings were escalating. And for the first time, he didn't seem to care about where he hit her.

She managed to peel off her clothes, pour two cups of Epsom salts into the tub, and slip in. Leaning back, she let the hot water massage her body. Her mind whirled to her teenage rape, and tears threatened to drown her. She shook her head and blocked the horror.

Rita couldn't let that happen to Hazel. She had to leave, get settled, and come back for her sister. But where? How would they earn a living?

She cupped warm water, splashed her face, and soaked. She cried until the shame drained her. When the water turned tepid, she crawled out, rubbed her bruises down with arnica and peppermint, and slipped into a fresh pair of jeans and a sweatshirt.

On the edge of her bed, she fingered a necklace her mother had given her—a cross layered over an eagle feather made from sterling silver. It was for her sixteenth birthday.

The day her world had turned upside down. She dabbed at her eyes with the sleeve of her sweatshirt. Again, she shoved grating memories aside.

She needed a plan.

Slowly, Rita pushed herself off the bed and padded to her desk. She eased into the rolling chair and opened the top drawer. After rifling through a few files, she came across a brochure. She pulled it out and leaned back. It was titled "Seven Tine." Tired of living a life of torment, she opened the trifold pamphlet.

Last year, Rita had attended a woman and ranch symposium in Pendleton. The keynote speaker, Sydney Moomaw Hardy, had been abused and abducted by her ex-husband and was making rounds to various conventions to share her story. What tapped at Rita's heart was when Sydney had said, "You do not owe your abuser another chance."

In the top drawer, Rita found a notebook filled with her notes. She took it out and flipped through it until she found a page she had read over and over. In big letters and circled several times were sentiments that had clung to her that day.

I'm not alone.

It's not my fault.

I am loved.

I am valued.

I am a daughter of God—the most-high King.

I can do all things through Christ who strengthens me.

The guest ranch was on the Colville rez in Nespelem. She grabbed her phone, looked up the Seven Tine website, and read about Sydney and the staff. Her eyes locked on Robert Elliot. Where had she seen him before?

And did she know anyone from the Colville Tribe?

Creator, is this where you want me to go?

CHAPTER 6

Rita padded down the hallway to the kitchen, her hair still damp. She flipped on the light and turned on the coffee pot. The wall clock read 4:00 a.m. While the coffee brewed, she flipped through the brochure. How far was the Seven Tine? Would Sydney be there?

Hazel entered the kitchen, rubbing her eyes. "What are you doing up this early?"

Rita folded and slid the brochure into her back pocket. How would she tell her sister she was leaving? Should she ask her to come too? Could she risk leaving Hazel behind? Would Bowie keep his word and come after her? Her younger sister's round face, high cheekbones, and delicate mouth made her appear fragile. On the inside, she was no different. "I need you to do me a favor."

Hazel poured herself a cup of the steaming brew and added a splash of pumpkin spice creamer. She leaned against the counter. "What kind of favor?"

"I'm taking a road trip. I'll help feed and doctor the calves, then I'm going to go see a woman about a horse." Technically, she was telling the truth. Sydney had horses, and some of the best contained Very Smart Remedy bloodlines. She poured a cup of coffee and added the same creamer.

Hazel's eyes grew round. She tipped her head. "What horse? Does Daddy know about this?"

"No, he doesn't. And it's a surprise. So don't spill the beans, okay?" Lying went against everything she'd been taught at youth group. Yet, she couldn't tell the truth.

To avoid added questions, Rita took her coffee to her bedroom and found a backpack in her closet. Packing light, she stuffed a couple of changes of clothes in it. What else?

"Why are you packing if it's a day trip?"

Rita stiffened. *Why? Ohhh.* "It's supposed to rain. I've been promised a trail ride on the horse I'm looking at and want dry clothes for the trip back."

"How are you going to sneak a horse trailer out of here?"

Why did her sister have to ask so many questions? Oh, man, Rita hated lying. Dishonesty was hard to keep track of. She needed time. Pursing her lips against the pain, she rose and turned to face her sister. "I'm only looking today. I have a couple of added prospects to look at."

"I want to go."

"No." Rita's tone sounded sharp and firm. So much so, she thought her sister might grow suspicious. "Listen, Bowie and I had a disagreement last night—"

"A disagreement, huh? You need to leave that jerk. You can do better than him. As beautiful and sweet as you are, you could have any man you wanted. Seriously."

"That's why I want to go alone. To clear my head. Figure out a plan. Okay?"

Hazel nodded. "Next time?"

"For sure." Rita zipped her backpack. Hopefully, Hazel would remember to keep her mouth shut. She went to the bathroom, dabbed on concealer, packed toiletries, and tied a black wild rag around her neck.

After a light breakfast of toast and bacon, the girls met their father in the barn near the main house at seven o'clock sharp. Rita kept her left side angled toward her dad, her head down.

"Saddle up, girls." Dean Runninghorse stood six feet tall. His clean-cut appearance and polished cowboy boots led townsfolk to believe that he was an upstanding rancher with a family any man would dream of having. His refined bay stallion, Ruger, was saddled and ready to go.

"Hey, Dad," Rita said, "I forgot something. I'll be right back, 'kay?" She didn't give him time to answer and would pay for it later. Second thoughts on escaping thumped her chest. She rushed out of the barn as fast as her stiff body would allow, jumped into her pearly-white, three-quarter-ton Dodge Ram, and drove away.

She needed a moment to calm her nerves and find the courage to leave. Plus, she didn't want everyone to see her face or have them ask questions. Especially her dad. She needed to stop shaking and pull herself together before catching up to her sister.

Oh, God, Hazel.

How could she leave her alone with their dad? With his aggressive ways and creepy friends? And with Bowie? Rita pulled over and pounded the steering wheel. "I have to do this to save her. Show her she can leave too. Find a better life. Crush the cycle." She pounded the steering wheel two extra times. A scream discharged from her broken heart.

The dashboard clock suggested enough time had passed for Hazel to saddle her horse and for everyone to head out for morning chores. Good. She still wasn't ready to face everyone. She started the engine and turned the truck around.

When Rita entered the barn, sure enough, everyone was gone. She went to Opal's stall and found the mare standing calmly inside, bridled and saddled. She double-checked the barn to see if someone was still around. The sign on the mare's stall door made her stop. Her heart plummeted. It read Pewter Tiger Lady, her registered name. Could she leave Opal behind?

What would happen to her once she was gone? Rita pressed her hand to the mare's neck. She swallowed hard, stood tall, and hugged the grulla's soft neck. "I'll come back for you too. I promise," she whispered and inhaled the horse's scent.

She prayed her mother would come too.

In the meantime, she had to fake her morning. Do her job. Then skedaddle. She took a deep breath and led her mare out of the barn. She shoved her sadness and guilt down her throat, making sure no one would have a clue, mounted, and joined the crew in the east pasture.

Dean Runninghorse came alongside his daughter, his mouth twisted. He looked like a character on an old Western but in modern attire that shouted I'm-a-rich-and-famous-wanna-be. "Don't be late again. You messed up the entire schedule. How can you be so selfish, huh? I don't know what was so important you had to leave us all hanging." He cursed at her.

Dean expected an answer. Shoot. She should've been prepared. "It won't happen again." And it wouldn't because she would be free.

"Get to work."

Rita found the first calf down a hill and around the bend, about three-quarters of a mile from the barn. She also found Austin Wright, who wore a tan Stetson, a tan wild rag, and a scowl.

Austin, a Umatilla ranch hand she'd grown up with, had the calf on the ground, his legs tied together. "What took you so long? Your dad reamed us all 'cause you're late. I even saddled your horse to speed you along. We all have things to do later—"

"Sheesh, Grumpy Pants. When have I ever been late? Huh? Like never." She eased herself out of the saddle.

"Yeah, I know. It's just—"

"You have a date with Shelly?"

Austin cocked his head, his mouth hinged open like a fish ready to take the bait. "How did you know?"

Rita laughed, hunched over, and pressed her elbows to her sides. She lengthened her spine, hoping to distract Austin from her pain. "That's privileged information." She shifted and let air out of her nose.

"You two quit yappin' and get the job done," Dean hollered from across the herd.

Austin's face turned red as he shook his head. "Where's your tote?"

"I'll get it." Rita recalled memories of the guys teasing her when she'd bought and organized the tote of medical supplies as though she were a vet. Even her father got in on the fun. It was one of the few times Dean wasn't so cranky. Or cruel. She stopped at her mare's side.

Normally, the tote hung from a latigo she'd fixed up and secured on the left side of the saddle's cantle. *Oh no.* Had she forgotten it? She'd hoped this day would be free of suspicion. And here her absentmindedness was doing a great job of generating attention.

"What's taking you so long?" Austin held down the squirming calf.

"I . . . huh, well . . . I forgot my tote. I'll be right back."

"You what?" He untied the calf's legs and let him go. "What's wrong with you?" His brows shot up. "And how'd you get the fat lip?"

"Never mind." Rita took hold of the reins. How would she get back on her horse without Austin noticing her stiffness? Shoot. She'd messed things up now for sure.

Dean galloped up to them and slid his horse to a stop. "What in tarnation is going on with you, girl? What's the holdup?"

"I'm sorry, Daddy." Rita kept her face toward Opal. "I hardly got any sleep last night. Truth be told," she cringed, "I haven't been feeling well."

"You coming down with the flu or something?" Dean shifted in the saddle.

"Maybe."

"*Maybe* ain't no answer. Either you are or you're not."

If Rita answered yes, would he send her home? If so, she could easily hook up a trailer and head out. Her gut told her to take Opal. It was never wrong. She searched the pasture. Where was Hazel? She was his favorite. The baby. Surely, she could convince her sister to help distract him. Beyond the herd, Hazel and Carson were about to disappear behind a knoll. Hazel was on a horse and Carson drove an ATV hauling a trailer with fencing supplies piled high. "I just don't feel well, Daddy. It's no big deal."

A gust of wind slapped the prairie grass. Rita held on to her buckaroo hat, tucking her chin close to her chest.

"We got a lot to do today." Dean spat a long string of brown juice at a pile of cow dung near his daughter's feet. "Suck it up, sister, and pull your weight. Austin, you come with me." He spun his horse around and said to her over his shoulder, "You're on your own."

His words punched Rita in the gut. How would she be able to handle the calves by herself? They were six-hundred-and-fifty-pound toddlers. She found a good-sized boulder and used it to help her climb into the saddle. She urged Opal back to the barn, flinching at every sway the horse made.

Rita found the tote in her pickup, next to a tube of arnica. She twisted open the container and slathered the cream on her sides. Hating to consume Western medicine, she swallowed two ibuprofen tablets and chased them with soda crackers and cheese she'd found in the barn office.

Coffee. She needed a swig of the dark brew to keep her going. After a few quick swallows of warm, instant Folgers, she tossed the medicinal cream, crackers, and cheese in her tote along with a bottle of water.

Darn him.

Having to work alone, how would she leave as planned? Rita had left her packed bags at the cabin to avoid suspicion. Why hadn't she brought them along? She still had to hook up the horse trailer.

"What are you still doing here?"

Oh, no. "I'm not feeling the best. Didn't sleep well." She braced herself for her mother's reaction. At times Joan Runninghorse liked to fuss over her daughters like an old hen. Hazel liked it. Rita did not.

"What's wrong?" Mom gasped when Rita faced her. The woman stood an inch shorter than her daughter, and her cropped silver hair and the deep creases in her skin made her appear older than she was.

"I'm okay, Mom. I think it's, you know, my moon time. I also may have pulled a muscle in my shoulder working that calf yesterday." She clutched her arm to make it believable. "We both hit the ground pretty hard."

Mom pressed her brows together. "I thought you just got over your cycle. Do you need to see a doctor? I'm headed to the clinic now. They'll understand if I'm late for work. I can take you."

A doctor. Could it be her way out? But she'd need a believable reason to take a horse trailer with her. *C'mon think.* But nothing came to mind.

"Maybe. I don't have time to go right now. It's not that bad. For the rest of the day, I can do light work. I'll have one of the hands help me." She gestured to the horse trailer. "Besides, I promised to haul a horse to Bowie's this afternoon." She chewed the inside of her mouth, hating the lies. Hopefully, her mom would go to work before she needed to load Opal.

"Bowie can get someone else to do his bidding." Mom raised her brows and gazed at the rolling hills to the side of the house. "Where's your father?"

"Down in the valley." Rita gave her mom a reassuring smile and stepped toward the horse trailer.

"Why don't I hook it up for you. You don't need to strain your shoulder."

With her mom's help, she could hopefully slip out unnoticed. All she had to do was make sure her dad kept busy and figure out a way to tend to the injured calves by herself. While her mother hooked up the horse trailer, Rita found the mounting block and heaved herself into the saddle. By the time she reached the calves, the pain would be slight, or so she hoped.

"Thanks, Mom." Rita reined her mare around. "You're the best." She urged her horse forward before her mother could answer, not wanting to cry in front of her mom. The guilt of leaving as planned pecked at her chest.

Rita prayed her mom would forgive her. Of all people, she should understand.

When Rita rode up to where she'd left the calves, Austin was herding the last of them into a small portable corral.

"What took you so long?" Austin shut the gate.

"What are you doing here? Where's my dad?"

"I talked him into letting me help you. Told him it would take too long for you to get this done by yourself." He motioned to a box laying on the ground. "Besides, there's been a change of plans."

"Oh?" Her pulse sped up.

"I got to looking at the calves that got tangled in the fence. They're about healed. I don't know what concoction you put on them, but it's working."

Calendula was the best thing she'd discovered for human and animal wounds.

"By the way, you owe me ten bucks. It was a wolf that shoved them into it."

"You got proof?"

"Tracks."

"Where?"

A sassy smile bloomed on his face. "I'll show you when we get done."

"What about Shelly? Don't want to keep her waiting, do you?"

"We'll have time."

"Okay, but I don't owe you anything. I saw cougar tracks and scat. You owe me twenty." She laughed, then coughed and groaned.

"You okay?" Austin strode to her mare and took hold of the reins.

"Yep. Just a little under the weather is all." Rita slid out of the saddle and gently dropped to the ground. When her feet hit, she doubled over and cried out.

CHAPTER 7

"I'm okay." Rita took in shallow breaths. Austin leaned down as if to help her, but she held out an arm to stop him. She couldn't take the chance of him touching her. When the dizzy spell subsided, she pushed to her feet and hung on to the saddle for support. "I think I'm dehydrated is all. I'll get a sip of water. Then we can get started." She rubbed her head and squeezed her eyes shut. "What are we doing today?"

"Shots."

Oh yeah. The box was right in front of her. These calves were seven months old, ready to wean and take to the market. Without a doubt, they needed their vaccinations.

"Are you sure you're okay?" He pressed a hand on her shoulder. The one that was supposed to be injured.

"Ow!" She wasn't sure she could keep up with the facade much longer.

He jerked his hand away. "What's wrong?"

"Yesterday, that late calf got the best of me." She wished this time he wasn't so compassionate. Austin always did have a tender heart though. "Get everything ready. I'll be right back."

He arched a brow but did as she asked.

Rita took a swallow of water, capped the bottle, and stuffed it back into her tote, hoping they could get the job done so she could leave. She picked up the first vial of bovine vaccine and shook it.

Austin held up a syringe and uncapped the needle. "Let's get this done."

One by one, they loaded the calves into a squeeze chute and gave them each a shot. When the last of the calves had been vaccinated, they were released with their mothers. Rita's sides were burning, and she made her way to her tote, ate some crackers and cheese, and took two ibuprofen. She wished she had brought her arnica.

"So, what's going on with you?" Austin snatched a bottle of water from his saddlebag and took a long swig. "That calf should have been nothing for you."

She spun her simple engagement ring around her finger. "Yeah, on a good day."

He gestured to her hand. "Everything okay with you and Bowie?"

Why would he ask? "It sure is."

Awesome. Had the others found out too? They weren't stupid, after all. She mentally listed the times her actions could have been tells. She'd been so careful to hide the abuse.

Austin gave her what looked like a disbelieving nod.

She slowly gathered the dirty supplies. "If we're done, I got to . . . um . . . I have somewhere to be."

He handed Rita her medical tote. "Take it easy." Concern bathed his voice.

"You too."

He mounted and headed toward the others.

She climbed into the saddle with a groan and reined her mare toward the horse barn. Time to leave the ranch.

Leaving thrilled yet scared her.

She prayed as she rode under the afternoon sky, asking Creator to keep her safe. She prayed Bowie would not try to find her, prayed for Hazel and her mother and their strength when they found out she was gone. By the time Rita got back to the barn, the temperature felt like it had dropped five degrees. She tightened her wild rag and turned up her coat collar.

Whew. Her mom's car was gone, and the barn was abandoned. All good signs. She untacked and brushed her mare. Then for a long moment, Rita entwined her fingers into the grulla's ebony mane as she memorized every curve and speck on the horse, drinking in her sweet scent. The horse would only slow her down. She didn't even know if Sydney Hardy would allow the mare to remain at the ranch. And she didn't have the time or the strength to load hay.

Moisture blurring her vision, she led Opal into the stall. She dried her tears with the heels of her hands. "I'll find a way to come after you. I promise," she whispered before trudging to her truck.

One last crank and the three-horse trailer freed itself from the ball. Rita rubbed her back, eased into the driver's seat, and sat for a moment, catching her breath. Leaning her head back, she closed her eyes. This was it. Committed to leaving, she hurried to the cabin.

Inside, she grabbed her backpack near the door where she'd left it. Once back in the truck, she twisted her engagement ring around her finger, slid it off, and tossed it into the jockey box. She started her pickup and tore down the lane—on her way to freedom.

But when rounding a corner, there was her father, sitting tall on Ruger's back, a deep scowl on his face. "Sorry. Not sorry." Avoiding eye contact, she stepped on the gas.

His look of betrayal—one that would never let her come back—burned deep into her bones. Somehow, she made her way through Pendleton and came to a halt at a stop sign and let three cars pass by.

Sydney's advice to conference attendees to get a protective order stirred inside her. But what she knew of them, the documents were worthless pieces of paper. Shredded pulpwood and ink were no weapons against a two-hundred-plus-pound ball of fury named Bowie.

She stomped on the accelerator and turned onto Interstate 84, the back of her truck fishtailing. She had to find a way to calm down. A car crash would only wreck her getaway.

She slid off her buckaroo hat and laid it on the seat next to her, hoping Bowie would be late getting home. Of all nights, this one would be good for him to stay out late and gamble, not finding out she'd left until morning. She eased off the gas pedal, turned up the radio, and let the music drown her fears.

But it didn't.

Rita turned around and headed for the courthouse. Some protection, she hoped, would be better than none.

CHAPTER 8

B owie Dark Cloud's cell chimed as he pulled up to his
house. Tired and hungry, he still answered the call.
"What's up, Dean?"

"Have you heard from Rita?"

"No. I just got back from Hermiston. Why?"

"She tore out of here late morning. About ran me over.
Haven't seen or heard from her since."

"I'll be right over." Bowie made it to the Runninghorse
ranch as dusk set in, jumped out of his truck, and took the
steps two at a time.

Inside the warm kitchen, Joan sat at the oak kitchen
table, dabbing at her eyes with a crisp, white handkerchief.

"She won't answer my calls." She held up her cell.

Bowie turned to Hazel. "Did she say anything to you?"

Hazel's gaze dropped to the floor.

"Did she indicate she was going anywhere?" Bowie
arched a brow.

Dean shook his head. "She was late this morning. And
seemed scatterbrained." His cell phone rang. He looked at
the screen and walked into another room.

Bowie studied Joan and Hazel. Joan looked as though
she knew something. He got her a glass of water, set it on the
table, and knelt beside her. Softening his tone, "Joan, did you
see her this morning?"

She shook her head, then dabbed her eyes.

Bowie curled his fingers into a fist and slammed it on the table. Joan flinched and cried harder. Bowie rose and paced. "I'm sorry. I'm . . . I'm just worried about her. C'mon, you guys have to know something." He settled his backside against the counter and crossed his arms. He'd have to corral his temper to get the answers he needed. "What did she say?"

Joan shook her head and, in a barely audible voice, said, "Nothing." She turned to the window framed by blue curtains.

He turned to Hazel. "You guys live together. She must have told you something."

She shrugged, her hands in her lap. "She didn't say anything to me."

What liars. "C'mon, you two are tighter than a vise grip," he said. "You have to know something."

Joan wrung her hands. "I think we need to call the police. What if she's hurt? It's cold outside." She stared out the window. "They take Native women all the time. What if she's been abducted?"

"I was with her all morning. Nothing appeared unusual." Hazel crossed her legs and bobbed her foot. "Besides, Rita's too smart to be taken. I agree with Mom. Call the cops."

"No one's calling the police," Dean said as he strode into the room.

Bowie agreed. There was too much at stake. "Why would she leave without telling anyone? That's not like her."

Joan's gaze lingered on the now-dark window. "I don't know why."

Bowie clenched his teeth. "I'll check the cabin. Maybe there's something there that will point to where she is." He stalked out the door, stood a moment on the porch, and lit a cigarette. Joan talked in a hushed tone. *They have to be hiding something.*

He drove to the cabin and found it unlocked. Good thing or he would have had to kick the door in. He strode inside and stomped to her room. Nothing looked out of the ordinary. He opened the closet. Her medical tote sat on the floor. He picked it up and rifled through it. Everything seemed in its place. As usual.

His fingers ran over her clothing, all neatly arranged by color. *What an OCD freak.* Then again, she'd keep his house tidy once they were married. A star quilt lay over her twin bed, not a wrinkle in sight. He grunted and went to her desk. He opened the yellow binder and thumbed through it. Nothing there but horse records, cross-breeding ideas, and ranch land management plans.

Yep, she'd be a handy wife. When he found her.

He opened the thin lap drawer. Inside she'd arranged various colored pens, paper clips, and small items only. The top side drawer had decorative paper, family photos, and record books. The second and third drawers stored high school keepsakes. One particular photo showed Rita and some punk at prom. He crumpled it up and slammed the bottom drawer shut.

A colorful brochure caught his eye. A corner peeked out from under her bed. On his hands and knees, he pulled it into view. "Seven Tine Guest Ranch? What the heck is this?" He opened the brochure.

His cell chimed. A text came up on the screen from Dean.

Chief Denton's on board.

CHAPTER 9

Three Hours Earlier

R ita tapped the steering wheel with her thumbs, her heart thrashing in her chest. What would happen when Bowie found out she had a temporary restraining order on him? She licked her lips, her mouth so dry she could barely swallow.

She tried to keep calm by singing along with a country song while she drove past the Hermiston exit. Good. His dirty-brown rig was still there and no sign of him outside— unless he hid and watched her drive by.

Please no.

How long would her fiancé—no, he was now her ex— plan on staying at the auction? Hopefully late. Trembling, she squinted at the bright sun on the horizon and flipped down the sun visor. She'd lost valuable time filling out the protective order.

Surely by now, her parents knew she wasn't coming home.

An hour and fifteen minutes later, she rolled into Pasco and pulled into a gas station. She topped off the tank, paid with cash, and used the restroom. After splashing her face with water, she stared at her battered reflection in the mirror. "What are you doing? If he finds you, you're dead."

But she couldn't go home.

According to her cell, Bowie had already sent eleven text messages. Most of them threatening because she hadn't returned his calls. He needed her to check out a horse someone planned to drop off at his place later that night. His expletives made her shudder. There were also a few missed calls and messages from her parents and Hazel, but she didn't have the nerve to listen to them. She had to keep going.

She exited the restroom and gathered bread, jam, peanut butter, and water in a shopping basket. She stepped aside and checked her billfold to see how much cash she had left. Forty dollars. She should have gone to the bank before she left. Or even better, the day before.

She took a chance and used the ATM, pulling out the balance—two hundred dollars. She added a stocking cap and gloves and made her way to the cash register.

A fortyish man about five-nine with dark hair strode in and swept his eyes over the store. She ducked and peeked at him over a magazine stand. But he had a mustache, not a goatee. She wiped her brow with the sleeve of her sweatshirt.

"Are you ready?" A plump, older woman with bright red readers and a scowl asked.

"Yes, ma'am. Sorry." Rita placed her items on the counter. Overheated and about to faint, Rita shrugged off her jacket and laid it over her arm.

Red Glasses seemed to take forever. She picked up the jam jar and examined it as if to make sure it was edible. She rang it up, lifted her chin to study the screen, and slid the jar into a plastic bag. At a snail's pace, she reached over and grabbed the next item.

Rita shifted her weight and tapped her fingers on the counter. *Good grief, sloths are quicker than this.* She was about to ask Red Glasses if she could pick up the pace when her cell chimed.

A notification for another one of Bowie's texts flashed on the screen. She shoved the phone in her back pocket, her face warming. When the last item was placed inside a plastic bag, she paid and got the heck out of the store as fast as she could.

Cool air massaged her face like a healing salve. Too bad it wouldn't heal her shattered heart. She loaded her items into the back seat of her pickup, crawled in, then hurried out of the station's lot, making sure no one was following her. She wiped her eyes, warm moisture blurring her view of the traffic. She hated to cry. It made her feel weak. "Darn him!" She hit the steering wheel.

Finding a secure place a few miles north of Pasco on Highway 395, she pulled over and took a sip of water. A bit hungry, she made half a sandwich, took a few bites, and tossed the leftovers out the window. After placing the rest of the food in the shopping bag, she tossed it in the back seat, leaned her head against the headrest, and closed her eyes.

She remembered 2 Corinthians 12:9, "My grace is sufficient for you, for my power is made perfect in weakness." Joan Runninghorse had made her daughters memorize the Bible verse as young girls. Now she knew why.

Pulling back onto the highway in the late-afternoon light, she prayed. It'd been a while since she'd talked to God. But according to His promises, He'd listen if she called on His name. So, call she did, asking for wisdom and protection.

Apple orchards, vineyards, and potato and wheat fields lined the dark pavement north of Pasco. Where the farmers had already harvested their spring wheat and had planted new seeds, the shoots were coming up green. But the closer Rita got to Mesa, sagebrush and blue bunchgrass replaced trees and vines.

As Connell, Washington, crept closer, a rock-lined coulee grabbed her attention. They called the ravine Esquatzel, a channeled scabland with basalt cliffs on either side and railroad tracks running along the bottom.

She could drive her rig over the ravine and be done with it. But if she killed herself, who would win? Definitely not her. She rolled down her window to get fresh air when a deafening pop echoed and her truck swerved, pulling her toward an oncoming eighteen-wheeler.

"No!"

CHAPTER 10

The semi blasted its horn as Rita cranked the steering wheel. "C'mon!" Right before Rita collided with the oversized rig, her truck jerked right, just missing the eighteen-wheeler. Thankfully, she was able to steer the pickup to safety onto the side of the road. "Holy smokes."

She clutched the steering wheel. "Thank you, Creator. Thank you." Breathless, she repeated the prayer over and over until her body stilled.

A sign indicated the Connell exit two miles away. Why couldn't her tire have blown closer to the exit ramp? She waited for a few rigs to blow past before opening her door. Ignoring her burning sides, she trotted to the tailgate while another car approached. She crouched. No spare. "What the heck?"

An amber horizon suggested that light was limited, and it felt like the temperature had dropped another five degrees. She crawled back into her warm cab. What now?

She could hunker down and keep the truck running all night. But then she'd be an open target. She could text her mom. But Joan was a rotten actor, often wearing her emotions on her sleeve. She couldn't take the chance of her dad finding out and bringing in Bowie for the search. Her only way out was to keep going.

After organizing a flashlight and the Leatherman multi-tool knife in the belly of her backpack, she placed her wallet and restraining order in the outer pocket for easy access. There was no room for the rose, tooled-leather purse her mother had given her, so she wound the strap around the rectangular bag and tucked it under the seat. Then using a bungee cord, she fastened a blanket she kept in her rig to the outside of her pack.

Her toes tingled, and she wiggled them in the cramped space of her thin cowboy boots. If she had been thinking, she would have bought winter boots in Pasco, at least finger- and toe-warmer packets. They had stood on the shelves by the checkout. Good grief. Why hadn't she planned things out better?

Rita reached for her buckaroo hat that her widowed grandmother had given her a few years ago for Christmas. How could she leave it behind? "It's shaped to fit your features," Nellie Runninghorse had told her granddaughter before moving to Mesilla, New Mexico.

Rita had worn that hat every day since and had cried for days after her grandmother had driven away. Desperately wanting to bring the hat along, she left it behind. It would be something else she'd have to lug around. She'd have to count on the police getting the hat and the rose-tooled handbag to her mom once they'd run the plates.

"Don't let fear of the unknown keep you from seeking safety" was something else Grandma Nellie had told her.

Rita blew out her frustration. What was she forgetting? Her ring. It could bring her a pretty penny. She checked the jockey box, took everything out, and set it on the passenger seat. She felt around until locating a circle of hard metal and held it up. "Ah, there you are." She stuffed it in her pocket and inched to the ground.

Before securing the truck, she made sure all of her windows were rolled up. Rushing air slapped her back as a semi blasted past, causing her to scream and slam into her Dodge. She groaned and buckled over until the initial pain passed. When the road was clear, she trudged up the highway—tired, cold, and livid. "Crazy. Freaking drivers."

A few cars whizzed by as the final shards of light dimmed. Should she find a spare tire or hitchhike? Would anything be open in such a small town? It was dark by the time she reached the Connell exit. The sound of a vehicle droned behind her and slowed as she made her way up the exit ramp. She stiffened, her pulse thundering in her ears.

Could it be Bowie? My dad? This quickly?

The sound of tires crunching rock about undid her. *Look. Don't look. Look.*

"Is that your white truck back there?" a woman said, her tone sounding kind but rough as though she'd smoked for years.

Rita angled her head toward the window. An elderly gal with silver, curly hair wearing a maroon, quilted jacket nestled in the passenger seat. The style of coat gave her away as someone who knew a thing or two about ranching. Grandma Nellie had a similar jacket. The elder's sunken eyes stared at her, a crease between her brows. A bundled gentleman wearing a tan scarf craned his neck around the woman, his hands gripping the steering wheel. He looked just as concerned.

"Stay right there." The woman shook a finger at Rita.

The coupe-sized car sped around her and pulled over. Rita strode to the passenger's side. At least they appeared to be trustworthy—a nice little couple straight out of *Little House on the Prairie.*

"I'm Faye Starr, and this is my husband, Albert. How can we help you, dear?" Faye smiled, her face soft and hopeful.

"My truck blew a tire, and there's no spare."

"My heavens. We can't have that now, can we?" Faye motioned to the back seat. "Where ya headed?"

"I . . . uh . . . I'm headed to Nespelem. Do you know where it is?"

Albert said in a loud voice, "What'd she say?"

Faye shouted back, "She's headed to Nespelem."

"Where's that?"

"I don't know. I'll ask."

"Why don't you ask her?" Albert asked.

Faye waved him off and turned to Rita. "Where is Nespelem?"

Rita shifted her weight from foot to foot and scoped out the car's interior. As far as she could tell, it was well taken care of.

"North of Coulee Dam."

Faye's eyes brightened. "Did you hear that, Albert? She's headed to the Indian town past Coulee Dam."

Albert's chest puffed. "Did you know I helped build the mighty dam?"

Rita had a feeling if she accepted the ride, she'd hear all about it.

"Well, get in. It's cold." Faye rolled up her window, and the door locks clicked.

Rita took off her backpack and got in. The scent of pine swirled thick as tar. She covered her mouth and took in short breaths until her nose became accustomed to the odor. Albert stared at her with a smile until she buckled her seat belt, then took off at a snail's pace.

"We're headed to our home in Ritzville," Faye said.

Home. Rita missed the comfort of her couch. And her sister's companionship. If she was at the cabin, they'd be watching *Heartland* reruns and eating pizza.

"What do you think of that?" Faye turned toward the back seat.

"I'm sorry, think of what?" Rita felt bad for not paying attention.

"We can drop you off at one of the quick marts in Ritzville. They're open twenty-four hours."

"That'd be fine." But would it? What then? Hitchhike the remaining way when so many Native women went missing? No thanks. She looked at the heavens. *Help.*

"I didn't catch your name, dear."

"It's Rita." She thought about telling them her last name but refrained. The less they knew the better.

"What a lovely name. Where are you from?"

"The Pendleton area."

Albert glanced at her in the rearview mirror. Rita squirmed. By now they had to have noticed her bruises. "Are you Umatilla then?"

"I am."

"We go to the Round-Up every year," Albert said with a smile. "Have for years."

Rita's heart sank. Would she ever be able to attend the Pendleton Round-Up again and shout, "Let'er buck!" when the broncs burst from the chutes? She didn't know why it mattered. She hated rodeo cowboys. She hated their catcalls when she'd walked by as a teenager. Hated her father dragging her around as he helped behind the chutes. For some reason, he'd picked her to be the son he'd never had.

It all made her feel cheap.

Degraded.

"Tell me about building Grand Coulee, Albert." Rita checked for suspicious tails before leaning her head back and closing her eyes.

He dove into the conversation with enthusiasm.

But her mind was on other things, like knowing the route after numerous horse training clinics in Ellensburg. She feared what should take them forty minutes or less would be much longer at the pace he was going.

Rita also knew the faster she got off this stretch of highway the better.

CHAPTER 11

"Rita, we're here," Faye said in a singsong tone as they pulled up to Circle K in Ritzville.

She rubbed her eyes and blinked a few times to clear her blurry vision. The car came to a stop in a bare lot between a store and an island of four gas pumps. A lit sign promoting sub sandwiches caught her attention.

"We don't have much but hope this helps." Faye held out a ten-dollar bill. "Whatever is troubling you, we'll be praying for you." Her eyes scanned Rita's face.

Aw. How sweet. "You both have been so kind, but thanks, I have my own money. And thank you for the prayers. They're appreciated." *Trust me.*

As she got out, the frigid air brushed against her face, awakening her senses. She'd need to remain alert now that she was again on her own. She waved at the Starrs and strode to the glass doors of the quick stop.

Inside she found warmth, food, and a pit in her stomach. She nodded at a fifty-something cashier. How would she get to Nespelem? At night? She found the ladies' restroom and went inside. After doing her business, she ran warm water and let it run over her hands. She soaped them up and scrubbed as if to wash away the anger, pain, and fear.

When done, she fished in her backpack, tugged out the tube of arnica, and lathered a good amount of salve on her sides. Rita asked the ragged-looking reflection in the mirror, "Why did you allow him to do this to you?" She sighed and washed her face, then sagged to the hard floor and leaned against the concrete wall. Her body begged for sleep and food. Darn. She'd left her food in the truck. How stupid.

A knock sounded on the door. "You all right in there?"

"Yeah. I'll be out in a minute."

"We don't allow drugs in here."

Drugs? What the heck? "None in here, sir," Rita said, her tone sarcastic. *What a racist pig.* She rubbed the back of her neck. After taking a minute to collect herself, she slipped the arnica tube into her pack and opened the bathroom door. The fifty-something male attendant stood near stacks of soda and eyed her.

She smiled, trying to remain ladylike, and headed for the coffee stand. Once a new insulated mug was selected, she filled it with a steaming dark-roast Costa Rican blend and added five pumps of hazelnut creamer. She took a sip and added two more.

The clerk came around the cash register that had been placed in the middle of the store and watched with his squinty, gray eyes as she perused the aisles. The weasel of a man reminded her of Festus in the *Gunsmoke* series she used to watch with her paternal grandfather. He was no Matt Dillon, that was for sure.

The glowing wall menu caught her attention. "Can I get half a sub?"

"Sorry, the cook went home sick, and I don't have my food handler's permit."

Shoot. Rita plucked a few protein bars off a shelf and found toe and hand warmers on the other side of the cash register. She selected several individual packets and laid her goods on the counter. The intensity of the burn in her sides was gaining strength. "I'll be right back."

After grabbing a few packs of ibuprofen and a couple of waters, she plodded back to the cash register.

"That it?" Festus asked.

"I believe so."

"Where you headed?"

"North."

He rang up a couple of items. "You need a ride?"

She arched a brow. Hope and uncertainty sparred inside her. She inched up her shoulder. "Maybe."

"Look, I saw you get out of the car and watched it drive away. By the marks on your face, I'm guessing you're in some kind of trouble. So, I'll ask again, do you need a ride or not?" He rang up the water bottles and placed them in a plastic sack.

"I don't need the bag, and, yeah, I'm on foot."

He took the bottles out of the sack. "I know a guy and, for the right price, he'll get you to where you need to go."

"The right price? What kinda girl do you think I am?" Rita's jaw muscles tightened. "First you accuse me of doing drugs in the restroom, and now, you stinkin' think I'm some kinda whore?"

Red-faced, Festus held up his hands as though she were pointing a gun at him. "No, no. No!" He wagged his head. "That's not what I meant at all. I have a grandson who needs to earn a few bucks. He's lazy. A good kid but doesn't like to work. Those stupid video games, ya know? He aspires to be a professional gamer. What does that even mean?" His face returned to its creamy hue. "I just want to help a girl in need, that's all."

Rita handed him the required cash, and he made change. "How old is he?"

"Nineteen. He stays up all night playing with his cyber friends." He tugged his cell phone out of his back pocket and held it up. "I can make the call."

"Look. I appreciate the offer, but I don't know you guys and—"

"What other options do you have?"

Rita drummed her fingernails on the counter. "I guess none."

Festus shifted his weight, acting like Matt Dillon and failing miserably. "The way I look at things, this is a win-win. You get a ride. My grandson gets a chance to earn his own cash for once." He studied Rita. "If you want, you can talk with my wife and see we are God-fearing folks. Desperate, but God-fearing."

Rita let out a heavy sigh. Pros and cons rattled her mind. Nothing could be worse than Bowie Dark Cloud catching up to her. And she understood desperate. If needed, she could defend herself with the knife in her Leatherman. "Okay. How much to take me to Nespelem?"

"Fifty bucks sound fair?"

She gulped and checked her wallet. "Thirty-five."

"Deal." Festus held out his hand, a smile hitching up the side of his face.

But Rita declined to shake it. She nodded, smiled, and shoved the cash into her pocket.

He made the same embarrassing look she'd seen the actor make in *Gunsmoke*. She waited by a window while the clerk made the call. He argued, making his case, and finally hung up. "He'll be right over."

Oh, goodie. "Can't wait."

Festus nodded, his brows pinched. "Be safe."

Rita placed her items in her pack and waited outside. The air was cold enough so that she slid her hands into the gloves and twisted from side to side, moving to keep warm and saving the hand warmers for an emergency. She took a sip of coffee and enjoyed the warm liquid sliding down her throat.

After ten minutes, a black SUV pulled up and parked in front of her. A shaggy teen with a lizard tattooed on his neck got out. "You Nespelem?"

"You've got to be kidding me," Rita mumbled.

Festus came outside. "This is my grandson, George."

"Hey, Gramps. Got the bills?"

Hey, Gramps?

Festus motioned to her. "She has them."

Rita blinked several times, her head tipped to the side. "I . . . uh . . ." With her teeth, she slid off her glove and shoved her hand in her front pocket. Pulling them out, she tried to convince herself to bail. Instead, she held out the cash.

George took it and stuffed it into his ratty front pocket. "Better get on the road. I'm missing out." He opened the driver-side door and got in.

Rita turned to Festus and arched a brow as she slid her glove back on.

"He's rough around the edges but is trustworthy. Don't worry, you'll be all right." He went to the car and opened the passenger door. "What's your name?"

"Rita." She went to the SUV but didn't get in.

"I'm George the first. He's the third." Pride showed on his face. "Go ahead and get in. He's a safe driver."

"I bet he is." Rita shook her head and got in. The car was at least clean. It probably belonged to Festus's wife.

George the third waved at his grandfather, a slinky smile on his face. Shivers raked across the back of Rita's neck. She reached for the door as he jerked the car into Reverse.

George the third jacked up the tunes and peeled out of the parking lot.

Rita gripped the door handle. *Oh, Lord, what have I done?*

CHAPTER 12

Colville Reservation

Robert stirred to the squawk of his alarm clock. The air in the small cabin his brother-in-law, Trey Hardy, had first used as his photography studio felt as frigid as a meat locker.

He dragged his weary self out of bed, threw on a sweatshirt and sweatpants, and padded to the woodstove, his bare feet thumping the chilly, hard flooring. Flicking on the living room light, he said to Posse, his red heeler pup who lay curled up in his blue-padded bed, "I left you in charge. What happened, huh?"

Posse glanced at him with droopy eyes, which wasn't normal.

Robert crumpled the last issue of the *Tribal Tribune*, topped it with kindling, and clicked the long-reach butane lighter. The flame consumed an edge of the paper. He blew on it, his body shivering. Once the fire took off, he went to the kitchen and brewed a pot of cheap coffee. He'd need it for the busy day ahead.

After a hot shower and a change of clothes, he again checked on the pup. Posse looked at him and whined. Had he been out yet? He knew how to use the doggie door. Small morsels of food brimmed his bowl, leftover from last night.

He'd had his parvo shots. Perhaps he'd already been outside, chasing varmints, and worn himself out.

"I'll let you rest for now, little guy. But soon enough it'll be time to milk Daisy. You like that, don't cha, boy? Yeah, I made fun of the Jersey, too, until I got my first taste of her creamy milk. Now I'm a believer. You are, too, aren't you?"

Listless, the pup stretched, revealing a distended belly. "I bet you found another deer leg. Or have you been chewing on a hide?" Chad had a carcass of a white-tailed buck hanging in the shop. The ranch hand must not have disposed of the unused parts yet.

He poured a cup of coffee, added two spoonfuls of sugar, and took a sip. "You ready to feed the horses?"

Posse shot out of his bed, yipped, and spun in circles.

Robert laughed. "There ain't nothing wrong with you, is there?" He leaned over to pet the dog as the whelp swirled around and set his dish in motion. His food scattered on the floor. But that didn't stop him from snatching up every last morsel.

Robert reached down and rubbed the little guy. He pulled on his canvas overalls and coat, then went for the door. "Let's go."

The warm clothing didn't stop the frigid air from blasting him when he stepped through the threshold. He pulled his knit cap over his ears and headed toward the barn, Posse on his heels. There was just enough light to see the bare trunks of the yellow-and-orange leafed aspens and cottonwoods. By the time the pair reached the outbuilding, Mandie appeared, bundled in a knit cap, gloves, and down jacket with a full milk bucket in hand.

She held it up as she passed by him. "Sleep in, Bronco Bobby?"

"No."

"Leading by example."

Although Robert couldn't see her face, he knew she was smiling. Her chuckle confirmed it. He shook his head and patted his leg. Posse jumped up as he leaned over and gathered him in his arms. They greeted the horses just as a flick of sunlight topped the hill. A few whickered, their noses poking through the bars of the upper-door grill.

Mandie paused and looked back on her way to the kitchen. "By the way, you left the barn door cracked open last night."

"Did not."

"Did too."

"Whatever," Robert said.

He fed the horses while Posse sniffed around the stalls, bouncing in and out of hay bales set out beside the stall walls. The pup peed beside a bale intended for their prize mare and afterward looked up at Robert with a look of pride.

"You better watch that one, squirt," Robert said. "She's a Valentine granddaughter and will make beautiful babies. You keep piddling on her hay, she might come after you."

Last year when the Seven Tine was about to go under, Trey had convinced Sydney to sell Twister, her valuable Blue Valentine colt—her last connection to her father. Trey had never gotten over the hasty deal. Guilt-ridden, he'd flown to San Marcos, Guerrero, Mexico, in late March and covered an earthquake with a magnitude greater than 8.0. He sold the photos to the award-winning *Nature Digest* and replaced the colt with a mare who was ready to breed with his folks' wedding gift—a Very Smart Remedy grandson.

The memory of Trey's account of the aftermath of the earthquake and stories locals had told him still turned Robert's gut—like when the sea had come onto land like a ravaging beast and dragged cattle into the ocean as though they were paper hand puppets.

He grabbed a couple of flakes of hay and slid open the door to find Blizzard, their newest blue roan stud colt, in the corner of his stall. "What's wrong, boy?" Every other day, the three-year-old had charged the wooden stall gate, pawed the air, and shook his head. He'd been handled twice. Once was to load him to bring him to the ranch, and once was to unload and stall him. To use his father's pet phrase, "Talk about a goat rodeo."

Blizzard lowered his head and pawed the cedar bedding. Puffs of steam rolled from his nostrils. A movement caught Robert's attention. "Whoa, boy." He dropped the hay in the wooden feeder and turned to face a squirming form under a thin blanket. "What the heck?"

A sharp scream erupted and a hand emerged, brandishing a knife. The colt stomped and charged Robert, then backed away. "Whoa, boy." He held out his hands.

A woman crawled from under the blanket. The right side of her face shone dark and swollen, and a cracked bottom lip protruded. She stood a few inches shorter than Robert, bundled in a teal down jacket, red knit hat, and thick work gloves. Worn cowboy boots fit her small feet, and a disheveled, single braid snaked down her torso.

She gave him what seemed like a look of recognition and said, "I'm here to see Sydney Hardy."

"Move out of there quiet and easy like. Blizzard's rank. Unpredictable." When she stood without moving, he added, "And put that knife away before you hurt yourself."

"Rank? Why, he's been nothing but a gentleman. Hardly knew he was around." While she scratched Blizzard's nose, he dropped his head and took a step toward her. "In fact, I thought he was a pony."

"For crying out loud. He's had us buffaloed from the get-go." Robert took a step toward the stud colt and jumped back when he bit at him and pawed at the cedar-scented wood chips covering the ground of his soiled paddock. Lousy stud.

Posse whined and trotted over to the woman. She knelt and scooped him up, and he became a red ball of wiggles. "What a cutie. What's his name?"

"What's *your* name, and what are you doing here?" How had such a beautiful mess of a woman ended up in his barn?

She glanced down and fiddled with her Leatherman. "I'm . . . uh. . . . Is Ms. Hardy around? I mean is she available?" Her face pinked.

Was she one of the abused women his sister held an open room for? Yeah, there was a vacant room, but Syd was gone. And he wasn't about to babysit for her. That was her wheelhouse. He turned to the barn's alleyway. "I . . . um . . ." He rubbed his forehead. "She's out of town."

"Guess I should've called first." Her shoulders drooped.

She looked so pitiful. Before he could stop himself, he blurted, "Mandie's here. She's the ranch cook. Let's get out of here. We can go to the lodge and figure things out." Robert picked up the blanket and carried it into the aisle while he studied Girl Warrior. She appeared to be thirtysomething and accomplished by the way she handled her Leatherman.

Before gathering her belongings and stepping out of the paddock, she rubbed the colt's neck. "You're a handsome creature."

Robert shook his head and slid the door shut. "So, what's your name?" He shook out the blanket.

"I'm . . . um . . . Rita." She wiped shavings off her jeans. "Uh . . . Runninghorse."

He handed her the blanket. "I'm Robert Elliot, Sydney's brother." What was he supposed to do with her? Sydney had made it crystal clear to the ranch hands that they were to stay clear of women like Rita at all times. She made darn sure they knew the ladies came scared, broken, and in need of a safe environment.

And under no circumstances were they to fraternize with the ladies. Ever.

So, he kept a respectable distance.

But the beauty behind the bruises made Robert break out into a sweat. He'd never reacted to one of Sydney's girls like this before. Why her? Why now? "Let's get you inside."

She looked at the barn's open door. "Do you have many guests?"

"Yeah. We're booked full."

"If she's not home . . . maybe I should leave."

"And go where?"

Rita toed the dirt with her boot, her voice barely above a whisper. "I don't know."

"Mandie sometimes works with my sister. She can get you settled in while I call her."

"When will she be back?"

"I'm not sure yet." Hopefully, either his sister would come back early, or she'd recommend somewhere else Rita could go. Because he needed to focus on bronc riding.

CHAPTER 13

There was no way Rita could stay without Sydney here. But Robert was right. Where would she go?

At least Mandie had treated her with kindness and compassion. Robert's body language had made it clear he didn't want her around without his sister at the ranch.

After rummaging through her pack, she took the last of her pain pills. The shavings in the stall hadn't offered enough padding, and she was super stiff and sore. Going to the window of her room on the east wing, she took in the fall colors igniting the countryside. Massive cottonwoods boasted deep amber leaves stemming from their coal-colored arms, and aspen and brush branches were smudged in red, orange, and yellow. A dusting of leaves littered the ground as though giving an offering to their prewinter death.

She hated feeling like a victim. She wanted to be on her mare, tending cattle. It's what she knew. It was her safe place in the world.

When her pain abated, she showered, left her hair loose to hide the bruises, and pulled on a pair of jeans and a V-neck sweater lined in tones of pink, white, and gray that Mandie had lent her. Finding foundation in the medicine cabinet above the sink, she applied a liberal amount.

To her surprise, she felt emotional. *Good grief. Why cry now?* The bruises were a long way from her heart and weren't about to change her circumstances. They'd heal. Eventually.

She went back to the window and fingered the pullover's soft yarn.

Muffled sounds drifted up the steps. She tensed. Probably ranch guests. She blew out a breath and tried to relax. *What would it be like to visit here for pleasure? Not having to flee life's cruelty?*

She desperately wanted to turn on her phone and listen to her mother's voice, but then she'd have to hear Bowie's threatening messages as well. Where would she go from here? It was all too much.

She jerked around at the sound of a rap on the door.

"Breakfast is ready. Do you want me to bring you a tray?"

Rita recognized Mandie's voice and opened the door. "No. I'll come down. I feel like a prisoner up here."

"Do you need anything else?"

"I'm fine. I appreciate your kindness." The corner of Rita's mouth edged up. But only a smidgen. "Do you know when Sydney might be back?"

"Not yet. She's on a working vacation." Mandie lowered her voice. "She's speaking at some big women and ranching convention in Montana. But don't worry, Robert called her and talked with Trey. I doubt they'll be gone the entire month."

"A month?" She blinked several times. "What will I do for a month? I can't stay—"

"Sure you can. You came with cowboy boots, didn't you? Must mean you know how to ride."

She curled her toes in the stiff boots. "Well—"

"You must have some kind of useful skills. Bobby said you're pretty wicked with a knife. Besides, we don't see an additional rig outside. How'd you get here? Where you from? There ain't no Runninghorses around here."

Her neck and face warmed. Thankfully, after she made George the third drop her off in Davenport due to his reckless driving, she caught a ride with a gentleman trucker to the Chief Joseph Rest Area perched north of the tiny town of Nespelem and walked the few miles to the ranch. "Well, I—"

"Bet you're starving. Being out in the cold and all." Mandie motioned for Rita to come along.

She crept down the split-log staircase that arched to the ground floor by the office, alert for anyone acting suspicious, not putting it past Bowie to have her followed.

Pendleton blankets draped the backs of leather furniture by the bay windows, and wagon-wheel lights hung over pine tables in the dining area, making her feel welcome. A mounted elk head hung above the stone hearth. On the other walls, a handful of stuffed deer and moose heads stared down at everyone through glassy eyes. Yep, it felt like home—minus the family friction.

Oh, and a cute, little gift shop was tucked in the crook of a second curved staircase. Too bad she only had a few bucks left. No way was she going to use her credit card. It was for emergencies only. Hopefully, the guest ranch would provide for her needs. If not, she didn't know what she'd do.

"Food's right there. Help yourself." Mandie motioned to a buffet-style breakfast. Guests were settled with full plates at tables in the dining room, their voices filling the Southwestern-style decorated space.

She took a plate off the stack and went down the line. The smell of scrambled eggs and greasy sausage made her feel nauseated. After choosing a huckleberry muffin and peach yogurt, she hunted for an empty table. But there wasn't one.

The leather seats by the crackling fireplace looked inviting. She took a step toward them but halted at Robert's booming voice.

"Rita, I mean, Miss Runninghorse—"

She shrank. *Great. Now everyone knows my name.*

"There's an empty spot over here." He waved her over as two cowboys got up and carried their dirty dishes to the kitchen.

She caught a whiff of alfalfa as the heels of their cowboy boots clicked past her on the wooden floor. The aroma made her pine for home. She turned her attention back to Robert, still waving.

Thankfully, only a few pairs of eyes were on her. She made her way to the table and eased herself into a chair. Mandie dashed toward them with a hot pot of coffee. She poured Rita a cup and glared at Robert as if shooting him a warning.

Rita took a small bite of muffin. Her body wanted the nourishment, but the turmoil chasing her insides made eating difficult. She managed another few nibbles and trailed them with a sip of black coffee.

Robert and Mandie seemed to scowl at one another for a long, uncomfortable moment before she turned to the next table. What was that all about?

When Mandie was out of earshot, he said, "I finally caught up with Sydney. It's definite. She won't be back for a couple of weeks. Or more."

By the look on his face, he didn't seem too happy. And neither was she. "What now?"

"You have a few options. You can remain here with Mandie until my sister gets back. Come on the road with me. Or stay with my other sister, Glenda, and her family."

Rita sighed. "On the road with you?"

"Yeah. To a rodeo in Idaho."

No way was she going to a rodeo. The other option was to toss in her cards and head home.

"You don't have to decide now."

She nodded. Could she work for hire if she stayed? She could use the cash.

Mandie came back with pumpkin spice creamer. "Try a dab of this. It will liven up your senses." She plopped the bottle on the table and gave Robert another grimace.

There was obviously friction between the two.

Rita shifted in her seat, trying to find a more comfortable position for her achy sides. "I can help with ranch chores."

"Or you can rest." Robert's eyes lingered on her face.

She ducked her chin. Clearly, her loose hair and concealer had done nothing to hide the bruises. She wished she'd brought her buckaroo hat. It might have done the job. "Idle hands are . . ." She broke off before she sounded too preachy.

Mandie grinned. "The devil's workshop. I get it." She poured a splash of coffee into their cups.

Robert watched Mandie walk back to the kitchen, the muscles in his jaws working. "Why don't you take a couple of days? Walk the property, think about your options, and let me know by Thursday night."

"Why then?"

"I leave Friday morning." He leaned back in his chair, a contented look on his face.

Rodeo cowboys were the worst. Especially cocky bronc riders. They were worse than bull riders, who seemed to respect the fifteen-hundred-pound ball of snot between their legs. "What's your event?" Rita managed in her sweetest tone.

"Saddle bronc."

Figures. She'd rather hang with Motormouth Mandie than go with Bronco Bobby. "I think I'll take your advice and scope out the place."

"Help yourself."

The next morning Rita sat on the edge of the bed and side braided her hair like she'd done every morning since she was eight. Of course Robert was a bronc rider. Just her luck. But wait. That's where she'd seen him before—at last year's Pendleton rodeo. Oh, yeah, he was good. That was when Bowie had her thinking he was worthy of her affection. What a stinking lie.

When she finished with her hair, she bundled up and headed outside, unsure of how to keep herself occupied. Hard work was all she knew.

First, she went to check on Blizzard. She hadn't even stepped foot inside the structure before she heard a sharp *whack* she recognized as a horse kicking wood panels. Hurrying past three horses with their noses poking out of their stall bars, she halted at the stud colt's pen as his back hooves struck a wall. "What's the matter, huh, handsome?"

"Better not mess with that one." A stocky cowboy with sideburns leaned against the doorframe of the tack room, a coiled rope in one hand.

Rita recognized him from the dining hall. Dressed in tan chaps, a brown felt cowboy hat, and silver spurs, it seemed obvious he was one of the ranch hands. He appeared to be in his early thirties with dark, clipped hair and brown eyes.

"I'm Chad." He moved to the stall, his shoulder a millimeter away from her.

She took a half step away from him, figuring he had no idea who she was. This surprised her, with Robert's announcement and all. "I met him . . ." She almost said last night. "He's got a kind heart."

"We talking about the same animal?"

So, the guy was another cynic.

She turned at the sound of footsteps, and Robert appeared around the corner. When he saw them, he scowled. "You got somewhere to be, Chad?"

The flustered ranch hand tipped his hat at Rita. "Nice to meet you." He headed toward the east exit.

Robert pulled Chad aside and gave her a quick glance. No way. Were they talking about her? Great. Soon everyone would know her business. Maybe it was best to leave Seven Tine. Having to hide her abuse for so long, she didn't know how to handle people knowing she'd been knocked around.

And then there was the danger of discovery. Was the room they had given her to stay in empty because word had gotten around that the owners and staff didn't exercise discretion? As Robert approached, she opened her mouth to tell him thanks but no thanks.

"Sorry about that. I had to let Chad know you were one of Sydney's special guests. Only the staff knows. We try to keep things under everyone's radar. We're pretty tight-lipped around here."

"Special guest? Is that code for 'abused, helpless women'?"

"No." He blushed and the space between his brows pinched. "It's not how it sounds."

Rita's face burned. "How is it supposed to *sound*?"

He fidgeted. "We alert the crew. Let them know to keep things quiet. Treat the women who come like any other guest, so no attention is drawn to them—to you—and look out for . . . you. We all try to keep our distance so you can maintain your privacy."

"Uh-huh. Like a plague."

"A what?"

"Never mind." She shifted her weight. Darn men. *They just don't get what we go through.* "What about Mandie?"

The corners of his mouth tipped up. "She's solid. She can be a bit much, but her heart's in the right place." He tugged a piece of hay from Blizzard's bale and played with it. "But I have to be honest with you."

She folded her arms to keep the shakes away. What did he need to tell her? Why was he hesitating?

"Bruises, like the ones you have, well . . . folks tend to ask questions."

"I can deal with that." She didn't like to but knew how. She'd watched some of her friends and their moms and other family members hide them for years.

"Isn't it uncomfortable for you?"

"Yeah, but I've been through worse." A bird flapping against the barn ceiling snagged her attention and reminded her of when she'd fought against her attackers. She'd gotten rid of one. Would she be able to eliminate the other?

CHAPTER 14

Highway 395, Washington State

Bowie Dark Cloud pounded his fist against the steering wheel. "That wench will pay for this." He stepped on the gas as he drove north. "Haven't I given her everything she wants?" He scratched his hairy chin.

"You're gonna have to rein her in before you get married," Gary Fullmoon said, "or you'll never be able to control her. She's a sly mustang."

"You got that right."

Bowie and Gary were like Turner and Hooch but in a wicked way. They spent many nights covertly gambling away the earnings from horse sales. Gary, wearing a ratty casino cap, was about five-foot-eleven and had never amounted to much. He'd barely passed high school with the ambition of a slug.

"What's that?" Gary pointed to a rig on the side of the road.

Bowie slowed down and pulled over behind a white truck. "Looks like Rita's. She did come this way." He hopped out of his rig and slammed the door. He'd bet his best horse she was headed to the guest ranch in the brochure.

Bowie clutched the door handle, and he pulled. "It's locked." He slammed his fist into the side mirror and broke it off. Hurling curse words, he strode to the side of the road, picked up a fist-sized rock by a clump of sagebrush, and chucked it at the passenger's window.

"You're crazy, man." Gary rubbed the back of his neck as he looked around. "We don't need cops on our tail."

"How will they know it was us? Huh?" Bowie opened the door. "Who's to say we didn't find her rig like this?"

Gary flung his hands in the air. "I ain't touching nothin'."

"You watch too many movies." Bowie searched the truck and pulled out Rita's tan buckaroo hat and leather purse. He held the hat up to Gary. "This is our bait."

"You gotta be kidding me. A hat?"

"It's not just any hat. She loves this stinking thing." Bowie tossed the rose-tooled purse to Gary. "See if there's anything of use in there." One way or another, he'd find Rita Runninghorse and drag her back.

CHAPTER 15

Colville Reservation

Robert groaned. "What am I supposed to do with her for that long, Syd?" Out the window of the ranch office, Rita stood alone, leaning against a panel hooked to the south arena. She stared off into the distance as though pondering her next move. "But I keep saying the wrong thing."

"What options did you give her?"

"To hang with Mandie, go to Glenda's, or go on the road with me."

"Go with you? Are you crazy?" A deep sigh droned over the line.

"Why not?" He paced the room. "She needs help. And encouragement. Not to be dragged around the rodeo circuit."

"Then come home. You can't expect us to deal with these women while you try to save the world."

"That's not fair. You know—"

"Yeah. I do. Sorry. It's just . . ." He exhaled a rush of air out of his nostrils.

"Please, Bobby, help me out. You know we need the money to keep the ranch going. This is the last convention of the year. Get her to stay and help Mandie. Call Chuck and Pastor Jake and let them know we've got another woman in need. If her abuser's anything like the last one, she'll need to keep hidden. I'll try to cut the trip short. Maybe they can move me up a day or two."

"A day or two won't make a difference. C'mon. What am I supposed to tell her?"

Sydney spoke in a calm tone. "Tell her that she's valuable. And safe. Make sure she knows she's not alone and feels loved."

"That's something I'd tell my future wife, not a stranger."

"Okay. You've got a point."

He massaged his temple, feeling a heaviness on his shoulders. "I'll have her hang here with Mandie. Or better yet, call one of the aunties. Elders have special powers, right?"

Sydney laughed. "Our aunties would smother her. Besides, she needs to be surrounded by big, strong men like you and the ranch hands." Sydney's tone softened. "The women's abusers can easily overpower them. Most who come are not only mentally and emotionally mistreated, but physically as well. C'mon. You know all of this, Brother."

"That's why you need to cancel your gig and come home. We can book additional events. Beef up advertising. Isn't that why we built the new hay barn? So we can have weddings and parties in the loft? C'mon. This is your thing, not mine." Robert tried to keep his tone in check. "It's not fair. I shouldn't have to put my life on hold."

"There're more important things in life than riding broncs, don't you think?" Sydney's tone turned sharp. "Life isn't just about you and your obsessions. These women are running for their lives. Please, cancel and stay at the ranch."

Cancel? "Not a chance. I can't believe you'd even suggest it. You know this is my career—"

"Career or hobby? You need to decide, the ranch or rodeo. We're growing at a rate where your help is needed on the weekends."

Robert curled his fingers into a fist and punched the air. "That's not fair."

"Life never is. But it's the grown-up thing to do."

He paced again. "I'll take her with me. That way, if for some off-the-wall reason her ex shows up, she'll be gone. No one will have to lie, and there won't be a scene. We've got a full house for the next three months." It was a win-win.

The line hummed for several seconds before Sydney spoke. "Think she'll go?"

"I think so. If not, I'll talk her into it. You know I'm good at that sort of thing."

"I hate to admit it, but you're right. You can talk a statue into buying a horse."

"It's a gift."

"Gotta go," Sydney said. "Keep me posted."

Rita hadn't moved from her spot by the arena. Great. How was he supposed to talk her into going with him? He'd approach her after lunch, which according to his watch, would be in fifteen minutes. So, no. Maybe after dinner. He needed time to figure out how to word things.

A light rap sounded on the office door. He opened it to find a couple of kids about ten. Brown Hair poked Red Hair and gave a nervous laugh. "What's up, boys?" Robert held back a chuckle, figuring it might be a serious matter.

"Will you teach us how to ride bucking broncs?" Brown Hair's eyes grew wide. "We seen you riding last night."

"You did, huh?"

Both kids nodded and elbowed one another. "It looks cool. Can you teach us?"

Robert grunted. "Your mothers would kill me. Now run along and wash up for lunch."

"Oh," they said in unison, frowns on their faces. They dashed away, shoving each other and dodging guests entering the lodge.

"Hey, slow down!" Robert shook his head, recalling his own shenanigans at their age. He turned to the window. Shoot. Rita was no longer by the arena. *Where did she go?*

He went to search for her but stopped. She was headed for the plates in the dining room. She tossed him a small smile. Her slouched shoulders gave Robert a twinge of compassion for her. What would it be like for a woman in an abusive relationship? Away from loved ones? He'd have to go easy on her. Give her space.

At the same time, it'd be nice to know more about her. Where she came from. Who was she running or hiding from? Maybe, just maybe, if he sat down with her and listened, truly listened, and formed what his sisters called a bond, then he could convince her to go with him. He needed the points. His budding career depended on it. Plus, he could keep an eye on her. Keep her safe. Again, a win-win.

After washing up for lunch, Robert filled his plate with a turkey sandwich and chips. He settled at an empty table, discouraged Chad and Rich from joining him with a shake of his head, and stood when Rita turned toward the dining tables. He motioned to an empty chair.

She nodded and headed his way. He swallowed, praying she would agree with his reasoning. He needed to get it over with so he could get on with his day—without the pit in his gut. His chest clenched when she stopped at the table. He rushed around to help settle her in and went back to his seat.

It didn't take but a few seconds for Mandie to appear with a pot of coffee, two cups, and a warning glare. She filled the mugs and plopped down in one of the chairs. "You bake?" she asked Rita.

A wide smile bloomed on her face and her eyes lit up. "I love to bake. I make cupcakes, pies, and cakes for various events back in . . ." Her gaze darted sideways.

"Good. If you don't mind, I could use another set of hands. My help took off for bingo."

Robert shook his head. *Good old Auntie Millie.* The woman loved to dob empty spaces with a bottle of ink. Robert opened his mouth to protest but was cut off by Rita's reply.

"I'd love to," she said. "When do we start?"

"After you eat." Mandie nodded to Rita's sparse lunch of half a ham sandwich and a few grapes. "This weekend we're having a pie social to benefit a family in need. Wanna help?"

"Absolutely," Rita said. "Thanks for offering." Again, her face brightened.

"Don't you have somewhere to be?" Robert asked Mandie.

She shot him a death look. Heat rose up his neck, knowing he was definitely not leading by example. Or respecting his employee. Why did Sydney have to come up with such ridiculous rules? They were impossible to live by. Stifling, really.

"I'll see you later." Mandie tapped the table and left.

"I'm excited. I've always dreamed of opening a bakery, but . . ." Rita dropped her smile.

"Why don't you?" Robert took a sip of coffee. "If it's something you're passionate about, I say go for it. Or go home. That's my motto. Win at all costs."

"At all costs?"

"Why not?"

Rita picked up her sandwich, examined it, set it back on the plate, and crossed her arms.

This wasn't the conversation Robert had formed in his mind. He finished off his meal and washed it all down with the rest of his coffee.

The way she'd handled her knife and made her way to the ranch, on foot no less, he would have thought she'd understand that life required sacrifices.

"I don't pretend to know what you're going through or who blackened your eye. We see some of that on this rez too. But I do know you need to be safe."

Rita lifted her gaze to him. Cocked a brow.

"I know you want to help this weekend, but . . ."

"But what?"

"My job is to keep you safe while Sydney's away."

"Your job—"

"I'm happy to step in until my sister gets back." Robert wiped his palms on his jeans. "What I'm trying to get at is . . . that your safety is my number-one priority right now. I have a rodeo this weekend in Coeur d'Alene. It's a big one for my career. I think you should come with me so I can keep an eye on you."

She stared at him, her mouth agape. Face red. "Keep an eye on me? As though I'm, what, a toddler?"

His jaw twitched as he realized how bad he was blowing it. "What if whomever discovers you're here?" What had Sydney advised him to say? "You're valuable and . . ."

Her eyes grew wide.

He cleared his throat. "Please know you're not alone."

The hint of a smile sprouted on her face, and she covered her mouth with her hand.

Robert suddenly felt like hiding under a rock. But then it rushed out of his mouth like water out of a firehose. "You're loved." *What?* "I mean—"

Rita burst out laughing. "I bet it took most of your morning to work up the nerve for such a profession."

His face blazed like a desert fire in August. Inside, his spirit groaned. "Like I said, this is Sydney's wheelhouse. To be frank, I think it's best you come with me. It's the only way to keep you safe. Especially if he finds out you're here."

"Thanks, but I'll stay here with Mandie." The shimmer left her eyes. "I'm sure he won't find me. There's no way he knows I'm here."

Great. How would he ever convince her to go with him now?

CHAPTER 16

Rita could no longer stand it. She sat on the edge of her bed, her thoughts running rampant. The knot in her stomach twisted until she pressed the On button of her cell phone. She plopped down in a covered wooden chair, the padding a Southwest design.

The clock on the nightstand ticked away.

By now, Bowie had to know about the temporary restraining order. *Wouldn't he?* And the document would only fuel his rage.

Her blood pressure inched up several notches as she waited for the phone to power on. And when it finally did, twenty-four missed calls and thirty-seven texts waited for replies. Most of the calls were from her mother and sister.

One was from her dad, and it sounded like he'd been drunk. His message lathered threats for her to come home, or he'd sell everything she owned—including Opal. Her heart pitched. She hoped her father's threats were empty. She prayed for her mother's safety and bit back tears.

She started in on the texts. Most were from Bowie. Her stomach dropped from the latest one.

> Found your truck. And the brochure. On
> my way to bring you home. Be ready.

The phone slipped from her grasp and toppled to the floor. She grabbed her backpack and dug through it. "It has to be here." She turned over the bag and shook it hard and fast. She combed through her items, looking for the brochure. "Where are you?" It must have dropped out. But how? She'd been so careful.

"Oh God! No!"

She rushed out of her room, her legs wobbly, and went for the stairs. Her boots clicked on the steps and when she jumped to the floor, a few elders who were fiddling with puzzles snapped their gazes to her.

Mandie looked at her and smiled. "You ready? I was just coming to get you."

"Not yet." Rita rushed into an office she'd seen Robert enter a few times. But he was nowhere in sight. She hightailed it to the barn. Chad looked up from brushing a horse. "You seen Robert?" Her lungs burned.

"He just took off to the river pasture. What's up?"

"I need to find him." She tried not to sound desperate. But she was. "Can you take me there?"

Before Chad could answer her, a dark blue, four-door, one-ton pickup rattled to a halt near the barn's front entrance, and Robert hopped out, Posse in his arms. He went around and strolled toward them. "Forgot my—"

"I'll go with you." Rita ran to him. "When do we leave?"

"To change pipes?"

"No. To Idaho. The rodeo."

He placed his hand on the small of her back, led her into the tack room, and shut the door. "Why the change of heart?" He lifted off his cowboy hat and mopped his sweaty brow.

"You were right. He knows where I am and is on his way."

"He's coming here? You sure? How'd he find you?"

"I must have left the Seven Tine brochure in my room." How could she have been so careless?

Robert tapped his Stetson on his head, handed the pup to Rita, and pulled his cell phone from the inside pocket of his jacket. "Hang on." He tapped the screen with his thumb and held the cell to his ear.

"Who are you calling?"

Robert held up his finger. "She's not answering."

"Who?"

"Syd." He made another call. "Hey, Trey, where's my sister?"

While Robert talked on the phone, Rita held Posse to her chest and walked in circles, leaving dust trails on the floor. They needed to leave before Bowie and any other goons with him showed up.

The horse trader didn't like to lose anything he believed belonged to him. He called her his Silky Dove, which was the Native name given to her by her maternal grandmother. In the beginning, she had adored his referring to her that way. But when he became possessive, she resented it.

Robert tapped the screen. "Sydney thinks we need to call Chuck."

"Who's he?"

"Our brother-in-law. And he's Tribal PD."

Rita shook her head. "No way. No cops. He'll kill my sister."

Robert's brows shot up. "Has he threatened to do so?"

"Yeah. He has. He's never actually touched her, but I don't trust him. Something in him has changed in the last few weeks. He's become more aggressive. I don't know . . ."

"What about you? Has he threatened to kill you?"

"Not so much in words. When he gets mad or doesn't get his way—or thinks I'm messing around on him—which I never would, he goes ballistic. Shoves me into stuff and . . ." She shook her head against the memories. "But it's always when no one's around. Things were getting worse before I left. Way worse." She'd never told anyone such personal information before. But Robert, he was different. Yeah, he wanted to pursue his dreams. As did she. Then again, he also seemed to want to help. Seemed to care.

"Let's go inside and call Chuck. We can't go into this blind." Robert asked Chad to hook up the ranch's living quarters three-horse trailer and escorted Rita to the lodge. Mandie started toward them, but he put up a hand and stopped her. He turned to Rita, "I'll meet you in the office. It's—"

"I know where it's at." She went into the lodge. Inside the office, framed photos lined shelves on a large bookcase behind a wooden desk. They seemed to share the ranch story. She strode past a somewhat tattered sofa, coffee table, and upholstered club chair scattered in rich florals. She stopped in front of the bookcase and picked up one of the photos.

A happy couple stood on the porch of a newly built lodge. Perhaps this was the beginning of Seven Tine? She placed the photo back on the shelf and perused the others, recognizing the woman in many of them as Sydney Moomaw Hardy. She stood by two people who must be her husband and daughter. The girl was a mirror image of her mother. Both were small framed with black hair and delicate features.

Behind Rita hung an aerial view of the ranch on canvas. She ambled over to the wall and was about to read the philosophy inscribed on the canvas when Robert appeared in the entryway. He closed the door behind him and went to the window, unrolling the blinds but keeping them partially open.

"Have a seat." He sat in the floral club chair and motioned to the couch. Once Rita was settled, he said, "Mandie knows you're coming with me."

"What did you tell her?"

"The truth," Robert answered.

"No one needs to know my business."

"She won't say anything. Not when it comes to women in need. And I only told her he might show up."

Rita nodded and crossed her legs. She hated being a woman in need. "So, what's the plan then?"

"We'll leave shortly. What else did your ex say?"

Good question. She bounced her foot, fingering the feather necklace her mom had given her. "I didn't read all the messages."

"Where's your cell?"

"Upstairs."

He stood. "Let's go get it."

"You stay here," Rita said. "I'll be right back." She shot out of her seat and barreled through the door before he could protest.

No sir. It was her private space. No men allowed. Not even one as kind and helpful as Robert.

She trotted up the curved staircase by the office and went inside the room, slamming the door behind her. On the area rug were the contents of her backpack. Shoving the items back inside, she noticed the modest engagement ring. She had to get Bowie out of her life. She stuffed the ring and the rest of her belongings into the pack, rounded up her phone, and headed back to the office.

Her belly in a knot, she entered the office, closed the door behind her, and handed the phone to Robert, who'd been looking out the window. "Here."

While he searched her cell, she studied the grounds through the slatted blinds, praying that Bowie wasn't actually coming to the ranch, that he was just trying to get her to respond to his texts.

"Looks like you've tolerated a lot of crap from Dark Cloud." The muscles in his jaw tightened. "Sorry. I didn't mean to be so blunt."

"No, you're right." She'd only told him what he needed to know. "It's been a living hell."

The ring tone Bowie had set on her phone crooned Marty Robbins's song "My Woman, My Woman, My Wife." Rita winced and reached for the phone. "I can't take it anymore."

CHAPTER 17

"**D**on't answer it." Robert pointed to the phone.
A shiver skirted across the back of Rita's neck. She
yearned for an affectionate touch. A hug. Some form of
physical comfort to stop the trembling and nausea. The kind
she was sure that Sydney would offer if she were here.

"I'll have Chuck help you get a protective order before
we head out."

"I got one in Pendleton. Besides, I said no cops." She
sucked in a breath, trying to calm her nerves and slumped
onto the sofa. Obviously, the temporary restraining order
offered no sense of security, which she had figured. The ranch
office seemed to cave in on her as her mind reeled. "Let's get
out of here."

She needed to go. Find a safe place before Bowie killed
her. She tried to stand but plopped down again. Her hand
flew to her neck as her breathing careened out of control.
She squeezed her eyes shut.

"Whoa. Easy does it," Robert said.

She put her head between her legs with her hands on
her head but couldn't catch her breath. Couldn't gain control.
Bowie's words entered her mind, *You make me hurt you, Rita.
You know that, right?* But it couldn't be her fault. He had free
will.

"Do I need to get a paper bag?"

Rita nodded, trying to concentrate on her ragged
breathing as she dragged in long gulps of air as her doctor

had taught her, trying not to pass out. Robert left and came back with a paper sack. She took it and blew, every muscle in her body tense. Someone had to stop Bowie. She had to get out of there. Her hands and feet began to tingle. If she didn't get a hold of herself—and soon—she'd pass out.

"I'm not going to let anything happen to you." His voice low and steady, Robert rubbed her back. "Breathe." His eyes held hers.

She tried to nod.

In a soft, soothing tone, he said, "Breathe."

She dragged air into her lungs as the bag deflated, then let it out. Oh, his hands were warm. Caring. Gentle. How a man's hands should feel.

Though her breathing was going back to normal, the urge to cry went full steam ahead. Years of pent-up fear and anxiety flowed with her tears. His sympathetic touch and encouragement helped her calm down. And twenty minutes later, she held the bag in her lap, finally relaxed. And totally mortified.

Robert handed her a box of tissues. She plucked one out, dabbed her eyes, and blew her nose.

"I know you're scared, but you have a better chance at nailing him if you turn him in. I'll call Chuck, and you can give him the truck's description. And license plate number if you know it. Chuck can contact your family—"

"Don't call him. Please." She shot to her feet and paced the room. She looked around and read Seven Tine's philosophy. Two words stood out: respect and prepare. It was clear Bowie didn't respect her boundaries—and may never. So, maybe she should turn him in.

She'd heard enough at the convention to know that she could trust Sydney. And if Officer Chuck was family, maybe she could trust him too. At least hear what he had to say. "Okay. I'll talk to him."

"You're doing the right thing." Robert went to the desk, picked up his cell, and made the call.

She wrapped her arms around herself and held on. *Lord, help. Do something.* As he talked, Rita formed emergency escape plans of her own. On the ranch, there were horses and trucks. She could borrow one and leave a note. Promise to return it later. She'd even seen a shotgun on the wall in the tack room. And she bet it was loaded. She had killed once to protect herself. Could she do it again?

"He's on his way."

"So quickly?"

"Yeah, he's on leave helping out with my sister, Glenda. She's recovering from surgery."

"Maybe we shouldn't bother him."

"Are you kidding me? Glenda's a handful." Robert laughed and settled on the sofa next to her. Close. But not too much. "Trust me, he needs the break." He glanced at the wall clock. "I'll get some coffee and a snack. I think better with food in my stomach. I'm sure Mandie has something hidden in the fridge."

"I'll help. I've never been good at sitting around and waiting." She had to get her mind off Bowie or she'd have another panic attack. She followed him into the great room. An unruly boy of about five bumped into her.

"What's wrong with your face?" He pointed his filthy finger at her.

Rita recoiled, her hand flying to her bruises to hide the evidence.

"Donnie!" A red-faced woman shooed him away. "I'm so sorry." The mother chased after the boy.

Robert strode to her, wearing a look of compassion. "You sure you don't want to wait in the office?"

"I'm good." She couldn't be angry with the boy. Kids were honest. She strode to the coffee bar and poured three cups of the steaming brew for herself, Robert, and Chuck. She doused hers with a plain creamer. Pumpkin spice seemed too festive for her angst.

She unbraided her hair and finger combed its thick length around her face. Since the afternoon weather had turned so cold and drizzly, many of the older guests were playing cards and games in the dining area. Parents tried to wrangle young kids for naps. They made her feel crazy exposed. Suddenly, a strong urge to flee engulfed her.

"How you holding up?" Mandie set an empty tray down and leaned against the counter.

"I'm okay." Rita pressed her lips into a counterfeit grin.

"No, really." Mandie touched her shoulder. "Tell me the truth."

The tender touch warmed her heart. "I'm scared."

"You're safe here, ya know."

"I'm not so sure. But thanks for caring."

Mandie set the mugs on the tray and carried it as both women headed to the office. Seconds later, Robert walked in with a tray of goodies, and Mandie went back to the kitchen.

"Scored some huckleberry pie." He set the dessert and a stack of plates on the coffee table and held up a knife and three forks.

The last thing she felt like doing was eating—even something as delicious as huckleberry pie. What she did feel like was weak. For years she'd kept up with the male ranch hands on her dad's place. Bucking bales. Fixing fence. Tackling weeds. Doctoring cows and horses. And dogs and humans. How could one man inject such fear into her?

Rita turned to a knock thumping on the doorframe of the ranch office. A husky man wearing jeans, black cowboy boots and hat, and a red pullover with a whitetail buck on the front strolled through the door. His smile and clean-shaven face lit up the gloomy room.

Robert turned around. "Thanks for coming, bro."

"Glad to help." Chuck clapped him on the back, and the men turned to Rita.

Their stares made her feel awkward. But she stayed planted in her seat on the sofa. She'd promised to hear him out. The quicker they talked, the faster they could leave. And thank goodness she'd let Robert convince her to return to the privacy of the office.

"Rita, this is my brother-in-law, Chuck."

He nodded, his hands clasped in front of him. "Nice to meet you."

Robert motioned to the floral club chair. "Let's have a seat." He settled beside Rita, his leg touching hers, and served pie.

She set hers on her lap, too anxious to take a bite.

Chuck cleared his throat. "Do you mind if Robert remains in the room while we talk or should he leave?"

Robert stopped chewing, his gaze darting from Chuck to Rita. The look on his face reminded her of a child asked to toss his favorite treat in the garbage.

She placed her hand on his leg. "I'd rather have him here." When his eyes grew round, she removed it. "I wish Sydney was here, but I understand."

Chuck nodded. "Talking to other women is probably easier."

"Way easier." She fingered the dessert plate.

"Why don't you start by telling me about yourself." Chuck set his plate on the coffee table and took out a small notebook.

About me? Good grief. What about Bowie? She sighed. "I work on my dad's cattle ranch on the Umatilla rez. My sister does too. I do just about everything, from fixing fence to doctoring cattle."

"You sound like a handy gal. You're a tribal member then?"

"Yeah. I am."

"And is Bowie Dark Cloud your fiancé?"

"Was. Before I left, I got a restraining order."

"Good to know. It will apply here as well. Tribal courts work together, and I can help you with—"

"I'm not going back. I can't face him." Her throat constricted. Why go back to court? Nothing was going to stop him from getting to her.

Chuck and Robert exchanged glances, and Robert gave him a slight shake of his head. "Is Mr. Dark Cloud a member of the Umatilla Tribe too?"

"Yeah. He is."

Chuck scribbled in his notepad. "Can you tell me about your situation?"

She didn't want to, but she went ahead and filled him in on the abuse, leaving out the rape and murder. She couldn't chance being put in jail. Even if it was self-defense. She couldn't chance Bowie taking out his rage on Hazel.

Chuck listened as a cop should.

When she was finished, he said in a tone filled with compassion, "What else can you tell me about Mr. Dark Cloud?"

His empathy had a way of wrapping right around her heartstrings and cracking the hard shell. There was no judgment. No ridicule. Mandie was right, she was safe and felt secure enough to show Bowie's texts to him. Her bruises were a testimony of truth.

After taking notes, he asked, "Anything else that might help?"

She gave him a description of Bowie, his truck, a few of his friends, including Gary Fullmoon, and his cell phone number. "Do you need a copy of the restraining order?"

"Yes, please."

"I'll be right back." She rushed to her room, ignoring the stares of nosy guests, unzipped her backpack, and pulled out the legal document. "Hope you can hold your value." She took it back to the office and handed the order to Chuck.

He took out his cell and snapped a photo of it. "Let me know if you think of anything else. In the meantime, we'll be keeping an eye out for him."

Exhaustion hit Rita like a freight train after Chuck left. She went to her room and curled into a ball on the bed, covering herself up with a knitted blanket that had been draped over the footboard. The rhythm of rain outside the window soothed her as she closed her heavy lids. She'd rest until Robert was ready to leave.

Just when she was almost asleep, her phone chimed. She lifted it to her face. Bowie?

After reading the message, she shot out of bed. She gathered her belongings and trotted down the stairs toward the lodge office. She caught Robert just as he was about to walk out the door. "Wait!"

CHAPTER 18

Rita waved her phone in the air. "It's him!" She followed Robert back into the office, and when he closed the door, she handed him her cell.

He peered at the text.

Almost there.

His gaze darted to hers. "Do you know where he's at?"

She shook her head. "Don't have a clue. And I'm not sure if he's bluffing or not." Oh, how she hoped his text was a sham. But he'd always lived up to what he said.

Robert pointed to her backpack. "Those your things?"

"Yeah, they are."

"Good. Let's get out of here." He led Rita to the foyer, plucked his Stetson off a hat hook, took hold of her arm, and led her out into the soggy outdoors.

Robert's touch was kind. Gentle. Secure. She couldn't remember the last time a man had handled her in such a protective manner, and it felt good.

"We'll take my truck." He nodded to his blue, one-ton Chevy Silverado parked beside the barn.

Chad came around the hood. "You're ready to roll." He opened the door for Rita.

She crawled inside and thanked him, then turned to Robert as he slid behind the wheel. "You're a bronc rider. Why are we hauling a horse trailer?"

"So you'll have a place to hang out while I'm behind the chutes." He fired up the engine and headed down the half-mile driveway.

His cell rang, and he took the call. "What's up?" He filled Mandie in and asked her to update Sydney. "Tell her I'll call when we hit Spokane." He tossed the cell on the dashboard.

The truck rolled to a stop under a wooden sign with both the Seven Tine Guest Ranch lettering and two seven-tined elk antlers tipped on Ts burned into the wood. Thick logs held the plank in place. At the top and on either side of the poles were matching pairs of what looked like elk antler sheds, faded and worn, also with seven points on each one.

"What if he's in town trying to flush us out?" She felt as though she was about to have a panic attack as a couple of vehicles passed by.

Robert turned south onto Highway 155. "Better to be safe than sorry. We'll cut across the east part of the rez and go through Inchelium. If he's in Nespelem or at the agency, we'll slip under his radar."

Her cell rang. What the heck? She slapped her leg. "My phone just went dead, and I don't have a charger."

"Maybe it's a good thing." Robert turned west just after the Chief Joseph Rest Area.

The bronze sculpture of the Nez Perce chief drew her back to the gentleman trucker who'd given her a ride. He was the opposite of Bowie Dark Cloud. One had brought her to safety, and the other, well, she was convinced that he wanted her dead.

They wound their way through a small section of town, past a HUD housing unit and a single-wide trailer house on their left and an old, whitewashed church on a hill to their right. They continued up a steep, curvy grade.

Only one car followed them, and it wasn't anything Bowie would be caught driving.

Once on top of the sagebrush-and-grass hill, Rita's pulse slowed. She leaned back against the headrest and closed her eyes, her tummy gurgling. She should have eaten the huckleberry pie.

"I heard your belly. Better take a look in the back seat." Robert kept his gaze on the road, the hint of a smile on his face.

She reached in the back and pulled a cloth bag toward her. Inside was a square container with her untouched pie, a thermos, travel mugs, and a gallon baggie of dried meat.

Robert adjusted the truck's heater. "Sydney makes the dried venison. You're going to love it."

Too bad the smell of peppercorn churned her stomach. But she did nibble on the pie as they looped their way over Cache Creek Pass. "How long until we're in Chelan?"

"A little over an hour. And it's Inch-uh-lee-um."

Her face warmed from the mispronunciation. "Inchelium. Got it."

By the time they turned north on Highway 21, she was weary and carsick from the winding pass. She struggled to enjoy the deep red, orange, and yellow leaves dangling from aspen trees lining the paved road and the shallow creek snaking along to her right. Robert slowed for three deer crossing the road.

"They sure are beautiful." Rita hugged herself. She wanted to feel beautiful. Feel worthy. When was the last time she had felt either? Had she ever felt pretty and treasured? Not by men, that's for sure.

"Not to mention they sure taste good." His gaze followed the deer.

"Do you hunt?"

He chuckled. "What Indian doesn't?"

"You got a point." Rita gave him a nervous laugh and turned toward the window. It felt good to laugh. It also felt wrong. Really wrong.

"And do you?" Robert's brows lifted. "Go after big game?"

At the moment, she felt hunted. "Yeah, I hunt. Haven't yet this year though."

"'Cause of your man?"

"He's my *ex*. But, yeah, because of him." In fact, she'd quit having fun in her life because of him. Because public displays of jealousy were never amusing. Rita kept an eye on the side mirror as Robert turned east at the Inchelium turnoff.

Keith Urban crooned "God Whispered Your Name" softly in the background as they started up Bridge Creek Pass. Surely, the song wasn't referring to her. God hadn't spoken to her in years.

"So, tell me all you can about Bowie Dark Cloud," Robert said. "I need to know what I'm up against."

Hmm. Where to begin?

It was dark when they pulled into Spokane. The line of buildings with glowing signage southbound on Division Street, a jumble of bumper-to-bumper cars and glaring lights, made Rita's head spin. Oh, Lord, how she missed the rolling hills of the Umatilla rez.

Robert's phone chimed. "What's up?" He talked for a few minutes, a scowl on his face, then ended the call. "Chuck caught up with Bowie."

So, he wasn't bluffing. She clutched her throat. "Where at?" How nice it'd be if he gave Chuck a hard time and landed back in the slammer.

"Near the agency."

"Where's that?"

"Do you remember coming through a small town with a huge building to your right before the trucker let you off at the rest stop?"

"Vaguely."

"It's Tribal headquarters. Just south of Nespelem."

"What did Chuck say? Did Bowie leave?"

"Um . . . he uh—"

"C'mon on, spit it out. I need to know. Did Chuck serve the restraining order or not?"

"Yeah, he did. And that's when your ex took off. Chuck said he'd been pumping fuel at the Trading Post. When he showed him the restraining order, he peeled out of the parking lot, and like an idiot, headed toward Buffalo Lake, which is southeast of the agency on a twisty, dirt road. Chuck pursued, but an elder pulling a fishing boat ran Chuck's rig off the road before the turnoff to a small resort at the north end of the lake. He rounded a corner and just missed the fisherman. Scared the poor guy out of his mind."

"Oh my goodness. Are they okay?"

"Yeah. They're both fine. But your ex got away. Chuck called it in, so there's an APB out for him."

"They should be able to get him then. Right?"

"I hope so."

She hoped so too. But the restraining order to Bowie equaled a red cloth to a bull. Good grief, would this cat-and-mouse chase go on for the rest of her life? "What if he ignores the restraining order and tracks us down?"

"We'll have to trust the cops will get him before then."

She snorted. So far it didn't look promising.

"What if they don't find him?" What if he found her first? Bowie wasn't one to give up so easily. He'd track her down like a hound dog on a fresh scent. But what she didn't understand is why? Why did abusers not want to let go?

"Try not to worry. It'll make you sick." He pulled into a gas station.

Too late. She already felt sick. "How much farther?"

"The fairgrounds are only about fifty miles away."

Rita went into the mini-mart and used the restroom. If she didn't force herself to eat, she'd pass out. So she gathered sandwich fixings, a few snacks, and water. Not having enough cash, she paid with her credit card. Back in the truck, she made them a PB and J.

Robert pulled into light traffic and headed south on the Newport Highway, then called Sydney with an update. When the call ended, he told Rita, "I'll take you over the scenic route."

"The scenic route?"

"Yeah, don't you like them?"

"Not really. After one of Bowie's episodes, he took me on back roads for a makeup drive. All he'd wanted to do was get physical with me. I've spent time after time fighting him off. Trying to save every ounce of honor for our wedding night. I hated those drives." And she hated Bowie.

"I'll stay on the main roads then."

"I appreciate it." The only thing that'd make Rita feel safe was to have Bowie Dark Cloud behind bars.

CHAPTER 19

B owie had sent Gary for burgers, giving him time to do a little research. Now that the cop was off his tail, and he'd found a brown and black '79 Ford F-250 pickup in good condition for a few grand in the podunk town of Wilber off US Route 2, he could concentrate on finding Rita again.

What luck to have driven through town and found the truck in a yard with a For Sale sign in the window—and for the owner to know a guy who'd be interested in Bowie's rig. Yeah, the truck gods were definitely on his side. There was a reason he hadn't gone gambling the night of the horse sale.

In the meantime, his Ford F-150 was tucked away in the back of the Lone Pine Hotel until the buyer could get the cash.

He laid low in the cramped business area of the hotel and wiggled the computer mouse, rubbing his hands as the screen lit up. He typed in "Seven Tine Guest Ranch." The ranch's website popped up, and he smiled. "What do we have here?"

What appeared to be family photos slid across the screen. He recognized Sydney from her headshot on the brochure. As he studied her, he pushed his black cowboy hat off his forehead, rubbed his head, and tapped it back down.

He clicked through additional photos and stopped on one in particular. The mug of the tribal cop who had served him the temporary restraining order was right there. He was dressed in off-duty Western wear and placed at the edge of the family on the steps of a massive lodge. A whole slew of them lined the stairs—young and old.

He chuckled. "Yes. I can run. I can hide. I can find her. Will find her and get back what belongs to me. I won't let her ruin my plans."

He printed off the picture, folded it, and slid it into his wallet. He studied photos of the ranch, every angle, every nook and cranny the website provided.

Gary came up to him. "You find much?" He placed a lidded cup and a bag saturated with grease and the smell of burgers and fries by the computer.

"Check this out." Bowie motioned to the monitor. Gary pulled up a chair and took a seat.

"Is this where she's hidin' out?"

"I believe so." Bowie grunted. "Get comfortable. I plan to be here all weekend."

"Got nothing better to do." Gary studied the photo on the screen. "Hey, isn't he the cop who stopped us?"

"Sure is."

"You showed him, bro." Gary laughed and sipped from his straw. "So, what's the plan?" He leaned back as though he were the mastermind of a mob.

Bowie put his phone on the cubicle. "We might have to go to this Seven Tine Guest Ranch and check it out. In the meantime, I'll keep digging."

"What do you want me to do?"

"Go to the room and leave me alone. I'll be up later."

Gary got up and headed to the elevators.

Bowie kept searching. He printed out a few photos of the ranch and smiled as he studied them. "Yep. We got her."

At ten the next morning, they rattled down the highway to Seven Tine in his new-to-him Ford. Bowie felt like a king, perched in the shiny rig. It was a step up from his battered F-150. It felt sturdy. Durable. Like he could outrun another cop—preferably with his fiancée in tow. "Us showing up will catch her off guard. She's never been a morning person. She'll be groggy. Making it easy to get in, grab her, and get out. Before anyone has time to call the cops."

"And if they follow us?"

"We can get away faster in this beast."

As they drove up the lane to the guest ranch, all Gary could talk about was how nice everything looked. He guessed how much money he thought the owners might have and how many horses, cattle, and chickens were on the ranch. Bowie's fingers curled around the steering wheel, wishing he'd come alone.

He parked near the guest ranch's porch and said, "Stay here." He settled his cowboy hat low over his eyes.

"Why?"

"Because I said so."

"But it's cold."

Bowie let out a gnarled laugh. "Don't be a wimp, Fullmoon. I won't be long. Start the engine if your tootsies get cold." He shook his head and got out of the truck. His lungs tingled as they drew in the frosted air and inhaled traces of farm life and wood smoke.

Movement in the barn snagged his attention. He pulled up his collar and shoved his hands into his canvas coat pockets. As he walked, he took in the lodge, barn, and rocky knoll behind it, every nook and cranny where a person might hide.

Inside the barn, a leggy cowboy with a pitchfork welcomed him. "Can I help you?"

Bowie recognized him from the online photos and held out his hand. "Your website says you have horses for sale. Sorry I didn't call first. But I'm passing through. Thought I'd take a chance and stop in. Take a peek."

The man took off his glove. "I'm Chad." The men shook hands. "Yeah, we normally set appointments. My boss takes care of all sales, and she's not here right now. Can you come back?"

Bowie shifted his weight. "Like I said, we're just passing through. If I could take a quick look, I'd be obliged." He was impressed with the eight-stall barn's cleanliness. It reminded him of Rita's tidy ways. Only she had the knack to make his barn shine so he could be as respectable as Dean Runninghorse, or at least fool folks into thinking he was. His future father-in-law had.

"Where you from?"

"The Umatilla rez."

"You're a long way from home." Eyeing Bowie, Chad put his glove back on. "I didn't catch your name?"

"Frank Hawley." In the past, the alias had worked well for him.

"I suppose it won't hurt for you to take a quick look. We have a full schedule, so I don't have much time."

"I don't need much." As they walked out the back entrance, Bowie noted every stall, the tack room, pens, animals, the grove of trees lit in autumn colors, and those not.

They stopped at a pen, and Chad pointed out the sale horses: a few stout, blue roan geldings. Then they went to another pen, and Chad showed him the mares: a red-and-white leggy paint, a shorter bay with soft eyes, and a gray.

Bowie lifted his cell in the air. "Mind if I take a few photos?"

"Actually, it's against the rules. But you can check them out online."

What a punk. "I understand." He tucked the cell into his coat pocket. Most horse owners he'd worked with never minded. "I see this place is a guest ranch. Mind if I look around? This would be a nice place to bring my fiancée."

"Taking the vows, huh? Congrats. Mandie should be in the lodge. She can answer any questions you might have."

Bowie was careful to thank Chad before he headed for the porch. Its size and winged design impressed him. Gary met him at the entrance. "What'd you find out?"

"Why aren't you in the truck?"

"It's too cold."

Bowie chuckled. "You just want your nose in the middle of everything, don't you?" He'd have to let his partner tag along so Gary didn't get into trouble.

Gary shrugged. "Well, what'd you find out?"

"Nothing yet."

"What's the plan?"

"We go in and check things out." Bowie marched up the steps, then warned Gary, "Keep your mouth shut."

Gary nodded. "When you said we'd be staying the weekend, I hoped we'd be staying here." He gave Bowie a stained-tooth smile and checked out the horsehead bench under the bay window.

"Like I said, shut up or you'll sit in the rig."

"Just sayin'."

The men went into the lodge. Bowie stopped at the welcome table in the boot-lined foyer and took a few brochures of the ranch and surrounding sites to make it look like he was truly interested.

Entering the great room, he slid off his cowboy hat and let a low whistle slide through his teeth. He inhaled a pastry aroma, making his mouth water. Apple? Cinnamon? The photos had not done the place justice. A large stone fireplace graced the south wall. Two sets of stairs on opposite sides of the room curved up to what he assumed were guest rooms. Games and puzzles littered a few tables—some started and others almost complete. To his left, a woman and four kids perused what looked like a fully stocked gift shop. And above them, head mounts of elk, deer, and moose graced the walls. He'd never seen such huge antlers before.

"Can I help you?" A short woman wearing an apron offered them a bright smile.

"Good morning." Bowie swept his hat over the floor. "We're passing through and wanted to get a brochure. This place looks like somewhere I'd love to bring my fiancée to for a romantic weekend."

A chuckle belched out of Gary's mouth. His gaze dropped to the side when Bowie glared at him.

"I can help you. I'm Mandie, by the way." She gestured to the dining area. "Why don't you grab a seat, and I'll get you cinnamon rolls fresh out of the oven." She flitted away as fast as she'd appeared.

Bowie found a seat in a corner. He tapped his fingers on the table and turned to Gary's curious expression. "What's the matter with you?"

"You think Rita's gonna want to marry you? She left for a reason."

"When I show her this, she will." Bowie pulled a small box from his inside jacket pocket and lifted the lid. A two-carat diamond ring glimmered under the light of one of the six wagon-wheel chandeliers.

Gary's eyes grew wide. "It looks expensive. Where'd you get the money for something so fancy?" He tipped his head. "Wait a minute. I thought she already had one."

"I have connections. And she does. But this one is bigger. Fancier." One she won't refuse.

"You mean you stole it."

Bowie scowled at him. "No, you moron. It means I know people who can give me good deals. She'll appreciate this one."

"Well then, it's the bait to hook her all right. Where do ya think she is?" Gary reached for the shiny rock.

Bowie snapped the lid shut and stuffed the box into the inside pocket of his jacket. He smiled at Mandie as she approached. As promised, she set a tray of freshly baked cinnamon rolls on the table.

"I see you have brochures. Let me know if you have any questions." Mandie smiled and motioned to the coffee bar near the batwing door leading into the kitchen. "And help yourself. I just made a fresh pot."

"I'll get the coffee." Gary rose and strolled to the bar.

Bowie thanked her and asked, "When will the owners be back?"

Mandie tipped her head. "How'd you know they were gone?"

"I've already been to the barn looking at horses with Chad."

She blinked several times. "Sydney's . . . um . . . I'm not sure. I think they'll be home in a few weeks."

"You've been a big help." Bowie bit into the warm cinnamon roll. "Best I've had yet." He winked at her.

She wiped her hands on her apron as Gary returned with two steamy cups. "Glad you like it." She hurried toward the kitchen and disappeared behind the southern batwing door. The swinging kitchen entryway—no, the entire lodge—reminded him of old Western movies, making him feel at home.

"She'll be gone a few weeks." Bowie chuckled, then washed the pastry down with a swallow of strong, black coffee.

Now, to find Rita.

CHAPTER 20

Coeur d'Alene, Idaho

By the time Rita and Robert pulled into the Kootenai County Fairgrounds, her body felt like it had been run over by a train. Her sides and rear end ached. And she was shaky from lack of food. She got out of the truck and stretched her stiff muscles, slowly rolling her shoulders and neck.

When her muscles began to relax she retrieved her backpack from the back seat and ambled to the living quarter's door of the horse trailer. She'd never shared a room with a man before. In fact, the last sleepover she'd had with someone other than family was in junior high with her friends Emily Nelson, Heather Snow, and Kris Arnold.

If only they were kids again. Together. Laughing. Telling stories. Sharing crushes.

Before Talon Hawkeye had ruined her.

Why had she let the friendships fade away when her nightmares began?

And until she stepped into the cramped, suffocating space, she hadn't freaked out about her privacy. Racked with fear, she rushed outside and knocked Robert to the ground.

"What's the matter?" He stood and brushed dirt off his jeans.

"I can't sleep in there. With you." She felt another panic attack coming on.

"What are you talking about? You can sleep in the hayloft. The table folds down into a bed. I'll sleep there."

She shook her head. "No-no-no way. Uh-uh." Her breaths came in short spurts and her head spun. Her legs weakened, and she dropped to her knees. Her backpack fell out of her hands. "I can't . . . can't breathe . . ." Her hand flew to her neck.

Gritty footfalls faded, then came back. And a hand bumped her shoulder.

"Here, breathe in this." He held out a paper bag.

She took the sack and pressed it against her mouth, feeling out of control. It smelled like stale fries and made her gag. "I can't—"

"Take deep breaths."

She nodded and expanded her lungs, fighting the urge to spew what little food she'd had on the road. She struggled to catch air, leaned back on her haunches, and blew into the bag. This couldn't keep happening.

Robert rubbed her back. At first, his touch made her cringe.

But after several minutes, she relaxed and appreciated his soothing touch. When calm enough to talk, she asked, "What on earth is the hayloft?"

"Up there." He nodded to the trailer's nose.

"I've never heard the gooseneck bed called the hayloft. Weird. But listen, I can find a motel." Rita hugged her pack, wishing it were Posse. She'd have to use her credit card again, but oh well.

"I can sleep in the truck."

"No. It's too cold." She couldn't let him freeze. He needed the win. With all he'd done for her, she wasn't about to block his path to victory.

"I've slept in worse conditions. It's no big deal." Robert's red nose called his bluff.

"Let's go back inside and see what we can come up with," Rita said.

"You feel comfortable going back in?"

Come to think of it, she didn't have enough left on her credit card to get a room, no matter the cost. "I'll give it my best shot." She cradled her backpack and stood. Robert led the way. The closer she got, the harder her body trembled. *Get me through this.* . . . Her Creator didn't take away her shakes, but He did give her the nerve to climb the one step and shuffle inside.

A queen-size bed loomed overhead. The ceiling was so low above it, she feared she'd hurt herself if startled awake from one of her nightmares. A table and leather bench seats perched across the door—the bed Robert had talked about. A short lane led to a cramped kitchen complete with a two-burner stove, microwave, and fridge and freezer combo.

Her father had a similar setup they'd used at fairs when she and Hazel were in 4-H club before they had to work on the ranch. While theirs was a two-horse trailer, this one had two drop-down windows and a door with a sliding window indicating three horse stalls. "I'd prefer sleeping here if you don't mind." She pointed to the table.

"Sure. What else would make you feel comfortable?"

Rita dropped her pack on one of the bench seats and strode past the kitchenette to the door leading into the bathroom, a very cramped space. To her left was a shower with a glass door and toilet, opposite a sink, mirror, and a thin but sturdy storage cabinet. Smack in the middle was a metal door.

She'd been in enough horse trailers to know the door led to slanted horse stalls. Being in the belly of the trailer made her feel like Jonah in the whale. Light-headed, she hugged herself and strode back toward the table.

Robert had remained by the entrance, texting someone.

She went back to the fridge and opened the door to find it stuffy and empty, which made her feel uneasy. She sighed and closed the door. Beside her backpack was a blanket. She unfolded and held it up. "Can we pin this up somewhere for a little privacy?"

"We can, but the door"—he gestured to the back wall—"leads to the stud stall. Sydney uses it as a dressing room. I think it's empty." He strode past her and opened the door. "Yep, empty."

"Works for me."

"We set then?" He closed the bathroom door and turned to Rita.

"Um . . . what about food?"

"We still have PB and J, right? Plus, I figured in the morning we could unhook, go out for breakfast, then do a little shopping. You might want to get warmer boots."

"Sounds good to me." Rita grabbed her pack to get ready for bed and realized she didn't have any toiletries. Too embarrassed to tell Robert, she went to the bathroom and searched the cabinet.

Not finding anything, she opened the thin, mirrored cupboard and found a ziplock bag with everything she needed on the bottom shelf. Did Sydney use the horse trailer as a backup when the room for women in need was occupied? Or was she using Sydney's personal stash? Either way, she'd replace the products when she could.

She found a washcloth and cleaned up as heat rose from the floor vent, warming her feet. She took her time and prayed, fretting about sharing a room with a man who was not her husband. The mirror reflected her bruised, weary face. Would a respectable man ever choose someone like her? Probably not. Feeling hopeless, she changed into the fleece pajamas Mandie had given her.

God bless Mandie.

On the other side of the bathroom, Robert's faint voice drifted through the door. By the time she was done, he was in sweats and a T-shirt and sitting on the loft bed, his feet dangling over the side with a thick book opened on his lap.

He looked up at her. "Can I get you anything before I turn in?"

"No. But thanks. What are you reading?" Good Lord, he looked sexy. His muscles stretched the T-shirt fabric. Hat hair wild and rugged. Sable eyes glistening. Her chest fluttered.

He rubbed his hand over the open pages as though caressing a woman he cherished. "The Bible."

It had been a long time since she'd cracked hers open.

The table and benches had been converted into a bed. A sleeping bag was laid out for her, a fluffy pillow in the middle. She turned the sleeping bag so the opening faced the loft and fixed the pillow. Not having a brush, she unbraided her hair and combed her coarse locks with her fingers, catching Robert staring at her.

For an instant, they locked gazes.

Though he'd proven his honor, the wanting look on his face made her insides tingle. She swallowed. Wanting—no, needing—a caring touch. A simple hug. But she knew she had to keep her distance. She slipped into her sleeping bag and lay back. "Will you read to me?"

"Sure." His finger slid down the page and stopped "For freedom Christ has set us free; stand firm therefore, and do not submit again to a yoke of slavery."

The words in Galatians 5:1 shook Rita's spirit, as though the Creator were speaking directly to her. Would she ever be able to break free from her yoke of slavery? Her arms prickled as he read. And by the tone of his voice, she could tell his convictions ran deep.

Like hers used to.

Until the rape. Good Lord, would she ever be free from her past? Free from Bowie? Free from her father's emotional control and manipulation? Free from the fear of men? Able to stand courageously on her own two feet?

She hoped to have her own ranch someday and a loving husband with a gentle touch who'd give her a herd of kids. For her vision to come true, she'd have to be far away from Bowie. Even if her mom and sister chose to stay in their oppressive atmosphere, she refused to raise her future children in the darkness that came with domestic violence—whether the exploitation was with words or fists.

Both devastated women.

Both demolished families.

Both destroyed children.

As Rita's eyes closed, she prayed for God's direction. Prayed Bowie would disappear. But she knew deep inside her core, this was only the beginning of his hunt to get her back.

And he'd do whatever it took.

CHAPTER 21

Frost stuck to her slick sleeping bag was the final straw to thrust Rita out of bed. She'd tossed and turned all morning. She dreamed Bowie had found her. Beat her. Dragged her back to the rez to find her mare gone, shouting everything was all her fault.

She rushed to the bathroom and turned on the water. But nothing came out. She hugged herself, taking in slow breaths, and shivered, then closed her eyes. "Stay calm," she whispered. All she wanted was the comfort of warm water on her face. She blew out a breath through her clenched teeth. "I'm safe." She drew in cold air through her nose. Exhaled. "I can do this. 'I can do all things through him who strengthens me.'" She repeated the sequence and the verse from Philippians 4:13 until her body relaxed.

"How ya doing in there?" Robert asked.

"It's a little nippy. But fine."

"When you're ready, we'll find a place to get breakfast and fill up the propane tanks."

She had assumed a ranch like Seven Tine would have things ready at a moment's notice. Apparently not, unless they'd recently attended a rodeo or gone camping and hadn't had a chance to fill up. Or they'd recently helped a few victims.

God knew there were too many abused women in the world.

The trailer bounced, and a door shut. Bumping into the sink, she dressed as quickly as she could. She fixed the bed back into a table, stuffing the pillow and rolled-up sleeping bag onto the loft bed. Some resemblance of structure was better than none. She fixed her hair into a long side braid and went outside to find Robert.

The horse trailer was unhitched, and the grounds were empty. Well, it was only Thursday. They had arrived a day early. Maybe she could catch up on some much-needed rest.

"Ready?"

"Yep." She winced as she climbed into the truck. The burn in her sides couldn't go away quick enough.

"I know a little restaurant that serves a mean breakfast. You up for it?"

"I'll try my best," Rita said. "Then if you don't mind, I need to do a little shopping."

"Yeah, we have all day." Robert pulled out of the fairgrounds and headed east onto North Government Way.

After breakfast, he filled the propane tanks and drove over to Coeur D'Alene Lake for a stroll on the resort's docks. Autumn colors lit the edge of the water, reflecting on the lake's surface like a ring of fire. If only they weren't working so hard to keep her safe, she could have enjoyed it, appreciated a romantic stroll with a handsome man. The last thing she wanted to do was head back to the rodeo grounds and hunker down in the coffin-like trailer.

"So, why rodeo? Why saddle bronc?"

"It's all I've ever wanted. Since I was little. My dad used to take me to rodeos. I loved watching the bronc riders. They were smooth and classy. Artistic. In a league of their own. Then I'd come home and pretend ride anything not nailed down. Spurred like the best of them with my five-dollar spurs. Then one day, he put me on a green Shetland. I think I was six or seven. The little bugger took me for the ride of my life. He bucked, hopped around like a chicken on fire, and I stayed on. Hung on because no way was I going to have all my cousins laugh at me. It was the best day of my life. I've been riding ever since."

"Sounds fun. And scary."

"It was scary. But once I gentled the pony, he never did buck me off. I knew I could ride anything."

"And you have?"

"So far. At least for the most part. I come off now and again. It's part of the sport. You have to get back on and ride the next one."

"I suppose it's true in life too."

"Sure is. What's your happiest moment in life?"

Easy one. "The day my dad bought me Opal."

"Your dog?"

"Nope. My mare. She sticks to a calf like a bee on honey. She's faithful. Has the biggest heart ever. She's helped me through some pretty tough times."

They stepped off the dock, and she picked up a rock. She tossed it into the water and watched the ripples. She loved how easy it was to talk with Robert. Come to think of it, she'd never felt this way with Bowie.

And when he suggested they get the shopping done so they could head back, she felt heavy. Although she understood the urgency to keep the pipes from freezing, she rubbed her arms, wishing she had extra time.

When they pulled into the fairgrounds, several trucks and trailers had sprawled out across the parking area. Robert parked and hooked up the propane while Rita slipped into her warm boots and put away the groceries.

The furnace clicked on and heat radiated through the floor vents. Soon, there'd be hot water for a shower.

The trailer door opened, and Robert came in. "Feels like it's warming up in here." He grabbed coffee fixings and put a pot on the stove. "This won't take long."

"While the coffee's brewing, I'll check out the arena."

Robert opened the cabinet doors under the sink and crouched. "Have fun. I'll make sure no pipes are broken."

Rita bundled up and went outside. At least the sun was shining, and the air felt warmer. She meandered through horse trailers of all sizes and colors—some in fine condition, others well used.

Inside the dusty arena, teenagers warmed up their mounts, swinging oversized loops above their heads. A few girls in the mix made her smile. A graying man with a felt cowboy hat the color of dirt wearing well-worn boots ambled through a gate and whistled.

He shouted out two names. The teens entered their respective boxes, the horses calm, their ears twitching between the steer in the chute and their riders.

Once the header's barrier was in place and the teens had their ropes ready, the header called for the steer to be released. A cowboy pulled the chute lever, the gate opened, and the steer burst through.

The header shot out of the box, rope swinging. He released the rope, and it sailed over the steer's horns. In one pretty motion, he dallied the rope around the saddle horn and veered to the left, setting up the steer for the heeler who was hot on his trail.

The heeler swirled his rope overhead and released it, aiming for the steer's back hooves. The rope wrapped around the animal's heels, and the cowboy pulled his horse to a stop. A quick time for teenagers. The steer stretched between the two ropes—a clean ride. Cheers erupted from the crowd, most appearing to be family members of the rodeo team.

Rita clapped too, yearning to be on a horse. She climbed the stairs and found a place to sit near a few middle-aged women who were deep in conversation. She took the cold, hard seat. Feeling out of place without her buckaroo hat, she bent over and rested her elbows on her knees, her gloved hands pressed against her mouth to keep it warm.

Two more ropers filled the boxes, and a fresh steer trotted into the chute.

In a warm-up pen behind the arena, a girl tangled with a resistant horse.

"She's had a tough go with that one." A woman in a red jacket with a Stompin' Hooves Rodeo Club logo on the back shook her head as she gestured to the pair. "I just don't know what to do with the darned mare."

Rita gathered the woman was the girl's mother. Her friends encouraged her to sell the mare. Some offered names of ranches with quality horses.

"But I don't have the money for the horse she needs," Red Coat said.

As the group talked, Rita learned that the woman's husband had recently passed away in a mining accident in a nearby town. She remembered hearing about a man being trapped in a collapse. The national news had covered the event and his extraction.

Rita cleared her throat. "Ma'am, sorry for eavesdropping, but I live on a working cattle ranch and rope myself. I start many of our colts and would love to give your daughter a few pointers."

The woman turned and studied Rita for a long while. "You sure?"

"Absolutely." She stood. "I'd love to meet them."

The women's gazes darted from one another to the mother and to Rita. All but one nodded. The skeptic gave

Rita a sideways scowl and muttered to the mother. "You sure? You don't even know her."

The way she said it made Rita feel insignificant. And it was probably due to her bruised face. But she didn't care. Not about to let the cynic beat her down, she lengthened her spine, keeping her gaze on Red Coat.

"Why not?" The mom stood and led Rita to her daughter.

"Cindy, this lady wants to help you with Jazzy." The teen rode the chestnut horse over to them. A white star adorned the mare's forehead, and she had a brick-red colored mane and tail.

Rita introduced herself and smiled. "So, what's going on with you two?"

Cindy dismounted and threw up her hand. "She keeps tossing her head and refusing to enter the box."

"Well, watching you from the stands, it looks like you have a disrespectful horse. I can help if you want me to."

Cindy glanced at her mom, and when Red Coat nodded, she said, "Yeah, sure."

Rita took the reins and spent an hour working with the pair using various natural horsemanship methods in a small warm-up pen. Rita preferred to use the gentle horse-training techniques that highlight a deeper bond between horse and owner/trainer. She had learned years ago to incorporate a horse's body language as seen in the wild, and knew these methods were kinder for the horse.

It took a bit for the chestnut to surrender her strong will, but after several lessons using the release of pressure at the right time to gain her trust and respect, the mare decided it was better to give in and work as part of a team.

"Okay. It's your turn." Rita handed the horse over to Cindy who mounted and trotted Jazzy round. "I like how you're keeping your hands soft. Good job."

"She feels good."

"Excellent." Rita gave her a few additional riding tips before offering a couple of roping suggestions.

Red Coat cheered when the horse finally listened to her rider, and Rita felt valuable when Cindy voiced her appreciation of the lessons.

The rodeo coach called for two new ropers.

Cindy found a partner and went into the arena. Rita held her breath as the mare approached the header's box and released it when she went in quietly and waited for her rider's signal.

When the chute opened, the chestnut bolted out of the box, hot on the steer's tail. Cindy tossed the rope, and Rita cheered when the coil landed around the steer's neck. She applauded again when Cindy's partner roped the steer's heels.

Red Coat hugged Rita. "No need to sell her now. You worked magic. How can I ever repay you?"

"Them doing well is payment enough. Have fun and keep supporting your daughter, and we'll call it even."

"I appreciate you."

With dusk approaching, Rita turned and faced the stairs to leave. Her cheeks heated when she noticed Robert watching her from a spot next to the arena fence, an admiring grin on his face.

Darned if his expression wasn't reeling her in and making her believe that, yes, one day she could find real love.

CHAPTER 22

Walking back to the trailer, Robert said, "I had no idea you were so horse savvy." He nodded. *Beautiful and talented.*

They weaved through shadows and scattered rigs.

"The way you asked the chestnut to perform a task . . . man. I've never seen someone with hands as soft as yours. How'd you stay so relaxed? And patient. You're obviously in your element in the saddle. I can't believe how quickly you got the mare to settle down. I've never seen anything like it. Wow . . . I thought Chad was good."

She blushed. But he didn't care. She'd earned his praises.

It was as if two broken spirits were communicating in perfect harmony, like when he'd found her with Blizzard. She was the only one the stud had ever accepted. It was an unexplainable trust. Rita Runninghorse was a true western woman with a God-given gift.

"It's easy when you love what you do. And did you see Cindy light up after she'd roped the steer? What a natural."

"Like you."

"I'm not so sure about that. But thanks for the vote of confidence."

"What's your dad's ranch like?" Robert noticed a change in her demeanor. Ouch. The subject was clearly off-limits. She'd shared a little. But he wanted to know more. What had her upbringing been like? What caused an amazing woman like her to pick a loser like Bowie?

"Like any other cattle operation, I suppose. He runs two hundred pair. Has three bulls and ten saddle horses." Her voice hitched when she'd mentioned the horses. Then she changed subjects like a pro. "Tell me about the Seven Tine." Rita sniffed. "I didn't get to see much of it."

"We have about one hundred acres. And lease both county and tribal property. When our dad and my sisters' mom passed away last June, we almost lost it all. You'll have to ask Sydney about it sometime. It's quite a story."

"At the convention, she told us about the barn fire, her parents' will, her mom's cancer, and Glenda's matrimonial deal concerning the ranch sale. We all laughed. And cried."

Robert led the way into the toasty trailer, the smell of coffee greeting them. He warmed up the tin pot and served them both cups of the steaming brew before settling across the table. "I've never heard my sister speak. She won't let anyone around when she practices. Not even Trey. But I know it has to affect women because you all come in droves. The reserved room is always full, and this trailer is often used as a spillover apartment." He sipped his coffee.

Rita cupped her hands around the hot mug. "How many have come through?"

"I'd say about fifty or so in two years." But none were as fascinating as she was. Not even close. She was stronger. Determined. And had a spark in her eyes that no one else had.

"Oh, wow."

He took another swallow of coffee and set his cup on the table, then leaned back. "My sister's amazing. Every woman Sydney and the domestic violence advocates have worked with has been set free from her abuser. Children are safe. Many of the abusers are behind bars or in treatment of some kind. The women now earn a living, have confidence, and seem . . . what's the word Syd uses?" He tapped the table with his thumb. "Empowered."

"I hope she can help me too."

Something he'd said put a spark back in her eyes. He smiled. "You should see the letters and emails she gets. It's crazy. But she likes the updates. It keeps her fire fueled."

"Good to hear. Is that how you guys were able to rebuild your stock so quickly? Her speaking engagements?"

"Yep. And Trey's photography business. Because Sydney offers hope in God, women pack conferences."

She wrung her hands. "I used to be involved in youth group as a teenager. Mostly middle school."

"What happened?"

"My dad made me stop going."

He made her stop going? "How come?"

"Wish I knew. About the same time, my mom stopped attending social events. Seemed withdrawn. I'm sure due to my dad's less-than-affectionate ways. My poor sister never had much opportunity to socialize outside of school either. It seemed around then that all hell broke loose in our family."

He remembered Sydney saying there were about six types of abuse. And isolation was one of them. Were Bowie and her dad mistreating her? The thought infuriated him. How could men be so cruel? Women should be cherished, like his dad had treasured Jennie.

Compared to the Runninghorse women's abuse, his dad hiding his fatherly identity seemed like chump change. A few months before the Moomaws had passed away, Robert and Sydney had discovered they were siblings. She and Glenda were full sisters, and Robert and the girls shared a father. But at least they were never isolated like Rita and her sister had been. He couldn't imagine a life so controlled.

Bright lights from a truck pulled in, circled around, and settled on the trailer for a long moment. Robert shaded his eyes, slid out of the seat, and opened the door. The truck spun around and fled. "Who was that?"

"I can't see . . ." Rita shook her head. She pulled down the shade and hugged herself. "Do you think it's him?"

Robert closed the door. "No. It can't be. He has no idea where we are. It's probably a bunch of rowdy teenagers." He scooted into his spot. "Besides, I'm sure Chuck scared him off."

"You don't know Bowie."

"No. But I've seen his type." Boy, did he want to pull her into his arms. Feel her soft skin. Smell her flowery shampoo. Assure her she was safe. Instead, he asked, "You hungry?"

"Not really."

"You've hardly eaten. Please, have something." He got up, opened the cupboard, and selected a large can of chicken soup. "How about some of this? I'll grill us up a couple of cheese sandwiches to go with it."

"Okay. The soup might settle my tummy."

After the light meal, Rita hopped in the shower while Robert did the dishes, then she crawled into her sleeping bag. Robert sat on the bench at the base of the loft, his Bible open. He prayed for Rita to find comfort and peace tonight and for God to allow her a deep sleep.

She turned onto her side and peered up at him with those beautiful brown eyes of hers. "Will you read to me?"

How could he say no? Especially if the Word would give her comfort. "I sure will." He flipped to the book of Psalms and read from chapter 32, verse 8. "The Lord says, 'I will instruct you and teach you in the way you should go; I will counsel you with my eye upon you.'"

He wasn't sure how long he'd been reading before she'd fallen asleep. He watched her breathe for a while. What had it been like for her to hitchhike the better part of two hundred miles to find solace?

He prayed God would give him wisdom when it came to Rita. Keeping her safe was one thing he wasn't willing to screw up.

CHAPTER 23

Rita woke when she hit the floor. *Oh, my goodness. Not again.* In this nightmare, she was running from Bowie. But then he'd caught her, threw her on the ground, and punched her time and again. She screamed. Called for her mom. For Hazel. For Robert. But no one came. She was trapped. Like a wolf caught in a serrated leghold trap with nowhere to go.

She untangled her legs and kicked the sleeping bag off her. *Good Lord, will the bad dreams ever stop?* With the sleeve of her fleece pajama shirt, she wiped her overheated face, focusing on what her dreams were trying to tell her or perhaps warn her about.

"You okay down there?" Robert hung his head over the loft bed, a flashlight in hand.

Squinting, she pushed to her feet and flipped on an overhead light switch. "Yeah. I think so." But not really. He hopped out of bed, got her a bottle of water from the fridge, uncapped it, and handed it to her. She took a sip, pressed the bottle to her forehead, and sat on the edge of the bed.

"Bad dream?"

"You have no idea." Rita hugged herself. *Oh, my.* He stood shirtless. Her face heating, she struggled to keep her eyes off his muscular chest and biceps. Six-pack abs. She blinked several times, willing herself to look away. "I have them almost every night."

He picked up her sleeping bag and laid it on her bed. "What can I do to help?"

Besides cradle her in those brawny arms of his? Giving her comfort and assurance? Inside, she groaned. It was early Saturday morning, and he needed his sleep. She inhaled his spicy scent and said, "I wish I knew. What time is it?"

He found his cell. "3:14."

"Oh goodness. I'm so sorry. You need to get some sleep. Go back to bed. I'm fine." She arranged the sleeping bag and pillow and crawled inside.

Robert settled beside her. "Obviously not. Do you need to talk?"

The warmth of his body next to hers brought comfort. Too much comfort. "But you need the win. So, yeah, I'm fine."

"I do. But right now it's not about me. So tell me, what can I do to help you?"

"All I need is sleep. Then I'll be okay." *Hopefully someday.* "You can go back to bed."

He sat for a few seconds, then pulled on his boots and coat and grabbed his flashlight. "I'll take a look around."

He'd check things out for her in the middle of the night? *Wow! What a sweetheart.* The door shut behind him, and a beam of light weaved around outside, disappeared, and resurfaced through the other window. The door squeaked opened, and her throat thickened when he came into sight.

"All clear." He stepped inside, shed his boots and coat, and hopped up to the hayloft.

The electricity in the cramped quarters could have lit the burners.

After a long moment, she said, "What can I do to make it up to you?"

"For what?" His voice sounded groggy.

"Waking you up?"

She wished she could see his face. Was he mad? Irritated? Frustrated? She hated not knowing. At least with Bowie, she knew where she stood. When angry, he'd toss things at her. His jealousy caused him to shove her against hard objects, like wood and metal. When happy, he gave her romantic dinners. Friskiness got her dreaded back-road drives. Counterfeit remorse bought her gifts and promised her the moon.

"Go back to sleep, Rita. You don't owe me anything."

By the sound of his voice, she should have stayed at the ranch with Mandie. What had she been thinking to hang out at a rodeo with a strapping bronc rider when she could have been close to a cop?

Her weighted eyelids drooped, but her thoughts kept reeling. She turned over to her side and sighed, then curled into a ball. She sighed again. Was it teenage boys? Or had Bowie found her again?

When she couldn't take it anymore, she flipped on the dim overhead light above the bed and wrapped a blanket around her shoulders. Robert's Bible lay open on the edge of the loft. She crept over and grabbed the book. Psalms spread out before her, so she read chapter 139. The passage talked about God knowing and loving her. How He'd knit her together in her mother's womb. But what caught her attention was the part where God claimed that she was fearfully and wonderfully made. Was He calling her special? Valuable?

If any of it were true, then why had He allowed the abuse? The rape? How could He care for someone and let them be violated?

But you chose Bowie over Austin Wright.

Yeah, Austin had asked her out plenty of times. But he was boring. And predictable. At the time, she wanted adventure. And Bowie had offered her the time of her life.

Her finger ran down the page and stopped on chapter 140, verse 1. Rita read it aloud quietly. "Deliver me, O Lord, from evil men." But wait. Had the Creator sent Robert to rescue her?

She read on. "Preserve me . . ." She covered her mouth with her hand and waited until the lump in her throat unclogged. She continued, "from violent men." Drawing her knees up, she dropped her head onto the book and silently cried out, *Yes, Lord. Please. Rescue me.*

CHAPTER 24

Robert was nowhere in sight when Rita woke up. She sank her feet into her new thermal boots and shot out the door. The truck was missing too.

Where could he have possibly gone? She went back inside, put on a pot of coffee, and looked for a note. Nothing. She'd have to trust God. Trust Robert. What else could she do? After a hot shower, she dressed and attempted to dry her thick locks over the floor vent. When most of the moisture was out, she side braided her hair.

Maybe it was time to leave. It was obvious she was in his way. But how would she get home? Hitchhike. That's how. She did it once. She could do it again.

Going back to Bowie and her life was all she knew. He wasn't so bad, was he? After all, he'd never broken a bone or landed her in the hospital. She'd have to be patient with him. Simple enough.

She could do it. Right?

Her mom had been a good example of an obedient wife. *I can be just as compliant.* Surely, she could get her job back if she begged hard enough. Her dad had relied heavily on her in the past. And she'd been the free vet—kind of—all she needed was the degree.

Would Bowie allow her to go to college? It wouldn't hurt to ask. Would it?

A diesel engine rattled in the distance. She lifted the window shade to see a brown-and-black pickup creeping through the grounds. Her mouth went dry. It wasn't Bowie's rig. But the weird thing was the driver kinda looked like him.

She dug in her bag for her Leatherman, wishing it were a shotgun, and unfolded the knife with trembling hands. *Calm down, Rita.* Her breath surged in and out. Not able to think, she wiped her damp forehead with the sleeve of her fleece button-down shirt.

Outside, another diesel rig sounded. She pressed her backside against the bathroom door. The racket drew closer and stopped beside the trailer.

She dropped to her knees and crawled to the back of the nearest bench seat, knife ready. The door flung open. The click of boots came close. She squeezed her eyes shut, not wanting to see his face, and prayed. Then she shouted "No" when she felt pressure on one of her shoulders.

The knife in her white-knuckled fist swung up, but something with the force of a boa constrictor squeezed her wrist and halted it from penetrating flesh.

"Whoa, it's—"

"Get away from me!" Rita fought against the restraint and tried to push to her feet.

"It's me, Robert."

Rugged arms swung her around and squeezed her arms against her torso. She fought, screamed, and sank her teeth into hair and skin, sweat and a metallic taste bathing her tongue. He shrieked and let go.

Knife in hand, she crawled to the bathroom, slammed the door shut, and locked it. She couldn't catch her breath. She had to find a way to get a grip and not assume every rig was Bowie.

"Use this." A brown paper bag slipped under the door.

She dropped the knife and flicked open the crinkly sack, pressing it to her mouth. She took in a deep breath, deflating the bag. Then she blew it out. She repeated the sequence until she could take in a deep breath, hold it for a few seconds, and release it. Heart still thumping, she pulled her knees to her chest and wrapped her arms around them, her head tucked inside the empty space. When would the blasted panic attacks stop?

"You okay in there?"

Rita shook her head, trembling too hard to answer.

"What can I do to help?"

She whispered, "I'll be out after a while." What was wrong with her? This morning she'd needed Robert by her side, needing his comfort. Now, all she wanted was to be left alone.

The sun was overhead by the time a soft rap on the bathroom door brought her out of her slumber.

"I got you something," Robert said.

She sat up and rubbed her eyes. How long had she been asleep? The smell of eggs, bacon, and pancakes wafted through the tiny space. "What is it?"

"If you come out, I'll show you."

She wanted to be by herself. But his soft voice enticed her. As did the gift.

Outside, the sound of rigs pulling in and parking vibrated through the walls. *Oh, my goodness. He probably needs to get ready.* She pushed to her feet and splashed cool water on her overheated face. She pushed the door open to find a barefoot Robert leaning against the refrigerator, a hand towel over his bare shoulder.

Oh, my. Not again. He was fit. Handsome. Alluring. *Don't ever rebound. It will only set you up for a bigger fall.* She shoved Grandma Nellie's warnings out of her head.

A green and yellow sunflower-adorned gift bag dangled from two of his fingers, revealing matching colored tissue paper. His smile matched the brightness of the package.

She took a few hesitant steps toward him and clutched the gift bag. "What's this?"

"Open it."

She went to the table and slid onto a seat, her back to Robert. Her throat thick, she set the present next to a rose handbag. "Where did you find this purse?" She felt the remains of her panic attack percolating in her chest.

"It was on the step this morning." He joined her by the table, a spatula in hand. "Someone probably found it and thought it belonged to us. Nice, isn't it? I feel sorry for the lady who lost it."

"So . . . you haven't looked inside?"

"Nope. I never rummage through a woman's purse."

Rita broke out in a sweat. "I'll check it out and make sure I find its rightful owner." How had Bowie found her? Would God ever rescue her from her psycho ex-fiancé?

"You hungry?"

"Not so much." Though she didn't have much of an appetite, she knew she needed nourishment. "But I'll have a little something."

Robert dished her up a plate. "You gonna open your gift?" He settled in the seat across from her.

"Oh, yeah. Sorry." Rita set the tissue on the table and lifted out a book titled *Unbridled Grace*.

"I saw it in the store yesterday but didn't think you'd like it."

She thumbed through the pages of the western women's devotions. Color photos of horses, words of encouragement, and scripture adorned the pages. "What made you change your mind?"

"I saw you reading my Bible this morning."

His adoring expression didn't help her resist him one bit. "You were *watching* me?" Shoot. Bad choice of words. It's what Bowie did. Watched. Stalked. Manipulated. No, Robert was nothing like her ex. Time and again, the triggers set her off. Would they ever leave her alone? She forced joy into her gray mood.

"Suppose I was. Sorry—"

"I love it." She embraced the book. She loved that he gave her a gift with no strings attached.

"I have to get ready." He rose.

"What time is it?"

He padded to the hayloft, checked his cell, and tugged his bag off the bed. "One."

Sydney rubbed the back of her neck. "When do you ride?"

"Rodeo starts at six thirty. But I need to check in, get my number, check out the horses—my draw." He gave her a reassuring grin and went to the bathroom.

He hadn't invited her to tag along to the rodeo—which was okay. Reading the devotional might just calm her nerves where the crowd might agitate them.

She cleared the table as the water pump whirred and planned on washing dishes after Robert's shower so the water pressure and heat wouldn't diminish. The leather rose-tooled handbag snagged her attention. She opened the purse and peeked inside. Nothing seemed out of the ordinary. She dumped the contents onto the table. There wasn't much: lip balm, notepad, pen, hairband, sunglasses, and gum. Something was missing, but she couldn't pinpoint it.

She uncapped the peppermint-scented lip balm and swiped it across her dry lips.

Still baffled, she flipped through the pad of paper. Nothing new was added to her ranch tally notes. "Hmm." When the water shut off, she placed the items back into the purse and positioned her pillow on top. Robert opened the door, his hair still wet. Her neck warming, she opened her backpack and pretended to look for something.

"Bathroom's free." Robert grabbed a bottle of water out of the fridge and headed for the door. "See you later." After scooting past Rita, he put on his Stetson and went outside.

Oh, his spicy scent. "Yep. See you later." She curled into herself. Was he embarrassed by her? Not blaming him, she grasped her pack and went to the bathroom. The reflection in the mirror highlighted red, green, and purple splotches on her face. No wonder he ditched her. How would he introduce her? "Hey, dude, meet the crazy chick who's on the run from the psycho who pounds on her."

She rummaged in the purse for her foundation. Wait a minute. That's what he'd taken out of her purse. And no wonder the ladies in the stands had given her condescending looks. She hadn't even thought to put some on.

Who takes a woman's cover-up? Then again, it was a habit. He'd taken her truck keys, cell phone, and the Montana Silversmiths ring Hazel had bought her for Christmas. But makeup? C'mon. What a creep. And to think she'd almost married him. No, she needed to stick with Robert and ditch thoughts about leaving.

She was re-braiding her hair when a soft rap sounded on the door. She gasped. Finding her Leatherman, she swung out the knife. She lifted the side of the shade but couldn't make out who was at the door.

"Who is it?"

"I met you yesterday. I'm Cindy's mom, Jackie."

Rita held the knife behind her back and opened the door. "Hey, how's it going?"

Jackie held out a bottle of brown foundation. "A good-looking man told me to give this to you." She blushed. "Said you'd need it."

Rita took the bottle of missing makeup. "What did he look like?"

"Tall. Dark eyes and hair." Jackie thought for a moment. "He had a well-groomed goatee."

Rita felt like she could pass out. "I . . . uh . . . appreciate it."

"You all right?"

All right? Heck no. Not even close.

Rita held up the bottle and gave her a lopsided grin. "Yeah. Again, thanks." She shut the door and sank to the loft bench. Yep. Bowie had found them. And was now playing with her.

Robert. She had to find him and let him know. Where would he be? She drew in a few ragged breaths. "C'mon. Think." After storing the cosmetics in her pack, she tugged on her insulated boots. "He had to check in. Check on the horses. By now he should be by the bronc pens." She shrugged into her coat, grabbed her hat and gloves, and headed outside.

With the crisp air stinging her lungs, she inhaled the scent of manure and hay and weaved through the maze of vehicles, animals, and humans—aware of her surroundings. Dogs barked and trotted toward her, making her jump. She shooed them away and kept walking. She found her way to the roughstock pens. Darn. He was nowhere to be found.

She searched the food vendors, ticket office area, and chutes. They wouldn't let her in the grandstands without a ticket, and she'd left her wallet in the truck, which was locked. She went back to the roughstock pens. Still no Robert.

Not sure what to do, she headed back to the trailer. She rounded a corner to find Bowie coming her way. Gary Fullmoon was with him. Bowie was on his cell and, so far, neither man had spotted her. She ducked between a truck and trailer as Bowie talked.

"I'm on my way."

"Where we goin'?" Gary's tone, as usual, sounded whiny.

Their voices faded before Rita knew what had turned them away. She peeked around the truck bed to find them rounding a pickup and disappearing. Too scared to follow, she rushed to the trailer and hurried inside.

"Hey, I've been looking for you." Robert set his rodeo number on the table and held up a spectator ticket. The space between his brows pinched. "What's wrong?"

"He's here." Breathless, she dropped to the loft bench.

"Who?"

"Bowie."

Robert lifted the shades and peered outside. "Did he follow you?"

"No. He left. Gary Fullmoon was with him. They didn't see me."

"He left?"

"Yeah. We need to get outta here. Now!"

CHAPTER 25

B owie unlocked the door and slid behind the wheel. "My brother called." He wiped his stinging eyes with his coat sleeve. Darned if he hadn't shed a tear since bullies had beat him up for being bashful and scrawny in the fourth grade, and he wasn't about to start now.

Growing up with a father in prison for killing a guy in a bar fight and with a mom who had to work three jobs to keep food on the table and clothes on her children's backs was less than fun. Being the oldest, Bowie grew up fast and without the luxury of school sports or any other kind of social contact other than his siblings. They were a pain in his butt. In time, he, too, had to work odd jobs when he was in middle school.

"What's going on?" Gary picked his teeth with his greasy fingernails.

"Dunnie bucked Mom off. She's in the hospital . . ." Bowie choked on his words.

"How bad is she?"

"She's not responding." Bowie cursed and wiped his eyes with his coarse coat sleeve. He blinked several times to clear his vision. How could this have happened? His mother, Edna Dark Cloud, was an accomplished rider. She'd had her children in the saddle since the moment they could sit on their own.

A few hours later, Bowie pulled into Saint Anthony's parking lot in Pendleton, Oregon. He rushed into the hospital, Gary on his heels, and found his mom's room. He stepped inside and stopped at the foot of the bed. His sister, Jo, sat at their mother's side, holding her hand. She looked at Bowie, her eyes rimmed red.

"Why don't you wait in the hall?" Bowie said to Gary.

Gary nodded, turned, and strode out the door, his boots clicking on the linoleum flooring.

Bowie made his way to his mother's side and addressed his sister. "Any change?" He hated the sterile hospital environment.

"No," Jo said, "she's still unresponsive."

He found a chair and settled in.

"Where's Rita?"

"She's tied up." He hadn't planned on dodging questions about his fiancée. He'd been so close to nabbing her too. He again read the text from Dean Runninghorse.

> Rita used her credit card. She's in Coeur
> d'Alene. Bring her home. I'll talk some
> sense into her.

Their brother Larry entered the room, two cups of coffee in hand. "About time you showed up. Where've you been?" He handed one to Jo.

Man, did Bowie need a smoke. "Busy with horse stuff and other things." He took off his coat, hung it over the back of the chair, and wiped his hands on his jeans. The restraining order rambled through his mind, and he clenched his fists. If only his mother hadn't gotten thrown, he and Rita would be together by now. He leaned over and stroked her silky hair. He prayed she'd wake up soon so he could get back to his woman and bring her home.

CHAPTER 26

Coeur d'Alene, Idaho

Rita stuffed clothes into her backpack. "It's clear he's not concerned about breaking the restraining order. I don't know who called him, but it must have been urgent or he would've stayed. Since my phone's been off, I think they used my credit card to track me. It's the only thing that makes sense."

"You said *they*. Who are you talking about?"

"The chief of police is Bowie's cousin. They have to be in cahoots with each other." And here she'd thought Chief Denton was a good guy. Apparently not.

Robert pulled out his cell. "I'm calling the cops."

"No!" Rita held up her palm. "By the look on his face, he's not coming back. Please, don't involve the police." She couldn't take the chance of them finding out she'd killed a man.

"It's clear he doesn't respect boundaries. Or laws. And I can't take the chance of him showing up at the Seven Tine. We have guests to protect." Robert swiped the screen. "I'll at least text Chuck and give him a heads-up."

There was nothing she could do. He was already typing with both thumbs. "What now?"

"We go to the rodeo. You can hang with me behind the chutes." He handed Rita a ticket. "Use this to get in."

She lifted a brow.

"It's safer to be with me, don't you think? In case your ex comes back."

"Okay. Hang on." She grabbed her backpack and went to the bathroom. After uncapping the bottle, she dabbed brown liquid where needed. "No one's going to look down at you now," she said aloud.

When she was satisfied with her appearance, she met Robert by the door, slid the ticket into her wallet, and tucked it inside her inner coat pocket. "I'm good to go." In reality, she screamed hot mess.

Blue skies and bright sun met them as they stepped onto damp dirt. Robert pulled his gear bag and bronc saddle out of the back seat of his pickup. "Hang on, I forgot my number." He dropped the bag and disappeared into the trailer. Moments later, he came out with his number and two safety pins. "Will you do the honors?"

"I suppose." How could she refuse the twinkle in his eyes? After securing the paper to his sponsor-emblazoned Western shirt, he slipped on his jacket and made sure the truck and trailer were locked.

He led her to the area behind the chutes and dropped his gear bag and saddle in the dirt. She breathed in the earthy scent of bull hides and dung. Robert patted a few of his buddies on the shoulders, and they laughed and compared the horses they'd drawn. Her chin tucked, Rita recoiled at the cowboys ogling her.

One came over and introduced himself as Payton Sundown. He wore a black cowboy hat, a turquoise Western shirt, and spurs.

"You're here with Bobby, huh?"

"Um—" She hadn't considered how they'd explain their relationship.

"Hey buddy, leave my girl alone." Robert draped an arm around her and didn't waver when she stiffened. He rubbed her arm and kissed the side of her face.

What on earth? Words clogging her throat, shock froze her ability to shove him away.

"This is Rita." Robert glanced at her, a bigger-than-life grin on his face, and she gave him a slight shake of her head.

"Nice to meet you." Payton tipped his hat. "Looks like you've stepped up your game, bro." His gaze locked on the side of her face.

She turned away.

When Payton strode toward the chutes, Robert released his grip on her. "Sorry. I don't want anyone messing with you. If they think you're mine, they'll leave you alone."

"Think I'm *yours?*" Was his claim supposed to put her at ease? She wrapped her hands around her tummy and squeezed.

"You know, my plus-one."

She took a step to escape the panic galloping through her bones and stumbled. Robert caught her and gathered her into his arms.

"I'm only trying to protect you." His minty breath brushed against her lips.

Nodding, her fingers curled around his arms. She righted herself and stepped back. "I'm fine." But when she reached for his unshaven face, she pulled one hand back, shoved them both in her pockets, and looked away.

"Come on, I'll show you which horse I drew." He put a gentle hand on the small of her back and led her to the roughstock pens. Then he rested a foot on the bottom rung of a metal panel enclosing the bucking horses.

"See the gray over there?" He pointed to a stout mare with a sour expression.

"She doesn't look happy."

"They call her Pitch a Fit." Robert snorted. "I called the guy who rode her last. He said I have a good chance of winning on her."

"She's nice all right. I hope you win." Rita leaned against the panel for a long moment, then pushed off and yawned. "I'm going to go find some coffee."

"I'll go with you."

Not wanting to be smothered, she held up a hand. "I got it." Rushing away before he could protest, she weaved through the crowd of cowboys and onlookers until finding a food vendor and ordering a cup. Then she ambled to the stands. She wasn't about to spend another minute around Robert's buddies with them gawking at her, judging her every move.

There was a somewhat isolated seat toward the top left-hand corner behind of group of middle-aged women—the perfect place to keep an eye on things in case Bowie did come back. Minutes after settling in, the announcer talked about the next bareback rider.

A cowboy pulled on a rope attached to a gate, and it swung open. A bronc burst out, bucking like the guy on his back was a hungry cougar. A few seconds into the ride, he got slammed to the ground, and pickup men went after the runaway horse. Rita flinched when he hit the ground, and the pains in her sides reminded her she was still recovering.

The contestant picked himself up off the ground and kicked the dirt. He plucked his hat from the arena floor, dusted it off on his leg, and shook his head. Standing on the platform behind the chutes, Robert scanned the stands. Rita leaned forward, hiding behind an older woman wearing a tan cowboy hat and lime-green glasses a seat below her and to the left. She was right, her nerves were on fire. Maybe it was time to go to the trailer. But it was locked. And Robert had the keys.

Green Glasses turned around and smiled. "You lose something?" Her gaze dropped to the floorboards.

"Oh, no. I need to get into our trailer, but my . . . my . . . boyfriend has the keys." The lie made her wince, though she liked the sound of being someone's girlfriend. Someone as thoughtful as Robert. "I'll wait until he's done riding."

"Oh, your man rides bareback?"

Rita shook her head and sat up. "No. He rides saddle bronc."

Green Glasses elbowed the lady next to her. "This little gal's man rides saddle bronc." Grinning and nodding, the remaining women in the group turned and stared. They introduced themselves and shared the events their husbands used to perform in. After a way-too-long moment of small talk, Rita excused herself.

She got another cup of coffee and found a spot at a picnic table. Bowie's expression fluttered through her mind. What had the call been about? How long would it be before he showed up again? Tomorrow? In a few days? Next week?

Robert wouldn't be up for a while. Trying to evade her hounding thoughts, she wandered around the grounds, checked out horses, and had a bite to eat but threw most of it in the trash. She turned around to find Cindy in front of her.

"Hey, how's Jazzy doing?" They walked to the edge of the stands.

"She's doing great." The teen's face lit up. "She's calm in the box. Listens to me. She's a totally different horse. Thanks again for working with us."

"Glad to hear it. You're a talented rider. Keep up the good work."

"I will." Cindy waved to a group of teens and darted away.

Rita wandered around until the announcer's voice boomed over the scratchy loudspeakers. Broncs were being loaded into the chutes as she clambered up a few steps and took a seat by a couple with a baby. Good. They'd be too busy to talk.

Robert stood behind the number three chute. He seemed distracted. She should have let him know where she was—or better yet should have stayed near him. She chewed her nails, waiting for his turn. After the second rider's score was announced, Robert climbed on Pitch a Fit. Rita gasped as the mare reared up, her hooves getting caught up on the gate.

One of the cowboys coaxed the horse back into the chute. Robert clutched the buck rein in one hand and held on to the top of the gate with the other. After a moment or two had passed, he nodded. The gateman pulled open the gate and Pitch a Fit came out bucking. Robert spurred and lifted his rein hand in a motion as smooth as a grandma in a rocking chair.

Rita clapped and hollered. She jumped to her feet, moaning at the burn in her sides from Bowie's mistreatment.

The buzzer sounded and a pickup man came alongside the mare. Robert leaned across the back of the cowboy's horse, clung to his back, and swung over, dropping to the ground. Rita whistled and clapped.

He caught a glimpse of her and waved with his fingers, both hands high in the air. She made her way down the stairs and rushed to the area behind the chutes. He met her with open arms, and they embraced. Then kissed. A quick peck at first. But as his sable eyes pulled her in, she wanted more. And when he leaned down and pressed his dusty lips against hers, she pushed into him, their hips connecting.

"Well done, Bobby." She recognized Payton's voice and broke the kiss.

Robert mouthed *sorry* to her. Someone tossed a flank rope at his feet. He picked it up and placed the cinch in his bag. "I need to get my saddle. Want to come with?"

Yes, she wanted to go with him. But she knew if she followed him to an intimate location, there'd be more kissing. The last thing she was looking for was a weekend fling. "I . . . uh . . ." She slowly twisted a half circle, not wanting to cause pain in her sides, and pointed a thumb over her shoulder, "Need to go to the trailer. Any chance I can get the keys?"

His grin faded, but he reached into his coat pocket and tossed them to her. "See you after a while. I'm going to hang back and help the guys."

"Yes. Of course, Bobby." Rita spun around and pushed through a throng of cowboys. Was she falling for him? How could she have such deep feelings for him so soon? Rebound. Nothing but rebound.

CHAPTER 27

Robert liked it when Rita called him by his nickname. It rolled off her tongue like honey. What he didn't like was her ditching him after his winning ride when he needed to apologize for kissing her in public. No, for kissing her, period. Why hadn't he listened to his sister's warning? His cell chimed, and he groaned but answered the call. "Hey."

"How's Rita doing?" Sydney's voice sounded weary.

"She's okay. Why?" He picked up his gear bag and headed for the horse pens.

"What happened?"

Shoot. Chuck must have called her. "What are you talking about?"

Her tone filled with impatience, she said, "Don't play games with me, Bobby. What's going on?"

"Nothing. Everything's fine here." He dropped his bag.

Sydney sighed. "Chuck called. Told me to get ahold of you. Please, fill me in."

Fill her in? He needed to find Rita. But his sister would only keep calling until he caught her up. "Well, she's had a couple of panic attacks. Chuck had a talk with her ex. Had to show him the temporary restraining order—"

"What? Where'd she get it from?"

"Pendleton. How odd. Chuck didn't tell you?" He nodded to a cowboy and turned to a bull's pen.

"He hasn't said anything. It's not his job, now is it?"

"What do you mean it's not his job? He's a cop."

"She's in your care."

He hated it when she was right.

"Mandie called and said a couple of guys acting strange came to the ranch. Chad confirmed it. He said a guy named Hank Mawley or something like that wanted to look at a horse. Got owly when he told the guy no photos."

"I'll ask Rita if she knows anyone by that name," Robert said.

"Do you think it's Rita's abuser? Did he freaking come on our property?" Her sharp breath clawed through the connection.

"I'm not sure. The restraining order's a joke."

"They always are. The good thing is, though, if something ever did happen, she'd have a paper trail. Where's Rita now?" Sydney asked.

"At the trailer."

"You left her alone?"

"Yeah, her creepy ex has already come and gone. He's—"

"He what?" She shrieked—so much that Robert held the phone away from his ear for an instant. "Why didn't you call me?"

"What could you have done? Sheesh, Syd, don't freak out. He's gone. Rita said he got a phone call and left. We don't think he's coming back."

"You don't know for sure."

"I have a gut feeling—"

"You always have a feeling, Bobby. For heaven's sake, get her out of there."

He tapped on the panel with his fist. "Can't. I ride tomorrow. I need this win. And you know it."

"She's in danger. Her life is more valuable than winning a rodeo. Don't you think?"

"She's not in danger. If he comes back, we'll leave. I promise."

"I hope you know what you're doing."

"When will you be back?" he asked.

"I'm not sure. I have three radio interviews and a meeting with an agent who wants me to write a book about my life with . . . you know, Cooper . . . including Leena and the . . . accident."

"A book deal? Wow. How cool. Are you going to do it?"

"Not sure I can."

"Why not? Think of all the women you can help. It could go worldwide."

"It's too hard. I want to leave Cooper in the past," she said. "And don't want the world to know my daughter killed her grandparents. Accident or not. Even if the boy who'd messed with the steering wheel was at fault. The media can be cruel and misleading. She's been through enough. It's taken her almost two years to get to a good place. I don't want to rip open her emotional scabs."

"I get it. I'll support whatever you decide."

"Take care of Rita."

"I will. Keep me posted when you think you'll head home. I got my next rodeo in a couple of weeks." Or so he hoped.

"I will. And Bobby . . ."

"What?"

"Stay in your lane."

The line went dead. Robert shoved his phone into his back pocket. "If she only knew." How was he supposed to corral his budding feelings for Rita? If only they'd met under different circumstances. It would've been so much easier.

CHAPTER 28

Rita sat lengthwise at the table, her back resting against the wall. How could she keep her feelings for Robert from blooming? *He's a rebound. And a distraction.* She hated everything hanging in the balance, her life suspended on a high wire.

She missed life on the ranch, her mare, and scribbling entries into her cattle tally book. Sitting around would drive her to the grave sooner than Bowie's fists.

The door rattled open, and Robert came in. "How's it going in here?"

"Fine, I guess." Her cheeks warmed. She sat up and took a drink of water. *Get a grip.* The scruff on his face made him look rugged. Handsome. She hugged herself. *He won't ever love me, anyway. I'm broken. Bruised. Used up and tossed to the wind.*

"Hey, do you happen to know a Hank Mawley?" He took a seat on the opposite side of the table.

"No, why?"

"Some guy came nosing around the ranch wanting to look at horses. No big deal."

No big deal? It had to be him. "Did Mandie call you? Did she describe him? What'd he look like?"

"I don't know. Chuck called Syd. I just got off the phone with her."

"What'd she say? It has to be Bowie. And Gary." Rita fingered her necklace and gnawed on her bottom lip.

"I'm sure it's nothing. But I'll call Mandie and get a description."

"What are we going to do?"

"Depends if you think they'll come back. Do you think they left for good?"

"No. Maybe. I'm not sure. It depends on who called and why." She sighed and shook her head. "Yeah. The call seemed urgent. And there was actual concern on his face." Something she'd rarely seen with him.

"You want to go for a drive? Take your mind off things?"

Getting off the grounds would be a nice change. So would picking up a charger for her cell. But then again, she didn't want to hear Bowie's voice or read his texts, not to mention give away future locations if they were indeed tracing her calls. "Sure. What do you have in mind?"

"There's no plan." His phone vibrated. "But I am kinda hungry." The space between his brows pinched as he studied the screen. Looking up, he frowned at Rita.

"What's the matter?" She shifted in her seat.

"Mandie said your ex called the ranch. Said your mom's in the hospital, and you need to go home right away. She was in a horse accident?"

No way. "A horse accident?" Rita shook her head. "Mom hasn't ridden in months. Dad sold her horse and won't let her ride any of the colts."

"That's cold."

"The point is he's lying." Shaking her head, she turned away from Robert. "Oh, what a dirty bugger. The call he took must've been about *his* mom. Not mine."

"He's trying to bait you home with her accident, isn't he?"

"Exactly. But I'm not going to fall for it."

"Let's get out of here."

"He won't come back," she said, her tone wavering. "Not while she's laid up."

"They close? Bowie and his mom?" Robert stood.

"You have no idea. They're tighter than a furious horse's lips." *Those apron strings should have been cut long ago.* "Um, before we head out, can we talk about . . . you know—"

"The kiss?"

"Yeah."

"I'm sorry. It shouldn't have happened. I'll keep my mouth to myself from now on." Red-faced, Robert grabbed his keys and strode out the door.

The next day, Rita stuck close to Robert and remained behind the chutes while he rode, her mind on the kiss. What if she didn't want him to keep his warm, sweet lips to himself? Yeah, he was so much better than Bowie.

Bowie was rough. Commanding. And a coward.

It wasn't beneath Bowie to send someone else to do his dirty work. Rita not returning his calls or phoning home didn't help either. She half expected Gary to show up with a couple of thugs to force her hand.

"Will you be all right?" Behind the noisy chutes, Robert put on his vest and buckled his leather chaps, which made him look taller. And brave. Daring. *Oh my.* The spurs practically jingled her name with every step. His black cowboy hat matched the black lettering on his sponsor-emblazoned, red shirt. It was definitely his color.

Don't fall for him. His kindness. Compassion. Yeah, well, way too late.

"I'll keep an eye on her for you." One of his buddies winked at her. He clapped Robert on the back with his meaty hand. He was stocky for a bronc rider, fit but compact with sandy brown hair and cat-like eyes.

"I think she'll be fine on her own." Robert kissed her, making her head spin. Then he whispered, "Sorry. Had to make it look real." He kissed her again and trotted toward a platform behind the chutes.

She forced a smile, folding into herself as Cat Eyes scoped her out. She turned away. He gave her the willies and reminded her of the sick feelings Bowie often gave her. But she lifted her chin anyhow. If he only knew what she was capable of. Like tossing a young calf on the ground to doctor it. Or roping with the boys, keeping up and sometimes surpassing their catches. And being the first one up and the last one to go home.

She could for sure teach Cat Eyes a thing or two if he tried anything.

The announcer's voice boomed over the sound system as he called out Robert's name. She didn't like where she was—couldn't see a thing—and took a step toward the bleachers. A hand caught her arm. She jerked away from the hold and spun around to find Cat Eyes, his hands up like a bandit facing a six-shooter.

"Whoa. I was just going to show you a good spot to watch Bobby." He backed up.

"Wait. I'm sorry. You startled me." She cocked a hip. "I'd appreciate the better view."

He led her to an empty seat behind the chutes. Rita had a spectacular view of the cowboys helping settle and cinch Robert's bronc. The announcer called this one "Shoot the Moon." She knew the term from playing pinochle with Grandmother Nellie but figured the name was along the lines of NASA.

Cat Eyes tipped his hat and hopped down the steps to join the others. She sank back in her seat, the entire arena in view. Robert nodded, and the gatekeeper pulled the rope.

Shoot the Moon broke loose.

The timer started.

Would he make the eight seconds? Her muscles tightened, and she shot to her feet.

One . . . two . . . three . . .

Bobby's feet spurred the bronc's neck, then swung behind him. Spur, pull, reach, lift. One smooth motion. Until a brisk snap of the horse's buck tossed his hat to the dirt, exposing his clenched teeth.

Four . . .

Would he hang on and pull off the win? She clapped and cupped her hands around her mouth and hollered, "Stick with him, Bobby!"

Five . . .

She waved her arms in the air, not caring how much her sides burned. "You got this!"

Onlookers nearby were also on their feet, clapping, shouting, and cheering. At that moment, joy bubbled inside Rita. For the first time, she understood his dedication.

Six . . .

Cat Eyes turned to her and raised an arm, his pointer finger in the air. She mirrored his gesture and stomped her feet.

Seven . . .

"Hold on."

The buzzer blared, and Rita waved both hands in the air. "Woo-hoo!" She clapped, happy to witness Robert's dreams springing into reality.

Once on the ground, Robert scooped up his hat, tapped it onto his head, retrieved his flank strap, and headed for the exit gate. His eyes searched until they found hers. A wide grin bloomed on his face and in her heart.

She hurried down the stairs, went to where he'd left his gear bag, and fell into his arms. His sable eyes stared down at her. "You were wonderful," she said.

"You think so?" He pulled her into a light hug.

"I do." She pressed into him, a hint of a dull ache in her sides.

"Good to know. I was convinced you didn't like bronc riders."

"I don't. Except maybe one."

"Oh yeah?"

"Yeah." Rita could never go back. Not to Bowie. Robert made her believe there were good men in the world. Ones who didn't hurt women. And they—no he—gave her the courage to break free and begin the healing process.

CHAPTER 29

Colville Reservation

Robert pulled into Seven Tine late Sunday night. Rita slept, her head against the window. He'd seen her cheering for him. Heard her voice above the crowd. Who was he fooling? Her big heart weakened his knees. As had her floral scent. Not to mention her soft lips.

But still, he should have kept his hands to himself. His mouth too. How could he have been so careless? Had he not learned anything from his ex?

Yet, he could watch her sleep for the rest of his life.

He loved how she wore her long, sleek hair in a side braid. He looked away and blushed when she caught him staring at her.

He pumped his fists at the thought of Bowie coming back. He made a mental note to call Chuck first thing in the morning, make a plan. He wasn't going to sit around and be defenseless.

He pulled to a stop on the north side of the barn. "Hey, sleepy head." He smiled and shook her shoulder. "We're home."

Home? She jerked awake and struggled to open the door. She fought back when he grabbed her arm.

"Whoa, we're at the ranch."

"He's coming!"

"He's not here. You're safe. With me." Poor woman. How long would she have to endure those nasty nightmares?

She looked at him for a long while, blinking several times, before her expression changed. Then she glanced around, wiping stray hair off her sweaty face. She licked her lips and asked, "We're here?"

"Yep. Just pulled in." He killed the motor. "I'll get your pack."

"No!" Rita caught his arm. "I'll get it." She smiled and hopped out of the truck.

Robert shook his head and followed her. She came out with a bundle in her arms, rushed to the lodge, and disappeared behind the closed door. "Okay. How weird." Definitely not what he'd expected. He shrugged it off as trauma induced.

He grabbed his bag, locked the truck and trailer, and trudged to his cabin. Inside, Posse met him with whines and kisses. Robert picked him up. "I missed you too." After a quick hug, he put the pup down and lit a fire in the woodstove, showered, and hit the hay. Bowie's call flooded his mind as he tossed and turned.

Finally, he got up, padded to the kitchen table, and flipped on his laptop. He typed in "Bowie Pendleton Oregon." His fingers drummed the kitchen tabletop as the internet worked. A list of sites with "Bowie Texas Livestock Barn" and "Bowie Auction Horses" came up.

What was his last name?

He typed in Gray Cloud and got nothing.

Robert tried "Bowie horses Umatilla." Images of various horses, pedigrees, and properties for sale in and around Umatilla, Oregon, popped up on the screen. He deleted the words and slumped back in his chair. Then he typed in "Bowie horse trader." He took a deep dive into anything related to "Bowie Sale Horses." The name Bowie Dark Cloud surfaced.

Robert squinted at an image of a leggy guy with a goatee, shoulder-length hair, and a swindler's smile.

"You have to be him." He leaned in and read. There was no mention of family. He scrolled down and opened additional links, not finding anything pertinent to his research. He looked up local newspapers and found the *Confederated Umatilla Journal*, which published monthly. He scanned the online version and the paper's Facebook page, coming up empty.

What about this? He typed in "Bowie Rita Runninghorse engagement announcement." Their photo flashed onto the screen. Bowie Dark Cloud, his face the image of ownership. Hers the statue of suffocation. Her eyes. They looked worn. Sad. Discouraged. Her smile was pasted on. And it broke his heart.

According to the article, they hadn't been engaged but a few months. Robert printed out the article and examined it. Rita's ring finger lay bare.

He tapped the paper. "You don't deserve her, you no-good scumbag."

CHAPTER 30

You don't deserve me. Rita jerked awake and rolled over. Would the nightmares ever go away? Would he chase her forever? She curled into a ball and pulled a pillow over her head.

With evil thoughts keeping her from sleeping, she slipped out of bed and let a hot shower wash away her worries. She dressed in jeans and a sweatshirt a size too large. She'd have to ask Mandie about washing some clothes. From her window, ranch hands fed animals in dawn's soft glow.

Blizzard. How was he doing? She slipped into her cowboy boots and plodded downstairs to check on him.

Mandie greeted her with a smile. "Good morning." She gestured to the beverage bar. "Coffee's hot."

"Perfect." Rita went over, poured herself a cup, and perused the creamers. Her hand hovered over the hazelnut, but she went with pumpkin spice, needing something more festive after such a nerve-racking weekend. Something to lend comfort if only for a short time.

A scream came from the kitchen and startled her. She plopped her cup on the counter, its blistering contents sloshing onto the wood surface, and rushed to the sound.

Mandie held a flour-caked toddler on her hip. Onyx-colored eyes shone through white powder covering the child and the floor. The little girl flashed Rita a pearly smile. She couldn't help but laugh.

"You have children?"

Rita covered her mouth and shook her head. Not living anyhow. She felt bad for laughing. Felt even worse for never having had the chance to meet her baby. She'd have to wait for heaven to introduce the two of them.

"On days like this, I wouldn't recommend it."

"How can I help?" Anything would be better than waiting around, fretting about Bowie showing back up.

"There's a broom in the storage room." Mandie nodded to a hallway. The child wiggled her way to the ground and padded after Rita.

She found the broom and turned around to find the toddler watching her with those big, curious eyes, brows raised. "Well, hello. Aren't you a little darling?" The little girl giggled and waddled back to her mother. Rita returned to the mess and swept. "What's her name?"

Mandie corralled the child and wiped her down with a damp cloth. "Nona."

"What a pretty name. What does it mean?"

"Ninth child."

"You have nine children?" Mandie didn't look old enough to have birthed nine babies. But the way she handled her daughter reminded her of the way her grandma was with her—loving and patient.

Mandie leaned against the island. "I've miscarried eight times. She's my only live birth. The doctor told me to quit trying. But I suppose I'm a little bullheaded."

Rita knew what it was like to miscarry. "You and your husband must be thrilled to have her."

Mandie grunted. "The deadbeat took off when I informed him the child was going to make it."

Okay, there were no words for how horrid she felt. "Oh, no. I'm so sorry. That's got to be rough."

"No worries. We make do just fine. Sydney's got my back. And so does God."

"From what I've been told, she's got a lot of our backs." As did Robert. The thought of his name weakened her knees. He was unbelievably handsome. Generous. Kind. And oh my. He was incredibly . . . off-limits.

She picked up a spatula and fanned her warm face, then turned away when Mandie raised her brows, giving her a hard stare.

"You got that right." Mandie tossed the cloth into the sink. "Thanks for helping me. My babysitter didn't show up and I can't seem to reach her."

"I have nothing better to do. I'm all yours."

"Really?" Mandie arched a brow. "I have to make dessert for dinner while keeping this one entertained."

"What did you have in mind?"

"I'm not sure yet. My usual go-to is chocolate cake."

"Well . . ." Rita grinned. "It happens I love to bake."

"Oh yeah?" Mandie pulled out a recipe book. "So, you weren't kidding the other day, huh?"

"Nope. I'm a rancher by day and a baker by . . . well . . . whenever I can fit it into my schedule."

Mandie set her hand on her hip. "I'm impressed. Does Bobby know—"

"Do I know what?" He strode to Nona and picked her up. "How's my little munchkin today?" The toddler giggled when he tickled her neck with his nose.

"This girl is a rancher by day and a baker by . . . whenever she can squeeze it in."

Rita's face flamed.

"So she said." He winked at her.

Rita folded her arms as if it would protect her from her pounding heart. If only they'd met years ago. The memory of his initial kiss in Idaho danced down her arms. His words sprang into her mind. *"Hey buddy, leave my girl alone."* She touched her finger to her lips. *"Sorry. I don't want anyone messing with you. If they think you're mine, they'll leave you alone."*

"What are you two planning to make? I bet Rita can teach you a thing or two."

Mandie wagged a finger at him. "You'll know come dinner."

His smile faded, and he turned to Rita. "Hey, you got your phone on you?"

"No. It's in my room. Why?"

"Chuck thinks his charger will fit it." He rubbed Nona's back, and the little girl leaned her head on the crook of his neck, her thumb in her mouth. "He wants to take a look at Bowie's texts. Wants them for evidence if he shows up again."

Mandie's eyes widened.

"I'll go get it." Rita started for the swinging doors, her mind vacillating between Mandie's curious gaze and the mention of Bowie's unopened messages.

Robert put Nona down, followed her into the great room, and stopped her at the base of the steps. The only person on the first floor of the lodge was an older gentleman who was reading by the crackling fire. "Hey, sorry. I should have talked to you privately."

"Yeah. No kidding. How embarrassing."

"I said I was sorry. Besides, Mandie's here for you too. She's—"

"Be right back." She climbed the stairs and stomped to her room. The vivid colors of the decor did nothing to brighten her outlook. It was bad enough having a male cop plow into her privacy. And now the ranch cook? Who was next? The wranglers?

Rita found her cell deep in her backpack and pulled it out. She found a pad of paper with the Seven Tine logo and a pen on the night table. After scribbling four numbers on it, she tapped the cell in her palm and met Robert downstairs.

"Here you go." She handed him the note. "Here's my pass code."

He took the phone. "You wanna ride over to Chuck's with me?"

"I already promised Mandie that I'd help her." Besides, she'd rather listen to the messages alone in her room where she wouldn't feel judged. "Let me know what's on there, huh?" Maybe hearing about it first would ease the blow.

He glanced at the slip of paper and shoved it into his pocket. "Will do." Then he grabbed his coat and cowboy hat off the back of a chair and disappeared into the foyer.

Feeling like she'd messed up, she made her way to the kitchen. Should she have gone in case Chuck had questions?

Mandie stood near the island in the middle of the room. "You can go with him if you want."

"Hey, a promise is a promise. I'm here to help. Besides, he can handle it."

Mandie studied her for a long moment. "I see how you two look at each other. Did something happen at the rodeo?"

"Nope. He was a perfect gentleman." *Good grief. Can she not mind her own business?*

"Bronco Bobby? A gentleman?" Mandie cackled. "In your dreams." She was still grinning when she turned to plop her daughter into a high chair with assorted fruit on the tray.

"Bronco Bobby, huh? His rodeo buddies call him Bobby too."

"No kidding." Mandie snickered. "They're a closely guarded secret around here. Never have met a one of 'em."

Payton's image came to mind. "You're not missing anything. Trust me."

While Mandie talked cupcakes, a knot twisted in Rita's stomach. How many calls had she missed? How many were from Bowie? Her mom? Hazel? How would Chuck react? Would he be able to help her?

CHAPTER 31

Robert handed his brother-in-law the phone. "I think she's nervous about what might be on here."

"Can you blame her?" Chuck leaned against his white speckled kitchen counter and plugged the charger into the phone. "We've got a winner."

The friendly kitchen atmosphere was adorned with burgundy, ivory, and green. Silk flowers graced a corner hutch and the kitchen table, and everything was put in its place. Neat and orderly. Like a cop's SUV.

Yep, she's definitely a winner. He'd meant, "Good deal." Robert knew that Chuck had been talking about his success with the charger, but he was thinking of Rita. She'd been a trooper. And working with the teen in Idaho, man, what a bighearted woman. Extra reasons to do whatever it took to protect her. And her God-given gift. Not to mention the sassy smile on her face while working with the girl's horse. Woo wee, one remarkable lady!

He needed to back off—before he stepped out of his lane.

"Oh yeah, I found this." He slid the copy of the engagement announcement from his inside coat pocket, unfolded it, and handed it to Chuck.

He studied the article. "You've been busy."

Robert lifted his shoulder up and down. "Couldn't sleep."

Chuck set the paper on the countertop. "While this is helpful, you need to let me handle this." He powered up Rita's cell. "Here we go."

Robert inched closer to his brother-in-law. He willed the phone to wake up faster, drumming his fingers on the counter. He stopped when Chuck frowned at him. A heavy sigh rushed from his nostrils.

"Be patient, bro," Chuck said. "This will take more than eight seconds."

Robert exhaled, leaned against the counter, and crossed his ankles. The sound of a vintage, floral wall clock near the window ticked as the second hand hitched its way around the digits.

"You have feelings for her, don't you?"

Robert stared at the burgundy curtains hanging from the kitchen window. "No . . . yes . . . maybe."

"Syd has rules for a reason, you know."

"I know. But I can't help it. She's different."

"How so?"

"She's smart. Creative. Driven." He wanted to say beautiful but didn't want to seem shallow. "There's something about her that connects us."

"I agree with Syd. Keep your distance, man." Chuck swiped the screen. "You don't happen to know her password, do you?"

"Eight, nine, one, two."

Chuck raised his brows.

"She gave it to me with the phone." He held up the slip of paper Rita had given him.

Once in, a voice announced the number of missed calls. Too many. Chuck tapped the screen. Joan Runninghorse had left several messages, concern thick in her voice, asking Rita to call a particular number.

And then Hazel's frantic voice blared through the speaker. "Where are you? Bowie's freaking out. He's threatening to 'make me disappear' if I don't give you up. I told him I didn't know where you were. He . . ." Chuck's gaze shot to Robert.

When she came back on, her voice quaked. "He beat me up, Rita. Where are you?"

Robert slammed his fist on the counter. "We have to find him," he said through clenched teeth.

"Your budding relationship with Rita is why you're going to let me take care of things." Chuck's tone was sharp. "You hear me?"

Robert nodded, but it was an empty affirmation. Rita had already gotten to him. He couldn't let Chuck take care of things by himself. And the next message that would soon arrive proved why.

CHAPTER 32

M andie handed Rita a recipe card. "You're going to love
these."

She took the well-used card and held it out, struggling
to concentrate on baking with the unopened cell phone
messages looming overhead. "Pumpkin Ale Cupcakes?"

"Yeah, you've never heard of them?" Mandie smiled as
she gathered flour and sugar and set them on the counter.
"I'm surprised."

"I'm normally not a huge pumpkin fan." Lately, not a fan
of food period.

"Oh? Must be why I'm almost out of the creamer."

Rita gave her a small smile. "I'm a work in progress."

A woman with short, curly hair and glasses knocked on
the doorjamb. Dressed in a maroon sweater and skinny jeans,
she looked to be in her forties. She had a blonde teenager
with a bright smile and the same curly hair with her. "You
need help with Nona? We noticed she's here today."

"You sure?" Mandie wiped her hands on the apron tied
snuggly around her middle. "Don't you have trail-riding
plans?"

"It's too cold and wet," the teen said. "I'd love to hang out
with her if it's all right with you."

Mandie introduced Rita to the mother-daughter duo.
The family had come from the Washington coast annually
for the past five years to fish and ride horseback. She handed
a wiggly Nona over with what seemed like a grateful sigh.

"We'll be close by."

"I hope my daughter grows up to be like her," Mandie said as the teen and her babbling toddler disappeared around the corner.

"Yeah. They seem nice." Rita handed the recipe card back.

Mandie motioned to a cupboard. "You get the canned pumpkin and spices, and I'll get the eggs, butter, and ale."

They were mixing batter when the kitchen's landline rang. Mandie wiped her hands on her apron and answered the call. A flash of concern crossed her face as she handed the phone to Rita.

"Is it Robert?" she muttered.

"I'm not sure who it is. The connection's not the best."

Rita pressed the phone to her ear. "Hello?"

"I know you killed Talon Hawkeye. And I'm gonna make sure you pay for it."

The line went dead as Rita sucked in a sharp breath. Did this mean she was headed for prison? Or was she a dead woman walking? Who? Why? She released the phone, and it tumbled to the ground. Her knees weak, her back slid down the island, her body trembling, every movement in slow motion. A wave of dizziness came over her, and she hit the cold, hard floor.

Mandie screamed, then shouted, "Help!"

Pounding footsteps entered the kitchen. Rita felt a gentle touch move hair out of her face and caress her cheek.

"I think she's okay."

Robert? Rita hoped it was him. The presence left and mumbled voices sounded. Doors creaked open.

"Everything okay in here?"

"Yeah. We got it."

Doors creaked again.

Rita felt sturdy arms pull her close. She caught a whiff of Robert's familiar spicy soap and lay her head against his firm chest. Felt the drum of his heartbeat. Tried to concentrate on it. Think about anything except the murder.

"Hey," Robert said to Mandie, "can you leave us for a bit?" He tightened his hold on Rita and smoothed her hair.

Mandie's staccato footsteps faded. Rita wanted to cry and scream but couldn't move. Who all knew her secret? How did it get out? She could never go home. Never see her family again because prison was not an option.

"What's going on?" Robert asked.

"They know." She turned into him, her fingers curling around the fabric of his button-up shirt.

"What do they know?"

"What . . . I . . . I-I did to him."

"Who?"

Her breathing sped up. "I killed the monster."

She felt Robert's muscles tense. He'd toss her out of his life and off the ranch now for sure. And she wouldn't blame him. Sobs racked her body.

"Shhh. I'm sure there's a good explanation." When her body settled, he asked, "Who's the monster?"

She shook her head and sniffed.

"What happened?"

"I got a call."

"From?" Robert asked.

"I'm not sure who it was. I . . . I didn't recognize the voice."

"Okay. Was it a man? Woman?"

"A man."

"What did he say?"

She wiped her face with the sleeve of her sweatshirt and looked at him. "He knows I killed the guy who . . ." She couldn't say it out loud.

Robert studied her as the rain pounded outside. "I can't imagine you killing anyone—"

"But I did."

"What happened? There had to be a good reason. And I'm guessing it was self-defense."

"I . . . I . . ." She pushed to her feet and rushed to her room. Once in, she slammed the door shut and stuffed her belongings into her pack. She had to get out of here. Bowie knew where she was and had been to the ranch for crying out loud. Where would she go? How would she get there? She sank to the hardwood floor and hugged her knees.

The memory of Talon Hawkeye's oily face and big nose scraped across her mind. He was a beefy guy who loved to eat as much as he liked to drink. Once upon a time, her dad and Hawkeye had been hometown basketball stars. Or so her father had bragged. They'd grown up together. Her father thought he could save him. But the evil in Hawkeye proved too powerful.

Rita dropped her face into the space between her knees and chest and squeezed her eyes shut, battling to leave the memories behind. If only she could forget the creak of the door as he snuck in, waking her up. Forget him coming to her bed in the middle of the night, his rancid breath reeking of whiskey as he ripped off her clothes. Forget about all he'd taken from her.

A soft knock sounded on the door, but she ignored it, not wanting to talk to anyone. The rap came again.

"Are you okay?"

Robert. She groaned.

The door opened a crack. "We need to talk."

"About what?"

He entered, closed the door, and slipped to the floor next to her. Hesitantly, he handed over her cell. "The same message was on your phone. With some others you need to listen to."

"I can't. Not now."

"Tell me what happened. Or I can call Chuck or Pastor Jake—"

"Don't call a preacher." She clenched her jaw. "All they've ever told my mom is to stay married. 'Divorce is sin.' It got her nowhere. She might be able to hold down a job. Keep up the house. But inside, she died a long time ago."

"I agree. Any type of abuse—especially violence—is not worth staying."

"What do you know about it?"

"It's rampant here, too, ya know."

She pressed her ear against her knees and took a deep breath. "I was sixteen. My dad's high school buddy"— his name stuck in her throat—"had come over to watch a football game. They got drunk. And loud. Tired of it all, I finally went to bed. Fell asleep." She pressed her fist to her mouth and choked down a scream, not sure if she could continue or not. After several minutes, she went on, "I woke up as he was crawling on top of me. I fought and pounded. But he muffled my screams with his dirty hand over my mouth. Years of mouthwash never did get rid of the taste. His forearm choked me as he pleasured himself. I remember gasping . . . these animal-like groans shooting out of my mouth. No one came. No one helped me."

She sucked in a ragged breath, closed her eyes, and exhaled the horror.

"When finished, he zipped his pants and said he'd kill me, my sister, and my mom if I ever told anyone."

"Where was your mom?"

"Asleep. My sister too. The next morning, I found my dad passed out on the couch. And his friend gone. Then a week later . . . I was in the barn." She grunted. "He came in like nothing had happened with the same hunger in his eyes. I'd been cleaning stalls. Had a pitchfork in my hand. It wasn't my plan, but it happened anyway."

She wiped her eyes, hating to relive the rape. "He came closer. I told myself to run. Get away. But all I could do was back up. Which boxed me in a stall. I still had the pitchfork in my hand. He pinned me against a wall. 'Let's get together again some time,' he said. His breath, rank with booze, made my gut churn."

Oh, Lord, don't let anyone else find out. She slowly blew out a breath, fighting off another panic attack. "My adrenaline must have kicked in because I shoved him, and he stumbled backward and dropped to a knee." She closed her eyes. "I still remember the look on his slimy face when he said, 'You wanna play hard to get, huh?' He pushed to his feet, smirked, and lunged for me. He got in a few good licks before—"

"The pitchfork plunged into him," Robert said, his tone husky.

Rita nodded. "The handle slid out of my hands as he went down. I'll never forget the look on his face as he died. He almost looked surprised I'd gotten the best of him."

"How'd you keep it a secret for so long?"

"Can't say."

"You mean you don't know or you won't tell me?"

"I don't know. Didn't think anyone knew."

"Okay. Well . . ." Robert steepled his fingers, pressed them against his lips.

"Does Chuck know?"

"No. The calls came in when I pulled in here. He has no idea."

"You can't tell anyone. Promise me you won't—"

"I won't—"

"I can still go to jail. Which would drag my family through the court." She was mainly worried about her mom and sister. "My life would be over."

And so would theirs.

CHAPTER 33

Moonlight spilled into Rita's room. But nothing could shove out the darkness in her soul. She tossed her cell against the wall. Hearing Hazel's call for help—*Oh, God.* Her heart felt like it was splitting in half. Thankfully, her sister was hiding out at a friend's single-wide trailer. Because there was nothing she could do for her.

But die.

It was the only way for Bowie to disappear from their lives for good.

She waited in a padded, wooden chair, staring out the window until she was sure everyone was asleep. There were no guarantees she wouldn't land in prison, even if Robert did keep her secret. And the Bible even said in Exodus chapter 20, verse 13: "You shall not murder." No killer was bound to make it to heaven, no matter how anyone spun Hawkeye's death. The urge to pray for forgiveness engulfed her, but she figured she'd run out of time. Yep, she was bound for hell.

Soon, the Umatilla cops would know, and they'd come looking for her. Yeah, she had a couple of options—go to prison or end it all here and now. She pulled on socks for added silence and slowly opened the door. The sound of a distant tick resounded off the lodge's walls, and night-lights lined the stairs and dimly lit the hallway.

The glow led her to the great room, her footsteps light and carefully placed. A feeling of despair crept into her bones. She went to every room on the main floor, hunting for pills—her first choice for death. An image of Jesus on the cross, bloody and torn to shreds, drifted into her mind.

Rita remembered the verse from 2 Corinthians 12:9: "My grace is sufficient for you."

I don't deserve grace.

Ignoring her reflection in the mirror, Rita opened the medicine cabinets. She found spare tubes of toothpaste, toothbrushes, and soap in the sunflower-themed bathroom.

I am your strength and your song. I will give you victory.

Her hands gripped the side of the vanity, and she shook her head and mumbled, "You have given me nothing."

I have given you life.

She snorted. "You allowed me to be raped and beaten and . . ." The knot jamming her throat blocked her words. She pushed away and padded to the bathroom between the kitchen and an exit, bumping into tables and chairs along the way. In the horse-themed space, she pulled open the medicine cabinet, sliced her finger on a jagged edge, and cried out. Her tongue stopped the flow of blood. She squeezed her eyes closed, trying to block the verses she'd memorized in youth group.

But the Bible story of Job broke through. She shook her head, refusing to believe that she and Job were anything alike. Job had lost everything and still remained faithful. She'd been raped and forced to kill against her nature. She'd walked away from her Creator.

With one hand, she riffled through the cabinet drawers and under the sink. Nothing. Nothing. Nothing! She leaned against the counter and let out a low moan, then slipped into the kitchen and found the cupboard holding the spices hostage. Rummaging through the bottles, she found over-the-counter migraine pills behind the cinnamon. "Ah, there you are." She opened the container. Three pills circled the edge.

She couldn't end anything with a few measly tablets.

Releasing a sharp groan, she tossed the empty bottle to the floor. Her breathing increased until she was hyperventilating. *No, not again.* She searched through drawers and cupboards for a paper sack, upending towels, utensils, and cooking supplies.

On the bottom shelf of the pantry sat a large bag of assorted chips. Dropping to her knees, she ripped one open, dumped out the contents, and covered her mouth.

She took several normal breaths from the bag, then removed it from her mouth and nose. She took a few deep belly breaths without the sack, then used the bag again. Repeated the cycle. Feeling light-headed, she sank to the floor.

What a failure. She couldn't even keep it together long enough to take her own life.

Her pulse pounded in her ears as she filled her lungs, held her breath for as long as she could, and pushed it out her puckered lips. Her lungs felt like they were on fire.

After three breathing cycles and feeling like the panic attack had passed, she pressed a hand to her neck and took in a few normal breaths while she gathered the tablets.

I will turn what is meant for evil into good.

Whatever. Sydney had said the same thing at the convention. *So where was the good?* Rita cleaned up the mess, then pulled a serrated knife from its wooden block. She pressed the steel blade against her wrist, cold and jagged. She turned it over to the dull side and ran it across her blue-lined flesh as though it were a fillet of fish.

Not having the nerve to go through with it, she tossed the knife into the sink. There had to be an easier way. One not including pain and blood. Back to pills. Didn't Sydney say she had battled migraines? At least used to. There had to be medications lying around. Just in case.

She padded to the office and held a breath as the door creaked open. "They have to be in this blasted place." Since it was the middle of the night, she took the chance, drew down the window shades, and flicked on the light switch.

At the desk, she rummaged through drawers concealing decades of ranch records and office supplies. Finding nothing of use, she went to the closet and opened the door. Tucked in a corner was a locked safe. And she bet inside was a pistol. If only she knew the pass code. Or where to look for it. She slid her hands around the cold metal box, hoping there was a slip of paper taped to it. But there wasn't. She sat back on her heels and fingered her feather necklace.

Come to me and I will give you rest.

Ignoring the pesky voice in her head, she rose, went to the west wall, and stood in front of the ranch photo. Were these rules? Or some kind of philosophy? She read them aloud, stopping on "Make goals and prepare for ruts in the road."

I will give you a hope and a future.

What? In prison? No thanks.

She sank to the couch. Self-defense or not, she'd taken a man's life. Yes, he'd damaged her. Physically. Mentally. Emotionally. Even if she was not held accountable by the courts, God would surely judge her.

"How could you ever forgive me? Make Bowie disappear?" There wasn't a way she could see through it all. And the nightmares were getting worse, not better, and her tummy was in a constant coil.

Wait. There was the shotgun in the barn. She darted outside, the chilly air scraping her face. Then she rushed to the barn. Déjà vu. The place where she'd found solace.

Horses whickered, and a nose by her shoulder poked through the stall slats, breathing warm air on her. Making her way to Blizzard's stall, she opened the door and went inside. At least she could say goodbye.

Just as she was breathing in his earthy scent, a light flickered on and startled her. The stud darted to a corner and lifted his head. "Shhh. It's okay, boy." She reached out to him. "I'm here." He pawed the shavings, his eyes wide and wild.

"I think I've found you here before." Robert's silhouette shone in the illuminated barn.

Rita swung around. "You scared the crap out of me. What are you doing out here?"

"I could ask you the same thing." She turned back to the stud and pressed her hand against his neck. Finally, he dropped his head.

"You first."

Robert leaned a shoulder against the stall door. "Couldn't sleep."

"Me either." With gentle pressure, she rubbed the colt's nose.

"You spoil him."

"He's special." She pressed her lips against Blizzard's forehead. "Aren't you, boy?"

"So are you." He sounded like he meant it.

Rita kept her back to him so he wouldn't see her reaction—like the flush of her face from her stomach flipping. She'd wanted to say, "So are you."

"Was anyone else roaming the lodge?"

Rita slowly shook her head. "No, why?"

"I saw the light flick off in the office."

Sweat broke out on her palms. "I . . . uh . . ."

"What were you looking for?"

She wanted to be honest with him. But couldn't form the right words in her head.

"Did you check your messages?"

She gave him a slight nod.

"Were you in the office?"

Again, she bobbed her head.

"Did you need something? I can help you, ya know."

She held her hands out to Blizzard and with a dull tone said, "I can't go to prison. I can't live with what I did. I was . . ."

His footsteps inched closer, and when Blizzard bit at him, Robert jumped back. "You were what?"

"Trying to kill myself." Saying it out loud made her recoil. And feel like a failure.

He gasped. "Why would you try to commit suicide?"

One of her shoulders inched up.

"Will you come out here and talk to me?"

She shook her head. "The guilt . . . it's too much." Rita reached up and scratched the colt's forehead. "It's the only way to keep Hazel safe."

"Please, let me help you."

"It's too late." She turned and walked past him.

He shut the stall door and caught up to her mid-barn. He reached out and took hold of her shoulders. "It's never too late. I'll keep you safe." He drew her close. "I can't lose you."

She wanted to believe him but couldn't. "No one can keep me safe." She pushed past him and raced for the lodge.

CHAPTER 34

Robert couldn't trust her to be alone, and it was too late to call Sydney. So he tried Chuck as he strode to the lodge and got his voice mail. Not knowing what else to do, he rounded up all the pills and weapons he could find and locked them in the ranch hands' gun safe in the shop.

Because she was worth it.

Which was why he then called Pastor Jake.

No, he wouldn't mention the rape. Or the death of Rita's rapist. She'd gone through enough. Besides, the dude deserved it.

He hated to wake him up at four in the morning. And he wasn't about to call the cops. As he waited for the preacher to answer, he went to the front of the lodge and stopped in front of Rita's dark, second-floor window.

"Hello?"

"Pastor Jake. I didn't mean to wake you."

"It's all right, son. What's up?" Concern flowed through the preacher's voice.

"One of our women in need tried to commit suicide tonight. Syd's out of town. I don't know what to do."

"Is she okay?"

"I think so. I found her in the barn with one of the studs." He thought—no hoped and prayed—it was nothing but a cry for help.

"Where is she now?"

"In her room."

"Okay, lock up all weapons and medication and stay with her. I'm on my way."

"I already did." Robert ended the call and sank to the porch steps. This was the first time any of the women had attempted suicide. At least on the ranch. And it was on his watch.

What if she attempted it again and succeeded in taking her life? Wetness burned his eyes. What then?

At least the retired preacher had training in suicide prevention and counseling and had helped many of the women at the ranch. Numerous times, he had brought a female tribal counselor to assist. But for some reason, they all preferred him. He had a safe, fatherly way about him. One which women—and even men—seemed drawn to.

He went to open the door of the lodge and found it locked. He shook the handle. *Oh no. Was she trying to finish what she'd started?* "Rita!"

He curled his fingers into a ball and pounded on the door. Not waiting, he sprinted around the lodge, jumping over decorative boulders and brush, and found the back door leading to the kitchen unlocked.

He burst inside and raced through the kitchen, then up the stairs, taking them two at a time. "Rita!" Finding her room, he tried to twist the knob. But it was locked. He pounded on the door. "Let me in."

Guests staggered into the hallway, gawking.

"Everything's all right. Sorry for disturbing you. Go back to bed." He went to knock again when Rita opened the door.

"What?"

He pushed past her and shut the door.

"What are you doing? I didn't say you could come into my room." She pinned a glare on him.

Oh good. She appeared to be okay. "Sorry for barging in, but I need to talk to you."

"No. Get out. I'm going to sleep."

A rap sounded on the door. "Do I need to call the police?" a man said, his voice stiff.

"No, sir," Robert said. "We're okay."

"Ma'am? I'll call if you need me to."

Rita shook her head and glared at Robert. Then in a sweet tone she said, "I'm okay. Thanks for checking on us."

After an instant, footsteps and muffled voices faded, and doors squeaked and clicked.

Robert leaned against the door and whispered, "Truth is I can't leave you alone."

"Says who?"

"Pastor Jake."

Rita turned on Robert. "You called your preacher? Knowing what they did to my mom?"

He swallowed hard. "He's different. Besides, I didn't know what to do. C'mon, Rita. You tried to kill yourself."

"You had no right." She turned away from him. "You better not mention the rape. Or Hawkeye."

"Of course not. I'm just concerned about you. I don't want you to hurt yourself." Oh, how he wanted to hold her. Make her feel safe and secure. *Stay in your lane.*

Nodding, she hugged herself and padded to the window, her back to him.

"Will you at least come downstairs?" He shifted his weight. "He's on his way."

She spun around. "At this time of night? What were you thinking?"

He swallowed hard. "I was thinking you might die."

Her expression softened. "I'll talk to him. But then you have to leave me alone. Got it?"

"Fine with me." Jake would do the rest.

They went downstairs. Rita shivered and rubbed her arms, so Robert lit a fire and handed her a blanket. She wrapped it around her shoulders and settled in one of the overstuffed chairs next to the sofa.

Robert wiped his hands on his jeans. "You want some tea?"

"Sure. Why not? Since you got me out of bed." She turned to the fire. "I was almost asleep."

"You were?"

The daggers in her eyes sent him to the kitchen. He plugged in a steel hot pot and found samples of tea in a basket on the counter. He selected Lady Grey and winced. Her mood was already sour, so he stuffed the packet back and chose another. Nightly Calm. Whoa, he wasn't about to tell her to chill out. She'd probably slap him if he handed her a cup with that dangling off the side. He tried to read the labels but couldn't pronounce some of the names.

"Who comes up with this stuff?" He picked through the basket until he found the right one. "Pure Camomile," he said and took a sniff. At least it smelled kinda earthy. This way he could offer her something soothing without suggesting she get a grip. He fixed the tea, and since she seemed to like the pumpkin creamer so well with her coffee, he thought he'd surprise her and add a few shots to the tea.

Happy with the tan, steamy brew, he sauntered to the couch as light beams swept across the lodge's picture windows. "Here ya go."

She took the cup and peered inside. Took a quick sniff. Then scrunched her nose. "What's in it?"

"Camomile tea and your favorite creamer." He hovered over her, expecting a sweet gesture of gratitude. Heck, he'd take a sigh of satisfaction.

She took a sip. "Yuck!" She plopped the mug down. Hot tea sloshed onto the coffee table. "That's nasty."

"Nasty? What'd I do wrong?"

"The creamer and tea don't mix. Sorry."

Pastor Jake strolled into the great room, and Robert gave him a you-better-watch-out-for-her look. The preacher smiled and patted him on the back.

Robert turned to her. "This is Rita Runninghorse. She's from the Umatilla rez."

She gave him what looked like a forced grin and a small wave.

Pastor Jake settled on the sofa next to her. "Which band are you from?"

She perked up. "Cayuse and Umatilla."

"My late wife, Ruby, and I often frequented the Pendleton Round-Up. Best rodeo around in my opinion."

Rita leaned forward. "Did you attend the Happy Canyon show?"

He nodded. "Loved every minute of it. From the story line between the early Natives and settlers to the regalia and Western costumes. The music and dancing warmed my heart every time. The reenactment is a top-notch production."

"It sure is." This time she gave him a genuine smile.

"Robert told me you've been struggling tonight." Pastor Jake crossed his ankle over his knee. "I've counseled many women who have sought safety at the ranch. Do you feel like talking?" Compassion filled his tone.

She lifted a shoulder to her ear, slumped back, and glanced from the minister to Robert to her lap.

When she didn't answer, he asked, "Do you need Robert to leave?"

Robert shifted his weight. *Leave?* He hoped not.

She gave him a sideways glance and shook her head. "He can stay."

With a sigh, Robert sank onto the couch. He knew enough to help fill in the gaps if needed so the preacher would get the real story.

"Robert," Pastor Jake said, "will you please get me a cup of coffee?"

"Yeah." Robert stood and turned to Rita. "What can I get you?"

"The same. Please." She paused. "Black is fine." She gave him a small smile and turned to the pastor.

CHAPTER 35

Rita didn't know where to start. Or how much to divulge. And the stupid tick of the mantel clock grated on her nerves. Good thing Pastor Jake made her feel like he truly cared. He put her at ease, but still, to speak it all out loud to a stranger made her pulse gallop.

"I-huh-well . . . after my ex-fiancé roughed me up, I found Sydney's brochure and came here."

The preacher gave her a slow nod. "You stated this man is your ex. Does he understand where he stands with you?"

"He should by now. Officer Chuck hand delivered a temporary restraining order to him."

"Super. Normally, I'd work with a domestic violence advocate to help with that process. How'd you get here?"

"My truck broke down just before Connell, and I caught a couple rides to . . . um . . . Ritzville and then, well . . . ended up in Davenport before catching another ride with a nice trucker. He dropped me off at the Chief Joseph Rest Area." There was no need to tell him about George the Third not taking her all the way to Nespelem.

Pastor Jake's brows shot up. "Sounds like you went through a lot to get here. How long has the abuse been going on?"

Robert brought them coffee and settled in an overstuffed chair across from Rita.

She filled him in on the basics. And only the basics. In her opinion, he didn't need to know the details.

"I'm sorry you've had a rough go at life. What made you want to end everything?"

"I-uh . . ." She couldn't tell him why. Couldn't admit she'd killed a man. Couldn't face going to prison. "Was scared. Not sure I could ever get away from him. And since he'd beat my sister and threatened to kill her if she didn't give me up, which she doesn't even know where I am, I figured if I wasn't around anymore, he'd leave her alone." Which was the truth. Just not all of it.

"Is she safe?"

"Yeah. She's with a friend."

"Okay. Good. If it's all right with you, I'll phone Sydney and Chuck and go from there."

"Yeah." She nodded. "That's fine."

He scooted to the edge of the couch. "Do you still feel like hurting yourself?"

"No. I don't. I haven't felt this much hope in . . . since . . ." She couldn't think of the last time. The stint with the youth pastor made her feel safe but never hopeful.

"I'm glad to hear you're feeling better. Here's my number. Call me anytime. Any hour." Pastor Jake handed her his card. "Mind if I pray?"

"Sure." A sense of calm blanketed her as he spoke. When he asked the Holy Spirit to draw her close and give her comfort, goosebumps broke out on her arms. Then fear pushed in. Would Robert keep his word? Keep her secret?

CHAPTER 36

Two weeks later, Rita found Robert in the living quarters of a horse trailer looking handsome in his black jacket and Stetson with a turquoise rag tied around his neck. She tapped the metal step to get his attention. When he swung around, she greeted him with two steamy cups of black coffee. "Permission to enter?"

His eyes lit up. "Absolutely."

She handed him one of the cups and climbed the step. "What are you up to?"

"I'm getting ready to head out to my next rodeo," Robert said. "Want to go with me?"

Another rodeo, huh? "Well, I've hardly slept for the past few days. So, yeah. Maybe getting out of here will help." In truth, Rita hadn't had a peaceful sleep since her last talk with Pastor Jake. Their session had ignited a smoldering battle inside of her—even hotter since Robert now knew she was a killer. But those beautiful sable eyes of his pleaded with her. "Where're you headed?"

"Redmond, Oregon. And from there to Vegas for the Indian National Finals Rodeo." He spoke as though it were the Super Bowl.

"You sure they don't need my help with you leaving?"

"Nope. Chad and one of his buddies have it covered. And since it's early, we don't have to rush to get there."

She glanced at the clock on the wall opposite the door. Seven in the morning, so yeah, they could probably take their time. "What about Mandie?" She hoped she'd have time to play a little with Nona before heading out. The toddler gave her hope that she, too, could one day have a child as beautiful and full of life as Nona was.

"She's fine. There're only a few guests."

Rita had enjoyed getting her hands dirty again. It was nice helping with the horses and fencing without the usual pain or aches that had come courtesy of Bowie Dark Cloud.

"So, do you want to come with me?"

Redmond, huh? And if there was plenty of time, could there be a way to hook up with Hazel? Convince her to come with us?

"Sure. Why not?"

He smiled. "Cool. Will you put the groceries in the horse trailer?"

They'd gone to Omak the previous day and stocked up on food, water, and toiletries and filled the propane tanks. Now she knew why. "So how come you didn't ask me yesterday? Or a week ago?"

His face pinkened. "I didn't think you'd come."

"Why not?"

"I wasn't sure when you had to appear in court for your restraining order."

She crossed her arms and shook her head. "I'm not going."

"What? Why not?"

"For one, it did no good. And I just can't go back. Can't take a chance of running into Bowie. Have him—or whoever—trap me for killing Hawkeye. Nope. Can't do it."

"You have a point. At least if you come with me, they won't know where you are. If you don't use your phone or credit cards. If you stay here, they know exactly where to find you."

"And I'm sure he's still planning. Waiting for the perfect time to pounce. So yeah, I guess I'm in. I'll finish here, then go pack." Which wouldn't take but a few seconds.

"Great. I'll be back in a bit." Robert placed a hand on her shoulder and left.

While setting a few cans of soup in the cupboard over the table, her mind went to Pastor Jake's warning about how hard it would be to leave her ex. How hard it'd be for him to let go. He talked about spiritual battles and the lies humans believe.

But this was no battle. Killing Hawkeye made it an all-out war. Which put her on the losing end.

And Bowie's threats of killing Hazel and her mom. Yeah, she was sure he'd meant every one of them. No lies attached.

With the chance of going to prison hanging over her head, how could she trust Pastor Jake's promise that, in time, she would heal? "God will pave the way. He goes before you," he'd said. "He will give you a hope and a future, Rita. All you have to do is trust Him."

The thing was she couldn't trust God to keep her safe. To give her a future. Not with Bowie on the loose.

Robert returned. "How's it going in here?"

She spun around. "Not so well."

"What's going on?" He handed her a can of clam chowder.

"I've been thinking about what Pastor Jake's been talking about."

"Oh yeah? Like what?"

"My future." She slammed the can of soup on the shelf. "How can I move forward when the past is still chasing me?"

"Tough one."

"Yeah. And Pastor Jake keeps telling me to 'be patient in tribulation, and be constant in prayer.' Heck, my prayer life hasn't been much over the last ten years or so."

"I get it. It's hard to remember prayer is an instant connection to our Creator. Yet He's always available. And always listens."

"Always?" she scoffed. "Where was God when Talon Hawkeye was raping me? Trust me, I cried out to God. Over and over. But He never answered. Never stopped him from . . ." Shaking, she dropped to a seat. "I get it with Bowie. I chose him. And didn't leave when the abuse began. But the rape? I didn't choose to be violated. No girl does."

"I can't tell you why God allows horrible things to happen." Robert took the seat across from her. "But I do believe God turns bad into good. I've seen how many women my sister helps every year. Then they go on to help others."

"Still. Where is God when we're being . . .?" She couldn't say raped or beaten or murdered another time.

"I'm sorry you have to go through this. Maybe getting out of here will help in some way."

"Maybe. Like you said, if I stay off my phone and don't use my credit card, I'll be okay. But . . ."

"But what?"

"I don't have a lot of money. However, I have my engagement ring. I can pawn it—"

"Save it. As much as you've helped around here this past couple of weeks, I probably owe you."

"I don't think so. But thanks. We'll work something out." She stood and put the rest of the canned goods into the cupboard. "We about ready?"

"Yep. I have a couple things to do. Then we can hit the road."

"I'll be ready." She went to her room and tucked her cell and Leatherman into her backpack, then added clothes. It felt like what she had in her backpack was all she had in life. And it wasn't much. She had to get Hazel.

Mandie met her at the bottom of the stairs, travel cooler and thermos in hand. "Nona's napping, so I packed you guys enough food to get you through the day. It'll be a long drive."

"You're the best." Sad that she didn't get to spend time with Nona, Rita took the items. She set them on a table when Posse stormed in and jumped on her leg, his tail wagging. She picked him up and giggled when he licked her face with his coarse tongue. "Any chance Bronco Bobby will let me take him?"

Mandie wiped her hands on her dream catcher apron. "Nope. 'Rodeo's no life for a pup.' His words, not mine."

"But I'd—"

"You ready?" Robert came out of the office. "And no. He's not coming." He rubbed Posse's head.

There had to be a way to sneak him in. Those big eyes melted everything inside of her. She'd be willing to take care of the pup. Heck, he'd fit into her pack. She brought him up to her nose and inhaled his grassy scent.

Robert took the ball of fur and handed him to Mandie. "Keep an eye on him for me, will ya? Chad's got his hands full at the moment." He picked up Rita's backpack and started for the door.

Mandie gave Rita an I'm-sorry glance and took the dog.

"No, wait. I'll watch him." Rita set the thermos into the crook of her arm, scratched the pup's head, and fast walked to the foyer.

"Rodeo's no place for a dog. Especially a pup." Robert shook his head as he opened the wooden door. "He's safest here on the ranch. Besides, he needs to learn his job." He held the door open for Rita.

"Guess you're right."

"I'm what?" Robert tipped his head and smiled.

"Crazy," Rita said. "Now. Let's get out of here before I run back and get him." She put the cooler and thermos in the back seat of the truck.

"Wait! I almost forgot." Mandie rushed down the porch steps with two travel mugs. "Pumpkin spice for you." She handed a tall, lidded cup to Rita. "And bitter black for you." With a smirk, she gave Robert the other one.

"Just like I like it." He put Rita's backpack in the back seat, hopped into the truck, and took a sip. He opened the door and spit it out. "Blasted, Short Stack!"

Rita got in. "What's wrong?"

"She put Tabasco sauce in it." He dumped the coffee in the dirt.

She laughed. "No way. Good one."

Robert wiped his mouth with his shirt sleeve. "Can't wait to get her back."

Mandie stood on the porch and waved, a huge smile on her face as they rolled away. Rita opened the jockey box.

Now, for the map and a plan to extract Hazel.

Her gaze landed on the .357 Magnum seven-shot revolver and a box of matching bullets under the neatly folded Western States map. Good thing she hadn't known it was there when they were in Idaho.

CHAPTER 37

Rita snapped the glove compartment shut. "Which way do you plan on going?" She unfolded a Western States map on her lap and traced a route from Nespelem to Redmond. "Through Yakima?"

"Yeah. We'll cross the river at Goldendale and come out at Biggs Junction. Then head south on I-97. It's the fastest route, considering I ride tonight."

Which makes it worse. Going through the Tri-Cities and onto Interstate 84 is pretty much out of the way.

"What're you thinking?"

"For a way to get Hazel."

"Going to Pendleton is out of the question. If you haven't noticed, it's in the opposite direction." Robert wound his way south on Highway 155 headed toward Interstate 90.

Rita tapped her finger where the small country town of Hermiston stood on the map. "What if we tie it to the Hermiston horse sale? My dad goes there all the time looking for the next great horse. Hazel and my mom usually go too." *Going through the Tri-Cities wouldn't be so far out of the way.*

"We don't have room for four people in the trailer, Rita. Besides, won't your ex be there too? Isn't he a horse trader?"

"Yeah, but . . ." *There had to be a way to rescue them both.*

"We just don't have the time."

"It was worth a try." Heartbroken, she slumped back in her seat.

"Sorry. I want to get to Redmond and settle in. I ride all weekend. Then have to turn around and head to Vegas. If we rush around, I won't be focused."

"I said it was fine." Rita continued to compare routes. Her fingers outlined the Umatilla Reservation boundaries. "Can I at least use your phone to call my sister? Make sure she's okay. Last time I talked to her, she was back working at the ranch. My dad found her and forced her to go back. He said if she didn't, she'd have to leave for good."

"I don't think it's a good idea."

"I at least need to hear her voice." She sighed. "I want her and my mom to know I'm safe. They deserve that much."

Robert nodded. "You're right." He handed her his cell.

She punched in her sister's number, tapped her lip with her finger. On the fourth ring Hazel answered.

"Hello?"

"Don't say anything. It's me."

"Where are you?" Hazel whispered. "Bowie found your truck, you know. Dad had it hauled home. He's furious. Says if you're going to leave him hanging out to dry, he'll sell Opal."

"What? Sell Opal? No way." Most definitely, he would. He had her horse. Her pickup. He had it all. All but her dignity—which wasn't up for grabs.

"Way. Where are you? Are you okay?"

"Don't worry. I'm safe. What about you?"

"I'm fine. Mom won't let Bowie come near the ranch. She threatened to kill him. Can you believe it?" In the background, Dean Runninghorse hollered for Hazel to get back to work. "I'll call you back. Soon. I promise."

The line went dead, and she tossed the cell on the seat between them.

"What'd she say?"

"Sounds like she's on the range and had to get off but will call back soon. Said Mom threatened to kill Bowie if he came around. But she shouldn't have. And—"

"Why not? Heck, I'd do the same, if not worse, if it were my daughters."

"Yeah, but for him a threat's nothing but a challenge."

Robert's cell chimed, and Rita picked it up. "It's her." She swiped the On icon. "Hey."

"That was close."

"Where are you?" Rita tapped her heel on the floorboard, her knee bobbing up and down. She winced as Robert pulled onto the narrow bridge below Grand Coulee Dam.

"Going back for hay. Dad's truck broke down." Hazel's voice sounded exasperated.

"How's Mom?"

"How do you think she is?" A hiss sizzled over the line. "She's a wreck."

"I'm sorry, Haze." Rita turned her face to the window. Jagged rock cliffs sped past.

"For what? You didn't beat me up," Hazel said. "Speaking of, I heard Bowie found you on the Colville rez. Is it true?"

"Kinda. He knows where I've been staying."

"Which is?"

Rita let out a heavy sigh. "I'm not going to say until it's safe." She wanted Hazel to honestly be able to say she didn't know if asked.

"Shoot. He's back. Gotta go. Call Mom."

"Hazel!" Rita dropped the phone on her lap. No. The call wasn't long enough.

Robert stopped for a red light at the Bridgeport Junction. When it turned green, he crossed the intersection and headed toward Soap Lake. Leaving town—and the security of a ranch with a built-in cop—made Rita feel exposed.

She tapped in her mom's work number. After one ring she hung up. "I can't do it."

"Do what?"

"Call my mom."

His brows rose. "Thought you wanted her to know you were safe."

"I do. But don't want her to beg me to come home." She regretted keeping Bowie's abuse to herself—regretted that her mom found out he'd beaten up Hazel. Of course, she was a wreck.

"But you're right, she deserves to know you're safe. If I were you, I'd call her before we lose service."

She made the call as she picked at the hem of her sweatshirt.

"Good morning, Yellowhawk Tribal Health Center, how may I help you?"

"Mom, it's me."

"Rita?" Joan Runninghorse lowered her voice. "Where are . . ." Her voice fragmented over the line.

"Mom?" The call died. "Ugh." Rita feared she'd made things worse.

"You'll have to wait until we get to Soap Lake to get service again."

They drove along Banks Lake, passing Steamboat Rock State Park. The astounding historic landmark encompassed six hundred acres of basalt rock in the formation of a flat ship. Then they snaked around the lake, hugging carved rock faces seeming to watch her.

The landscape scratched across Rita's mind as they traveled along the coulees. Oh, how the rocky scabland resembled how she felt. Deserted by God. Unable to help her mom and sister.

Helpless.

CHAPTER 38

Umatilla Reservation

Bowie rested on his mom's sofa in her modest but clean double-wide mobile home. "I'm not leaving until you're stable."

Today was his day to look after her since she'd been released from the hospital, and he was already sick of her house plants taking root in every empty space, even from a handful of ceiling hooks near windows. He should be out finding Rita.

Edna Dark Cloud had woken up shortly after her CAT scan. The results showed a concussion, and she'd had migraines nearly every day since the accident. But there were no broken bones.

She'd spent a couple of nights in the hospital and was released on the third day with a bottle of pain pills and a follow-up appointment with the family physician. And now she reclined on the sofa beside her eldest son, her feet on a weathered, white coffee table, a cup of tea with an orange aroma in her hands.

Edna shook her head, her curly, silver locks swaying. "I'm fine, Son."

"No, you're not." His mom was too frail, her skin hanging off her bones like an underfed ninety-year-old. He needed to get her to eat food that would stick to her ribs. Enough of the watery soups and salads.

"Honey, if you love Rita, for heaven sakes, go get her." She patted his hand.

"I'd like to, Mom. But we had an argument, and she's pretty upset. I'll give her time to cool off. Then take her for a ride to Pilot Rock. She likes it there."

"Oh, Son," Edna crooned. "You are one of the kindest souls I know. She loves you. Otherwise, she wouldn't have said yes." Her shaky hand lifted the cup to her pale lips. A drop spilled onto her shirt. "Heavens. Look what I've done. This isn't like me." She winced and pressed a hand to her head.

"You're right." Bowie got a towel and blotted the orange-scented stain. "I'll go after her."

"That's my boy."

"But not until you're back on your feet."

"Can you get me my medication? My head hurts."

Bowie checked the time, popped a tiny pill from a metallic blister pack, and handed it to his mom. "Here. Take this."

Edna took the medication and chased it with her tea. "You know your sister will help me. Go bring Rita back so we can plan a wedding. I'd love to have grandkids." She leaned back and closed her eyes.

"I know you would." It didn't mean he wanted them. Kids would get in the way—unless promising to have a few would get Rita back.

After a few days, the temporary restraining order would be dismissed. He planned to show up for court. He had the feeling Rita wouldn't. Inside, he smiled. He'd do whatever it took to win her back. All he had to do was get one foot in the Runninghorse door and his hands on their money. Then all his problems would disappear, and he could take care of his mom.

CHAPTER 39

Soap Lake, Washington

She'd do whatever it took to get rid of Bowie. And keep him away from Hazel. And her mom away from her dad. Dean Runninghorse's impatience was escalating. At least according to Hazel. Rita put the call on speakerphone as her sister pleaded for her to come home.

"He actually hit her." Hazel had panic in her voice. "All because she threatened Bowie. What's with those two? Why does Dad protect him and not Mom? It doesn't make sense."

"I don't know." Rita rubbed her temples with trembling fingers. "I'll find a way to get you and Mom out of there." Her leaving had lit a fuse, and now he was taking his rage out on their mom. It would only be a matter of time before her dad went after her sister. "It's all my fault. I should have stayed."

"I'm afraid he'll kill her." Hazel had a twinge of defeat in her voice.

"I'll see what I can do. We'll talk soon."

The edges of the mineral-rich Soap Lake foamed like pie topped with whipped cream. Clumps of sage, rabbit, and bitterbrush along with basalt cliffs surrounded the lake. Rita pointed to a park along the beach. "Pull in there."

"Why? We're making good time."

"Robert . . . please?" Had he not been listening to Hazel?

"Hang on." He braked, cranking the steering wheel to the right, and rolled to a stop in an empty parking lot. "What do you have in mind?"

Rita opened the map, her finger tracing red lines. "According to this, we can cut off up ahead and from Moses Lake head to the Tri-Cities and on to Pendleton."

"And why would we do that?"

"Have you not been listening?"

"Yeah, I have. But there's nothing we can do. Surely you have family there to help."

"Really? Let my family handle it? You've got to be kidding me. This is my mom we're talking about. You of all people—losing yours—should understand. C'mon. She's in danger."

"And so are you." He shifted his weight and faced her. "Let the cops deal with your dad. Did she even call them?"

"The cops? Humph." She shook her head. "Nothing happens with domestic violence victims. I think because you see so much success with Sydney, you don't understand what we go through. The laws suck. I—we—need to go get them. Please, between Bowie and my dad—"

"You know what will happen if you go back."

She sniffed and wiped her eyes with her shirtsleeve. "I can't leave them there. Wait for my dad to kill my mom."

"Don't you think you're overreacting?"

Overreacting? "Are you kidding me?"

"Did he put her in the hospital?"

"No, but—"

"Then she needs to leave. Why can't she stay with someone else?"

"You think it's so easy, don't you?"

"Sydney—"

"Almost died. Didn't she?"

He worked his jaw.

"He's getting worse. Until now, he's never left visible marks on her. He's the kind who threatens, manipulates, demeans, isolates. You heard Hazel. He hit my mom. Even before I left, he was angry all the time." Her chin trembling, she pulled a napkin out of the travel cooler and blew her nose.

He checked his cell. "There's no way I'd make it in time if we take a detour." A thin line formed on his lips. "We have almost six hours to go. About three hundred miles."

"I understand how important rodeo is to you." She opened the door, a rush of cold air blew into the cab, and got out. "I found my way to the Seven Tine. I can find my way home." She slammed the door shut.

Robert jumped out. "You're not hitchhiking."

"I'll do whatever it takes to protect them." She walked around the truck.

He met her by the front bumper and clutched her arm. He yelled over the rattling engine, "Get back in the truck."

"No." The urge to run surged through her. She had to get to her family. Save them from—

He drew her in and kissed her. Not like he had in Idaho to keep the other cowboys away. This was passionate. Protective. Like he meant it. She couldn't remember a time when she'd been kissed with such hunger.

Robert—?

He smelled so good. Of leather. Horse. And a hint of cinnamon and nutmeg. Making the kiss taste of desperation, of needing, and maybe even a fear of losing her. The thing was she didn't want to lose him.

Her hands found the collar of his long-sleeved shirt, and she tightened her fist around the fabric. Held on as he deepened the kiss. For an instant, she didn't move. Did nothing but enjoy his strong arms around her waist. Drank in his urgency.

Right up to the point he broke off the kiss. "My job is to keep you safe."

His job. Duty. What, according to Sydney Hardy? She pushed away. "I get it. My job is to keep my sister and mom safe."

Robert groaned. "No. It's the cops' job."

"Like I said before, no cop or restraining order can stop the fire fueling a man's blind rage. You see the result of abuse all the time. How many women did you say have come to the ranch? A couple hundred?"

He let out a deep sigh. Shook his head. "What do you have in mind?"

"Go to Pendleton. Get them. And get back on the road. It's a simple plan and won't take much time." Though she knew it would be pushing Robert to get to his rodeo on time.

He scrubbed his stubbled face. "You know it won't be so easy."

"Let's get on the road. We can form a plan as you drive."

"You realize they'll see us coming. And what if they turn *us* in to the cops?"

"Trust me. Dean Runninghorse wants nothing to do with cops. He hates all law enforcement for putting him in jail for shooting a wolf who'd killed three of his cattle four years ago. He'd rather handle things privately. And they won't see us if Mom and Hazel can meet us somewhere."

"Do you think they can get away? And do they want to? Not all women are willing to leave their abusers."

"Hazel will come with us for sure. Thanks to Bowie beating on her. But honestly, I'm not sure my mom will leave my dad." Courtesy of her preacher's cockamamie warnings about divorce.

"All right then. Let's go get them. I'd want to do the same if it were my mom and sister."

She shrieked, planted a big kiss on his lips, and hopped into the rig.

Robert pulled out of the parking lot and headed toward Moses Lake. "God help us."

Rita grabbed his cell and texted Hazel.

We're coming to get u.

Pasco, Washington

A couple of hours later, they rolled into a gas station and mini-mart. Rita called Hazel, and she picked up on the third ring. "You ready?"

"Dad's making us go with him to the stockyard." Hazel's tone sounded hurried.

Rita put the call on speakerphone. "In Hermiston?"

"Yeah."

"Perfect. It's closer, and no one knows what Robert looks like." And they'd blend in with his rig.

His eyes widened. "Me?" He shook his head. "No way. This is your—"

Rita put a finger to her lips and scowled at him. "What time?"

"We're almost ready to leave."

"Okay. We'll meet you there."

"Oh, and hey . . ." Hazel's voice hitched. "He's bringing Opal."

"No!" She squeezed her eyes shut. "Have her ready to load." When there was no answer, she held the phone out. The call had dropped.

"Great. And now a horse too? Good Lord, Rita. What's next?" Robert shook his head and got out to pump diesel.

She felt bad for pulling Robert into her family's mess. But a twinge of hope shoved out her guilt.

Could this be the day they'd all break free?

CHAPTER 40

Hermiston, Oregon

An hour later, Rita's shoulders tightened as Robert pulled into the stockyard and parked his pickup near the edge of the road, ready for their getaway. "I don't see his truck and trailer." She opened the door.

"Wait a minute." Robert grabbed her arm. When she glowered at him, he released the pressure. "We can't go in blind."

"You can't keep grabbing me."

"I know. I'm sorry."

She shut the door. "Anyway, you're right. What do you have in mind?"

He arched his brows. "Me? No, ma'am." Then shook his head. "This is your deal, not mine. I don't even know what your family looks like. The question is, what do *you* have in mind?"

She dug her cell out of her backpack, powered it on, ignored numerous missed calls and texts, and flipped through her photos. C'mon. She chose a good one of Hazel lounging in a swing on their cabin porch during a warm July evening and handed the phone to Robert.

"You two look different. Except for your mouths."

She showed him a photo of her, her mom, and Hazel beside a yellow rose bush on the south side of their house. "Yep. Same mouths and eyes." Rita was the tallest at five-seven and had the longest and darkest hair. Hazel wore bangs, her shoulder-length locks the color of fertile soil. Silver streaked her mom's black, cropped hair.

"Unfortunately, I look like my dad." She scrolled through her photos. "I guess it's no shock I don't have one of him."

"What does he look like?"

She scrunched her nose. "A dime-store cowboy. Black Stetson and boots that shine like a new penny, creased jeans, and a 1998 calf-roping championship buckle from the Pendleton Round-Up." She laughed. "He wears the stupid thing as though it brings him some kind of superpower. The only thing missing from his getup is a set of jingly spurs."

"Check out the guy by the black Dodge." He tapped his window.

Rita's heart leaped into her throat. "That's him all right." She hid behind the map when he glanced their way. "Do you see my sister or mom?"

"No one's with him. He's walking away."

She slapped the map on her lap as her father disappeared into the red structure. "I'll look for Opal, and you try to find my mom and Hazel."

"And then what, Nancy Drew?" Robert asked in a mock whisper.

"You making fun of me?"

"Kinda. Maybe. Yes. Because this is insane." He tapped the steering wheel twice with his fist. "We need to get on the road."

"You promised." She gave him a pleading look.

"Promised is a strong word." He sighed. "Okay. You have fifteen minutes."

"And then what?"

"If we don't find them, I'm out of here."

"Fine. Let's go." She hopped out of the truck and headed for the panels on the south side of the building.

"Rita!" he said in a loud murmur.

She spun around and said in a low growl, "What?"

He tossed her a tan cowboy hat. "Wear this. And tuck your hair inside."

"Good idea." She wound her braid into a bun on top of her head and tugged the straw hat low over her eyes.

"Rita."

"What?"

He lobbed her a pair of brown sunglasses. "Put those on."

"Thanks." In full disguise, she crept between trucks and trailers, making her way to the horse pens.

In the distance, a woman slouched near a pen, a wide-brimmed straw hat covering her face. Rita would recognize the orange, floral, button-up shirt anywhere. It was her mom's favorite. As Rita crept closer, it became clear that her mom was stroking the nose of a horse. A grulla. She gasped. *Opal.*

"Hey . . ."

She startled as a large hand clamped over her mouth. *Robert.* She knew his scent.

"Hazel's in the sale barn."

Their dad holding her hostage, no less.

She nodded, her muscles loosening when he released his grip. "My mom's over there. In the orange shirt and straw hat. See her?" She nodded to the horse pen. "See the grulla. That's Opal."

Robert blew out a low whistle. "No wonder you want to keep her."

"Text my sister to come outside."

He tapped his screen. "Done."

"See the guy in the tan coat?"

His gaze followed her finger. "Yeah."

"He's a good friend of the family. If he sees me, it's over. Distract him, and I'll go for my mom."

He nodded, approached the man, and struck up a conversation. With her head turned away from them, she rushed to her mom and faced Opal. The horse whickered. "Hey, girl," she said in a low tone.

"Rita?"

"Shh. . . . Be quiet, Mom."

She nodded. She'd done a horrible job trying to cover her bruises with makeup that was two shades too light. Red rimmed her puffy eyes. It took every bit of restraint for Rita not to hunt her father down and shoot him on the spot. She cleared her throat. "We need to get Hazel without Dad knowing. I have help. C'mon We need to get you guys out of here."

Her mom shook her head. "Hazel told me what's going on. I can't go with you, honey."

"Why not?"

"You know God doesn't allow divorce."

"Mom . . ." Rita clenched her teeth. "God hates abuse. Besides, divorce isn't a salvation issue. Let's get Haze and go."

"I have to trust the Lord to change your father's heart."

"Change his stony heart? Not a chance. You need to stop listening to your stinkin' preacher." She lowered her voice. "He's crazy. God doesn't expect us to stay in a place with men who will eventually kill us. Maybe if you leave, Dad'll wake up. Then you won't have to divorce him."

Rushed footsteps came up behind Rita.

"Dad's distracted," Hazel said. "Let's go."

Mom hugged Rita, then handed her a lead rope. "Call me when you can."

She clipped the lead onto Opal's halter, opened the pen, and regarded her sister. "Grab her and follow me." Hazel took their mother by the arm and went with Rita, who nodded to Robert as they strode past. Seconds later, he trotted ahead and opened the trailer door.

She released her horse, flung the lead rope over her back, and the mare stepped up into the stalls.

Robert shut and latched the door. "Ready?" He glanced at the women.

"Take Hazel with you." Mom hugged her youngest daughter and stepped backward.

Her dad's voice boomed through the parking lot. "Joan!"

"Go!" Mom turned and hurried toward the horse pens.

"Get in," Robert said to Rita and Hazel. "Now."

The sisters sprinted to the truck and jumped in as Robert fired up the engine. He shoved the rig into gear and stepped on the accelerator. "Hang on, ladies."

CHAPTER 41

The passenger's side mirror showed no sign of anyone tailing them.

Rita turned to face Hazel in the back seat. "Did you see Bowie at the sale?"

"Yeah, I did." Hazel peeled off her maroon Carhartt jacket and laid it on the seat. "Guess his mom got bucked off her horse and was knocked out cold. Sounds like he's been taking care of her." Puffy, purple traces scattered across her face were evidence of Bowie's thrashing.

Thank God she'd come with them.

"That's why he left in such a hurry," she told Robert. "No wonder."

"What are you talking about?" Hazel leaned forward and gripped the back of the front seat, her knuckles fading to white.

Rita brought her sister up to speed concerning the last few weeks, then added, "We have to find a way to get Mom away from Dad."

"I know," Hazel said. "She's too loyal. And Bowie's mom is blind as a one-eyed bat. She can't see how evil her son is. He's got her fooled. Just like the preacher's got Mom fooled."

"She's brainwashed if you ask me." Speaking of the misled, she asked, "How bad is Edna?"

"She landed in the hospital, unconscious, but was out a couple days later." Hazel slouched back. "How long until we get to Redmond?"

"About four hours," Robert said. "We can only stop once and for only a few minutes. Or I'll miss my ride."

Rita motioned to the travel cooler. "Take what you want."

"About what time do you think you'll ride?"

He shook his head. "I'll be lucky to get there, find my draw, and get on."

"Your draw?" Hazel scrounged in the cooler and closed the lid.

"The bronc he'll be riding." Rita smiled at him, her gaze lingering on his scruffy whiskers and intense look.

"Oh, yeah. Duh."

Hazel had never been interested in the rodeo. She loved music, but Dean never would allow her to study an instrument. Their father had forced her sister into the saddle at an early age and kept her there. Ranching was Rita's passion, not Hazel's. Her interest lay in the fiddle. She played around with a friend's from time to time and even sounded pretty good.

Hazel's gaze darted from the cowboy to her sister and back again. "What's going on between you two?"

"Nothing." Rita turned her head toward the window. She knew it was a lie. Minus his rodeo addiction, Robert was the kind of guy she could see herself with someday. They both had a deep-seated passion for ranching and horses and faith, though his trust in their Creator was a lot stronger than hers at the moment.

Redmond, Oregon

Robert drove through the security checkpoint of the Deschutes County Fairgrounds and Expo Center, parked the pickup behind the Juniper Arena, and jumped out. "I'll catch up with you guys later." He grabbed his bronc saddle and gear bag out of the truck's bed and disappeared through the jumbled shadows and contestant vehicles.

Surrounded by darkness, Rita sighed. "Guess I better check on Opal."

Hazel leaned forward. "What are you going to do with her? Do you even have hay?"

"I don't. I'll see if I can buy some off a barrel racer or something." Rita grabbed the lead rope and opened the door, the pungent odor of juniper making her gag. She slid out of the truck and stretched her back and legs. Night noises caused her to shiver.

Hazel joined her, and they went to the back of the trailer. The mare had yet to make a peep. Rita unlatched the door and opened it wide.

"Got light switches here," Hazel said from the side.

An interior light illuminated the stalls, and the horse gave a soft whicker. Rita crouched under the butt strap and climbed in, her hand brushing Opal's topline as she stepped to her head. After taking a moment to rub the horse's forehead, she clipped on the lead rope.

"Want me to unhook the butt strap?" Hazel peered inside.

"That'd be great." But before Hazel could unlatch the strap, the mare plowed backward and ran into it. She slapped her on the rump, and the mare jolted forward.

Groaning, Rita elbowed the horse. "Get off my toes." Opal backed up a step, again bumping into the butt strap, but this time Rita remained to the side. The grulla kept her sharp hooves to herself.

"Whoa, girl. C'mon now." The pain in her toes spiked, but she couldn't blame her horse. She had to be tired and hungry. She backed the mare out of the trailer and into the light shining from the spot lamp. Head high, Opal glanced around and whinnied. A few horses returned her call.

"Hey, look. A stud stall." Hazel jumped inside, strode to the front, and opened the aluminum divider.

Her mournful groan resounded from the other side of the trailer wall as Rita tied the mare to a D ring metal tie attached to the outside of the horse trailer. She joined her sister in the stud stall and slumped her shoulders. "At least there's a bucket."

"And a portable horse corral. It must be battery operated."

"With our luck there's no juice."

Rita grabbed the black rubber bucket and watered the mare. Hazel disappeared and came back with an armful of hay. "Where'd you get it from?"

"In the barn," Hazel answered.

"You can't take someone else's hay."

"I left five bucks."

"Good grief, Hazel. It's still not okay."

"Chill out. We're desperate."

She had a point. And they were all tired and frazzled.

They set up the portable corral around the back of the trailer so Opal could find shelter inside the stalls. They closed the stud stall divider and left the others open.

Once the horse was settled for the night, Hazel said, "It's kinda creepy way out here. Let's go watch your boyfriend."

"He's not my boyfriend." Rita limped inside the living quarters, treated her toes with arnica, and took the bench seat facing the door. "And no, I'm tired."

"He seems way nicer than your scumbag of a fiancé. And I see the way you look at each other. I'm not blind."

"Ex-fiancé."

"Whatever." Hazel plopped down across from Rita and looked around. "I can't just sit around in this tiny space. I'll go nuts."

"I get it. But I don't want to take the chance of exposing us walking from here to the arena. If Bowie was able to find us in Coeur d'Alene, he can easily track us here." She fingered her necklace. "Besides. My toes are killing me. Opal got me good."

"You're right. He's like a stinking bloodhound. How do you think he found you?"

"The only thing that makes sense is his cousin, Chief Denton, is tracking my cell phone and credit card."

"You think he's a dirty cop?"

"I'm not sure. They do have the same blood."

"Being family doesn't make him crooked."

"Like I said. It's the only thing that makes sense. And if they don't have anything on me"—*except the murder*—"then, yeah, it makes him crooked for tracking me with no probable cause of anything. It's against my civil rights." *Shoot.* Did Chief Denton know about Hawkeye? A shiver snaked up her back and tingled across her neck.

"Have you used your cell or credit card since we left?"

"No. Wait. I turned it on to show Robert photos of you guys." *Stupid move.*

"Why'd you turn it on?"

"So he'd know what you guys looked like. Do you know how hard it was for me to talk him into going to Hermiston?"

"Well, looks like your paranoia is justified."

Rita shot her a scowl. "Robert should be up soon."

"So, tell me about him." Hazel rested her elbows on the tabletop. "Is he as nice as he seems? Or like Bowie, is it a front?"

"It's not a front. And he's nothing like Bowie. From the beginning, Bowie had a short fuse. And was super jealous. Robert, for the most part, is patient and gentle. His only fault is he's super hooked on rodeo."

"Yeah. I can tell." She paused. "I'm glad you called off your engagement. I wish he'd give up and leave us alone. How are you going to get rid of him?"

"I have no idea." For a short moment, she took in Hazel's blackened and bloodshot eyes and cracked lips. *How would it feel to kill two men?* There was the gun in the glove box.

"You'll find love again, Sister. True love. Good men are out there. You just have to keep looking. Or maybe he's right in front of your face."

"I'm no princess and life ain't no fairy tale."

"Oh, c'mon. You have to believe not all men are lyin'-cheatin'-beatin' scumbags."

Rita turned sideways, her back against the wall, and drew her knees into a hug. "Too much has happened. I'm not sure I can trust anyone." Though she desperately wanted to trust Robert.

"Yeah, but Robert seems so nice. Not every man would go out of his way in hot pursuit of his flashy dreams to rescue a horse and a sister for a pretty lady."

Rita grunted. "Even Bowie was nice. He went out of his way to do things for me. At least at first."

"Please tell me you don't still have feelings for the slimeball."

"I don't. He did a good job of beating them right out of me."

"You can't run from love forever. There's a good man out there for you. For us both. I know there is."

Rita believed her sister meant every word, but she wasn't so sure there was truth to any of it. And she didn't want to quash Haze's delusional dreams, so she let it go. Too many of her sister's desires had been spoiled. She wanted Hazel to have hope—the kind of hope that had long ago faded for Rita.

"So, can we go to the rodeo? Maybe Robert hasn't ridden yet."

Rita checked her wallet. "I only have a ten."

"Don't worry, I have cash." Hazel pulled a wad of twenties from her coat pocket and slapped them on the table. She pulled extra bills from both front pockets, then took off her boots and added handfuls to the pile. Most of them were hundreds.

"Good Lord, Haze. Where'd you get all of this from? Please tell me you didn't rob a bank on the way to the stockyard."

"Dad's secret stash." She waggled her eyebrows.

"He has a secret stash?"

"*Had* being the key word. I followed him one night a few years ago. He was wasted and didn't know I was awake. Last night I checked to see if he was still using it."

"How much did you take?"

"All of it." Hazel's eyes sparkled.

Rita groaned. "We can't spend it."

"Why not? What has Dad ever done for us?"

"Because it's not ours. Plus, we'll have to pay him back."

"I ain't paying him back. No way." Hazel gave her a sassy grin. "Think of it as severance pay. We've earned it."

"Haze—"

"Look. It's all we got."

"I suppose you're right. I'll keep track of what we spend and pay him back."

Hazel rolled her eyes. "Always the honest one."

Rita grunted. *If she only knew.*

CHAPTER 42

The sisters wound their way through the circular grounds to the entrance gate of the First Interstate Bank Center, rodeo tickets in hand. Rita felt grungy. She brushed horse hair from her coat and jeans. Hazel didn't have clean clothing, and Rita didn't have much to spare.

Inside, the girls went upstairs and strode past a line of vendors, then stopped by a section of railing overlooking the arena. The open space made Rita feel extra vulnerable. Below them stood several empty, single, green seats but not two together. There was no way they were splitting up. "How about over there? It's not the best but will do." She motioned to an area close to the edge of the chutes.

"Nothing like feeling exposed." Hazel scanned the arena, her eyes locking on the lit jumbotron.

"I know, right? Hopefully, this will be a good distraction and not make either of us more freaked out than we already are."

They found their seats and settled in.

Hazel squinted at the cowboys behind the chutes.

The final team roping pair of the night had missed their calf and the announcer asked for applause, then announced the next event, "Saddle bronc riding."

Rita checked out the crowd then stiffened when a bronc reared up and crashed his hooves against a metal panel. "I'm not sure this is relaxing." She leaned forward, her attention landing on a man wearing a green jacket, his hands in the coat pockets, and a white Wildhorse Resort and Casino logoed cap. *No way. Is . . . ?*

Acid burned her throat, and she swallowed. It couldn't be. She ducked her chin, her hand over her face, wishing she had on Robert's straw cowboy hat, the one he'd tossed to her in Hermiston. "Oh, crap. It *is* him."

"Who, Bowie?"

"No. Gary."

"Gary who?"

"Fullmoon. You know, Bowie's freaky sidekick."

Hazel squinted and leaned forward. "It looks like him but a taller version. I don't think it's Gary."

"Go check him out."

Hazel's eyes grew round. "Why me?"

"Because—"

"He knows me, too, remember?"

Rita wrung her hands and snuck a peek. The man turned around. He seemed to sport a bigger belly than Gary. But she wasn't sure. "You sure it's not him?"

"Why? Do you think Bowie saw you at the stockyard and followed you?"

"Or had me followed." Rita sat back as the announcer talked about the bronc rider in chute number one. "I'll go check him out."

"Bad idea, Sis."

"It's not like he's going to do anything in a crowd."

"You plan on asking him, 'Hey, man, enjoying the rodeo?' At least get us a couple of sodas." Hazel pulled out a twenty and held it up.

Rita took the money. "Be right back." But by the time she had climbed up to the concourse, Wildhorse was gone. She made her way to a concession stand and stood in line, her smashed toes aching. Anyone who slightly resembled Gary or Bowie made her jumpy. When it was her turn, she gave her order and paid with her dad's cash.

Guilt tugged at her over the transaction.

She grabbed the cold drinks, moved out of the way, and took a sip of the lemon-flavored soda. After powering up her cell, she emailed herself a note for the overpriced expense. *Oh crap. Why did I turn on my phone?* Then again it didn't matter if Bowie already knew where she was. Notifications for several missed calls and texts popped up on the screen. For a moment, her finger hovered over the On icon, wanting to know if any of them were from her mother. But she pressed the Power Off button and rushed back to her seat.

"Here." She handed Hazel her drink.

"Is it him?"

"He was gone by the time I got down the stairs."

"Then what's wrong?"

"I emailed myself the expense of the pop."

"You turned your phone on?"

"What's the problem if he's tied to Bowie?" Rita sipped the soda and choked on the sugary drink.

"What if he wasn't? They'll know we're here for sure."

"I know." She mentally chided herself for turning on her cell.

The announcer called out, "Robert Elliot, a cowboy all the way from the Colville Reservation in Eastern Washington. This cowboy—"

"Think he'll stay on?" Hazel asked.

"Probably. He's pretty good."

Rita's cell vibrated, and she swiped the screen. Hadn't she turned it off? *Shoot.* She'd forgotten to tap the confirmation icon. A text came through from an unrecognized number.

How's the rodeo?

Rita gasped.

"What's wrong?"

Should she tell Hazel? Stay? Leave? "I . . . uh—"

"He's up." Hazel elbowed Rita.

She lifted her eyes just as Robert shot out of the gate. After a few good jumps and the buzzer sounded, Robert was flung to the ground, his cowboy hat sailing into the air. The thud of his shoulder slamming the dirt made her wince.

"Oh no!" Hazel's gaze darted from Robert to Rita. "Do you think he's hurt?"

He sprang to his feet before she could answer. The crowd cheered at the announcer's suggestion to give Robert applause after getting bucked off before the eight seconds was up. But the clapping, foot stomping, and cheers added to Rita's already jittery nerves.

Hazel touched her arm. "You okay?"

"I'm not feeling well. I think I'm just tired."

"You want to go back to the trailer?"

And be away from the crowd? "No. I'm fine." She took another sip, swallowing hard.

Hazel scrunched her nose. "Let's get out of here."

"No. We need to stay put." She needed to snag Robert's attention so he could escort them back because she'd left her Leatherman in her pack.

Which left them as easy targets.

After the last bull tossed his rider, the crowd began to disperse. The girls trudged closer to the chutes, and Rita squinted. "I don't see him. Do you?"

Hazel shook her head. "Think he went back to the trailer?"

"Or he's checking out the horse pens."

"Let's try to get back there."

As Rita weaved through the crowd, she noticed a man who looked to be in his forties with a mustache, black cowboy hat, and navy-blue jacket following them. For a brief moment, they made eye contact, and she shuddered and sped up, elbowing those trying to cut in front of her. When she came to a side exit, she turned around.

Oh no. Where was Hazel?

She stood on her tiptoes on her uninjured foot, studying every bobbing head. "Hazel?" Her sister was nowhere, and neither was the guy following them. She backtracked but didn't find her. As the center cleared, her throat clogged.

The ladies' bathrooms stood vacant. The concession stands were closed. *Oh, God. Where is she?* Her breathing ramped up as Rita scrambled downstairs to the lobby and burst through the exit door, weaved through the crowd, ran past the Juniper Arena and to Robert's trailer. Light shone through the shade-drawn window. Breathless, she yanked the door open and rushed inside.

Hazel's scream filtered through the curtain of fog in Rita's mind.

"You scared me half to death!" Hazel pressed a hand to her chest.

Rita slammed the door, moisture blurring her eyes. "Where were you?" And where was Robert when she needed him?

CHAPTER 43

W here had Rita gone?
He'd seen them peering over the railing. And instead
of staying put, they disappeared. Shrugging into his new
Columbia River Circuit Finals jacket, he slung his saddle
over his shoulder, picked up his gear bag, and made his way
back to where he'd last seen the sisters.

No sign of them. They weren't anywhere in the bare event
center. *Awesome.* He made his way back to the trailer.

Darn the one remarkable distraction who had cost him
the go-round. No. He couldn't blame her. It wasn't her fault
for being so beautiful. Vulnerable. Giving him an intense
need to protect her. And her sister. He had to figure out
a way to release the burden to God and not worry about
winning or losing. This was his biggest struggle because it
was his greatest dream.

Angry voices filtered through the thin walls as he
approached the trailer. He stowed his gear in the back seat of
his truck, took a deep breath, and went inside.

Rita stood by the kitchen sink, her face red and sweaty.
Hazel leaned against the fridge, a smug look riding her face.

"What's going on in here?" he asked. "Good Lord, I can
hear you all the way across the parking lot. And how did you
get in here?"

Hazel shrugged. "It was unlocked."

What? He was sure he'd locked it. Either way, with these
two, he'd have to hide a key.

Rita lifted her chin to Hazel. "She took off after the rodeo—"

"Whatever. You've been uptight ever since you got a text. I saw the scared look on your face when you glanced at your phone. It had to be a message from Bowie."

"Shut up, Haze." Rita pinned a steely glare on her.

"Stop it, you guys," Robert said, then regarded Rita. "What text?"

She waved him off. "It was a wrong number."

Face twisted, Hazel said, "I doubt—"

"Wrong numbers don't usually rattle a person this bad." Robert lifted his brows.

Yep. She was lying. Her tells were pretty obvious—biting her bottom lip, sideways glances, pink cheeks.

"I'm not rattled."

Hazel snorted. "Whatever. You've been paranoid. Especially since you—"

"I said shut up." Rita took a step toward Hazel when a knock sounded on the door. She froze and looked at Robert with wide eyes.

He put his hand out and opened the door to a security guard who looked like a stockier version of John Legend. In his hand was a long, black flashlight.

The guard smiled and rested a foot on the step. "How's it going? You have a good night?" His eyes fell to Robert's CRCF jacket.

"Tonight was a little rough, but there's always tomorrow."

"I hear ya there." He let out a deep chuckle. "Listen, man," the guard said, his tone kind, thoughtful, "sorry to have to say, but you need to keep your horse in a stall. They should have told you when you checked in."

The guard backed out of Robert's way as he came down the step and shut the door. "No problem. We picked up this mare at the last minute. By the time we got here, I had to grab my gear and saddle up, if you know what I mean."

"Hey, I understand."

"Are there any empty stalls?"

"I believe one or two." He shined his flashlight toward a white trailer near the open-air horse barn situated opposite the arena on the circular grounds. "A nice lady named Lucy will help you out in the office."

Robert shook the man's hand. "I appreciate it. I'll get her moved right away." He strode to the trailer near the barn and knocked on the door. A spunky, middle-aged woman with pink glasses and curly, brown bottle-dyed hair greeted him.

"Good evening, ma'am." He tipped his hat. "I need a stall if you have any available."

"Come on in." Lucy shuffled to her desk and clicked on her computer screen. "I sure do, sugar. I've got two open. They come with one bale of shavings for fifteen dollars a night. If you need more, each bale is five bucks extra. How many would you like?" She lifted her gaze and smiled.

"Bales for two nights, please." Robert pulled three twenties from his pocket. "And do you happen to have extra hay?" He handed her two.

"No hay. But there's a Coastal Farm & Ranch a short hop from here on Highway 97. They're usually well stocked. If you don't like that one, there's a couple on up the road." She took his forty dollars and made change. "You'll be in barn five and stall number twenty-six."

Robert thanked her and left. It wasn't the ideal place to put Opal, but at least there'd be ample lighting to see the barn from the horse trailer. Hopefully, it would ease Rita's tendency to worry.

She met him at the electric fence's wire gate. "What'd he want?"

"We have to move your horse to a stall."

She frowned, pulled bills from her jeans pocket, and flipped them open. Mostly ones peeked through her fingers. "What do I owe you?"

"I got it." He held up a hand.

"I'm not looking for a free ride."

No, but she was a woman on the run and needed help. "We can square up later." He went to the other side of the trailer and flicked on the spot lamp.

Rita clutched his arm, and he faced her. "No, now." Her eyes pleaded with him. "Please."

"It's fifteen a night."

She held out five ones and a ten. "I have more in my wallet."

"Rita," he said, his voice soft. "It's okay. You can take care of it later. Or not at all. I'm here to help you. No strings attached. Besides, I still owe you for helping out on the ranch, remember?"

She dropped her chin.

Robert took a finger and lifted it and waited for her to look at him. "It's all good. Save your money. You might need it later."

She nodded, her speckled, tawny eyes searching his, an ache, a hope, a longing in them so tender it nearly broke his heart.

He held her shoulders. "I'm not sure what the text was about. But trust me, I'll do whatever it takes to keep you from harm." When she looked away, water glistening in her eyes, he pulled her to him, and she went willingly. He hoped this was how she felt about him, not a reaction from her fear. His fingers slid down her silky braid.

She melted into him, her arms curving around his waist. "I was so scared when I couldn't find Hazel. Someone was following us. And then she disappeared. We're not safe, Bobby. We're not safe."

Why did she have to feel so natural in his arms? "Who—"

"What's up with you two?" Hazel glared at them.

"Nothing." Rita stepped away.

"She was scared when you took off," Robert said.

"I didn't *take off*. We got separated. I figured coming back here was where she'd look for me."

Robert stepped closer and spoke to Rita. "How much does she know about your past?"

"Most everything."

"But not everything?" When she shook her head, he said, "She's a grown woman. Don't you think she can handle the truth? At least she'll get why you're so freaked out."

"There's no way I'm telling her about the . . ." Rita glanced at Hazel.

"Why not?"

"I'm standing right here, guys? Tell me what?"

"Let's get your horse settled," Robert said. "Then we'll talk."

"Or not." Rita untied the lead rope from the D ring while Robert unhooked the gate. "We need to move Opal to a stall. Will you grab her bucket and hay?"

"Not until you tell me what's going on." Hazel set her hands on her hips.

"I will. Let's get her moved first, okay?" Rita clipped the lead to the mare's halter and led her out.

"You found hay?" Robert unlatched the gate to the wired fence.

Rita shot Hazel an interrogative look. "Enough for the night."

"Lucy said there's a ranch store close by to get hay."

"Who's Lucy?" The sisters said in unison.

"The lady who oversees the horse barn." Robert dumped the bucket and followed behind.

He hadn't gone looking for love, that was for sure, but she made something stir deep inside. Something he was willing to fight for.

CHAPTER 44

Rita wrung her hands as she waited for some kind of reaction from Hazel after telling her about the rape.

They sat at the table in the trailer, and she took a swig of water, letting it roll around in her mouth before swallowing. Under the table, Robert's fingers tangled in hers. He squeezed, and she returned the pressure.

Hazel's eyes looked red rimmed. "Did you ever tell anyone? Go to the clinic? See a doctor?"

"No, I didn't. The only thing I was worried about was how to keep him away from me. I was way too scared to tell Dad."

"Did you at least tell Mom?"

"I was terrified to say anything. Too ashamed, really." She wasn't sure she'd ever be able to shed the dirty feeling. Not even with God's help. And she prayed no one would ever find out she had killed him.

"So, what do we do now?" Hazel peered at Robert. "Keep rodeoing like nothing happened?"

Robert angled his head. "What do you mean, like nothing happened?"

"He's been doing nothing but protecting me this entire time," Rita said. "He didn't have to drag me along. I'm sure he'd love to unload us and send us back to the ranch."

"Let's all settle down," Robert said. "I'm not sending either of you anywhere. This has been a lot for you to take in, Haze—"

"Ya think?"

Rita broke her hand away from Robert and slapped the table. "Watch your mouth—"

"Hey, c'mon now. We'll get through this, you guys,"—he lowered his voice—"if we all work together and watch each other's backs. I'll notify the police—"

"No cops!" the sisters said together.

"We've already talked about why." Rita fixed a threatening glare on Robert.

Hazel raised her brows. "What's the plan then, Marshal Earp?"

Robert narrowed his eyes. "For starters, don't ever call me that again. Then stick with the group." His expression softened. "Have you never heard the saying there's safety in numbers?"

"Like I said. We got separated."

"I have a companion pass. It will get one of you into the rodeo. You'll have to buy a second pass. I've got extra cash in my jockey box."

"We have money." Hazel eyed Rita as she spoke.

"It's not ours and you know it," Rita said.

Robert leaned back and tipped his face to the ceiling. He took in a breath and looked at Hazel. "Whose money is it?"

"It's severance pay from our dad." The corner of Hazel's lips tugged upward.

"In other words," he said, "you stole it."

Rita fingered her necklace. "What we don't use, we'll pay him back. I don't want to owe him a dime. But for now, it's all we've got." Would their father find the cash gone? Come after them? Be mad enough to call the cops? Put them in jail for aiding and abetting and ruin Robert's career?

Robert stared at Hazel for a long moment. "How much did you take?"

When she didn't answer, Rita said, "Sister, tell him."

"About a grand. Maybe more."

"Criminy." Rita groaned. "What if he discovers it's gone?"

"He won't."

"And what if he blames Mom? Then what? Huh?"

"I wasn't trying to make things worse for her. I was thinking of us." Hazel's chin quivered. "Besides, I thought I could talk her into coming with us."

Rita rubbed her forehead. "I know. I'm sorry."

"Let's get a good night's sleep," Robert said. "We can talk about this in the morning. Did you two have dinner?"

Rita shook her head.

"No wonder," he muttered.

Rita wished she had a pillow to throw at him but knew he was right. An empty stomach and hot nerves proved a noxious combination. She rose and fixed clam chowder while Robert grilled cheese sandwiches.

Hazel stirred her soup. "Where's everyone going to sleep?"

"Good question." Both she and Hazel couldn't fit on the table bed. They'd have to sleep in the loft and Robert on the table. She lifted her chin to find him with an amused look on his face.

"I have a blanket, and there's an open spot in the back," Robert said.

"The back of what?" Hazel craned her neck around Rita.

"The trailer. I'll clear the horse apples—"

"No way!" The corner of Hazel's upper lip curled.

Rita and Robert burst out laughing, and Rita motioned to the floor. "There's room down there."

Hazel's eyes shot darts at her sister.

"C'mon now, no one's sleeping on the floor." Robert jabbed a thumb behind him. "You ladies can sleep in the hayloft. I'll take the table."

Oh, how Rita loved his sense of humor. And his generosity. Here it was his accommodation, and they were taking over.

"About contestant perks. They have dinners before the rodeo starts. We can eat at the arena tomorrow night. Tonight was chicken-something. Tomorrow night's prime rib." He flashed the ladies his pearly whites and winked at Rita.

The gesture caused warmth to rise up her neck and spread throughout her bones. She desperately wanted to trust in love again.

CHAPTER 45

The scent of bacon, eggs, and coffee aroused Rita out of her slumber. She reached over and felt a hard lump beside her. It wasn't Hazel cooking in the kitchen. She rested on her elbows and found a shirtless Robert, working away in the kitchen, a towel over his shoulder.

Yeah, she could get used to having a man like him around. Both handy and sexy. Never had Bowie been so thoughtful or caring.

Robert looked up and gave her a saucy smile that about undid her.

She gave him a small wave of her fingers. Oh, yeah. She could definitely get used to this. She climbed out of the hayloft and passed by him on her way to the stud stall to change clothes, allowing her hand to brush his soft skin. When she entered the privacy of the cramped space, she closed her eyes and breathed in the residue of his spicy aftershave. Could he be the man for her?

In the cold stud stall, she quickly changed into jeans and a T-shirt, then slipped her boots on. Goosebumps formed on her arms as she shrugged into a sweater Mandie had loaned her. Coffee. She needed coffee. But first, the bathroom. She opened the door and found Hazel at the sink putting on mascara.

Her sister dipped a wand into its base and swirled it around. "Do you think Bowie's having us followed?"

"Who knows for sure? But don't you think it's creepy to see a guy who looks so much like Gary Fullmoon? Then there's the dude wearing the blue coat and black cowboy hat. He was definitely trailing us."

"I didn't see him. You sure?"

"Oh, yeah. He made sure I saw him." Certainly her imagination wasn't overreacting.

Hazel shook her head. "I kinda want to hang out here today. I don't even have clean clothes. I packed a bag. But left it at the cabin. Dad would have known something was up."

"I agree. But we're too isolated out here. It'd be safer in public. And we can get you clothes this morning when we get hay."

"Okay. I see your point. And yeah, new clothes would be nice."

Hazel nodded and finished putting on her makeup, then followed her sister to the kitchenette.

"Smells good in here," Rita said. She felt like she might be able to eat. "Thanks for cooking." His handsome smile made her melt inside. She kept her distance, not wanting temptation to suck her into something she'd regret.

"No problem. I need to keep busy. There's a lot at stake today."

"We'll stay out of your way so you can focus." The girls slid into the seats. Wow. He'd even set the table. Rita scooted over, leaving space for Robert.

Hazel perked a brow, a hint of a smile on her face. Rita ignored her.

"Don't worry about it. I'll unhook, and we can go get hay and whatever else you ladies might need." Robert caught Rita's gaze as he served them breakfast. After filling their cups with coffee, he motioned to the space next to Rita. "Mind if I sit by you?"

"Not at all." She patted the cushion, ignoring her sister's sassy look, and put the hot cup to her lips. She was about to offer grace and pray for his ride when Hazel opened her big mouth.

"So, are you going to tell him about those guys, or am I?" Hazel stabbed her fork into the scrambled eggs.

"What guys?" Robert asked, his tone anything but happy.

When Rita choked on her coffee, hot liquid spilled onto her hands. She skewered Hazel with a steely glare.

Robert slid out of his seat and darted to the kitchen, yanking paper towels from the holder. He handed her a wad. "You all right?"

"Yeah. Thanks." She sopped up the spilled coffee, tossed the towels into the garbage, and settled back at the table.

Robert slid back onto the padded bench, concern on his face. "What guys?"

"We may have been followed last night," Rita said.

"Where? Out here?"

"No, in the arena." Rita picked up her fork and herded her eggs around the plate.

"Why do you think you were followed?"

"And who do you think sent the text?" Hazel tipped her head.

Why did her sister have to keep opening her big mouth? She didn't have the answers. And because Bowie had threatened to kill Hazel, she wasn't about to involve the cops—other than Chuck.

Rita sank against the padded backrest. "There were two of them. One in a green jacket wearing a Wildhorse Casino cap. The other guy wore a black cowboy hat and a blue jacket. And I don't have a clue who sent the text. I didn't recognize the number."

"You think Bowie knows we're here?" Robert asked.

"Who else could it be? Our mom?" She recoiled at her sarcasm. "Sorry. I just . . ."

"You're sure they're from your rez?"

"Wildhorse is the spitting image of Bowie's buddy, Gary Fullmoon. And I have no idea who the guy in the blue jacket is."

"Did either one of them approach you?"

"Well . . ." Rita stroked the feather on her necklace with her thumb and forefinger. "No. But they were watching us."

"Which makes you think they're tailing you?"

"Well, yeah. The guy in the blue coat made sure I saw him. Besides, it's a gut feeling." By the look on his face, she assumed he thought she was overreacting. It was obvious he didn't have a clue what she'd gone through, probably never would, and she didn't know how to get him to understand her paranoia. But she didn't care because she wasn't taking any chances. Not with Hazel in the mix.

"Her gut's never wrong," Hazel said. "Trust me."

Robert drummed the table, then looked at Rita. "Okay. Keep your cell phone on and—"

"You want me to keep it on?"

"Yeah. You seem sure your ex knows you're here, so what's the problem?"

"I guess there isn't one." She wasn't a hundred percent certain—but still. She turned to Hazel. "Did you bring yours?"

"I can't find it. I must have left it in Dad's pickup."

"Stick with your sister then," Robert said.

"But what if we get separated again?"

"We won't." Rita would make sure of it.

"But what if we do?"

"Then stay near the entrance," Robert said. "It's well lit and security sometimes hangs out there." He found a slip of paper and a pen, jotted down his cell number, and gave it to Rita. "Just in case one of you needs it."

"Can't we pray or something?" Hazel said to Rita. "You used to pray all the time with me when we were little. When Daddy . . ." She glanced down, a flush racing up her face.

"Yes. I'd love to." Rita led them in a short prayer, asking Creator to protect all of them. And it helped release the tension in her shoulders.

"Tonight," Robert said, "we'll eat in the hospitality room. You two can hang out there until the rodeo starts. Make sure you use the restroom before you take your seats. If you want snacks, get them first. Then stay put until I come for you."

"But we don't use the same entrance gate," Rita said.

"Good point." Robert scrubbed his chin. "I'll escort you to the ticket office. I need to use the northwest corner entrance and check in. But I can meet you inside."

"Okay." Hazel's eyes grew round. "But what if Bowie is here?"

Rita reached across the table and held her hands. "As long as we stay in a crowd, they aren't going to do anything."

"I agree with Rita," Robert said. "At this point, all Bowie seems to be doing is keeping tabs on her. He might just be playing with her with no intent for harm."

Rita nodded, trying to keep Hazel calm. But deep in her bones, she knew if Bowie caught up to her, she'd wind up dead. Hazel too.

Robert draped an arm around Rita and pulled her close. "Remember, Chuck's working from his end. We need to trust him." He pressed the side of her head to his lips for a quick kiss. "Time to cowgirl up, ladies."

Robert had a way of giving her strength and courage when she needed it most. She sank into him for a second and thanked God. Wanting Hazel to relax a little, she said, "It means to suck it up and get it done."

She and Robert laughed.

"Duh." Hazel rolled her eyes, but she, too, let out a soft chuckle.

"Now," he slid out of the seat, "let's go find some hay."

"And new clothes." Hazel flashed a few hundreds. "It's on Daddy."

CHAPTER 46

Rita swiped peppermint-scented balm over her lips and shoved the stick into her front pocket. Robert was right. Time to cowgirl up and stop letting fear rule her life.

Between the indigo and amber sky settling over the high desert plains, new clothes for Hazel, and fresh hay for her horse, a thin—kind of sheer—blanket of tranquility enveloped her.

Robert grabbed his saddle and gear bag out of the pickup and locked it. He held out the keys to her but did not release them.

"Hang on a minute." He unlocked his truck, found a flashlight, and shined the beam on a ledge behind the rear tire. He separated and held up a single key with the top encased in black plastic. "This one's for the trailer. I'll hide it back here. Hopefully, you won't need to come back but just in case." He rested the key on the shelf, clicked off the flashlight, and handed it to her. "Okay, you guys ready?"

Was Rita ready? No. Was she willing? Oh, yes. *Goodbye, fear. Hello, faith. Ready or not.*

Then why did she feel so naked without her buckaroo hat? It'd make a great shield. Then again, it'd be the perfect target. As they strode through the grounds, she kept an eye out for Bowie Dark Cloud's hand-picked ferrets.

Dusk-to-dawn pole lights flickered to life as they made their way to the First Interstate Bank Center. While Hazel bought her ticket, Robert pulled out his Professional Rodeo

Cowboy Association's companion pass from his wallet and handed it to her. "Use this."

Rita's senses flicked to high alert when Hazel went to buy a ticket. So far, she hadn't recognized anyone in the crowd, nor did she see the guy who resembled Gary Fullmoon or Blue Coat.

"I'm ready." Hazel waved her ticket in the air as she joined them. Rubbing her arm, she glanced around. "You see Bowie's lowlifes anywhere?"

"No," Rita said, trying to sound confident. "Let's go."

"I'll meet you guys inside." Robert rubbed her shoulders.

She nodded, giving him a hint of a smile, and stepped through a glass door to warm air and the earthy scent of livestock. As she inhaled the familiar aroma, it brought her back to the family's Umatilla ranch. Back to cleaning stalls and doctoring animals. To the sadness in her mother's eyes. Her father's harsh words. The sting from Bowie's hands.

She stuffed the urge to panic down her throat and took in a few deep breaths. *Faith over fear.*

"Where are we supposed to meet him?" Hazel scanned the lobby. She shed her jacket and hung it over her arm.

"I think up there." Rita headed for the stairs. A choking sensation gripped her throat as she climbed the concrete steps. With each click of her boots, the room closed in on her. The smell of grease and popcorn made her want to throw up. *Where could he be?* She picked up the pace.

"Wait for me." Hazel tugged on the back of her jacket. "We're supposed to stay together, remember?"

But Rita couldn't wait. Panic pressing in on her, she raced up the remaining steps, burst onto the second level, and turned left, nearly crashing into a vendor table covered with precious, Western art. "Oh, I'm so sorry. Didn't mean to—"

"It's all good. Are you all right?" A woman wearing a tan, Nevada-styled hat with a flat brim and concern in her eyes said as she straightened a set of painted coasters.

"Yes. I am." *No, I'm not. Get it together.* Rita smoothed the black tablecloth, then twirled around to voices—laughing, talking, toddlers having meltdowns—and bumped into Hazel. Where could she go to catch her breath? Jewelry, cowboy hats, jeans, rodeo shirts, art. You name it, they had it.

"You having a panic attack?" Hazel asked.

"Get me out of here."

Hazel looped her arm around Rita's and took her to a quiet space between vendor booths.

"Faith over fear. Faith over fear. Lord, help me," Rita whispered, concentrating on her breathing. She dragged in a deep breath through her nose and pushed it out through her mouth. She repeated the process a few times. "I'm not sure what came over me."

"You've been through a lot, Sister." Hazel rubbed Rita's back.

"We both have." Merchandise in nearby booths caught her eye. She nodded to them. "Let's check these out while we wait. Who knows, maybe we can find a disguise or two." They went two vendors down and stopped at a table filled with ProRodeo gear.

Rita selected a cap and pulled out her wallet. It wasn't her cowboy hat, but it would do the job. "You want one?"

"Yeah. And a T-shirt. It will help us blend in." Hazel picked out a blue, scoop-neck, long-sleeve shirt.

Rita paid for their items, forgetting about keeping track after Hazel had insisted on splitting up their dad's cash that morning, and tugged the hat's bill over her eyes. "We better go back to the top of the stairs. Robert should be there any minute." They weaved through the thickening crowd.

"Where's he coming from?"

"I'm not sure." Several men wore black cowboy hats similar to Robert's. But so far none had his confident swagger. She turned around to see Robert striding toward them, the corner of his lips turned down. They locked eyes. *Uh-oh.* His held fire in them. Hot, searing heat.

Robert took her arm and led her to the wall. "We were supposed to meet downstairs. Why'd we make a plan if you're not going to stick to it?" The vein on his neck protruded as he handed Hazel a rodeo program.

She took the booklet and hugged it as though it were a security blanket.

Shoot. They should've stayed in the lobby. Rita hadn't meant to scare him. "I'm sorry. Guess I got confused."

"She had a panic attack." Hazel gave her a look of apology. "Do you need to go back to the trailer?"

"No. I'm fine. It was a mild one. I don't know what came over me. But I'm good." She'd fight for her renewed faith to stomp out her fear. *I know you killed Talon Hawkeye.* The thought made Rita shudder and pray for strength.

"Let's go." Robert led them to the hospitality room where they filled their plates with a prime rib dinner.

A man offered her a glass of champagne, but she shook her head. "No thank you." Her nerves sizzling, the offer tempting her. Instead, she found a soda and waited for the other two. She caught a whiff of the familiar cedarwood and sage tones of a pungent cologne.

"Ah, there's Miss Beautiful." Payton Sundown approached her from a crowd of cowboys with women dressed for a cover shot hanging off their arms. He was alone, wearing a broad smile. His gaze swept Hazel.

Rita narrowed her eyes. "This is my sister. She's off-limits."

Hazel's face blanched, and she looked away.

Payton tipped his hat. "I see beauty runs in the family. Hopefully cynicism doesn't."

Rita clenched her teeth. "Let's find a seat, Haze." And to Payton, she said, "Catch ya later." She snorted. Preferably not. Then she herded Hazel toward a few empty chairs.

"Apparently I'm not invited to your table." Payton's voice rang above the others.

Ignoring his remark, she settled into her seat. After Hazel and Robert took theirs, the one lone empty spot by Rita made her cringe. *Don't let him see it.* At least Hazel sat between Robert and another woman. "Sorry to have embarrassed you, Haze. But he's a creep." She hacked into her meat, took a bite, and tried to savor the flavor.

Robert glanced up. "He's not so bad."

Rita frowned at him. "He's a womanizer."

"He's harmless—"

"No man is harmless." Rita severed another piece of meat. Stabbed it.

Robert clinked his fork on his plate. "No one?"

"Maybe not you. Jury's still out." She tossed him a rueful smile. But still, most of the men she knew seemed to turn their scorpion-like tails and sting women with their poisonous tips. She went to take another bite when Payton plopped down beside her. She turned to Robert, her face burning. He lifted his shoulder.

"Who'd you draw?" Payton asked Robert.

Robert seemed to hesitate. "Crazy Lady."

Rita shook her head and speared a buttery asparagus spear.

"You?"

He peered at Rita and gave her a sassy smile. "Hot Betty."

The corners of Robert's mouth inched up.

She glared at him and took a swig of soda. Yeah, she should have taken the glass of champagne, then introduced them both to Crazy Hot Rita.

Hazel finished her meal before Rita and seemed fidgety. "Let's go check out the vendors." She nudged Robert with her elbow. "We have time, don't we?"

He checked his phone. "Yeah, you have enough time to check out a few before the rodeo starts." He caught Rita's gaze and leaned close. "You think it's wise though?" he whispered.

"It's better than sitting here with him." She gave a slight nod toward Payton. "And stewing over whether Bowie's here or not."

"You got your phone?"

She checked the inside pocket of her coat. "It's right here."

"Call me if you need anything."

"Will do." She craned her neck around Robert and said to Hazel, "You ready?"

"Yep. Sure am." Hazel stood and grabbed her jacket off the back of the chair.

"You ladies have fun, now." Payton winked at Hazel.

Robert squeezed Rita's hand under the table and leaned close. "Stay alert. I'll be here if you need me." His lips brushed her ear.

Tingles pricked her neck. If only she wasn't so irritated.

She followed Hazel to a booth with racks loaded with Western designer jeans. They picked through them, Rita trying to remain aware of her surroundings.

Hazel picked out a couple of pairs. "What do you think? I don't like the ones I'm wearing. They're not real comfortable."

"Yeah, they're cute." Rita fingered a pair with pearls, lace, and rhinestones detailed on the back pockets. "Not real practical though."

"Oh, those would look good on you."

"Not sure I care about looks. To me, they're tools of the trade."

Hazel rolled her eyes. "You're too stuffy."

Was she? Rita fingered the thick fabric. It was thicker than she normally wore. "You think these would last longer than mine?"

"Oh, yeah. For sure. All embroidered jeans last longer." Hazel snatched the pants out of Rita's hands. "I'll buy them for you. You never get anything nice for yourself. Besides, no one'll be looking for a woman in fancy jeans and a rodeo cap."

"No. They're too expensive." Rita tugged at them, but Hazel held firm. Bowie would've accused her of trying to flirt with guys wearing bejeweled pants. The last time she wore a cute summer dress to lunch, he'd blown a fuse.

"Come on. We're headed to the Indian National Finals. In *Vegas*. You can't go looking like a redneck."

"What's wrong with the way I dress?" *Was it so bad?*

"Really, Lou?"

Rita rolled her eyes at the pet name. It'd been a long time since Hazel had referred to her as Louise McCloud from the hit series *Young Riders*. Heck, Lou was practical. Gutsy. And goodness, she wore her plain look like nobody's business.

Then again, the decorative back pockets caught her eye.

"I bet *Robert* would find them sexy."

"Hush, Hazel." But would he like them? When held just right, the rhinestones sparkled in the light. "I suppose it won't hurt this one time."

"Dad owes us for all the crap he's put us through." Hazel got in line.

Maybe she should use her credit card.

Hazel marched back over to Rita, lifted her brows. "I know what you're thinking. Don't. He stole our childhood. He was about to sell your horse. Don't feel sorry for him.

He's not worth it. He should have protected you from Bowie. And . . . and—"

"He didn't know."

"What do you mean he doesn't know? I figured—"

"I told you no one knows about the . . . you know. Hawkeye." Rita lowered her voice as a security officer strolled past. "Except me, you, and Robert. I don't want anyone else to know." She crossed her arms and licked her lips with her dry tongue.

"Okay. Sorry. I get it." Hazel stepped back in line.

The announcer's voice blared through the sound system, announcing a team ropers' time, when Blue Coat sauntered past, his gaze pinned on Rita. She bit her lip. Hazel still stood third in line to pay. Rita swung around and muttered, "Hurry up."

Rita's attention was zeroing in on Blue Coat's back when Hazel handed her a plastic sack. "Here ya go. Try to enjoy them."

"Let's get out of here." Rita linked arms with Hazel and ushered her to their seats.

Hazel laid her coat against the backrest and put the sack on her lap. "What's wrong with you?"

"I saw him."

"Who? The Fullmoon look-alike? Or Bowie?"

"No, Blue Coat. He made sure I saw him too." Rita slumped in her chair, her head down.

Faith over fear was not working.

CHAPTER 47

Rita wasn't sure if she could sit through the rest of the rodeo or not. So far, the evening had been a blur. She wanted to be with Robert. Glean his strength and confidence. Away from him she felt like a sitting duck. "How many team ropers are left?"

Hazel shed her jacket and held out the day sheet. "Two." She ran a finger down the page. "Look, here's Robert's name."

Yep, there it stood out. Robert Elliot on . . . Twisted Tea? What happened to Crazy Lady? Oh . . . *Darn you, Bronco Bobby.* "I'm gonna kill him," she said under her breath.

Though her eyes tracked the ropers, her mind was stuck on her folks. Had her dad discovered the missing money? Was her mom in danger? She pulled out her cell, swiped the screen, stiffened at the same unknown number in a text.

She put the phone on her lap and shook her head. Then she picked it back up, opened the message, and sucked in a sharp breath.

> How was your prime rib? Looking forward to seeing you. I miss you, babe.

Prime rib? How did he know what she had for dinner? "No freaking way." She searched the arena, the shakes tearing through her.

Hazel looked at her. "You're white as snow. What's wrong?"

Not wanting Hazel to freak out, she said, "I'm worried about Mom. We should have made her come with us."

"We can't force her to do anything. She's a grown woman, for heaven's sake." Hazel studied her. "What's wrong?" Her gaze dropped to Rita's cell. "Did you get another text?" When Rita turned away, she asked, "You did, didn't you? What'd it say? Was it from the same number?"

"Forget about the text. Should we have Auntie Cee Cee check on her?"

"Nah. Let's keep things quiet. You know Auntie loves to gossip."

Rita sighed. "I don't know what to do."

"Who sent the text?"

"I don't know who sent it. But I'm pretty sure it was Bowie. He called me babe." *It had to be him.* Rita turned and scanned the crowd for the guy in the Wildhorse cap.

"You think he's here?" Hazel examined the spectators.

Wildhorse stared at Rita from two rows behind and to her right. He tipped his chin at her. She swung around and leaned forward. "Shoot, it's him."

"Who? Bowie?"

"No, Wildhorse."

"Again? Where is he?"

"Good grief. You want me to point him out to you?"

"Yeah." She turned and scanned.

"No." She sighed when Hazel gave her a look. "He's two rows up and to the right."

"I don't see him. You sure it was Wildhorse? I don't see anyone wearing a green jacket."

Rita twisted around. "He was there. I swear."

"I think your imagination's working overtime."

"No, Haze," Rita said through gritted teeth. "I saw him."

"Okay. I believe you. What's the plan then?"

"To sit and watch. Stay put."

"For how long?"

"As long as it takes. Until Robert comes to get us. You were there when he said to wait for him." Her cell vibrated. Another message, but from a different number.

> Meet me by Opal's stall in five. Or you
> might find her dead.

Dead? She couldn't get there in five minutes. But she had to try. And what about Hazel? Take her and stay together? In this situation, was there safety in numbers? Or should she leave her behind and keep her safe in a crowd? "I'll be right back." She went to stand, but Hazel held her in place.

"Look, Robert's on his bronc."

Shoot. Rita needed to leave.

CHAPTER 48

*S*he better stay put.

Making his way to the chutes for the evening ride, Robert, sporting his new Columbia River Circuit Finals jacket, walked with his fellow bronc riders. His bronc saddle slung over his back. They strode between the bronc pens and the concrete wall below the stands. The fringe on his chaps slapped his legs with each step. He should be excited. But he wasn't.

Where were they sitting? He needed to know she—they—were safe and sound. Needed to see them. Yeah, she was a ranch woman who knew how to handle herself. But still, she was small. And in a fragile state of mind.

He regretted letting them check out the vendors. He should have put his foot down. But would either of them have listened? They were adults. And it wasn't like Rita was his wife or anything.

Besides, he needed to focus on his bronc. He felt bad for telling Rita the horse's name was Crazy Lady. Well, kinda. It may have even been downright mean to tag onto Payton's horseplay. But he couldn't help it. Their exchange of words popped into his mind:

"No man is harmless."

"No one?"

"Maybe not you. Jury's still out."

Enough already. He'd drawn one of the rankest horses and needed to keep his head in the game. If he rode her, he could win.

Robert climbed the stairs to the platform and dropped his saddle, halter, and flank strap. He'd be the fourth one out. He took off his jacket. His red, sponsor-covered shirt was similar to the other bronc riders. He faced the stands, searching.

Payton clapped his back. "You looking for your little filly?"

He started to say that she didn't belong to him, then remembered in Idaho he'd made it look like they were a couple. "Just thinking about my ride." A downright lie. In reality, he couldn't get Rita Runninghorse out of his head and, without a doubt, wanted her to be his girl. And maybe someday, his wife.

Payton laughed. "Yeah, right, bro. If I had a woman as fine as Rita, I'd be looking for her too."

"*If* you had one as fine as her."

Robert scanned the crowd again. There were elders and middle-aged spectators, along with teens, kids, and babies. Where the heck was Rita?

He squinted. Wait. Was that her to his left, looking scared out of her mind? What was he doing at the chutes? He should be with her—now—on the road back to Seven Tine. Why had he been so selfish to drag her along?

The panels rattled to life as horses were loaded into the chutes. After finding Twisted Tea, he grabbed his saddle and gear bag and headed toward the chestnut force of bunched nerves he'd soon be riding. He rested his hands on the top rung, drumming his fingers on the silver tube of the chute panel.

Get your head in the game. He came here to ride. To win. Not to babysit a hardworking, gorgeous woman and her sister. Rita would have to take care of herself. His career depended on this ride. His future too. He couldn't let an amazing woman with an overactive imagination derail him.

He pounded the rail with his fist.

Ride hard or go home.

CHAPTER 49

R ita stopped at the top of the stairs and turned to the
cowboy on his bronc, her body trembling. She could
surely spare eight seconds. *C'mon, Bobby, stick with 'im.*

She remained long enough to make sure he covered the
horse for the eight seconds, then raced for Opal's stall, not
waiting for his score.

Her boots clanked on the concrete as she shoved past
rodeo fans holding beers, hot dogs, and buckets of popcorn
oozing rich butter. Blowing past a security guard, she took
the steps two at a time, burst through the glass doors, and
prayed the guard wouldn't follow her. Shadows swayed as she
sprinted across the lawn and down the gravel lane.

Rita rounded the corner of the larger livestock complex
and came to a halt fifty feet away. Was the text a ruse to get
her outside where they could snatch her in the dark? Had
they found her horse? How stupid to blindly believe the text.

But since she'd stopped near the barn, she hid in the
shadows of decorative bushes and waited. When the coast
seemed clear, she'd check on Opal to make sure she was safe.

The crunch of footfalls on gravel crept closer. She
crouched lower. Waited. Barrel racers led horses in and out,
the click of their metal shoes echoing on the gravel.

Looking through poky branches, she saw a tall man
step into the light. *Could it be?* He turned around, and Rita
gasped. Bowie looked toward her but didn't seem to see her.

Two kids walking past stopped, blocking her view. They talked about visiting the Redmond Caves across the street and down the road that morning. How huge they were. *Big enough to fit a horse?* One boy mentioned they'd been within walking distance. *Perfect.* He pointed to the dark space behind Bowie and moved on.

Where had Bowie gone?

The three-quarter moon and a handful of stars provided enough light for her to grab Opal and make it to the caves. She could hide out until they gave up and left. Then she could find Robert and beg him to leave.

Four cowboys walked toward the barn. She jumped in behind them, sticking to the outside. Most of the stalls stood empty. Darned if her mare's pen didn't sit at the end of the second lane. The men stopped midway, leaving Rita exposed. Her head down, she fast walked to Opal's stall, bumping into a woman leading her horse. "Excuse me." *Wait, Emily?*

She'd already turned the corner, and Rita didn't have time to see if the woman was indeed her friend Emily Nelson or not. When she made it to her horse's stall, she reached for the halter, her fingers fumbling the lead rope. "Come on." A knot kept her from pulling it loose.

"Can I help you?" a man said from behind her.

She stiffened and stifled a scream. Realizing it wasn't Bowie's baritone, she said, "I got it." She kept her face to the pen as the footsteps faded. Again, she worked the knot and wobbled backward as it broke free. Gaining her balance, she haltered her horse, then led her out the back way and across the road into the black expanse of night. No way was anyone going to take her horse from her.

They made their way through sagebrush, other native brush, and juniper trees, the pungent odor tempting her to sneeze. She held a finger under her nose and removed it when the urge had faded. After stumbling on a rock, she dropped to her knees. The mare spooked, pulling the lead rope out of her hands and Rita off balance. Her face slammed into the rocky ground.

After a long moment, she rolled over and sat up, her hands hanging over her knees. Her palms stung from the rope burn. A jagged rock had ripped her jeans. Her fingers probed the hole and found warm liquid. "Darn it!"

After wiping her hand on the side of her pants, she shoved to her feet, found the mare, and clutched the lead rope. Then she stood for an instant to get her bearings. Okay, where was the small parking lot? The boys had said the caves were to the right of it.

Behind her glowed the lights of the fairgrounds. Rita continued north paralleling SW Airport Road. On foot was taking too long and her knees ached, so she fixed a looped rein, hopped on Opal's back, and urged her forward. Up ahead, the small airport's runway lights illuminated the horizon. The caves had to be between the fairgrounds and the airport.

She hunted, going deeper into the night, occasionally checking to see if anyone was following her. Minutes later, headlights approached, slowed down as if sifting through the night, and sped away.

"Where are the blasted caves?" she muttered.

She kept searching but came up empty. Then it dawned on her the boy had pointed to the left of the airport. She weaved in and out of rocks and scabland brushes, getting closer to SW Airport Road. The hair on the back of her neck rose just before she heard something skitter around Opal's feet. The horse shied sideways.

Rita's fingers clung to the mare's mane, her knees clenching her sides. Cars and trucks sped past. She preferred grassy rolling prairies, not snakes and lizards. She prayed she'd be back at the trailer and safe in Robert's arms soon.

Behind her, another pair of headlights bounced their way down the road. She circled, searched, wound around clumps of sagebrush and jagged rocks, her muscles tight. An instant later, a rig pulled off the road and killed the lights.

"God, help me find those caves."

CHAPTER 50

"Don't play with me, Jeff." Bowie regretted having Gary Fullmoon's brother help out. The guy proved to be dumber than a post.

"I'm telling you it was her. We made eye contact. I was only a few seats away." In the shadows of the open-air barn, he pulled off the Wildhorse Casino cap Bowie had given to him and rubbed his head. "Can I keep the hat?"

"I don't care what you do with it," Bowie said. "We had a deal."

"And I'm telling you I saw her. She wore a ProRodeo hat like this one." Jeff waved his cap in Bowie's face. "She was with her sister."

Bowie smiled and said in a low tone, "I knew she'd hooked up with Hazel at the sale." Thankfully, his cousin Chief Denton had agreed to ping Rita's phone and track her credit card and get him a tracking device to implant in Hazel's coat. Courtesy of Dean Runninghorse. Yep. She now stood within reach.

"Which stall did she go to?"

"I'll show you." Jeff led him to the stall the mare had been in. "There was a nice-looking horse in here."

Bowie spit on the ground.

"Can I have my fifty bucks?" Jeff held out his hand.

"For what? I don't have proof she's here. There's no horse to prove anything. I haven't actually seen Rita or Hazel yet. All I got is your word. And so far, I'm not impressed."

"But I did see 'em."

"I haven't."

"After she and her horse ran outa here, she took off over there." Jeff pointed to the desert across the road.

"What's out there?" Bowie strode out of the barn.

"Nothing but snakes and lizards." A slow smile spread across Jeff's face. "And the Redmond Caves."

Bowie hooked his thumbs in the corner of his front pockets. "Caves, huh?"

"Yeah, come on." Jeff motioned for Bowie to follow him. "I'll show you."

CHAPTER 51

"Rita? Where are you, honey?"

Bowie? Oh, God. No.

"I know you're out here. Can we talk?"

A pickup door slammed shut. Then another. Were there two of them? As Opal picked her way through the rocks, Rita prayed they'd find a cave.

A bit farther, she pulled her mare to a stop and slid off. It looked like a cave entrance loomed a few feet from them. She led the grulla closer, but when the horse pulled back, the lead rope again burned her palm. A screech of pain slipped out. *Shoot!* She covered her mouth with her cold hands and listened.

A man called from nearby, "I think she's over there."

Who was talking? It wasn't Gary Fullmoon. Was it? Though it kinda sounded like him.

Either way, it was two against one.

"C'mon, girl," Rita whispered. She grabbed the lead rope and coaxed the mare under the cave's overhang. Terrified of bats, she crept just deep enough to go undetected.

Footsteps crunched in the distance. Opal lowered her head and pawed the ground. "Shhh." Rita stroked the mare's neck. The horse settled and licked her lips.

"Rita, babe, we need to talk." By the sound of his voice, Bowie was getting closer.

She stepped back, and the grulla skirted to the side. When a bat flapped overhead, the mare reared up and came down hard. She stomped several times. "Whoa, girl. It's okay," Rita whispered. Then she shivered, pressing the side of her fist to her lips to keep quiet.

"Come on out, honey." Bowie's tone was soothing, as though coaxing a frightened colt into a round pen. "Let's go home and work things out. We have a wedding to plan." He paused. "I forgive you for the restraining order. We can work this out." He paused again. "I have a big surprise for you."

I bet you do. No thanks.

The crunch got louder. When Opal wiggled under the overhang, Rita pressed a hand to the horse's neck.

"Can't wait to get you back. I miss you." His voice sounded like it was on the other side of the cave wall. And a beam of light swept over the arid landscape.

All he had to do was round the corner, and she'd be boxed in. She couldn't let him trap her. Not again. Not ever. Rita swung onto her mare's back and kicked her sides. "Yaw!" Her horse flew out of the cave with her hanging on, so close her leg brushed against a solid form.

"Hey!"

From the sound of a body hitting the ground, whoever she hit had toppled off balance.

"Stop her!"

She raced for the lights on the rodeo grounds, praying Creator would guide Opal's steps. She had no idea what loomed out there or where the other caves perched.

Head low, her mare darted about, jumping over rocks and shrubs. When she came to the road, the driver of an oncoming car laid on the horn. Horseshoes clicked the pavement. *Oh no!* The screech of tires on asphalt cut the air, and the aroma of burned rubber stung her nose. "Go!" She kicked her grulla and hung on.

The mare pitched to the side, sending Rita airborne. She tucked and rolled, her shoulder smashing against something rock hard. The clunk of the mare's hoofbeats in the sandy dirt faded, and lights blurred as she gasped for air.

Overhead, stars twinkled as if encouraging her to get up and move. Lying on her back, she shuddered as an aircraft roared past and sloped toward the lit-up runway. Covering her ears with her hands, she groaned. Shooting pains snaked through her shoulder. She rolled over and curled into a ball.

By now, Robert and Hazel would know she was missing. It wouldn't take them long to figure out Opal had disappeared too. But then what? Would they find her before the coyotes and snakes did?

Probably not. She had to get up and make her way back. No one knew where she'd gone. She should have stayed put. Horses were replaceable. People weren't. And now Hazel had a target on her back. Rita shoved herself to her feet, braced her shoulder with her hand, and took a step forward. *Stay together.* The only thing Robert had stressed. Oh, man, had she blown it.

CHAPTER 52

Robert found Hazel in a panic by the center lobby's glass doors. "Where's Rita?"

"She got a text." Hazel hugged herself. "No two. She got two of them. She jumped out of her seat—before you rode—and took off. Left me behind. I've never seen her this upset. It had to have been Bowie. We have to find her!"

Left her behind? What was she thinking? Robert touched her arm, his gut in a bind. "Let's go back to the trailer and—"

"No. We need to find the cops. Rally a search party."

"We don't know why she left yet. It could have been about your mom—"

"My mom?" Hazel shook her head. "No way. Rita would have told me. She wouldn't have run off like someone was chasing her. Or had threatened her. Or . . ."

"Or what?"

"Had threatened Opal."

"She'd abandon you for a horse?"

"In a heartbeat. She loves that mare."

He looked away, a hard swallow feeling like a fist in the middle of his throat. "I find her choosing a horse over her own sister hard to believe."

"What if Bowie has her? What if she's lying hurt somewhere? Or dead? Bleeding out from a knife stuck in her. You know, the kind he threatens her with all the time? You think—"

"Everything okay?" An officer's gaze darted between the two.

What knife? "Yeah—"

"No. It's not." Hazel slapped Robert's arm. "My sister's missing."

"Oh?" The officer shifted his weight and glanced at Robert. "Has she been drinking, ma'am?"

"Drinking?" Hazel let loose a piercing cackle. "No, she *wasn't* drinking. She doesn't use alcohol or drugs."

A part of Robert truly believed Rita had been lured away. *But by who? Her ex? The guy with the Wildhorse cap? The one wearing the blue coat?* "She received a text—"

"Two texts." Hazel wrapped her arms around herself.

"Ma'am," the officer said, "have *you* been drinking?"

Robert peacefully lifted his hands. "None of us—"

"Me?" She got in the cop's face and blew. "Do you smell alcohol?"

The officer kept his feet rooted to the concrete. "I do not."

Robert couldn't believe how calm the man was. He would have slapped her in the patrol car. What a pistol. *Please, don't involve the police.* Rita's pleas slid into Robert's thoughts. "We were going to drop off my gear and look for her. I'm sure everything's okay."

"There are officers patrolling the area twenty-four seven. Holler if you can't find her."

"Will do." Juggling his gear, Robert grabbed Hazel by the arm and dragged her outside.

"What are you doing? We need to go back. They can help us look. Put out a missing person's report." Hazel jerked her arm free.

He desperately wanted to involve the cops. But he'd promised he wouldn't. There were two reasons—to keep Hazel alive and to keep the woman he loved out of prison. "He's right. Let's wait and see if—"

"What a load of crap." She stopped on the lawn and paced. "What if Bowie has her?"

"We'll find her." He motioned for Hazel to lead the way. After he stowed his gear in the pickup, he turned to Hazel. "Let's check the barn."

They went to the now-packed barn and found Opal's stall empty. Some of the barrel racers were cooling off their horses, and others were comparing their rides.

Hazel glanced around. She pulled out her cell and showed some of the girls Rita's photo. "Have you seen her?" No one had.

Robert moved outside, and Hazel followed. "Do you hear that?"

She tilted her head. "Hear what?"

"Shh," he said with a sharp tone.

She plopped her hands on her hips and whispered, "I don't hear anything."

He held up his finger, and then pointed at a moving shadow several yards out coming at them hard and fast. "Opal?" He jogged toward the horse. When he got within a few yards of the ball of fright, he waved his arms over his head and called the horse's name as though catching steeds at an Indian relay race.

Opal, breaths whooshing, veered toward Robert and slammed past, knocking him to the ground. He rolled over and jumped to his feet to find Hazel snatching the mare's lead rope and pulling her around with all her might. Wide-eyed, her damp coat glistened in the light of the pole lamp.

"She okay?"

"I think so."

He made his way to them and rubbed his hand over the grulla's wet body. "Where's Rita, huh, girl?"

"I'll take care of her. You go and find my sister." Hazel's chin quivered as her gaze pinned on the darkness behind them. "She has to be out there somewhere."

"I'll find her." Robert took off into the desert, not knowing what he'd find out there or who he'd discover, if anyone. Or how bad off she'd be.

CHAPTER 53

Robert cupped his hands and hollered, "Rita!" When there was no answer, he crossed the road and jogged into the shadows of the desert, the air now cool. She could be anywhere. Again, he called her name.

"Over here!"

The outline of a small figure waved an arm, and Robert raced over to her. He found her perched on a boulder, one of her arms cradling her shoulder. "What happened? Are you all right?" He fell to his knees, his anger dissipating with the twist of her face. Strands of her hair flared from her lopsided cap. Dirt streaked her face. She looked pitiful but adorable.

"I don't think anything's broken. Might be out of place though."

All he wanted to do was gather her in his arms and hold on. Instead, he helped her up, placed his arm around her, and guided her back to the grounds. "What are you doing out here?"

"Bowie texted me. Said he had Opal and to meet him at her stall or he'd kill her. I didn't know what to do. Wasn't thinking. Just reacted. Panicked. I love her so much. She's always been there for me. And I didn't want to drag Hazel out here. Put her in danger."

"You should have stayed put." His voice rose, then softened. "Hazel has Opal. She's—"

"You left her alone?"

He snorted. "You might want to rethink your accusation."

"You're right. Sorry." She stumbled and cried out when he squeezed her shoulder, trying to steady her.

Feeling bad, he held her for a very long moment. She felt so right, her body warming him like the heat on a summer's night, her dirty hair still giving off a hint of a floral aroma. Hated to release her but knew Hazel would be frantic. So, he let her go, and they started back.

About a half-hour later, they were on the edge of the grounds headed for the horse trailer. Thank goodness for the dust-to-dawn lights. She could actually see the ground. Trudging through the sand and rocks and every scary thing out there about did her in, and the pain in her shoulder now throbbed. She wished she'd had a ride like her dirtbag ex.

"Where are we going?" Rita tried to veer right toward barn five.

Robert felt her stiffen when he blocked her. "Hazel should be in the trailer by now." But no light shone through the shaded windows.

"No. She would stay with Opal until I got back."

"Why would she stay out in the cold? She's probably out. Toasty in her sleeping bag."

"Asleep? Hardly. I know my sister. Take me to the barn." She dug in her heels. "Please."

He released her arm and abruptly turned to face her. "You need to rest—"

"Rest? No way. I need to see my horse. I know Haze is with her. That's why the trailer's dark."

Robert took off his cowboy hat and raked his gritty hair with his fingers. What a stubborn woman. "Fine. Let's go."

When they reached the stall, the mare stood inside, munching on her hay. Where was her sister?

"Hazel?" Rita checked the surrounding lanes and just outside the barn entrance. She called for her sister again.

Robert shook his head, hoping Hazel had simply wandered off for a minute. "Where are you?" He rested his hand on a panel rail. In his line of sight, a paper nestled between the gate and the panel. He pulled it out. "Hey. I found something."

She hurried over, holding her arm. "What is it?"

He handed her the note.

She unfolded it and read aloud. "I have Hazel. I won't hurt her unless you make me. You know we're a perfect match. Call me or you know what will happen to her." She crumpled the paper in her fist. "It's all my fault. I should've left her in Hermiston."

"Your fault? Do you think you control your crazy ex?"

"I could have kept her safe."

"Don't flatter yourself. He would've come after her no matter what. And you. It's why he's here."

She leaned against the panel and wiped her glistening eyes.

By the look on her face, he'd offended her again. He rubbed her good arm. "Listen. I've learned abusers have their own issues. You didn't cause him to hurt you or take Hazel. He did it all on his own. C'mon, Rita. Even I know you'd never intentionally put anyone in danger. Especially your sister."

Her look softened, and she let him hold her. "What are we going to do? You know we can't involve the cops."

Robert pulled his phone from his back pocket. "I'm calling Chuck. He may know someone who can help." He made the call and strode to the edge of the barn.

CHAPTER 54

"C'mon, answer," Rita muttered.

Though eager to phone Chuck, if only for a pep talk, she wasn't sure what Robert expected to get from the call. Good grief. It would take him at least seven hours to get here and this wasn't even his jurisdiction.

And there was no way she'd involve the cops. Too risky. For her and Hazel. Her shoulder burned, and the rest of her felt stiff. She wanted Bowie out of her life—and maybe even dead so he couldn't ever come after her again. The last admission surprised her.

When Chuck finally answered, Robert looked at Rita with hopeful eyes. "Hey, we need your help." He filled him in, then said, "Uh-huh." He nodded. "Okay. Thanks, man."

While Robert pocketed his cell, Blue Coat stepped into view. She gasped and gave a slight jerk of her head in the cowboy's direction, hoping Robert would catch on. She wanted to use her words, but they stuck in her tight throat. Reaching for his arm, she—wait. What?

He turned around, smiled, and extended his hand. "Oh, hey. You must be Ethan Harris."

Ethan Harris? Rita recoiled. How on earth did Robert know Blue Coat's name? She looked forward to the explanation because she'd been convinced the cowboy had been stalking her.

"This is Rita Runninghorse. Her sister, Hazel, is missing."

No. Abducted.

He turned to her. "He's a friend of Chuck's from the academy and a private investigator. He's been keeping an eye on you."

"Me? Why?"

"Chuck was convinced Bowie would show up here," Ethan said. "Sounds like he was right."

"But-I-uh . . ." It seemed pretty suspicious for him to—so conveniently—show up in Redmond. It must have shown on her face.

He smiled. "I live in Bend and come here every year, know the place. And owe Chuck a favor." He leaned an elbow on a panel. "I often work with the local police and am happy to help you guys out."

"If you've been keeping an eye on me, why didn't you show up here before I fled to the caves? And how'd you miss Bowie kidnaping Hazel? Where've you been?"

"I got a call from Chief Denton and lost track of you. I believe he's from your rez?"

"You know he's crooked, don't you?"

"I have my suspicions. But—"

"Glad he hasn't buffaloed you." Rita nodded. Good or bad, having so many eyes on her gave her the heebie-jeebies. She didn't know who to trust.

"So tell me, when was the last time you saw Hazel?" Ethan asked Rita.

Robert cleared his throat. "Let's go back to the trailer and talk."

Once in the warmth of the living quarters, Rita took a couple of ibuprofens and filled Ethan in on events of the last few hours. The more she talked, the harder her body shook. How could she have abandoned Hazel?

"Is your shoulder okay?" Ethan asked. "Do you need to see a doctor? Maybe get an X-ray?"

"I'm fine." Good Lord, she wasn't so fragile that she needed medical attention.

Ethan's phone rang, and his gaze dropped to the screen. "Give me a second, will ya?" He got up and went outside.

"He's a PI, huh?" Rita rubbed her forearm.

"Yeah, he was on the force before going into business for himself. Chuck said we can trust him."

She grunted. "What else did Chuck say?"

"He plans to meet us in Vegas."

"Isn't his wife recovering from surgery?"

"Yeah, but she's doing well. He said one of the aunts wants to dote on her and is fine with him leaving for a couple days." He touched her arm. "You need to be checked out."

"Thanks for your concern, but I'm good."

Ethan nodded to Robert as he came back inside and settled in a seat at the table. "That was Chief Denton. Sounds like your husband's a piece of work."

"He's my *ex*-fiancé." Thank God they weren't married.

"Good to know," Ethan said. "Apparently, bookies are after him for nonpayment and officers are looking into complaints of him swindling good people with lame horses and—"

"No way. I check each one of them. They're sound."

One of Ethan's brows rose. "Are you a vet?"

"No, but I used to work for one and know a lot." Heat crept up Rita's neck, realizing how foolish she sounded. Having worked for a veterinarian was far from being one.

"I'm sure you do," Ethan said. "Here's the deal, Chuck said you're headed to Vegas. He'll meet you there. Tribal Police will continue to investigate, and so will the county sheriff. They're contacting various sale yards to help get the word out. They'd planned to set up a sting operation to catch him in the act until—"

"The act of what? Selling lame horses? Taking money he can't pay back?" She almost laughed.

Ethan gave Robert a she-has-no-clue kind of look. "Chief Denton thinks he's selling more than horses."

No way. She would have known. "Like what?"

"Drugs."

"He's a lot of things but not a drug dealer. The accusation's pretty farfetched." Wait. Was she defending him? Or just mad she'd never noticed or been suspicious?

And was her dad involved too? "Oh, my goodness." She turned to Robert. "I wonder if the cash Hazel found is drug money." Was there additional money stashed away somewhere? Either way, if her dad found it missing, who knows what he'd do.

"What money?" Ethan asked. "How much does she have?"

She closed her eyes, somewhat light-headed, and told him about the cash. "Is my dad working with Bowie? Has anyone been watching him? What about my sister? Doesn't this add kidnapping to Bowie's list of offenses?"

"It will if he's got her. Can I see the note you guys found?" Rita handed it to him, and he scanned it. "Is this his handwriting?"

Rita chewed on her bottom lip, inched one of her shoulders upward. "I'm not sure. I'm embarrassed to say, I've never seen anything he's written. Looking back, he's been a pretty secretive guy."

"Okay. So we don't know for sure who has your sister, right?"

"My gut does." Rita's gut was never wrong. It felt like a knife twisted her insides. Would they even find her sister? Alive?

He gave her a sympathetic look. "And I don't know anything about your dad. Give me his name and I'll check into him. I'll also find out if they're connected in some way."

Why did Hazel have to steal the money? Rita should've kept it hidden. Not spent a dime.

Ethan cleared his throat. "What I need you to do is call Bowie—"

"Call Bowie? What for?" Rita's body quivered.

"To set up a time and place to lure him in," Ethan said. "Think you can make the call?"

Probably not. She swallowed.

Robert grabbed her hand. "No way are you using her as a pawn."

Ethan looked at Rita. "You up for it?"

"You want to use me as bait?" *Oh, Lord.* In an instant, a panic attack came on. She felt like a boa constrictor had wrapped its scaly self around her thorax. Robert left, came back, and handed her a small paper bag. She put it around her nose and mouth and breathed in. Then out. In. And out.

"Will she be able to make the call?" Ethan asked Robert.

Robert shook his head. "Find some other way."

"You don't have to be there, Rita," Ethan said. "If you can get him to agree to meet you, I'll do the rest."

When her breathing returned to normal, she said, "Yeah. Okay. I'll do it." If something ever happened to Hazel, she'd never forgive herself.

CHAPTER 55

"You ready?" Ethan Harris sat across the table from Rita in the living quarters section of the horse trailer. Robert sat next to her, his hand on her leg.

After giving Ethan Bowie's cell number and her dad's name and number, she did everything in her power to keep calm. Robert had even set a paper bag on the table for her just in case. "I hope so. But I need to know something first."

"What is it?"

"If they suspect Bowie's dealing drugs, selling lame horses, and owes loan sharks money, why is he not in jail?"

"There's not enough evidence to hold him. These things take time. No one wants to arrest someone and not have the charges stick."

"Is that what your call with Chief Denton was about?" The pain in her shoulder pulsed. In about fifteen minutes, the ibuprofen and arnica should kick in. Or so she hoped.

"I can't share our conversation with you."

"Because it's an ongoing investigation?" Maybe Denton wasn't as crooked as she'd thought.

"Yep. You ready to make the call?"

"As ready as I'll ever be." Rita closed her eyes and inhaled a deep breath.

"Use your head," Robert said. "I know you can do this."

His touch gave her the confidence she needed. She nodded and made the call, her fingers trembling. At the sound of his voice, she hung up.

"What happened?" Robert glanced from her to Ethan.

"It went to voice mail. I didn't know what to do."

"Call back," Ethan said. "If the same thing happens, leave a message."

And say what? She blinked a few times to clear her vision, called him back, and tapped the speaker icon. After a few rings, Bowie answered.

"Where's my sister? Is she okay?" Rita fought to keep her voice from wavering.

"So far. Tell me where you're at, and I'll come get you. But if you bring the cops, you know what'll happen to her." Her hands trembled so hard, she had to put the phone on the table.

A plane buzzed overhead, and seconds later the roar came across the line. She picked up the phone and rushed outside. Sure enough, an airplane was descending toward the runway. She turned toward the guys, who had followed her outside. She ended the call. "Did you hear the plane?"

"I did. Good job." Ethan smiled. "What does his truck look like?"

"It's a dirty, brown Ford F-150. Pretty rough looking."

"Got it." Ethan looked at Robert. "You coming?"

"Darn right I am." He grabbed his coat, and they raced off, leaving Rita behind.

"Hey, what about me?" When they kept going, she stomped inside and plopped down at the table. She wanted to be there when they rescued her sister. Needed to hold her.

"Darn them for leaving me behind." She paced. Then she went outside and studied the pitch-black horizon. The stars. The partial moon. She prayed they'd get Bowie.

Going on eleven o'clock, she went inside and made herself a cup of rich-smelling coffee and drank it black. She wasn't about to sleep while her sister was in captivity.

Rita paced from the loft bench to the bathroom door and back again. She checked on her mare, inhaling the cool desert air. She roamed the barn and was startled with every click and snort. After a while, she went back to the trailer, plunked down on the seat, and sighed. *Have they caught up with them yet?*

What was taking them so long? She checked her phone. Three missed text messages. One voice mail. She tapped the voice mail button. "Why did you hang up on me?" She laughed. But not from joy. "Because you're an idiot," she told the phone. She went to the next one. "Let's meet so you can keep Hazel alive." Bile rose in Rita's throat, and she swallowed, the sting sliding down her esophagus.

Yep. The same old stinking manipulation.

What had Sydney said at the convention? Oh, yeah. "It's never your fault. Greater is He than what comes against us. So stay strong." Yep, she'd have to stay strong for Hazel. She said a short prayer for her. Sydney had encouraged women to recognize manipulation and resist its power of persuasion.

But then again, this involved her sister. It wasn't just about her. She couldn't ignore him this time, sure he'd kill Hazel.

Headlights swept through the trailer. Rita held her breath, hoping the lights belonged to Ethan. She pressed a hand to the base of her neck and hid in the bathroom shower. If it wasn't them, she could escape through the stud stall.

The sound of a motor turned off. A faint creak sounded, and the trailer dipped four times. Muddled voices drifted through the bathroom door. It dipped again, twice, and the sound of a door slamming bounced into the bathroom. Steps grew louder.

"Rita, you in there?"

She released a breath and hunched over for a short moment. When composed, she rushed out of the shower and opened the bathroom door to Robert holding out his arms. She fell into his embrace and clung to his strength, breathing in his musky scent. "Where's my sister?"

"They were gone by the time we got there."

"No!" Sobs burst from her throat.

"Don't worry. He'll find her." His hold on Rita tightened. "Ethan wants us to get out of here tonight."

She pushed back and shook her head. "No way. I'm not leaving without my sister."

"Staying will put you in danger."

"Or are you in a rush to get to the next rodeo?"

He flinched. "There's nothing we can do here. We need to let Ethan and the cops handle it."

"I get it. Cowgirl up."

"Good grief. That's not what I meant."

Didn't he? "Then what did you mean?"

"To stay strong. You've been incredibly brave so far. Don't cave now." Robert held out his hand to her, but she brushed it away.

Rita shook her head. "I can't go." She grabbed her backpack. "I'll head to the nearest hotel and—"

"You're not going anywhere." He rushed past her and blocked the door. "You think he's going to hand Hazel over and everyone'll live happily ever after? This isn't a fairy tale, Rita."

"I know it's not."

Robert's cell chimed. He slipped it from his back pocket and swiped the screen. "It's Sydney." He tossed it onto the loft bed.

"Aren't you going to answer?"

"I'll call her back."

"I'm not changing my mind." As the big sister—the protector—it was Rita's job to look after Hazel. And that's exactly what she intended to do.

With or without Robert Elliot.

CHAPTER 56

Robert pulled off his Stetson and raked his fingers through his hair. How on earth was he going to convince her to come with him? His cell chimed again, and he went outside.

"Chuck, what's up?"

"Hey, I just got off the phone with Ethan. They have a plan to lure Bowie back to the Umatilla rez. You take Rita to Vegas and keep her safe. Sydney's on her way home."

"I'm not sure I should go. This has all gotten out of hand."

"You need to take Rita and get out of there. Bowie's still in the area. Who knows what he'll try to do? Especially if the cash Hazel took is tied to him and drug money. Ethan's still checking into their dad."

"He told you about the money?"

"He told me everything."

"I don't know. This is no longer about wanting to be a hero. It's now about protecting a woman from her ex. With drugs and bookies and kidnapping now thrown in the mix. . . . And Rita's refusing to leave without her sister." He hated to see the pain in her eyes. Hated watching her fall apart. She glared at him and closed the shades. The silhouette showed her head dropping to the table, her shoulders bobbing. It about undid him.

"You keep her safe, let the cops rescue Hazel, and trust me, man, you'll still be the hero. Think you can talk her into heading out?"

No longer caring about being a hero, he'd do anything to protect Rita Runninghorse. "I'll try."

"Try harder, bro. I'll keep tabs on the sister. Besides, I don't think he'll hurt her. She seems to be his bargaining chip. And from what Ethan dug up, this Bowie character is interested in getting Dean Runninghorse's money. That's why he's desperate to marry Rita."

"What money?" Robert walked in circles, not wanting to get too far from the door in case she still intended to bolt.

"Looks like he has money his family doesn't know about, and maybe Bowie found out about it. He's made some big investments in racehorses and real estate, and they seem to be paying off. He's got the money tucked away in a bank in Washington state with only his name on the account."

"What about drugs? Does it look like he's involved with Bowie and gambling?"

"I'm not sure yet. But I'll keep you posted. In the meantime, work your magic and convince Rita it's time to get on the road."

She got up and headed toward the back of the trailer.

Ending the call, Robert decided to get the horse first.

Opal's head drooped, her eyes closed. Robert grabbed her rope halter and opened the gate, waking up the mare. "Hey, girl, time to go." He stroked her neck and pulled the halter over her nose, fastening it beside her jaw. After dumping what water remained in a bucket, he stuffed leftover hay in it and led the grulla to the back of the trailer. He flicked two switches, and the overhead lamp showered light on them.

A door slammed shut, and Rita rounded the corner. "What the heck are you doing with my horse?"

"Chuck called. We have to go." He unlatched the stall door and told her what Chuck had said.

"I told you that I'm not leaving without my sister." She clutched her horse's lead rope.

He let out a deep sigh. "Listen. Taking you with me is the only way to keep the cops out of your hair. If they find out you killed Hawkeye—which I'm sure your ex will be willing to share with them—you'll be arrested. Then you won't be there for Hazel. Is that what you want?"

"No. It's not." She released the lead rope. "This sucks. You get to play Bronco Bobby, and what do I get?"

Robert secured the mare and turned to her. "It's what I do. And you get to stay alive." He picked up the bucket and remaining strands of hay and tossed them into the side door of the stud stall. The bucket bounced, splaying what little hay they had on the rubber-matted floor. He hooked a padlock through the two latches, secured the lock, and jerked the base down for good measure, hoping she wouldn't take off.

Thank heaven she remained there, the spotlight shining down on her not-so-sweet-looking face when he went back to the double doors. He grunted and flicked off the switch. "Get in." He stomped to the driver's door and slid behind the wheel. Surprise and delight swirled around him when she wrenched open the passenger door. "C'mon, get in." But she didn't.

"You turn off the propane? Secure the coffee pot or anything else? Or do you plan on letting your belongings fly through the living quarters as you speed down the road?"

Shoot. He'd forgotten. He pounded the steering wheel, making her jump and stumble backward. She slammed the door shut and headed for the service road, wearing her backpack with her blanket tied to the bottom, the one he'd found her in the day she showed up at Seven Tine. He hopped out of the pickup and chased after her. "Rita, wait."

She broke into a run.

Robert passed her and spun around, blocking her with his outstretched arms and causing her to stop. "I'm sorry. I didn't mean to upset you."

She pursed her lips, her nostrils flaring. "Get out of my way."

"What can I say. I'm an idiot. I'll control my temper from here on out."

"I didn't realize you had one until now."

His drive to protect her was making him crazy. "I know. I'm sorry. The only way this is going to work is if we stick to the plan and work as a team."

"Stick to what plan?" Rita grunted. "Winning the INFR?"

Oh, she drove him nuts. He took a few deep breaths. "Do what you want. I'm headed to Vegas."

"Of course you are."

He whipped around and, like an idiot, slammed into her injured shoulder, making her scream and cry and bend at the waist. She groaned. A deep-throated moan. The kind from pain and frustration and fear. Red-faced, she reared up and slammed her fist against his chest, shoulder, side of his face, wherever she could make contact. He ducked, his fingers encasing her wrist.

"I'm all she's got!"

"I know." Robert drew her into his arms. "I know. They'll find her, Rita. They'll find her."

She nodded, hiccupping sobs. She clung to him for a long moment, her knees seeming to want to buckle. And to his surprise, her lips found his. Something powerful and possessive shot through him, and he tightened his grip on her. She pulled him close as he deepened the kiss.

He tasted hunger and horror. The kind of fear that makes a person do things they normally wouldn't. Then he caught a whiff of her hair. Something soft and floral. Something as sweet as roses on a summer day. Yeah, purely he and Rita, alone under the flare of moonlight. And it made him feel like he could rescue her no matter what came against them.

A deep groan pulled him away from her, his breathing rapid. He pressed his head to hers. "Sorry. Not sorry." No, he didn't regret the kiss at all.

"Same here."

After one last intimate moment, he led her back to the pickup, turned over the engine, and dialed up the heat. "You need anything?" Her head turned to the window. She clutched her injured arm and shook her head. *Yeah right.* He secured the trailer, grabbed bottles of water and a bottle of ibuprofen, and jumped into the pickup. He took her hand and gave her a light squeeze. "She's going to be okay."

Red-rimmed eyes stared back at him. "Where will we go this late? With a horse?"

"Let's get out of town, and we'll pull over and figure it out." Robert handed her a water and the medication.

"My horse needs hay."

"We'll find some."

She took out the Western States map in the glove compartment and studied it. "By my calculations, it's almost nine hundred miles to Vegas. Looks like we need to hit Highway 20 out of Bend and head toward Burns."

"We can stop along the way and get a little shut-eye. We'll be fine."

"You sure? What if he finds us?"

"Turn off your cell and he won't."

She did.

Robert released the parking brake and slid the lever into Drive. "I'll take care of you both." He had to make good on his promise—prove to her that he was reliable and trustworthy. It's all he had to offer. At least for now.

CHAPTER 57

Highway 376, Nevada

A loud boom jarred Rita awake, and a familiar whoosh sounded through the windows. Then there was a flap, flap, flap sound as though slapping the pavement. Oh, sheesh. Not again. She prayed there'd be a spare this time.

She rubbed her eyes, tired from the little sleep they'd gotten parked off of a side road near Brothers, Oregon. She'd been too wound up to sleep, sure Bowie had someone following them—or was doing it himself.

Yeah, the cops could try to lure him back to the rez, but it didn't mean he'd take the bait, not if he was tied to the drug money Hazel had found.

Robert guided the pickup to the side of the road and turned on the emergency flashers near a sign that read: Big Smoky Rest Area, Two Miles. Why couldn't the tire have blown closer to the rest area? Rita slid out of the truck and into the afternoon warmth of the desert. It was seventy degrees, according to the thermometer on the dashboard. She stretched her sore body from the long, exhausting ride of long straight stretches with nothing in between but sagebrush and pavement.

She sighed and went to the trailer to rub her shoulder down with arnica, then unloaded Opal and grabbed a bucket. "I'll go find some water for her."

"I'll get this changed as fast as I can." Robert pulled a bag from the trailer's side compartment.

Rita tied Opal to a D ring on the desert side of the trailer. Once the mare was secure, she went to the stud stall and stuffed the last of the hay into a feed bag. Darned if she wouldn't have to pay twice as much from a feed store in Vegas—extra money she'd owe her dad.

By the flat tire, Robert had the trailer and truck separated and the spare waiting on the ground. Sweat drenched his T-shirt. "Will you hand me the jack?" He set the lug wrench on the ground.

She picked up the tool and held it out to him, admiring his ruggedness—with a capital R—as he changed the tire. She recalled his soft lips from last night's kiss. How foolish to have thought she could find Hazel by herself and remain safe.

Looking around, Rita put a hand on her hip. "Where are we going to stay tonight?"

"We'll find something when we get there."

"When we get there? You plan on hauling this rig all over the city to find a hotel or something? At least for one night, can't we stay in the parking lot of . . . where's the rodeo?"

"At South Point. Will you hand me the lug wrench?" Robert took it and loosened the first lug nut. "Let me change the tire so we can get back on the road. Then we can talk about where to stay." He continued to work the lug nuts loose.

"What are we going to do with my horse?"

He stood and waved the wrench in the air. "Let me change this tire first, then we'll figure it out. I promise."

"Can she stay at the venue?"

He let out a groan. "I don't know. I've never hauled a horse down here before."

"You should have found out. You had plenty of time the last couple of mornings."

"Guess I should have done a lot of things differently." He shifted his weight, took in a deep breath, and said in a calm tone, "Remember, you're the one who insisted on bringing her."

"You're the one who brought me to Hermiston."

He went back to fixing the tire, the vein on his neck bulging.

"I'm sorry. I should've been the one to look for a place to keep her, not you. I can't expect you to take care of us both. You've done so much already." She sighed. "We should have left her in Hermiston." *Maybe me too.*

He stood, sweat drenched and dirt streaked. "No. You did the right thing. From what you've told me about her, horses like Opal are hard to find. Not only in color and conformation but also in disposition."

Not to mention emotional support.

"I know you're scared and tired. But we have to keep our heads on straight to make it through all of this." He gave her a light hug.

She rested her head on his glorious chest for a few seconds and listened to his heartbeat. "Thanks for being my rock."

He kissed her head and let go. "Now, will you let me finish this?" He turned back to the truck.

Rita went to the trailer, untied her mare, and ambled into the desert landscape.

Eyes wide and head high, the mare sniffed the sage and peered at her with a sour look on her face, as though asking if she was expected to eat the pungent, silvery-gray brush? Where on earth would she keep her horse for seven days? She pulled her cell from her back pocket and turned it on.

"No way." She didn't expect to have four bars.

She returned her grulla to the trailer, grabbed a water bottle from the fridge and a sack of salt and vinegar chips, and settled on the step of the living quarters. She searched for horse stables in Las Vegas. *Oh, good.* There were twenty of them. Most of the stables had four and five stars. A few had three. She called the first number. An answering machine came on, and she left a message. Then she went down the list, finding each stable full. She slammed the cell against her leg. "What are we going to do?"

She enlarged the search. She tapped in "horse motels in the Vegas area." Six popped up. "Yes." The Open Heart V Farm looked perfect, close to the South Point Arena & Equestrian Center—which had to be the place Robert mentioned—and had ten covered pens. The equestrian center sat in back of the South Point Hotel Casino & Spa. She hoped they weren't already filled. She called the number, and on the third ring a woman answered.

"Please tell me you have space available."

"For how many nights and how many horses?"

"Seven nights and one horse." *Please have an open stall.*

"I sure do. Got a cancellation this morning."

"Great. We'll be there sometime tonight." Rita gave her the needed information to reserve a spot and hung up. "Yes!" She grabbed a chip and plopped it in her mouth.

Robert strolled to her, water bottle in hand. He crouched at her feet and took a swig. "What are you so excited about?"

"I booked one of those horse motels near South Point for thirty-five a night."

"You turned on your phone?"

"Oh. Shoot." She looked around at the barren landscape. "Hopefully he won't figure out where we're headed."

He wiped his hands on his grungy jeans. "If you would've been patient, I would have told you I booked a room weeks ago. Two beds. Told my buddy he'd have to find another place to crash. And had planned to call to find out if there were open stalls available."

Two beds? One room? No way. "You can drop us off at the horse motel and keep your reservation. As long as it's okay if I crash in the trailer."

The space between his brows formed a V. "Like I'd let you stay alone." He leaned forward, as if expecting a kiss.

She rested her hands on his chest. "You stink." It took effort to keep him at bay looking so sexy with his wild hair and a swipe of grease smeared on his face.

He leaned down anyway and rested his sweet lips on hers.

Rita leaned back. "You need to get cleaned up so we can get back on the road."

"I will in a minute." He kissed her again. This time with passion and fire.

She tasted salt on his lips, her fingers finding their way to his firm back. She savored every delicious moment. Then again, she pushed him away.

"What about your hotel room? You can't get a refund this late, can you?"

"I don't care as long as we're together."

"It sounds like a bad line from an old movie."

He entwined their fingers together. "Maybe so. But it's true." His sable eyes bore into her. "If we stay at the horse motel we should be off Bowie's radar." If she could remember to keep her cell off. "I'm banking on Ethan's plan working."

"If he thinks marrying me is the answer to his financial problems, I'm not so sure. He'll come after me. Not go back to the rez. He's got Hazel. What would he do with her?"

"I don't know. We have to trust Ethan and the detectives working the case. I'll go hook the trailer back up so we can hit the road." Robert helped Rita to her feet and strode away.

Was the money drug related? And tied to Bowie? Would her mom know? She picked up her phone and called her mom's cell as she walked toward her horse.

"Hello? Rita?"

"Yeah, it's me, Mom." Joan's tone made her regret calling.

"How are you? Where are you? Where's your sister? Are you both safe?"

"We're fine, Mom." At least she was. The lie made her recoil.

"Your father, he's changed. You girls leaving woke him up—"

Or he discovered the missing cash.

"It's time to come home, honey."

Dean change? Ha. Not in this lifetime. "Not yet, Mom."

"We'll help you get away from Bowie. Dad realizes what he's done to you. He's sorry for a lot of things."

"I bet he is." She knew her dad all too well. Yeah. Her mom's story was a scam, and her dad was still a swindler.

"Give him a chance."

"I have to go, Mom. I'll talk to you soon."

"I love you, honey. We both do."

She disconnected the call and held her phone to her forehead. *Love you too.*

"Ready?" Robert hollered from the front of the truck.

Rita powered down her cell, loaded the mare, and slid onto the passenger seat. Her mother's plea made her want to go home. She'd never been away for this long. She missed the comfort of her mother's loving touch. Her pot roast and huckleberry pie. She wiped away a rogue tear with her thumb. What she wouldn't give to see her right then.

She missed Hazel too. Was she fine? Like she'd promised her mom?

Please, God, protect her.

CHAPTER 58

Las Vegas, Nevada

They pulled into the Open Heart V Farms on Sunday night at around nine. Rita felt worn out from the long drive and insane traffic through town yet felt relieved to be at the simple horse motel.

Robert pulled up the dark driveway, past a two-story house, and parked. A middle-aged woman dressed in jeans and a hooded sweatshirt met them at the rear of the horse trailer. "You must be Rita Runninghorse."

"I am. I'm so thankful you had an open spot."

The woman stepped aside when Robert flicked on the spotlight and opened the stall door. "I'm Maggie Dennison. Where'd you all come from?"

"Redmond," Rita said. "He rode in the Columbia River Circuit Finals."

"Oh, how'd you do?"

"Not too bad." Robert unloaded Opal.

Maggie let out a low whistle. "Nice looking horse you got there." She walked around the mare, examining every inch as though prepared to make an offer. "You a roper?" she asked Robert.

"Bronc rider."

Her gaze shifted to Rita. "Oh, you must turn cans then?"

"Nope. I've never barrel raced. We picked her up along the way." She didn't like how easily the lie had slid out of her mouth. Then again, her statement was true.

"Get a good price for her?"

She turned to Robert, who looked as though he was stifling a smile, then faced the woman. "She was a steal."

He beamed like a proud parent. "Where do you want her?"

"The third stall's fine. And you can park your rig right by the blue Dodge." Maggie motioned to a pickup illuminated by a pole lamp near the south end of the open-air barn.

"Great," he said to Maggie before turning to Rita. "I'll take care of all of this if you'll go take care of the bill." He reached into his back pocket, pulled out his wallet, and handed her his credit card.

Rita lowered her voice. "I'll pay you back my half."

"No need."

He walked away before she could protest. She caught up to Maggie at the back door and followed her inside the weathered house. Under the dim lighting of a porch lamp, she could see that the place needed new siding and a manicure.

"Excuse the mess. My husband passed a few months ago, and I can't seem to keep up by myself. I don't have the money to hire help, but I'm hoping after this week, that will change."

"You ever think of raising your rates? Thirty-five a night is pretty cheap." She handed Maggie the credit card. "Do you know where we can get hay?"

"Mountain Springs Tack and Feed off North Lamb Boulevard has the best hay around." Maggie handed her a receipt. "Here ya go."

"Um . . . we ran out of what little hay we had. Can you spot me a couple flakes?"

"Sure. There's hay in the shed on the north end of the barn."

"I appreciate it." Rita dug in her pocket and pulled out a five.

"Put your money away. This one's on me."

What a nice woman. She'd pay her back somehow. Maybe mow the lawn or weed the flower beds. As long as Maggie wasn't offended. She stuffed the bill back in her pocket. "I'll see you in the morning then."

"Just to warn you, I'm up bright and early and don't fancy late nights and loud music."

"Fair enough." Rita went back to the trailer, dragged herself up the step and went inside.

"She was a steal, huh?" He chuckled. "Good one."

"Stop laughing. I don't want to make a habit of lying."

"You weren't. Not really."

True. Taking back what was already hers wasn't stealing. The crunch of tires on gravel sounded outside, growing louder as though coming right at them. Rita held up the window shade as headlights flicked off. The truck looked brown. Or maybe black.

Crouching behind her, Robert peered out the window. "It must be one of the horse owners. Probably here for the rodeo."

"You think so?"

A tall man with a black felt cowboy hat emerged from the driver's seat, the pole lamp near the stalls backlighting him. She stiffened and held her breath. When he lifted his chin, she gasped.

"How on earth?" Rita shot out of the trailer, ready to put her fear six feet underground and let courage finally reign.

CHAPTER 59

"Where's my sister, you no-good piece of crap!" Robert slipped out of the trailer and edged along the passenger side of the pickup. He opened the door and the glove box and pulled out his pistol, then stuffed it into the back waistband of his jeans. For a brief moment, his fingers curled into a fist as he strode to Rita's side and touched the small of her back.

"This the playboy?" Bowie spat on the ground and scowled at Robert. "Think you can replace me, huh?"

"Can't be replaced with something that's not yours."

Maggie, wearing a bathrobe and a glare harder than a ticked off Brahman bull's, approached them from the house. "Everything all right? I don't want no trouble here. I'll call the cops if I have to." She waved a cell in the air.

No. Not the cops. "He was just leaving." Rita pressed her lips together, praying he'd go quietly.

Bowie reached for Rita, but Robert slapped his arm away. "Time to go, buddy."

Bowie sneered at him. "This isn't over." Then he gave Rita a puppy-dog face. Pleading. His tone sounding soft. Soothing. "Don't ruin *us*, babe."

"There's no us, Bowie. We're done. You need to leave before she calls the cops. You don't want the police involved, do you?"

Maggie held up her cell and tapped. "Nine, one—"

"No need for the police, ma'am." Bowie held up his hands and jumped into his truck. He kept his gaze leveled on Rita as he circled past.

What a piece of work. Trembling, she looped her arm around one of Robert's in a death grip and pressed her hip to his. "Sorry, Maggie."

When the headlights of Bowie's truck disappeared, Maggie turned to Rita. "What's going on? Is he stalking you? Do I need to ask you to leave?"

"He's been a bit of a problem," Robert said. "But knowing you're a woman to be reckoned with, I'm sure he'll stay away."

Rita blew out a ragged breath. "Can I fill you in over morning coffee?"

Maggie studied her for a long, unnerving moment. "Like I said. Bright and early." She padded back to the house, mumbling.

Robert escorted Rita back to the trailer, his pistol still in his waistband, and called Ethan. "Change of plans."

True to her word, Maggie was doing morning chores at the crack of dawn.

Rita got up, trying to be quiet, and made a pot of coffee.

"What time is it?" Robert poked his head up and rubbed his puffy eyes.

"Go back to bed. You have a long day ahead of you." He was the only man who made her feel safe. But the funny thing was, she felt the need to protect him as well. Or maybe pamper was a better word.

"I can nap later." He crawled out of the hayloft and took clean clothes to the bathroom. While he showered, Rita made him eggs, bacon, and toast. Still upset from their run-in with

Bowie last night, she made herself oatmeal and raisins with strawberry yogurt before cleaning up.

"Let me do the talking when we go over to Maggie's." Robert pulled on his boots. "We don't need to scare her any further. I have a feeling you were lucky to get a spot here, and we don't want to lose it. The barn's pretty full."

"How on earth do you think I'm going to scare her?"

"You were pretty heated up last night. I don't have an emotional connection with your ex." *Other than wanting to pound him.* "I have a better chance of staying calm."

After she dressed and fed Opal, Rita grabbed the coffee pot with cute horsey potholders, and Robert guided her into the house, his hand on the small of her back. She was beginning to feel like they were a couple and kinda liked it.

Inside, Maggie motioned for them to sit at a small kitchen table. Baskets and plants lined a wooden shelf on one side of the sink, and a small island and two chairs sat in the middle. White, wood, and leaf-green trim colored the interior.

"I need the truth. I can't afford to have a ruckus on my place, or I'll have to kick you and your horse to the curb." She plopped down in a chair on the other side of the table.

Robert cleared his throat. "This is simply one man refusing to let go of the past. He's not a contestant and won't come back. Trust me. He's headed home, licking his wounds."

"I hope he doesn't come back. Like I said, I'll have to call the cops and have him arrested. And have you two escorted out of here." Maggie nodded to Rita, her gaze shifting to Robert. "Looks like you got the girl, anyhow. Good for you."

"Something like that." He patted Rita's thigh.

She stiffened and held his hand still. Bowie showing up last night doused the desire for romance. Even at the smallest level. This totally irritated her because she found herself falling for Bobby and didn't want to give him a standoffish vibe.

Maggie rose, found two clean cups in a paint-chipped cupboard, and set them at the table. Rita warmed Maggie's cup with pitch-black coffee and filled the other two to the brim.

Maggie gestured to the center of the table. "There's cream and sugar if you fancy it."

Not able to handle his touch, Rita brushed his hand away. "We'll be gone most of the time anyhow." She sipped her coffee and winced at its acidic taste.

Maggie eyed them. "Tell me again, what are you here for?"

Robert spent the next thirty minutes talking about the Indian National Finals Rodeo and told a few bronc-riding stories. Rita offered to help with a few chores in the mornings, which Maggie happily accepted.

They chatted a little about landscape ideas. Once Rita was sure their host was comfortable with them remaining on her property, she thanked her, and they left.

"You can't promise he won't be back," Rita said as they made their way back to the trailer.

"I have a feeling he'll stay away with Maggie threatening to call the cops." Robert's phone chimed. He slid it out of his back pocket, chatted for a few minutes, and hung up. "Ethan says they set up a meeting with Bowie for tomorrow morning at ten."

"How'd they convince him to meet up?"

"With high-end horses and a brick of heroin."

"No way. Wasn't Bowie a little suspicious of them wanting to hook up here?"

"I don't know. Don't care. If he bites, the charges will stick. And he'll be out of our lives."

Our lives? Shimmers danced up her arms as a sliver of hope settled in. "Yes. Having him gone would be good. And maybe a bit of a miracle. Did Ethan say anything about Hazel? Do they know where she is?"

"No, he didn't. We'll have to trust Ethan and the cops to find her."

Trust. She was still struggling with it and wasn't sure if she'd ever learned to have faith in love—or men—ever again. At least not until Bowie was behind bars and she had time to heal.

She stopped and faced him and nudged him with the warm coffee pot. "Why tomorrow? Why not today?"

"Good question." Robert hadn't thought to ask why they waited until the following day to meet with Bowie. "It must take time to get a team of law enforcement rounded up. Or get the drugs. Or horses."

"Ugh. Waiting this long stinks."

Back in the horse trailer, Robert found her at the table, the space between her brows pinched. "Since we're a day early, we'll have to lie low. Let's go get hay, then help Maggie around here. It'll keep our minds off things." He set his hat on the bed, crown down, settled across from her, and leaned forward to stroke the back of her hand.

She pulled away and slouched against the seat. "I wouldn't mind going to the grounds and getting the lay of the land."

He hated it when she recoiled at his touch. Bowie showing up last night must have thrown her for a loop. He scrubbed his bristly face. "Why? So you can snoop around? See if Hazel's there? C'mon, I'm sure your ex has no idea why we're here."

"Are you kidding me? I'm sure by now, he's figured out who you are, what event you ride, and with the internet's help, are in the INFR at South Point. It doesn't take a rocket scientist to put two and two together."

"I still don't think it's a good idea. Besides, we already promised to help Maggie. We need to keep our word and keep on good terms with her. You don't want to get kicked out of here, do you?"

"No. I don't." She let out a sigh. "You think Hazel's okay?"

"Why would he hurt her?"

CHAPTER 60

Monday Evening

"I don't know what to wear." Rita wanted to pull her hair out. Between the stuffy trailer and her country clothes, she was about ready to toss in the towel. She had thirty minutes to get ready for a ceremony where they handed out back numbers to contestants, and her skin was already sticky from the dry Nevada heat.

Why a special event for the finals?

Helping Maggie in the yard and hanging around the trailer had done nothing to settle her nerves. She'd convinced Robert to take her to the South Point grounds after picking up a few bales of hay, but that hadn't helped either.

What had she been thinking? Bowie wasn't stupid enough to keep Hazel there. To make things worse, she'd worn herself out and had fallen asleep, something she never did in the middle of the day. "You should have woke me up."

"You needed the rest," Robert said from inside the bathroom. "You've managed to work yourself into a frenzy, and it's not helping you or your sister."

Okay, she needed the rest. But her patience was running thin, all because Ethan Harris hadn't called. From her understanding, PIs were supposed to be like bloodhounds. She turned on the kitchen sink faucet and splashed cold water on her face, patted it dry with a paper towel, and got out the bottle of foundation.

"Why a fancy ceremony? Why can't you just pick your number up in the office?"

"Because it's the finals."

She gave him a questioning look.

"It's like the Super Bowl of Indian rodeo. C'mon, have a little fun."

No time for fun. Not with Hazel missing. "And what do I wear, anyway?"

"Jeans and a shirt," Robert said from the bathroom. "It's no big deal." He came out wearing creased jeans, polished boots, a shiny championship belt buckle, a light blue Western shirt, and a navy-blue blazer.

He looked as though he'd already won the event and was headed to celebrity parties. Smelled like it too. She sank to the bench, her elbows on the table, and pressed her hands to her face. "I suppose the other girls will be wearing dresses. I'll stay here," she muttered.

His spicy scent beat him to her side.

Robert took off the blazer and laid it on the table. "Is this better?" He slid into the seat across from her.

She hated how her conflicting emotions gnawed at her. Grateful is what she should be. With a warm roof over her head, food in her belly, and a gorgeous man at her side. It didn't get much better.

Through her slatted fingers, he still looked like he'd stepped off the cover of a glossy men's magazine. "Not really." Rita felt like a frazzled country hick. In her closet at the cabin hung two dresses. She'd worn them once. One for her high school graduation, and one for a relative's funeral. She'd thrown away the summer dress she'd worn for Bowie. For tonight, she threw on a lavender button-up shirt and called it good.

"You're making too much of this. I'm just getting my number, and I want you by my side." He pulled her hands away from her face, his sable eyes connecting with hers. "It would be an honor to escort you."

Why did he have to make her feel so darn special?

Too good to be true. Where had his initial self-indulgence gone? He use to seem pretty full of himself. "Yeah, I'll be fine wearing this."

"You'll be way more comfortable than me." Robert held out his arm for her. "Shall we?" She smoothed his shirtsleeve and smiled. Then in one fluid motion, he slid on his Stetson and pressed his mouth to hers for a long moment.

His warm lips made her forget about long-legged women in short skirts and updos. And his minty mouth drew her to him, but she broke the kiss and brushed a stray hair from her heated face.

He pressed his lips to her ear and whispered, "I like you just the way you are."

She traced his clean-shaven jaw with her finger, his dreamy eyes boring into her bones, and wet her lips.

"Try not to worry tonight," Robert said, his tone still low. "Worrying won't change the outcome and will only drive you crazy."

Oh, how she wanted to kiss him again. Instead, she leaned her head against his chest and soaked in the strong arms wrapped around her. She closed her eyes and fought telling him that she was falling for him. What if this was a whirlwind romance? Would he drop her once they returned to Seven Tine?

Love proved too risky.

Rejection out of the question, she released him, and they walked to the pickup. "What do we know about the sting operation?"

"Ethan was going to call me and fill us in."

"When?"

He opened the passenger door. "He didn't say."

Not knowing made her toes curl in her boots. She climbed into the rig and shut the door.

Robert got in, started the rig, and drove to the end of Maggie's driveway, stopping for thick traffic. He turned onto South Las Vegas Boulevard and headed toward the South Point Hotel, Casino & Spa.

"How long is this shindig going to last?" Rita did like the idea of being his plus-one. She wanted to scoot over and snuggle next to him, draw from his strength and comfort. But in the end, she didn't want to be someone's weekend rodeo fling.

She turned her head to the window, fiddling with her necklace. Vegas was not what she'd expected. A city in the middle of nowhere, surrounded by rugged mountains. Dirt lots and hobby ranches dotted the southern tip of the strip. *How odd.* But she did enjoy the country feeling.

"We don't have to stay for very long. I'm pretty beat."

She didn't want to ruin his night, so she gave him her best smile. "This is going to be fun."

They arrived at South Point and found the Grandview Lounge beyond flashing multicolored slot machines, card tables, and sports-betting areas. The room looked dark and loud, filled with contestants and . . . oh my.

Yep. She'd been right. Her jaw dropped at the sea of high heels and flashy jewelry. Women dressed to the hilt, many wearing low-cut dresses and skirts the size of a sticky note, hung on the arms of their slick-dressed cowboys.

She tried to back out. But Robert looped his arm around hers and led her farther inside. She muttered, "I'm going to kill you."

"I had no idea. They just said to dress nice but casual."

Yeah, casual for the cowboys. Their ladies were another story. "I'll wait outside. Don't hurry. I can check out the grounds." She tried to break away, but he kept her arm knotted with his.

"Stay with me. Please."

"I feel like a fool . . ." And oh, so dreadful and plain.

"You're twice as beautiful as these guys . . . ladies . . . and their painted faces and blinding jewelry. You're fine just the way you are. I prefer sincerity over big hair, high heels, and glitzy nails."

"And long legs. Don't forget those." She said as a lanky woman in a mid-thigh halter dress slung past.

He led her to the bar.

A big girl, she could spur through her humiliation. Right?

CHAPTER 61

Tuesday

For Rita, today went off without a hitch. She supposed for Robert too. So far, she'd survived the back-number ceremony, day one of the rodeo, and the morning working in Maggie's yard. Her lawn and flower beds at least looked presentable. She planned to finish the job Wednesday morning.

The rodeo felt like a regular circuit event. Nothing special. No themes. No sign of Bowie or Gary.

Or Hazel.

Rita hated having no distractions. Fear and doubt haunted her that day and night. At this point, she'd do anything to get her sister back—and never have to see Bowie again.

She couldn't even get into the vendors and their sparkly jewelry or stylish clothing that dotted the arena concourse. The cowboy hats only reminded her of the special buckaroo hat she'd left behind.

Stupid move.

Wednesday Night

Rita panicked at the thought of being in the spectator stands another night alone—without Hazel—as rodeo fans bumped her, stepped on her toes, and shoved past as they scrambled into the event center.

While Robert went to dump his saddle behind the chutes, Rita found cowboy hats among the throng of vendors on the concourse. She perused their assortment, perturbed she wasn't allowed to go with him. For some reason, it didn't feel right to attend a rodeo without one. Plus, the added head covering might help her feel more camouflaged.

She'd hoped by now Ethan would have called with news of her sister. For crying out loud, this was day two of the finals. Had something gone wrong? Had Bowie been a no-show? Why hadn't Ethan called?

Opening ceremonies were in an hour, and boy, did she feel vulnerable. She twisted the companion bracelet around her wrist. Irritated, she'd have to wear it all week to gain entrance into the rodeo. The darn thing felt like a pair of handcuffs confining her, making her feel claustrophobic and imprisoned.

Spectators dressed in colorful ribbon shirts and skirts caught her attention. According to the program, the theme was "Traditional Day" or "Red for Missing Indigenous Women." She'd always wanted a ribbon skirt and wanted to make it herself. But there'd never been enough time in the day.

She selected a wide-brimmed Atwood hat and paid with her dad's cash. A few booths down, she found a woman selling western wild rags. She fingered one in turquoise, orange, and black silk fabric. Bold and noticeable wouldn't keep her disguised. She chose a drab black and white floral instead and paid for it with her credit card. With vendors living in various states, the charge wouldn't disclose her location.

Now, to find a spot to the side of the crowd where she could lean against the wall and wait. Rita hated waiting. She slipped the wild rag around her neck, tied a buckaroo square knot, and traced one of the silky tails with her fingers, a familiar feeling from childhood. She and her sister used to practice tying the knot on each other.

Oh, Hazel. Where are you? Thinking about her produced hot tears, but she wiped them away, not wanting to give in to the sorrow and fear and guilt.

Several minutes later, Robert walked toward her leading a couple of men. "Hey, these are my buddies, Tyler and Kaden. This is my friend Rita. Tyler rides broncs and Kaden bulls." Tyler, short and thin with a barrel chest and cropped hair, gave her a small wave. Kaden, taller and twiggy with chiseled features, smiled at her. "They live on the Colville rez too." All three cowboys wore eagle feathers attached to the beaded headbands of their hats.

As handsome as Robert looked in his green ribbon shirt, she found it hard to concentrate on what he was saying. The garment, adorned with green and black ribbons and a black elk on his chest, whispered class.

He handed her a large paper bag with handles. "I got you a little something."

"Me? What for?" Goodness. Another gift? But she hadn't gotten him anything. And now she felt like a schmuck and a freeloader. She'd have to find a way to pay him back for all his generosity.

She opened the crumpled sack and pulled out a lilac-colored ribbon skirt with parallel ribbons a few inches above the hem in shades of purple, white, and black. Embroidered roses vined between running horses on the lines of connecting ribbon. One of them a smokey gray like Opal. She swallowed hard, not knowing what to say to such a beautiful gift.

"Dig deeper." Robert's gaze was pinned on her as though his buddies didn't exist.

Huh? Rita fidgeted, embarrassed at such an extravagant gift. But when Robert gave her another nudge, she laid the ribbon skirt over her arm and retrieved a lavender tunic to match.

Tyler and Kaden let out low whistles. Kaden prodded Robert with his elbow. "Looks like you're more than friends, bro."

Robert's buddies laughed. And it didn't seem to faze Robert.

His face lit up. "Figured we could get a photo before grand entry."

No man had ever given her a gift this valuable just for the heck of it. Or did he want something in return? "What do I owe you?" She reached for her wallet, afraid of being manipulated—and possibly trapped by her need to be loved.

The light in Robert's eyes dimmed. "Nothing. It's a gift." His face turned a few shades of red as he shifted his weight and gave her his best crushed-hearted smile. "Why don't you try them on. You've got time." When she didn't answer, he said, "I'd like a photo with you before I have to change shirts."

The cowboys teased Robert and Rita about being just friends, making her neck prickle. She opened her mouth, ready to give them a piece of her mind but noticed the embarrassed grin on Robert's face. Oh. Did he have feelings for her? Like she did for him? Real feelings, not a weekend-fling kind of deal? "I'll be right back." She pressed her palm to her sweaty cheek as she headed to the women's restroom to change.

In an empty stall, she fingered the silky ribbon of her skirt. It seemed as though he'd read her mind. And the running horses—one in her mare's grulla hue—told her he hadn't simply plucked one off the rack. He'd put genuine thought into the outfit.

Noting the time, she pulled on the skirt over her pants and fixed it to cover her ragged boots. She rolled up her pant legs. Better.

Before they'd left, she tucked her Leatherman into her right boot, just in case. It made her feel like an outlaw, not a lady. But the soft tunic gave her a sense of womanhood. A belt or jean jacket would have completed the ensemble. Something she could add later. When satisfied with how things looked, she rushed back to Robert.

Added whistles floated through the air, and heat warmed her face.

"You look nice." Tyler jabbed a thumb toward Robert. "This guy's on a roll, man. If he keeps kicking butt, he'll not only have a fine-looking woman, but he'll have the title too."

"Oh?" He hadn't talked about how he'd been doing. She figured maybe not as well as he'd hoped, hence the silence when it came to his standings. In her quest to remain hidden, she hadn't thought to ask. How inconsiderate of her.

Kaden took their photo with Robert's cell phone. "These are good. You two make a nice couple."

Robert didn't bother to correct him. Quite the opposite. He beamed as though they were together as he draped an arm around her good shoulder.

After Kaden handed the cell back, he and Tyler headed to the chutes, leaving Robert and Rita alone. He turned to her, less than an inch away, and ran his fingers down her wild rag. "Nice scarf. It looks good with your new skirt and hat." He lifted a finger to her jaw and traced it. "You are one beautiful lady." He bent down and gave her a firm kiss. "I don't need this kind of distraction," he whispered.

"You've been winning?" Her fingers traced the ribbon on his shirt. She could feel the thump of his heart as they slid to the elk. Hers kept pace.

"I've held my own."

"Congratulations. And thanks for the skirt. I've always wanted one."

"No one will be expecting you to wear it either."

"You got a point." How on earth would she be able to keep hold of him when they got back to Washington?

"Will you be okay?" He brushed his lips over her fingers.

"I have to go for the contestants' meeting."

"I don't see why not." She rubbed his forearm.

"I'll see you when I'm done."

She nodded, not wanting to let go of him.

Robert didn't ride for about an hour, so Rita made her way down the escalators and through a corridor between the hotel and casino, passing folks dressed in their Western and Indigenous attire and went straight to the hotel's elongated registration desk.

Used to a quiet country life, the buzz of bells and whistles and voices, not to mention the smoke, made her feel dizzy. She waited in line between wooden columns and tried to admire the metal chandeliers hanging overhead. When her turn came around, her boots clicked on the shiny, starred floor. "May I have a hotel map, please?"

"Of course." The receptionist smiled and handed her one. "Let me know if you need anything else."

She went to the Catalina Island Bar, eyed the impressive array of alcoholic beverages, and ordered a lemon-lime soda. Hawkeye's rancid breath on her neck and face the night he attacked her had ruined any desire for alcohol. Still, a stiff drink would've helped her nerves. Half expecting trouble at some point, she settled at a table, took a sip, and pressed the condensation-covered glass to the side of her face.

She studied the small hotel map and googled South Point, then shuddered. *Shoot.* There were too many places Bowie could hide. She counted eleven restaurants, a fitness center, pool, spa, bingo hall, movie theater, bowling, twenty-two breakout rooms, an arena, parking garage, and an indoor barn. Her gut coiled into a tight knot. The place overwhelmed her. Good Lord, Bowie could remain hidden for days.

According to a clock on the wall, she had enough time to investigate the outdoor pool. She dumped her plastic cup in the trash, folded the map, and tucked it into the bag holding her shirt. On her way, she weaved in and out of slot machines, gamblers, and hotel and casino staff.

A busty woman with blonde curly hair and dark roots, ivory skin, and a short knit dress stopped her. "Your skirt's beautiful. Does it have some kind of meaning?" she asked, a slight slur to her words.

The alcohol on her breath smelled like rum and coke. One of Bowie's favored drinks. "It's a traditional ribbon skirt. It's a modern expression of my Native roots."

"You're so beautiful. May I . . .?" She held up her cell phone.

Rita shook her head, blocked the camera with her hand. "No, please. I-uh . . ."

The woman frowned and staggered away.

By the angle of the camera, Rita figured the woman had snuck a photo anyhow. Maybe she should have allowed her to take a snapshot of just the skirt because her face was off-limits. *Too late. Darn it.* The last thing she wanted was to be plastered all over social media.

CHAPTER 62

R ita made a beeline toward the glass doors leading to the pool, which would close soon due to the cold nights. She shoved them open and breathed in the fresh, desert air. Palm trees and lounge chairs edged the curvy pool. A handful of children and adults enjoyed the turquoise water, hot tub, and padded seats. *What a beautiful hotel.* If only she were here for pleasure.

She took off her boots, tucked the Leatherman in her right one, and rolled up her pants legs higher. After sitting by the edge, she dipped her feet into the cool water, closed her eyes, not realizing how tense she'd been, and inhaled the pungent aroma of . . . chlorine. Yuck.

A stiff breeze caressed her face and neck and just when she began to relax, just a little, a shirtless cabana boy dressed in tight jeans and flashy cowboy boots with gorgeous green eyes knelt beside her.

"What can I get you?"

Rita gave him a small smile. "I'm fine. Thanks." She turned back to the water and sighed. She dreamed of what life with Robert Elliot might look like.

"There you are." He kept his voice calm and loving. Deceptive. "Flirting, I see."

She stiffened. Where'd Bowie come from? Good Lord. The lunatic had to have had eyes on her the entire time. But how? Who? Would he try anything with an audience? Surely not.

"You look absolutely gorgeous in your new outfit. But I'm surprised with one piece of it."

Shoot. She'd left her knife by the lounge chair. But wait. His speech sounded slightly slurred. A sign his reflexes would be slower. Good.

"Will you at least get out of the water and talk to me?" He knelt beside her, an arm behind his back. Was it a gun? Knife? *Oh, Lord, help me.*

His soothing tenor reminded her of a slithering snake, low and deadly. Tired of being hunted like an injured doe, she braced herself for his next move, not feeling one ounce of affection, pity, or compassion for him. Maybe it was blind faith, but she didn't feel fear either. Just rage.

Yeah, Bowie had a hard childhood, and for a long time, she'd held empathy for him. Never again. At some point, he needed to make the choice to help or heal people. Not hurt them. She decided he no longer had the power to hurt her.

"I have a gift for you."

Of course he did. His way of reeling her back into his good graces. And he knew it worked—most of the time. But his control over her now lived in the past. Prepared to resist him, she kept her gaze pinned on the shimmering pool. "I'm not interested."

He dangled her buckaroo hat over the pool. Like bait. Or a snare.

His words came to mind: *"But I'm surprised with one piece of it."* She bet he was.

"I was wrong to take Hazel. She's on her way back to your dad's ranch. Your folks are worried about you. I told them I'd bring you home. And I'm willing to do whatever it takes to win you back. Honey . . . please . . . I promise nothing like this will ever happen again. I love you—"

"Jealousy, manipulation, threats, isolation. None of it is love, Bowie."

"We can work through our past, babe. Heal together."
He took her by the elbow, lifted her to her feet, and ran his
hands down her arms. "See, I'm not even mad. We can have
a happy life together. I need you. Can't see myself with any
other woman. And I know you need me. No one else could
ever love you like I do." He set her buckaroo hat on her head
and tossed the Atwood aside. "A perfect fit." After glaring
at the cabana boy while he strode by, Bowie pulled a small
velvet box from the inside of his jacket.

Rita put space between them, hoping no one was listening
to their conversation.

"I know how much this hat means to you. C'mon now. I
saved it for you. And the purse. And now you have a bigger,
better diamond. The engagement ring you deserve." Bowie's
eyes creased when he gave her a wanting grin and stepped
close.

Too close. She caught a strong whiff of rum and coke and
recoiled at the spirit-filled stench and his freshly trimmed
goatee. And he thought a bigger ring would rope her in? Not
today. Or any day. *Oh, God, help me stay calm.*

"Look what I bought to add to your cowboy hat." He
reached behind him, then brandished a hatband made of
small, turquoise-blue nuggets threaded between purple, red,
and white seed beads.

Buy me off? She grunted. "Sorry. I can't accept—"

He yanked her close and forced a rough kiss on her
mouth, hurting her lips as they pressed against her teeth. The
rum and coke made her want to puke. It was worse when he
tried to deepen the kiss. Squirming, she tried to shove him
away, but his grip proved as strong as an anaconda's.

When he finally broke the kiss, she stepped back and
raised her hand to slap him. He dropped the hatband and
grabbed her wrist, his mouth in a tight line as if fighting off
the urge to lose his cool. After a short moment, the corners

of his lips tugged up, and his eyes softened. "C'mon now, babe. Let's make a go of it. We can get help."

"Not sure there'd be enough counseling for you."

"Like I said, whatever it takes."

Yeah, whatever. What a freaking liar. Oh, how she wanted the knife in her boot. Wanted her freedom. Wanted Robert.

Bowie leaned down, a breath away, and whispered, "We're getting married tonight."

Married? Tonight? A scream broke from her lips, and she shoved him toward the water as hard as she could. Bowie lost his balance and grabbed at her. She lifted her ribbon skirt and kicked him in the groin. The ring sailed through the air and landed in the pool. When he hit the water with a loud splash, sending screaming swimmers to the pool's edge, she gathered her belongings and sprinted toward the exit gate.

Once out, she dashed down the alleyway between the pool and the Priefert Pavilion, pebbles pricking her feet, and hightailed it to the casino side entrance doors, juggling her belongings. She swung open the glass doors and dashed straight to the nearest ladies' restroom. After locating an open stall, she went in and locked the door, her lungs and nerves on fire.

She slid off and hugged her buckaroo hat—the closest thing she had to family—forcing herself to drag in deep breaths, blowing them out until her lungs were empty. If only she could stop trembling.

Someone tapped on the door. "You okay in there?" The woman sounded like an elder. Soft. Caring.

Rita nodded. "Yes, I am. Thank you for your concern, ma'am."

"You sure?"

"Yes. I'm sure. And I appreciate your concern." *Now, please, go.*

"You got shoes?"

Rita wiggled her toes, then cringed at the thought of her bare feet on a cold, germ-infested floor. "My boots are right here."

"All right then. If you're sure."

"I'm sure."

The click of the woman's footsteps faded.

Exhaling, Rita pulled on her socks and boots and settled her buckaroo hat back on her head. She went to the sink and splashed cool water on her face. She smoothed her ribbon skirt.

The mirror revealed rogue strands of midnight-colored hair framing her heart-shaped face. With a drop of water, she combed them into place. Her red-blotched face looked as ragged as she felt.

Had Bowie sent Hazel home? Or was it another one of his bald-faced lies?

She searched for her phone, not finding it anywhere. Oh, no. Had she left it at the pool? Had it fallen out of her pocket? She bolted from the bathroom, past the sickening scent of cigarette smoke, and headed toward the event center. She couldn't go back to the pool. By now it had closed. She couldn't retrace her steps. Not yet. Not with Bowie on the loose.

Never had she felt such a powerful ache to find safe arms. Instead of taking the escalator, she ran up the steep, carpeted staircase. In the lobby, she found Robert leaning against the wall, his gear bag and saddle dumped at his feet, phone in hand. The look on his face, a mix of disappointment and worry, made her heart drop to her toes. She'd missed his ride. It looked as though he couldn't speak. Couldn't move. Couldn't breathe.

Or was it she who felt paralyzed?

He looked up and strode to her. "I've been trying to call you. Where've you been?"

Out of breath, she said, "I lost my phone. C'mon." She grabbed his arm and started for the lost and found desk to find her phone. She had to find out if Hazel indeed had been sent home.

"Wait." He went back, slung his saddle over his shoulder, and got his gear bag. "Where are we going?" They stepped onto the escalator.

"To find my phone. I had a run-in with Bowie and—"

"You what? Where?" Robert glanced around.

"Out by the hotel pool."

"What the heck were you doing by the pool?" When they exited the escalator, Robert herded Rita into the hallway near the lost and found desk.

"I came to check out the hotel and got a map of the grounds. The flashing lights, dings, and drunks got to me, so I went outside and dipped my feet in the water. I meant to relax for a few minutes before watching you. Can you call Ethan? Bowie claims he sent Hazel home. But he's lying. I know it."

"I'll make the call. But first, tell me what happened," he said, his voice filled with concern.

Rita hugged her jacket. "He gave me the usual cockamamie story, trying to convince me to marry him tonight. I shoved him into the pool and ran for it."

"You shoved him in the pool?" A hint of a smile tipped his lips.

"Yeah, with the help of my foot to his . . . well, you know what."

"Huh. You little scrapper." He winked at her and made a call. "Hey, Ethan, it's Robert. Bowie attacked Rita tonight. And claims Hazel's on her way home."

CHAPTER 63

Robert ended the call. Outside the hallway, contestants wearing their INFR jackets and rodeo spectators filled the space near a gigantic bronze statue of a cowboy on a horse. "They lost track of Bowie. He was a no-show."

"A flipping no-show? These are professionals. How can they lose him, for crying out loud?" She slammed her hands on her hips.

"They'll find him. And I doubt he'd be stupid enough to come back." *He'd be embarrassed to have a wisp of a girl toss him in the drink.* He chuckled, then shifted his weight. "Listen, I won tonight and plan to go to my interview at the championship buckle ceremony. From the podium, I can see the crowd. See if he's around or not."

"While you give your interview, I'll try to find my phone." She turned and darted away.

"Rita, wait." She disappeared through the crowd. Good thing lost and found sat behind them. What was she up to? He pushed out a deep groan and headed for the Grandview Lounge, a bit irritated she'd missed his winning ride. And now she wasn't interested in his interview as the go-round champion. A big deal—experienced only at the finals. Go figure.

He took an end seat in the contestants' section near the stage of the dim room. Music played, and voices chirped. His eyes scanned the packed crowd. No sign of her. The announcer welcomed everyone and called up the night's bareback champion. They discussed his ride while the replay showed behind them on a big screen.

As they talked, Robert swung his gaze around the noisy crowd and locked eyes with Rita. She made her way to him and crouched.

"You find it?" Robert asked, thankful she'd come.

"No."

"You see Bowie?"

"Nope. But after him showing up at the pool, I doubt a crowd will scare him off." She stood and strode back toward the bar serving as a barrier between them and the casino.

He agreed with her, which tied his gut up tighter. Cameras flashed, the bareback rider and stock contractor left the stage, and the announcer called up the winning steer wrestler. When they were done, the champion barrel racer took her turn. He struggled to concentrate on the conversations.

How would Ethan find Dark Cloud before Rita's ex cornered her again? He couldn't be with her twenty-four seven. And he certainly couldn't force her to stay put. The last thing he wanted to do was go up on stage and leave Rita alone. No, he'd take her back to Maggie's, call Chuck, and figure out what to do. He leaned forward to stand up and haul Rita out of there.

"Let's get our saddle bronc champ up here," the announcer said. "Put your hands together for Robert Elliot from the Colville Reservation."

No. No. No. He needed to get Rita out of here but found himself standing and moving toward the podium as the crowd cheered. His pulse thundered as he hopped up the stairs.

The announcer shook his hand, and asked, "So, you got to be here a couple nights. Got to look at all the horses. Was this horse kinda who you hoped to have in your lottery, so to speak?"

"Yeah, these horses are fresh and have a lot of buck in them. I've been watching videos of him, and he's probably one of the stronger ones in the pack."

He'd imagined this day for years. Had planned to talk about the bronc and how he handled it. Use humor to reel in the crowd. Take in the night, moment by moment.

But his mind stuck on Rita, whom he suddenly couldn't find. Yeah, she was a big girl. But darn her if she went rogue again. He squinted. Wait. A woman tilted her face up, and he blew out a breath. *Thank God.* She sat in one of the back chairs, flanked by two women.

"Talk us through this ride," the host said as the replay rolled on the big screen.

No. He didn't want to talk anyone through the ride. The sooner they left, the harder it'd be for Dark Cloud to find Rita.

And then . . . hell opened its doors. It paved the way for Bowie Dark Cloud to step into view for a few seconds, give Robert a smirk, and disappear behind a horde of cowboy hats.

"I-uh . . ." *Am going to make sure he never touches Rita again.* "Tried to hold him on the second jump . . ." *What? Did that even make sense?* He spurred through talking about his ride as the replay scrolled across the screen, sure he wasn't making a lick of sense.

When the replay was finished, the host brought up Troy Carson of D & D Rodeo to talk about the bronc. Yeah, the stock contractor deserved his time in the spotlight, but man, this was the longest two minutes of Robert's life. He accepted a boxed buckle and eagle feather from Miss Indian Rodeo, smiled as a photographer snapped photos, and rushed off the platform.

Cowboys stopped to applaud him as he struggled to make his way to where Rita had been sitting. And when he finally arrived, the chair stood empty. Not again.

He searched the crowd, his pulse kicking up a notch. When he couldn't find her in the lounge, he rushed to the pool. Closed! *Where could she have gone?* He went back to the casino and weaved through slot machines and gaming tables, searched restaurants and bars. After coming up empty, he climbed several stairs to the upper level and checked the theater, bowling alley, and bingo hall.

Nothing.

He made his way back to the lounge in case she'd wandered back, his senses on high alert, afraid Bowie had gotten to her first.

CHAPTER 64

"Hey, Rita."

She turned to find her long-time friend from the Umatilla rez, Emily Nelson, coming out of the lounge. Dressed in a floral ribbon skirt, the bottom half adorned with the backs of Indigenous women holding hands between horizontal strips of red, white, and black ribbon and cowgirl boots, she asked, "You okay?"

"I can't find my . . . um . . . friend." She felt helpless without her cell phone. She hadn't found it when she'd quickly retraced her steps back to the pool, the lane between it and the Priefert Pavilion, and the sidewalk to the casino. The inky night didn't help matters.

"Want me to help you look for . . . him?" Emily leaned a shoulder against the outside of the lounge's railing, a beer in hand and a sassy smile on her face.

About to say yes, she caught Robert striding toward her, nostrils flaring. "Oh, there he is. Listen. I'll catch up with you later."

"Call if you need anything. My number's the same."

"Will do." Rita marched toward Robert, still miffed about having to stay for the interview. But then again, they were not an item. She took responsibility for all things Rita Runninghorse. On a quest to conquer his rodeo dreams, he rode broncs. Plain and simple.

"Where've you been? I've been worried sick."

"Didn't know I needed to check in."

"This isn't about checking in or me controlling you." His hand on the small of her back, he led her inside the foyer near where the buckle ceremony was held. "When I couldn't find you . . . I thought he . . ." He turned his head and mashed his lips together, eyes glistening.

"But you said he wouldn't come back."

"I didn't think he'd be stupid enough to show his face again. But while on stage, I saw him by the bar." Robert curled his fist into a ball. *He's relentless.*

"What? Where'd he go?" The room felt like it was spinning. She clutched his arm to steady herself.

"I don't know. He made sure I saw him though." He put an arm around her waist. "Let's get out of here."

Payton walked up to them, keys in hand. "Hate to interrupt, but we're heading out. You comin'?"

With Dark Cloud after the woman he loved? "No. But thanks."

Payton clapped him on the back. "Congrats, man. I'll text you where we'll be in case you change your mind." He waved his cell in the air as he swaggered away.

"Let's go." When they reached the truck, Robert called Ethan. "Yeah, he showed his ugly face again. Made sure I saw him."

Rita prayed the PI would find Bowie. And soon.

Thursday Afternoon

Why hadn't Ethan called yet?

Rita needed to find Emily Nelson. But darned if the security guard wasn't hovering around the door leading to the indoor barn. She rode up the escalator, swung around and came down the other side, trying to figure out how to finagle her way inside. When she got back to the landing, he was gone. And no one stood at the podium chaperoning the escalators. What fortune.

After slipping inside, Rita found Emily Nelson saddling her horse outside the mare's black-paneled stall. She stroked the palomino mare's neck, trying not to breathe in too much of the odor from horse waste hanging in the stagnant air. Horses' hooves clicked on the concrete as competitors led their mounts outside.

"Hey, I lost my cell yesterday. Can I use yours to call my mom?"

"You sure can." Emily handed her the phone.

Rita went over to the outdoor Farnam Arena where she could breathe in fresh air and called her mom.

"Hello?"

Dad?

"Um. . ." *Shoot. Why did you open your mouth?*

"Rita? Where are you? Where's Hazel? You girls need to get home. We—"

She ended the call. Okay. If Bowie had sent Hazel home, she should have been there by now. So where was she? Rita went back to the stall and handed Emily her phone.

"Everything okay? You look a little pale." Emily asked her as Kris Arnold and Heather Snow approached them. Oh, how'd she missed these ladies! And here they were, together again after years of being estranged—and in the worst circumstances ever for a reunion.

"Yeah. Thanks for letting me use your phone." Rita offered Kris a smile, hoping her friend wouldn't see how upset she was. "Good to see you. Looks like you guys are doing well, huh?"

Kris gave Rita a warm hug. "We're holding our own. Good to see you too."

"I'll catch up with you in a minute," Emily said to Kris, then turned to Rita. "Come with me." They went outside and stopped beside the panels holding calves. "I've known you too long. Now tell me what's going on?"

"Nothing. Just tired is all."

Emily studied her. "You party last night?"

Was she kidding? "No. Went to bed after we, uh, I got back."

"Where you staying?"

"Nearby."

"Nearby, huh? Where's this *friend* of yours, anyway? From what I saw last night, he's one sexy dude."

"He's just a friend." She wanted to explain her predicament, but it wasn't the time or place.

"I'm not buying it, Rita. I saw the way you looked at each other. Can't fool me, sister. How'd you two meet?"

"You better go warm up. I'll tell you about him later." Knowing later would never come. *Shoot.* Just when she'd reconnected with her friends, she'd have to avoid them. No way would she get them involved and have Bowie come after them too.

"Fair enough." Emily swung into the saddle. "It's good to see you again."

"You too." Rita felt awful as Emily urged her horse into the arena.

She enjoyed watching them warm up. Part of her wished she was back home, herding cattle. So far, the barrel horses had all been turning tight, with only one can knocked over. *But wait. Was Heather Snow going into the arena?*

She, Heather, Emily, and Kris had been inseparable as kids but had drifted apart by their sophomore year. Until now, she'd never had the chance to reconnect with them—thanks to her dad and Bowie. Sydney had taught her isolation was one of the seven types of abuse.

Stalking wasn't on the list but definitely felt like an abuse of personal boundaries.

As Heather made her final turn, a man wearing a Wildhorse Casino cap and a black T-shirt came into view beyond the barrel-racing pair as they flew toward the finish line. Was it the same guy she'd seen in the Deschutes Fairgrounds in Oregon?

Rita tried to get a better look at him when Emily and her yellow mare burst into the arena and raced around the first barrel. She inched down the arena's half wall, but the man had disappeared.

Finding one of the rolling doors open, she slipped into the indoor barn and rounded a corner to find Wildhorse several stalls away, trying to appear inconspicuous. "Hey!"

At the sound of her voice, he disappeared between two sections of stalls. She jogged around the area, seeing horses in the aisles or locked in their stalls, and went for the exit to the hotel and casino. Darn. He'd lost her again. She had to find Robert.

He wasn't in the event center, so she made her way to the casino. He wasn't there either. After searching for nearly an hour, she needed fresh air. The dings and cheers and chatter and cigarette smoke choked her. She went to the pool and eased into a lounge chair under a shade tree and rubbed a sharp throb near her temple.

She leaned back and closed her eyes, covering them with her arm. A twinge of hopelessness mingling with anxiety made her want to gag. She cringed from the noise of kids screaming and splashing.

"There you are." Robert sat down beside her. "I've been looking for you."

"Same here."

Robert took off his cowboy hat and wiped his face with the sleeve of his Western shirt. "Where've you been?"

"The guy who was with Bowie at the caves is here. I caught him watching me while I was with a few friends from home by the outdoor arena."

"The guy in Redmond?" He glanced around.

"Same one. But I have an idea. Come with me." She led him to the registration desk. "Is a Bowie Dark Cloud registered?" She frowned when the attendant shook his head. Her mind played with various names Bowie could have used. Even Frank or Jeff. Then it hit her. "Do you have a Frank Hawley listed?"

"Sure do. Would you like me to ring his suite?"

CHAPTER 65

Rita waited until Robert went behind the chutes to drop off his gear.

She headed to the hotel lobby, feeling like an amateur sleuth in an old Western movie wearing a cowboy hat low over her eyes and a wild rag around her neck, ready to be pulled over her nose if the need arose. Bowie had been clever to use his father's first name and his mother's maiden name.

A pair of Wild Wolf slot machines caught her attention. She clutched her arms and zeroed in on a man beside them. Was it Bowie? She stepped back to see Wildhorse watching her near images of gray-and-tan wolf faces with their haughty eyes.

He trapped her gaze for an instant before he turned and went for the hallway leading to the hotel elevators. Instead of following him, she fast walked toward the corridor leading to the arena. A couple bumped into her, splashing their beers on her sky-blue button-up shirt. Between the alcohol and the smoke, she smelled like a cheap nightclub.

Bowie cut her off just past the bronze cowboy and his horse. "Come with me."

Rita turned to flee, but his beefy hand wrapped around her arm. She lifted a foot and slammed it into his shin. He groaned and slapped her so hard, she crumpled to the ground.

"You witch." A slow, low groan came from his mouth as he yanked her up by her hair. Clutching Bowie's hands, Rita screeched as she rose to her feet.

"Hey, let her go!" A burly man and three other men the size of bouncers stormed toward her.

Bowie let go and fled, leaving Rita dizzy and breathless, her head burning.

She turned to find Wildhorse staring at her from several feet away. She got up and started for the indoor barn.

"Do you need help?" The burly dude stopped and held out his hands.

Over her shoulder, she hollered, "I'm good. Thanks." She tore down the hallway. *Please let me in.* With the security guard's attention on a cute gal dressed in slinky Western attire, she followed a cowboy into the barn and found Emily watering her horse and Heather leaning against a metal panel. "I need your help."

Her expression must have startled Heather and Emily because they escorted her into an unlocked stall filled with hay bales and grooming supplies. Inside Rita blurted, "My ex-fiancé just attacked me in the casino, and one of his creepy friends is following me. Can you text Robert? Tell him I'm down here?"

Emily watched the aisle. "What does he look like?" She slapped her riding crop in the palm of her hand.

"Bowie's tall, tough looking. Wears a black Atwood and a goatee. He kinda looks like Jacob Nighthorse on *Longmire*. The other guy's in a black T-shirt and a Wildhorse Casino hat."

The click of heavy footfalls came close. Emily grabbed Heather by the arm, their bodies blocking Rita crouched behind them. When the footsteps faded, she stayed down for a few extra minutes, just to be sure.

"It's clear," Emily whispered before turning and kneeling beside Rita.

"Was it Bowie?" Rita asked. "Or Wildhorse?"

Heather handed her phone to Rita. "Here. I think I got a good enough shot of him."

Rita nodded. "Yep. That's Wildhorse. I'm not sure who he is. Have either of you seen him before?"

Heather took her phone back and studied it. "Isn't he Gary Fullmoon's brother, Jeff?"

"Is it?" Rita hadn't seen him in years. Hardly knew him.

"Oh, I know who your ex is," Emily said. "Isn't his mom Edna?"

"Yeah, she is. How do you know her?"

"My mom and Edna used to hang around when I was little. She'd come over for coffee, and they'd play cards and shoot the breeze. Yeah, Bowie's creepy. And so are Gary and Jeff. You need to call the police."

"They're already involved. I need Robert to come get me and to call Ethan."

"Who's Ethan?" Heather furrowed her brows.

"Some PI guy Robert's brother-in-law knows." Rita sighed. "I can't explain things right now. I just need to get out of here."

Emily handed her cell to Rita. "Here, use this."

She took it and called Robert, glad she'd taken the time to memorize his number back in Oregon. It went to voice mail. "Darn." She texted him a message to call security and meet her in stall number 1016.

"We'll put our horses away and come wait with you," Emily said. "Did you have him call security?"

"Yeah, I did. And you don't need to come back. I'll be okay."

Emily shook her head. "Still the same Rita, Miss Independent."

"I came and asked you for help, didn't I?"

"You did."

Boots clicked on the concrete. *Don't let it be him.* Rita stiffened and held on to Emily's arm until the sound passed.

"It was some chick," Heather said.

"We're staying until they get here," Emily whispered. "I'm not taking any chances."

Rita appreciated Emily's stubborn streak. Heather too. "I'm sorry for allowing my dad and Bowie to isolate me. It won't happen again. I miss you guys."

"It better not," Emily said with a feisty smile. "We miss you too. What do you plan on doing?"

"I'm not sure. Robert rides tonight, so I'll stay put in the stands until he's done." She wasn't about to take off by herself again. Too risky.

"My family's here. You can hang with them." Emily told her where they preferred to sit.

Rita hugged her friends. "Thanks for being there for me. Especially because I don't deserve it."

"Don't talk nonsense. I would have done the same thing," Heather said.

"Yeah, me too." Emily nodded. "Don't be so hard on yourself."

"It's not so easy. Being trapped—threatened—and . . . well . . . to leave was just plain tough. Until recently."

Emily and Heather exchanged glances, and Emily's cell buzzed. She handed it to Rita.

Robert. Thank God.

I'm following Wildhorse. Stay put.

"You guys can go," Rita said. "It might be awhile." She gave Emily back her phone and settled in the corner of the stall.

She drew her legs up and hugged them and rested her head on her knees.

Keep Robert safe.

CHAPTER 66

The stall door slid open, and Robert poked his head in. Thank God she was still there. "Hey." He went in, crouched beside Rita, and put a hand on her thigh. "How ya doin'?"

She gave him a small smile. "I'm fine now that you're here."

"Sorry I took so long. After meeting up with security, we saw Bowie again. I gave them Ethan's number, then followed Wildhorse. Found out what room they're in."

Rita touched his arm. "Did you find Hazel? Did you see her?"

"No, I didn't. But I think she's on the grounds."

"Show me the room." She started to get up.

But he pulled her back down. "No, it's too dangerous. I let Ethan know. He's on his way along with the cops."

"We can't wait for Ethan."

Oh, yes, we can. "We can't get in their way and blow it. Bowie slipped them once. He can do it again. Let's be patient and let the pros do their job."

"Yeah, but—"

"But nothing, Rita. Be patient."

She chewed her bottom lip.

He lifted her chin. "What happened? You have a bruise on your cheek."

She turned away. "It's where Bowie slapped me."

"The dumb son of a gun." Ethan better find him before he did.

The stall door flung open. He swung around and sprang to his feet, fist in the air. Emily poked her head in, shrieked, and ducked.

Rita jumped to her feet and held on to Robert's arm. "She's a friend. Em, come in."

Emily and Heather slid into the cramped stall, and Rita made introductions. "Thanks for coming back, you guys."

"Guess we'll head out since he's here," Emily said. "Sit with my family tonight. They're expecting you."

"I will." She hugged her friends before they left, then followed Robert out of the barn into the fresh, warm air. "What are we going to do? Stake out the room?"

"Like I said before, we're going to stay out of the way and go back to Maggie's. You're going to go love on your horse and relax until the rodeo."

"Relax. Right. Great plan." Rita snorted. They made their way to Robert's truck and got in. "You have no idea what I'm going through. I can't simply sit around and relax." She wiped her damp brow.

He couldn't concentrate on his riding worrying about her. Robert's throat tightened. "Maybe rest is a better word." He pulled out of the parking lot and headed south.

Back at the Open Heart V Farm, Rita jumped out and went to the barn. Robert joined her, studying her hat as she brushed her horse. "I do like your buckaroo hat better than the Atwood." He winked at her.

She chuckled. "My grandmother gave it to me. Bowie found it and thought he could use it to win me back."

"How'd he get a hold of it?"

"The tooled purse you found? That's mine too. I left them both in my truck when I broke down. Figured the cops would get to it first and it would end up back at my dad's ranch. I'm thinking Bowie got there first, broke in, and took them both."

"He's such a dirtbag." Though he could think of much worse names to call him.

"Do you know how difficult it is to know you're damaged goods? I mean, who's going to want someone like me?" Tears leaked from her eyes and streamed down her face.

Robert wiped them away with his thumbs. "I would want you. Remember when you asked me if I thought you were like a plague?"

"Yeah." She sniffed, dabbed at her nose with the cuff of her shirt.

"Well, you're the complete opposite. And I'm scared too, Rita. I'm scared to fall in love again." Although he knew it was too late. He'd already fallen head over heels for Rita Runninghorse. Every day he was with her, she proved to be the one he could settle down with. Forever.

"What do you mean by *again*?"

"I, too, have an ex-fiancée."

"What? Why didn't you say something?"

"I don't know. Maybe because I was so focused on helping you. Maybe because I'm embarrassed." He went into the pen and rubbed Opal's neck.

"Did you leave her? Or was it the other way around? Was it because of rodeo?" She bit her lip.

"She left me for a bull rider. Said bronc riding wasn't exciting enough." He chuckled—the kind of laugh that shoved unwanted emotions back down his gullet.

"Oh, wow." *What a fool.*

"Yeah. I thought about quitting—"

"Over a girl?"

"Yeah. But Chad gave me such a hard time over it, I kept riding to prove him wrong." After a long moment, he asked, "Do you think you're damaged goods?"

"Yeah. I do." She rested against her mare.

Robert gently slid off her hat and drew her into his arms, inhaled her humiliation and insecurities and vulnerability, and kissed her sweaty head. "You're the best thing that's ever happened to me." He hated Bowie. Hated Hawkeye. Hated Dean Runninghorse. And he didn't know any of them. But he knew he hated what they'd done to her.

"I am?" She lifted her face to him.

"You're the craziest, most amazing, fiercest woman I've ever met."

"But how can you love a killer like me? I'm no good—"

"It was self-defense, honey. That monster took away your childhood."

"Then why does it feel like God's punishing me?"

CHAPTER 67

Friday Morning

Near ten, Rita blinked her eyes open. Had she read the wrong time on a new burner phone? Robert had bought it for her the previous day to use to call for help if needed. Having the cell phone made her feel safer physically but not mentally or emotionally. It felt like she'd been on a four-day bender—or at least what she'd heard being on one was like—after crying most of the night. And she hated feeling so . . . so weak. She sat up to a stuffy, empty trailer.

So much for being the best thing to happen to Robert Elliot.

She pulled on her boots and slipped into a T-shirt and jeans, then shoved her sunglasses on her nose and went to check on her mare. A stiff breeze met her at the door. She found Opal munching on the last of the hay in her feeder, appearing to be as happy as a puppy with a full belly. "Did you have a good night, girl?"

Leaning against a panel, she noticed Robert's truck was gone too. Maggie's Open Heart V Ranch cut-out metal sign swayed and creaked. And right before she felt the urge to panic, Robert's truck rumbled up the driveway and halted by the trailer.

Two doors slammed shut as she closed the horse pen. Who was with him? Closer to the truck, she found Chuck and Robert heading to the trailer.

Robert noticed her and grinned. "You're awake." He opened the trailer door and waited for her to enter first.

"Hey, Chuck. What's up?"

"How 'bout I tell you over a hot cup of coffee?"

"Sounds good to me." Rita climbed the step and went inside. For some reason, Chuck's presence made her edgy. The look on his face didn't help. Or the static she'd felt as she'd passed him on her way into the trailer. She gathered the supplies and made a pot of strong coffee.

"Rita?" Robert's voice boomed.

"Huh?" She turned to him.

"Do you think you can handle it?"

"Sorry. My brain's working overtime. Handle what?"

"Let Ethan do his job and stay out of the way?"

He had to be kidding. "I'm sorry, whose way have I been in?" She poured three cups of coffee, inhaled the aroma, hoping it might settle her raw nerves, and took them to the table. Robert scooted over and she took a seat next to him.

"They're close to nailing Bowie," Chuck said. "Ethan wants you to stay here. He thinks it's safer."

"How's staying at Maggie's safer? Bowie knows we're here. If he can't find me at the rodeo, what makes you think he won't come here looking for me? Seems he's tracked our every move. And I'm not going to get her involved. She's a sweet woman who doesn't need our problems."

"It's better if you stay here," Chuck said, "because, well—"

"Because you won't quit playing Miss Detective," Robert said. "To be truthful, Chuck's here to keep an eye on you."

"Good Lord." Rita elbowed Robert. "I don't need no stinkin' babysitter." She leaned back and shook her head.

"The reason I'm here with you is"—Chuck leaned forward—"because they think Bowie killed a man last night."

"He did? Who?" She leaned forward, her chin quivering.

"Jeff Fullmoon."

"You've got to be kidding." She put a fist to her mouth and closed her eyes for a moment. "He's Gary's brother and was with Bowie in Redmond. They came after me in the desert. And he's been the one sneaking around, keeping an eye on me here."

"What were you doing out in the desert?" Chuck pulled out a notebook and pen from his shirt pocket.

Rita caught him up to speed. "If Jeff's dead, where is Hazel?" Her voice rose with each question. "Who's watching her? Gary? How many men does he have with him? Is she safe? Where is she?"

"Ethan thinks he's at the hotel and—"

"They're on the fifth floor," Robert said. When Chuck's brows rose, he added, "I followed them."

"Neither of you listens very well, do ya?" Chuck let out a deep sigh and regarded Robert. "Syd's on her way back. She's pretty upset you haven't been returning her calls or texts."

"There's nothing she can do. Besides, I've had my hands full." His gaze flashed to Rita.

She gave him a rueful smile.

"No, but she loves you. Doesn't want to see either of you come back in a body bag." Chuck took a swallow of his dark brew.

Rita wrung her hands in her lap. *Sydney's coming back?*

Robert reached over and placed his hand on top of hers. "What I don't get is why would Bowie kill Jeff?"

"For whatever reason, he may have turned on Bowie and threatened to turn him in. We're not sure. But, from what the detectives can deduce and after talking to your dad, Rita, they think Bowie's after Dean's estate. That's why he's after you. And why he took Hazel and is using her as bait. He's broke. Desperate. He's in way over his head. It looks like he'll do whatever he thinks will get him your dad's money—"

"What estate? My dad doesn't have the money people think he does. Do you think my folks are in danger?" She needed to call Tribal PD and have them camp out at their house.

"No, I don't think so. But there's—"

"Then what?"

"Let him finish," Robert squeezed her hand.

She broke the bond, feeling as though anything else would put her in a straitjacket.

"Bowie's been betting on racehorses and has won some but not enough to dig himself out of the hole he's gotten himself into. And the cops think there's been foul play."

"Doping?"

Chuck nodded. "Sounds like it."

No wonder he had her check out the horses and not a real vet. She didn't have the means to drug test them, only to make sure they appeared sound. She'd let her father flatter her with playing veterinarian, just as she had as a child. From her teen years working with a local vet, she gained enough knowledge to get the job done—and possibly cripple the animals for life.

Good Lord, what had she done?

And how on earth would she be able to sit around all day and night with a cop? With a cop who would arrest her if he ever found out she'd killed a man?

CHAPTER 68

Friday Night

Rita should have been there with him for his night of celebration. Robert had won two go-rounds, and he had a good chance of winning the night's ride on a bronc called Lucky Strike, according to the cowboy who'd ridden him last.

Rita prayed he would. A little luck would be nice. She needed a plan to distract her keeper and slip out. Another minute cooped up in the stuffy trailer wasn't in the cards.

On the table sat Rita's new burner phone. Truth be told, she liked having a way to keep in touch with him. The cell also gave her the means to flee the confines of the trailer and Chuck Williams.

She'd have to escape on foot, which would work because South Point was close—maybe two miles away. She wanted to watch Robert ride and support him for all he'd done for her. And, yes, stake out Bowie's room.

It was better than playing rummy. She drew a card and grunted at the nine of spades. So much for her hand. What a bust. She discarded a two of hearts, her mind reeling.

Gary Fullmoon had to be with him. Had to be the one keeping an eye on Hazel. If she could find him, he'd lead her to her sister. She'd lost all hope in Ethan and the cops. They didn't seem to be doing much of anything.

"You want to go to the rodeo?" Chuck tossed a three of diamonds onto the discard pile and checked his cell. "I can't win this game for nothing."

Rita picked up his card and laid down a four of clubs. "What happened to you insisting we remain holed up here?"

"Robert's got a good chance of winning tonight. Besides, I think sitting here is worse on you. And according to this," he held up his cell, "Bowie has once again seemed to evade everyone."

"You think he left? What about hotel security cameras?"

"I'm not sure where Hazel and Bowie are. Ethan's working with the cops, and they're keeping an eye out for them. The police need added proof or nothing will stick. And, yes, they're going through security tapes as we speak."

She put the cards away and slid out of the seat. "I'm in. Maybe we can bring a little luck to our bronc rider." And maybe she could ditch Chuck and snoop around the hotel and casino.

"Our?" Chuck pulled on his jacket.

"You know what I mean." Rita zipped her coat, settled her buckaroo cowboy hat on her head, and headed for the door. Yeah, she could break away after Robert rode, go for popcorn and a root beer, and search for her sister. Her mind whirled with possibilities.

Steer wrestling had wrapped up when Rita and Chuck took their seats.

She thumbed through the rodeo program. "Look here, this nine-year-old girl from the Colville rez is coming in as champion of the King Mountain Indian Rodeo Circuit. Good grief, she's in the woman's division." She studied the photo. "Tiny thing, isn't she? Hmm, Rocksie Marchand. Good for her."

"Oh, yeah. I've known her grandparents for years. Her mom's quite the rider too. Races on a flat track. Great family."

Rita ran a finger down the performance sheet and stopped at breakaway roping. "I'd love to enter this event." She gestured to the first contestant of the night swinging her rope in the arena near the calf chute, warming up for her turn. "I rope calves on a regular basis. It's good for the horses."

"Why don't you rodeo then?"

She rested the program on her lap. "My dad's all about working sunup to sundown. Money is his god."

"When we get you back to the ranch, I'm sure Sydney would love to work with you. She's a master roper."

"Maybe we could do a little team roping." Provided the nightmare ends. Guilt from having a good time riddled her. She should be looking for Hazel. She checked her phone. No new messages from either Ethan or Robert. Big surprise.

"Don't worry, they'll find her." Chuck clapped as the announcer drawled out the woman's score: two minutes, forty-nine seconds. He blew out a low whistle. "Think you can beat that?"

"Good question. I'll have to try." *Don't worry, they'll find her.* If only she could believe him. She suddenly felt like coming undone. She took in deep, slow breaths. *Get it together.*

"You okay?"

She nodded, closed her eyes, sucked in a slow breath. Let it drift out of her mouth. "I get worked up is all." *Oh please, don't have a panic attack here.*

"I know it's hard to sit and do nothing. Especially when a loved one is missing. But between Ethan and Metro, they'll find her. Okay? Trust them." Metro—Las Vegas Metropolitan

Police Department—was a combination of city and county law enforcement for the city of Las Vegas and Clark County.

Right. Trust them. Not likely. And it wasn't about their performance. Trusting people just wasn't something she excelled at.

Chuck held up a pen. "You can use this to keep track of their scores and times. It'll be a good distraction."

Rita took it. "You're right. I might as well relax and try to have fun. What's the fastest Sydney's ever roped a calf?"

"Last year she entered a local rodeo and snagged a time of three point fifty-four."

"Well, then, I reckon it's the time to beat." Speaking of measurable moments, Robert should be up soon. As soon as his ride was over, she planned to slip away and do a little investigating of her own.

Chuck laughed. "Reckon you'll try your best to beat it."

"Must be your cop intuition talking, huh?" She'd always loved a good competition. Except in this instance. Worry coursed through her like venom in a bloodstream. Grandmother Nellie had drilled into the granddaughters, "Worrying never changes the outcome, so don't waste your time doing it." If only it were that easy.

"From what Robert says, you're one determined lady."

"I am." She watched breakaway roping a little longer, her bladder so full she bounced her leg. "Listen, I need to use the ladies' room. I'll be right back."

"I'll come with you."

"I'm a big girl, Chuck."

"I'm hungry, Rita."

She made her way to the ladies' restroom, glad for a minimal line. When her turn came, she did her business and washed her hands, letting the warm water wash over her skin. She dabbed her face with a damp paper towel and adjusted the Leatherman rubbing against her ankle.

Her buckaroo hat settled low on her forehead, she pulled her black-and-white floral wild rag out of her pocket, tied it on, tossed the paper towel into the trash, and headed to the hotel and casino for a quick look-see before Robert's ride. *Sitting and waiting is for the birds.*

CHAPTER 69

R ita darted out of the bathroom and into Bowie's grasp. "You won't get away this time."

Before she could scream for help, he wrapped his arm around her and poked her side with something sharp. It felt like his deer-skinning knife. "Don't make a scene. One mishap and you and your sister are dead."

Acid seared her throat as his alcohol-caked breath gusted in her face. He led her to the corridor leading to the hotel. "Where are you taking me? Where's Hazel? If she has one bruise on her—"

"I don't think you're in a position to threaten me, honey. And if you don't cooperate, I'll have to hurt Hazel, and it'll be all your fault."

"Did you kill Jeff Fullmoon?"

"He was going to rat me out. And if you don't do as I say, I'll kill you too."

For crying out loud, where was Chuck? He'd seen Bowie before, showed him the temporary restraining order. Her own words assaulted her. *I don't need no stinkin' babysitter.* *Oh, no. Had he gone back to their seats?* She tried to wiggle out of Bowie's grasp. But he held her tight, reigniting the burn in her shoulder.

"None of this is my fault, you no-good—"

"Settle down, Silky Dove. Or you'll ruin our wedding night."

Her chest flipped. *Wedding night? No freaking way.*

"I have a preacher waiting in our room. Paid a pretty penny for a private shindig. We're getting hitched whether you're ready or not. Tonight." His guttural chortle made her queasy.

"Why get married? I don't have anything you want." For whatever sick reason, she needed to hear his confession.

"Oh, but you do."

"The suspense is killing me. Do tell."

"A rich father who'll make all my troubles disappear."

Rich? Hardly. "If I agree to marry you, what makes you think I'll stick around? Or if I have access to any of my dad's presumed money. I've never seen evidence of him having a padded bank account."

"You'll stick around because you want to keep Hawkeye's murder a secret."

Yep. He'd sent the mysterious texts from a burner phone. "How do you know?"

"I'm the one who got rid of his body for good. You can thank me tonight. After we're married." He yanked her into an empty elevator, pinned her in a corner, and leaned close to her ear. "I have a photo of you burying him. Your face is as clear as a sunny day." He rubbed her shoulder as though they were newlyweds.

Rita's knees weakened, and she felt like she'd puke right there in his ugly, twisted face. When the doors slid open on the twenty-fifth floor, he looped his arm around her neck, hauled her out of the elevator and down the hallway to a corner room, and pounded on the door. Gary's dark, beady eyes met them on the other side. A smile slithered over his face, and he moved aside to let them into the main living room portion of the suite.

A table and chairs, orange couch and matching love seat, wall-mounted TV, and an oval coffee table with a marble top filled the quaint space. Between the love seat and the dining table, doors hung on either side of the walls—one closed and one open.

Rita surveyed the place. *Love seat. No hint of love in this room.*

"If you're so broke, how are you paying for this? Drug money? Did you gamble and win?" She turned to Gary. "And where's Hazel, you godforsaken piece of garbage?"

Bowie shoved her toward the sofa. She stumbled to her knees, her hands slamming against the carpet. The sharp edges of her Leatherman scraped against her ankle bone. Shoot. Her pants leg blocked it.

But by her face lay a well-worn, rank-smelling pair of cowboy boots. She grabbed one by the shaft, sprang to her feet, and swung hard and fast, striking Bowie in the side of the chin. Red-faced, he slapped it out of her hands. She lunged for it, but he kicked her in the side.

Her forearms slammed against the marble tabletop, and she hit her head on the edge of the couch. Fighting to catch a breath, she groaned and curled into a ball, her body on fire. A metallic taste oozed into her mouth.

Muffled screams came from one of the other rooms, the one on the other side of the TV. *Hazel?* A surge of energy bursting through her, she shoved to her feet, the room in a slow spin. Her hands flew to the sides of her head, and she squeezed her eyes shut, bent over, and willed her body to snap back to life.

Thank God, she's alive.

Bowie seized her arm—his grip one of duty and force, not affection and commitment—and dragged her into the bedroom behind the couch. "Okay, Preacher, do your thing."

Preacher, huh? Why was this man of God not lifting a finger to help her? What kind of monster was he?

The minister, who wore a straw cowboy hat, tan boots, and had a paunch, fumbled his book open, concern sparking his gaze. His jaw slack, he said, "I don't think the lady wants to marry you, sir."

Bowie jabbed his knife at him. "Keep going."

Gary Fullmoon burst into the room, waving a handgun in the air. "Do what the man says." He glanced back when louder muffled sounds escaped through the open door.

"Hazel!" She jerked away from Bowie, but the barrel of Gary's six-shooter leveled at her head stopped her.

"How could you, Gary?" she shouted. "Hazel, stay strong!"

Gary smiled, backed out of the room, and slammed the door shut, leaving her alone with Bowie and the preacher.

Bowie spun her around so her back pressed against him and clamped his hand over her mouth, the blade of his knife pressed against her neck. "Shut up, Rita." He nodded to the preacher. "Get on with it."

She bit his hand and, when he jerked it away, said, "Don't do it. You're right, this is against my will."

The preacher sidestepped closer to the door as he read from his book. "Love is—"

"Love isn't—"

"Shut up. Both of you!" Bowie grabbed her around the neck.

The preacher kept his eyes on Rita, sweat beading on his forehead. With a swift motion, she shifted her weight and kicked Bowie in the shin with the heel of her boot, then elbowed him in the groin. As he buckled, the sting of Bowie's knife blade grazed her neck.

She spun to face the preacher, but he'd vanished. She lost her balance and slammed into the wall. *No way.* She held her arm and stumbled for the door. "Help me!"

Bowie scrambled for the door and slammed it shut. "Close enough." A monstrous laugh erupted from his mouth. "I've got the license. Preacher's already signed it. You can scribble your name on it later." He turned the rest of the way around and wet his lips. "It's our wedding night, babe. I've been looking forward to this for a long time." He unzipped his pants. "This should seal the deal."

She threw her hands out to block him. What deal? How far did Bowie's corruption dig into the pit of hell? "Don't do this . . ." She backed up.

Memories of Talon Hawkeye sneaking into her room late at night—his rancid breath in her face and his grungy hands all over her, ripping her innocence away—scraped her mind. She never could shed his bitter scent. A scream lodged in her throat as Bowie stepped toward her.

He shoved her onto the bed and crawled on top of her.

"Get off me!" Rita struggled as he lowered his mouth to hers, his stale breath as rank as Hawkeye's had been, and ripped off her shirt. She turned away. *God, where are you?* He hadn't been with her before, and He didn't seem to care now. Was her life so invaluable to Him that He couldn't save her at least once?

When her arm broke free, she beat on Bowie, not caring where her fist landed.

"Help!" She pounded him with all she had. "Get off me!" One of her fists connected with his nose and blood splashed across her face. She spit the metallic tang out of her mouth.

He curled his fingers into a fist and slugged her in the head, the impact taking the fight out of her—but for only a few seconds. His arm pinned against her chest, he tried to work her pants loose. She took the heel of her hand and went for an eye.

He grabbed her wrist and squeezed. "Hold still or I'll kill you here and now."

She popped him again, this time on the side of his face. With a string of swear words, he pressed his forearm against her neck. She gagged, wiggled, fought. She squeezed her eyes shut and tried to scream for help, but no air came from her windpipe. If only she could gasp for one breath, she might make it. If only . . .

Seconds later, she went limp.

Another second later, the pressure of his body lifted off her as a deep groan drifted through the room. "Get off her."

Robert?

She opened her eyes to him and two others pulling Bowie off her. Rolling onto her side, she clutched her neck. *Chuck? Ethan?* She coughed.

"Rita?" The deep timbre of Robert's voice drifted through the room.

She sprang off the bed and flung herself into his open arms. Her fingers clung to his shirt, her head buried in his chest. The aroma of horse, dirt, and spices filled her senses, calming her tremors.

"I got you." Robert held on. "It's over."

"What are you doing here?"

"Chuck texted me before I rode and said you were missing. I came right away."

"What about your ride?"

"I don't care about the ride," he whispered. "I care about you, Rita. I love you."

His warm breath swept across her head. "I love you too."

He kissed her, took off his shirt, and helped her into it, then wrapped his arms back around her.

Hazel burst into the room, the area over her mouth blotched. "Rita!"

She slid out of Robert's arms and clung to her sister. "Are you okay? Did they hurt you?"

Hazel shook her head as she clung to Rita, choking on her sobs.

"I've got you, Sister. I've got you." Rita held on. Just held on.

Hazel was alive. It's all she cared about right then.

Ethan handed Bowie over to a LVMPD officer. As the cop escorted Bowie out, he turned to Rita. "I'll find you when I get out. And don't forget, you belong to me. You're now *my* wife." He pinned a glare on Robert as if in warning.

"I'll never be your wife." It would never end, would it?

Chuck sat with Hazel on the sofa, her eyes watching Rita's every move as though they'd again be separated.

"The preacher didn't want to do it," Ethan said. "But once inside, Gary put a gun to his face. He's the one who called the cops."

"He did?"

Robert disappeared into the bedroom Bowie had held her in.

Ethan nodded. "And Chuck called me when he couldn't find you. We saw hotel security take off and followed them here."

Robert came back with a damp washcloth and handed it to Rita, and Ethan walked away. Robert led her to the window.

She wiped her face with the warm cloth and walked into his embrace. "It was Hawkeye all over again," she whispered. "Good Lord, Bowie had a preacher ready to marry us. He's freaking crazy. Why in heaven's name does he think he can force me to marry him?" She took in his musky scent, her hands pressed against his tight back muscles. "I thought the preacher ditched me."

"He's in the hall and won't leave until he knows you're safe."

"Oh?" She closed her eyes in humble gratitude.

Yes, Creator loved her. And He even protected her this time. For the first time, she felt valued by Him.

CHAPTER 70

Saturday Night

Dressed in her ribbon skirt and tunic, Rita held Hazel's hand.

Hazel also wore a ribbon skirt Robert had gifted her with. The floral fabric in hues of maroon, green, pink, and white enhanced the beauty of her sister's gentle spirit.

In the hotel lobby, the sisters waited behind the procession of Indigenous drummers carrying the beat on a large powwow drum set on a wagon and sang as men and women danced in their traditional regalia. Men's ankle and wrist bells jangled, and women's jingle dresses clinked as colorful ribbons and feathers whirled through the air.

Rita had left her buckaroo hat in the trailer at Maggie's because tonight she wanted to show her face. Show her strength. And walk for women in abusive relationships and for all those still trying to break free. *I'm tired of hiding. Tired of others overpowering me either physically, mentally, or spiritually.*

Tonight, her turn came to show bravery—for herself and for her sister.

She reflected on how free she felt as the drummers' voices pierced the casino. She prayed for healing over her parents, Hazel, and herself. She prayed Robert would be the one strand of hope she could find in a relationship. She thanked

Creator for protecting her and asked for forgiveness for not believing He would.

When the performance finished, Hazel squeezed Rita's hand, and they strode through the casino and started down the corridor between the two buildings. As Rita passed by the cowboy-and-horse sculpture, she forgave her father.

She held on to hope.

Hope in her Creator, her culture, traditions, and family. And in love.

"The Lord is my strength and my song, He has broken my chains and has given me victory." She thought of the verse from Exodus 15:2 that she'd read in Robert's Bible last night after waking up restless at three in the morning. She'd clung to it ever since. She needed Creator's strength. His healing touch. And now, through the traditions of her people, she came to Him in song, free and empowered.

They rode the escalator up to the arena lobby. The moment Rita stepped onto the carpet, she released the dam of pain, anger, guilt, shame, and bitterness she'd held for years.

A sense of healing swathed her like a newborn in a cradleboard.

And right then and there—as they formed a circle in the lobby and continued the celebration—she chose to forgive Bowie Dark Cloud and Talon Hawkeye. Tired of holding onto her hate and fear and resentment, she lifted her face to the heavens, closed her eyes, and sang with the drummers, her hands splayed out at her sides, palms up.

Rita invited healing into her soul.

And not only did she feel honored to practice her heritage in such a public way, she felt privileged to be one of Creator's daughters. Reconnecting with Him gave her a peace she'd never had before. Not even as a child.

Robert and his final ride of the season slipped into her mind. She hoped and prayed he'd win. He'd worked so hard to be a successful bronc rider, equally toiling to keep her safe. And to give up yesterday's ride knowing she'd gone missing— no words could describe how valuable it made her feel.

When the drummers stopped singing and dispersed into the arena, she opened her eyes, turned to Hazel, and held on to her for a few glorious moments. "Shall we find our seats?"

Hazel nodded, her eyes red rimmed.

The sisters settled near the chutes. Spectators wore red, white, or blue in honor of the veterans. No wonder Robert wore a red shirt. Minutes later, Chuck scooted past three fans with what looked like popcorn and drinks for all. Behind him sidestepped a woman with dark, shoulder-length hair and a cowboy hat blocking her face. The opening ceremony continued as Chuck plopped down into a seat, an empty chair between them.

Who was the woman?

When she finally looked up and smiled, Rita inhaled a sharp breath. *Sydney Hardy?*

"Look who I found roaming around, lost like a butterfly in the desert." He chuckled and let the woman pass.

"Hello, Rita," Sydney said. "I'm pleased to finally meet you."

Oh my goodness. She'd come. Words lodged in her throat. Sydney looked more stunning up close compared to on stage at women and ranching conventions. Light glinting from her smoky eyes, she proudly wore a blue ribbon skirt with two rearing horses, a tipi in the middle, and running horses across blue, white, and yellow ribbons. Her waist boasted a rodeo buckle with a roper on the front.

Sydney settled in a seat beside Rita. "Heard you've had a rough go of it. I've also heard you're one tough nugget. How are you doing?"

Rita nodded. "I'm fine. Thanks to Robert."

"I heard my brother broke every one of my ranch rules." Sydney winked at her.

"No, ma'am. He saved my life." Rita fingered her necklace. "He rescued me." *In so many ways.*

"I want you to know when we get back to the ranch, you have a place to stay for as long as needed. We've got plenty of work and could use a ranch hand like you."

"Thanks. I'll keep your offer in mind." But would she be willing to house Hazel too? She introduced the women. "To tell you the truth, I'm not sure what we'll do."

"I understand. Just so you know, Hazel has a place to stay as well until you girls get things figured out."

The offer lightened Rita's shoulders. Years of weighted oppression quickly vanished. She'd do anything to help women, as Sydney—and Robert—had helped her and Hazel. She looked forward to whatever Creator had in store for her.

The lights of the event center dimmed, and spotlights swept the arena floor. Four black boxes spit fire, and a loud boom ignited the letters INFR in a crackling blaze. After inducting five past contestants into the Hall of Fame, the announcer introduced the staff and the competitors vying for their event championships. When Robert's face flashed on the jumbotron, Rita shot to her feet and whistled, searching for him through a layer of sulfur-scented smoke.

She didn't care if her display of affection came on thick. He'd supported her, and now her turn came to return the gesture.

After the contestants cleared the arena, powwow dancers and four Native women of the color guard wearing traditional regalia carrying the US, POW, US Army, and US Marine Corps flags dispersed throughout the arena.

Rita, her hand pressed against her throbbing heart, stood with the others, proud to be an American and a woman overcoming her abuse. Not a victim. But a victor. Tears blurring her vision, Sydney took hold of her hand, squeezed, and let go.

The announcer recognized Spotted Face, a world championship drum group. When the lead drummer began to sing a prayer song, she released remnants of pain and anger she'd been harboring for years, her pulse keeping time with the boom of the drumstick. She'd never felt prouder of her Indigenous heritage. And she was sure added healing would come—after she revealed her deepest regret to Robert.

When the song ended, Rita cheered as war whoops and high-pitched trills filled every shadow of the arena.

Next, the Canadian flag and anthem were honored, and a competitor from the Kootenai-Salish tribe of Montana sang the National Anthem. While the woman sang the words, "The land of the free," one by one, Rita felt the spiritual shackles of bondage break and drop from her wrists, ankles, and throat—a purification of sorts.

The arena cleared for the first event, bareback riding, and those still standing sat down. Rita made small talk with Sydney and Hazel and cheered for the contestants until it was time for the saddle bronc event.

Her body tingled when they called Robert's name. *Bronco Bobby.* She let out a soft chuckle, sitting on the edge of her seat. Who would have ever thought she'd fall in love with a bronc rider? "Come on, now, Bobby, ride this bronc," she said under her breath.

The longer it took for Robert to come out of the chute, the more Rita fidgeted.

"What's the hang-up?" Hazel watched with intent eyes.

"I don't know," Rita said. "But this is killing me."

Hazel stared at her, a feisty smile on her face. "You've fallen for him, haven't you?"

With a flash of heat radiating up her neck, Rita shrugged. "Suppose I have."

"You tell him so?"

"It's not your business, Haze." She bumped her sister with her shoulder and grinned.

"Well, when this is done, if you don't, I will. You two are made for each other."

She thought so too.

The announcer's voice boomed as the chute flung open. Robert's bronc burst out. Rita jumped to her feet, cupping her hands around her mouth, and hollered, "Ride that bronc!"

To the rhythm of the horse, Robert spurred and lifted his rein arm, his chin tucked to his chest.

Rita clapped and hollered. An instant later, Chuck, Sydney, and Hazel sprang to their feet, stomping and cheering right along with her. Eight seconds later, the buzzer sounded, and a pickup man pulled Robert to safety. He slid off the tall, bay horse and lifted his hands into the air, pointing to the heavens.

Yes, sir, glory to God.

CHAPTER 71

It seemed like hours for the bull riding, the final event of the night, to end. According to the scores, it appeared Robert had come in second place with a ride of eighty-six points. As selfish as it seemed, Rita smiled, knowing she could see him right away.

No buckle ceremony. No interviews. No crowds. Just the two of them.

Hopefully, there would be time to say what needed to be said. Time to sort out the important from the not important and sort out her emotions.

Robert met them all by the cowboy-and-horse statue, bronc saddle slung over his shoulder and a broad smile on his face.

Rita's cell rang. *Mom.* She handed it to Hazel. "You can take this one."

"Hey, Brother," Sydney said, "you rode hard. Congrats. I'm proud of you."

But his attention was glued on Rita, and it made her feel weightless. He regarded Sydney. "Thanks. Glad you made it." He gave her a brief hug.

"Me too. Looks like we have a lot to discuss." She peaked a brow.

His face reddening, he pinned his gaze back on Rita. "Suppose we do."

Chuck clapped his brother-in-law on the back and congratulated him. Hazel fist-bumped him, turned to Rita,

350

and with glistening eyes said, "Dad's not involved in the drug money and has agreed to go to counseling."

"That's great." Yep, God was finally showing up. As her youth pastor used to say, "His timing, will, and way."

After the sisters hugged, the trio left Robert and Rita alone with plans to meet up at the Garden Buffet restaurant.

Robert led Rita up an escalator to an empty conference center and dropped his saddle and gear bag on the floor. "Thanks for sticking around to watch me ride."

"I wouldn't have missed it," she said, her voice low and intimate.

He took hold of her hand, entwining their fingers together. "Do you think you'll be coming back to the ranch?"

Rita gave him a slow nod. "I think so. I'd like extra time with Sydney. It would be nice to work with someone other than my father."

"How long you plan on staying?"

"As long as it takes. Sydney's words, not mine." She pressed into him, feeling like she could live there forever—if he'd keep her after what she planned to tell him.

"Good. I think you and I need to talk about us."

"We do. But first . . . there's something I have to tell you."

"There's nothing else I need to know. I love you, Rita."

"You might not after—"

He put his finger to her lips. "There'll be plenty of time to talk when we get back."

She removed his hand. "I need to get this off my chest. Please."

"Okay. What can't wait until we get back?"

"I . . . um . . ." She turned her head.

"It can't be worse than killing a man," he whispered, a lighthearted grin on his face. "In self-defense, that is."

Yeah, he was trying to get her to lighten up. Too bad it wasn't working. "After Talon raped me . . . I . . . well, I got pregnant."

His Adam's apple bobbed. "What happened to the baby?"

Salty tears stung her eyes, and she wiped them away with her fingers. "I lost it. And the sick part? I was . . . quite relieved." There. She'd said it. But her regret still pricked her chest.

"How far along were you?"

"Not far." She prayed God would continue to bind her wounds and glue the shattered pieces together bit by bit. The voices of cranky children bubbling up the escalators sank right into her bones.

He wrapped his arms around her. "Does your mom know?"

"No one knows. Not even Haze. I have a child in heaven and don't even know what it is." Her fingers fisted his shirt. "I pack a lot of baggage, you know. You might want to rethink keeping me around."

"Never. I agree you carry a heavy load. But it's nothing we can't handle together."

"I was hoping you'd keep me around." She inhaled his earthy scent. "Sorry you didn't win."

Robert kissed the side of her head, his lips lingering in her hair. "I may have come in second tonight, but I'm hoping I've won you. Which is better than any buckle I could ever earn."

Rita lifted her face to his. "You mean it?" He looked so handsome and rugged, his black hair peeking out of his black Stetson, pure love in his eyes.

"I mean, not you as a prize, but—"

"Shut up already and kiss me."

He chuckled, moved his hand to the back of her head, and pressed their lips together. So gentle. So sweet. She tasted his love and commitment. His devotion. Her hands ran up his solid chest, found his collar, and rounded his neck. He pressed into her, deepening the kiss.

And she let him.

Free of fear, of bondage, of abuse.

She looked forward to a new life, to a hope and a future with Robert and ranching.

And of course, rodeo.

ACKNOWLEDGMENTS

It takes a team to write a heart-tapping story. I could not have written this book without my team of experts and beta readers or my Redeemer and His guiding Spirit. May this story give broken and battered women hope and breathe life into healthy relationships for them.

Thanks to my editors Larry J. Leech II, Susan Cornell, and Susan Powell for your vital edits that have helped me become a better writer. You are much appreciated! Thanks to Michele Trumble, Elaina Lee for her gorgeous covers, and the rest of the Iron Stream Media team for their assistance and dedication. Thank you to my son, Corey, and daughter-in-law, Tiffany, for agreeing to be my cover models. This is a special touch to the cover.

Thanks to first readers Debra Whiting Alexander, Linda Jacobs, and Anne Schroeder. Your suggestions have made this story so much better.

Deepest gratitude to my husband, Joe Peone, who set me straight with bronc riding scenes. Babe, I loved to watch you ride and understand why you stopped.

Thanks to one of our sons, Eddy Cohen, who helped me with calf illness, vaccines, and injuries; to Fran Marchand, Colville Tribal member and 2014 INFR Saddle Bronc Champion, for your expertise and knowledge of Pro-West, professional, and Indian sanctioned rodeo events, as well as the Indian National Finals Rodeo in Las Vegas. Thanks for answering the plethora of questions and providing photos along the rodeo trail. You are an inspiration for Indigenous Peoples. Thank you for allowing me and my readers to follow your 2015 road to the INFR.

Thanks to Liz Curtis for helping describe the area between Pasco and Connell. I've driven it many times over the years to ride horses at Curtis Arabians. Thanks to Emily Smith, MSN RN, with CHI St. Anthony Hospital in Pendleton, Oregon, for answering my questions concerning head injuries and the hospital's treatment plan and to Heidi Brooks and Melody Biehl for helping me navigate the Deschutes County Fairgrounds and Expo Center, Interstate Bank Center, and the Redmond Caves.

Thanks to Ashley Zacherle, Colville Tribal member and three-time Pendleton Indian Relay winner, for your assistance with horse lodging and the layout of the South Point Equestrian Center in Las Vegas, Nevada, for answering all my questions and providing photos of the venue prior to my arrival at South Point to fact-check my book, and for allowing me to mention your daughter in this story. She earned it.

Thanks to Charli Knight, Colville Tribal Public Defender, and Officer Thomas Cohen III, Colville Tribal PD, for teaching me about tribal law and the tribal court system where battered women are concerned; to Donna Hoyt, General Manager for the Indian National Finals Rodeo (INFR), for teaching me the ins and outs of the INFR's week-long event. Your attention to detail helped make the ending of this story authentic. Thanks to INFR staff members Tashena Hastings, White Mountain Apache, and Tangy Acorn, Oklahoma Cherokee, for answering all my questions at the INFR rodeo. Tashena, Tangy, and Donna Hoyt were incredibly generous, and I'm honored to know you.

Thanks to those who have answered questions and have chosen to remain anonymous. You know who you are, and I appreciate your help.

DISCUSSION QUESTIONS

1. Rita often forgot to call on God for help, especially when things became hectic. Who do you call on for help and when?
2. Which character in the book did you empathize with the most?
3. How important are personal boundaries? Is it hard for you to tell someone no? Do you enable or rescue?
4. After Robert rode Shoot the Moon in Idaho, Rita vowed she'd never go home. How hard of a decision do you think it was for her? What would you do in her situation?
5. Being a victim of abuse can cause multiple fears. What role can fear play in our lives? How can we battle it?
6. Rita tended to look to Robert for her security. Is depending on others good or bad? Why?
7. Rita made the hard choice to leave her mother behind. It can be difficult to accept someone's free will. If you were in a similar situation, would you have done the same? Or would you have stayed with your family?
8. Are you familiar with signs of abuse? If you know someone you suspect is being abused, how can you help them? What resources are in your area?
9. Rita's sister Hazel was abducted. If you knew someone in the same position, how would you get the word out in an effort to help bring a loved one home?
10. It can be hard to forgive those who are abusive. What role does forgiveness play in our lives?
11. While in the horse trailer with Chuck Williams, Rita was impatient, claiming the police weren't doing

much when, in fact, they were busy behind the scenes trying to catch Bowie. Have you ever struggled with patience? When? If so, how did you overcome it?

12. Which scene in the book made you the most emotional? Why?

13. What is a source of hope for you?

A NOTE FROM THE AUTHOR

This book was extremely hard for me to write. It was inspired by the murder of my niece. In her early twenties, she married her abuser and within a few years he had beaten her to death.

I wanted to write a story not only to help me heal from the violent crime, but to help women who are in destructive relationships. Abuse, whether emotional, mental, physical, financial, sexual, or spiritual, is never love. Violence is selfish manipulation. It steals the victim's self-worth and isolates them from family and friends. It lies, deceives, and betrays.

Do you know how much Creator God loves and values you? I hope you'll take the time to discover how important you are to Him.

So, let's talk about what love is.

Love is kind, tender, patient, truthful, respectful, selfless, and humble. Love uplifts and encourages. It never tears a person down.

I'd like to encourage you to recognize the difference between what love is and isn't and to seek help if you are in an abusive relationship.

https://www.thehotline.org/

Check out my resource page: https://carmenpeone.com/resources/

Sign up for my newsletter and receive a free novella, *Gentling the Cowboy*: https://carmenpeone.com/books/gentling-the-cowboy/

OTHER BOOKS BY CARMEN PEONE
Inspirational Romantic Suspense
Captured Secrets

Young Adult
Contemporary
Girl Warrior

True to Heart Trilogy - Historical
Change of Heart
Heart of Courage
Heart of Passion

Gardner Sibling Trilogy - Historical
Delbert's Weir
Hannah's Journey
Lillian's Legacy

For information on YA Book Curriculum See Carmen Peone's Website:
https://carmenpeone.com/books/curriculum-young-adult
-workbook-series/